THE BARROW SHIP

JOHN WILKINSON

Blue Poppy Publishing

Edited by Sarah Dawes
Cover art by John Wilkinson
Cover design by Tom Wilkinson
Interior design by Oliver Tooley
Body Garamond 12pt, Cover DIN Condensed
Blue Poppy Publishing, Ilfracombe, Devon

ISBN: 978-1-83778-013-6

To Thomas and Deborah
this story is most lovingly dedicated.

Acknowledgements

Very grateful thanks to my most sagacious friend, Allan Frewin Jones, for his unerringly generous and astute professional insight, constructive editorial candour and unwavering creative enthusiasm.

Big thanks to Louise Pugsley and her wonderful class, for listening week after week and wanting more. Also to Lucy Tredant for the use of her marvellous library.

Loving thanks to Angela C. Wilkinson and Simon J. Harris, for an eternity of listening and never losing faith.

Heartfelt thanks to Claire Barker, whose magical advice at the formative stages of this project did so much to propel it.

Much love and gratitude to Izzy Turner and Clare Turner, for their enduring support, for reading and rereading, and for so many kind words to add to my heart's vocabulary.

Warmest thanks to Sarah Dawes and Oliver Tooley for their creative support, unstinting patience and professional diligence.

Part One:

Before and After

1 (Before)
The Tears of the Crocodile

It had been three days since the boy had looked at his dead father folded in the shower cubicle. For weeks the city had been weighed down with an unrelenting heatwave. The boy watched the scraggy pigeons on the fire-escape billing, cooing and circling endlessly. He had eaten the last crust of white bread with half a tin of grapefruit segments.

Someone knocked at the door. There had been no visitors and no telephone calls.

Whoever it was knocked again, this time louder and more insistent.

The boy slid off his plastic chair and went to the door. He listened. There was the muffled thumping of music from an apartment down the hall, pounding in perfect time with the rhythm of his heartbeat.

"Don't worry," said a softly solicitous voice on the other side of the door. "I'm here to help you."

The boy heard the person cough. It sounded like a man. The boy had to stand on tiptoes to see through the spyhole. The man was looking straight at him.

He had tears in his eyes.

"You need to open the door." The man's face was florid and round.

The boy saw that the man's lips were bulbous, purple, as if they had been tattooed. He had a funny black hat. He had a dog with him. The boy could hear it barking sharply. The man stooped out of view and the dog went silent. When he reappeared, the man was further from the door.

"Your father is dead, my child. He is gone, leaving only his useless corporeal vessel."

"How did you know?" the boy asked the stranger in a whisper, feeling a sense of something beyond his control.

"After very many years of devoted service, one gets, let's say, a nose for these things."

"You've got a gun," the boy said, struggling to maintain his strained position.

"It's a ticket machine. Think of it like that. It dispenses tickets to get people out of trouble. It can transport folks from one place to the next."

"You can't come in. I won't open the door."

"That's fine. I'm not here to watch cartoons and eat stale cornflakes from the box. Your father is with your mother now, happily reunited, but they are lost without you. If you want me to take you to them, you will have to do as you're told and open the door."

"Open the door." The boy heard himself say it. He was trying to see the stranger's gun. The man had tucked his long black coat behind the gun's beautifully carved handle. The boy thought the man looked as if he was much too warm in that big coat.

"Have you ever killed anybody?" the boy asked.

"I have," the man replied with a smile. His eyes still looked wet.

"Are you going to shoot me?"

The stranger's laugh gurgled deep within the fleshy folds of his throat.

The boy saw two girls pass by behind the man in the hallway. The stranger picked up his dog, supporting the animal on his left arm and allowing the slack of its lead to hang at his side.

"Your mother begged me to come here to collect you and take you to her. Please don't disappoint her. She so desperately needs you with her."

There were more tears on the man's ruddy cheeks. His tears looked red.

The man had a gun, and he was crying.

"I must go now," the tearful stranger with the ornate pistol said. "It would seem such a wasted journey to return without you. I have a ticket with your name on it. What shall I tell your mother? She will be inconsolable."

And he was gone. The boy strained to see. The stranger was gone.

The boy panicked. He opened the door. It hadn't even been locked.

"Step through, child," the stranger said, holding out his hand.

2 (After)
I Am Her

Sylvanie wrote: I am her.

She had slept badly, and it was early. Movement flickered across the sprawling city as it began to shake itself awake. She felt indignant. Indignance felt like something that generated power.

Again she put pencil to the page of her homemade notebook: I am not her.

Sylvanie looked out at the whitening sky, opening her eyes as wide as she could, staying like that until her eyes hurt.

I am not myself, she wrote. I'm the one who stayed. I was supposed to. I had no choice.

I don't know who might want to read this in the future. Maybe they'll think they know me. Everyone in the entire world thinks they know me. They know my name and what I look like. They see me all the time on the TV and in the newspapers. There's loads of pics of us, even crap school photos. Danny with his hair combed. Looking like it's an idiotic wig. Most of those pictures I've never seen before. People say stuff about us like they know us. What the hell do they know, when our own families question whether they really knew any of us at all. Privately. Publicly. One photo they keep showing is of me, Finch, Maze and Danny in hysterics because Finch told Danny he'd shot himself in the foot over some crummy quadbike deal, then I told him he'd shot himself in the leg as well, and Maze said he'd blown his own arse completely off. We all started looking for Danny's arse. It was the summer before he went to college. Some kid on holiday took the photo. That kid will probably be famous now, interviewed like everyone else who's ever or never met us, making up some totally bogus bullshit.

When they come back, me and Finch will sit in the bus shelter watching the world and his dog go by on carnival floats for ever and ever amen.

Sylvanie slapped her notebook shut, turned it over in her hands and opened it again.

She wrote: On the day I made this book with Mum, Maze's pet fox, Royston Quantock, started yowling down in the porch, so me and Maze took him for a walk. Only up the bumpy track as far as the beech tree with the ruin of our epic treehouse. When we got back I moved Kinky – my cat with the crooked tail – into my room so Royston the Red could be upstairs with us, curled up on a cushion on the floor. He put his nose under his brush, but kept his big glossy, glassy eyes open all the time, watching every move we made and listening to every word.

Sometimes I have felt ridiculously angry and frustrated. Sometimes I have felt important. I know what happiness is, how fragile it is. It feels like a balloon that someone you love just keeps blowing and blowing into. I haven't got a clue what happens next. Sometimes I think that Mum feels she's lost me. I can be sitting beside her on an ugly sofa that doesn't even belong to anybody and I know she feels she's lost me. I keep telling myself not to lose myself. Sitting in the waiting room. Sometimes I am overcome. Like a saint. Sometimes I get scared. Like a little kid. There are other rooms waiting. And there's other people waiting in them.

3 (Before)
A Headful of Moonlight

It was pitch-black when Maisie left Hannah and Sylvanie's cottage with the notebooks and Christmas cards she had made. She borrowed a heavy torch. It wasn't particularly cold and the air was still. Mother and daughter stood with the porch light on and both doors open as Maisie went down the path with her red hoodie up and Royston Quantock sloping along behind her off his lead. Two or three bats repeatedly described a fluid circuit around the cottage and several pale moths were tempted by the bare electric bulb. From where Sylvanie and her mother stood, no lights other than Maisie's torch were visible. No moon or stars. Everywhere, all imaginable destinations, seemed possible. It also seemed possible that there were no other places to walk to, to travel to, and that the liquid darkness had dissolved all reality beyond the reach of meagre torchlight.

"She'll be home before she knows it," Hannah said.

"With her pockets full of fallen stars and a headful of moonlight," Sylvanie said.

4 (Before)
Metamorphosis

"It was weird when you guys were swimming toward me underwater," Sylvanie told Danny and Maisie. "Your faces were pale. You were like frogs metamorphosing into human beings."

"Give them time," Finch said. "Come back in sixty million years."

"Your hands and arms are so brown they almost dissolved in the peaty water," Sylvanie continued, "and your faces came at me out of nowhere."

"Basically, she's saying you're pond life, mate," Finch told Danny. "The swamp is your natural habitat." He focussed a pair of imaginary binoculars on Danny. "It's a privilege," he said in hushed tones, "to be able to observe this rare mutant beast in its own environment."

"I'm a wild animal," Danny growled, leaping to his feet. "They can't chain me. I can't be tamed."

"You can't be more embarrassing," Maisie said.

Danny roared and beat his chest with his fists, red club marks appearing rapidly. He pumped himself up until the veins on his neck stood out. There were six or seven other teenagers on the opposite bank who applauded and cheered when he did a bandy-legged dance and back-flipped into the dark pool.

Maisie stood up and looked down over their rock.

"The beast is free," she proclaimed with priestess-like solemnity.

The surface of the pool stilled and the uncannily calm water appeared to solidify. All eyes turned to the point of entry. Everybody waited, holding their breath.

Danny finally broke the surface as if in slow motion, lifting a smoked-glass cloak of water with him and holding a boulder roughly the size of his own head. He brought it clear of the water in both hands.

"You wanted the world," he said, not in the least breathlessly, and heaved the rock up to Maisie and Sylvanie.

"We gracefully accept the gift of this great stone, noble knight," responded Sylvanie, regally, feeling the weight of the dark boulder and trying to comprehend the struggle Danny must have had to get it to the surface. "We asked for the world, and you, good knight, have fulfilled the duty you swore."

Danny grinned. "I never bloody swear. Goodnight." And again he was gone.

"It feels like my eyes are really open when they're open underwater," Finch said, when Danny eventually reappeared at the furthest downstream edge of the pool. "It's like I can *feel* everything I see going past my eyeballs. I kept them open when I was under."

"You're still under," Sylvanie told him. "Under ... achiever."

"Under … pants," Maisie added. "Under the anaesthetic from the brain transplant."

Maisie and Sylvanie pinned Finch down and attempted to forcefully complete the operation with which they imagined professional neurosurgeons must have struggled. They gave up after telling him that they couldn't find a donor organ small enough to be a match.

It began to rain, darkening the stones and roots beside the pool, making the grass flicker and the broad leaves of docks, balsam and nettles plunge and shudder with the impact of droplets mediated by the alder and willow canopy along the riverbank. Danny climbed out of the river. Sylvanie lay motionless on the warm rock while the others panicked with towels, clothes and phones. The heavens opened and heavier raindrops percussed her skin. When she rose, there was a dry shape, briefly, on the stone where she had been lying.

"It's your soul, Syl," Maisie said, stuffing her massive Disney beach towel into her backpack. "That's probably the last you'll ever see of it."

The pale form disappeared.

"It was like the reverse of a shadow," Finch said pensively, taking his cue from Sylvanie, who seemed determined not to hurry. "I should have taken a photo of it," he told her. "But you can always do it again sometime."

"I can do something else," Sylvanie said. "I can do something *like* it. I can't do *it* again. If you failed to capture the moment, then the moment is still at liberty."

"Look," Finch said, pointing over the river, out across the fields. "There it goes."

"I'll get me bliddy shotgun," Danny said.

They sat at the back of the bus on the way home. In her notebook, on pages that were damp at the edges, Sylvanie wrote: We are changed. What we look like through the water. Reflected in it. No mirror can be trusted. Shapes shift. Finch took amazing shots of Danny and Maisie. They're lifting their arms from their sides to above their heads as they push themselves up out of the river. They both kept doing it. They gave themselves fantastic pairs of transparent silver wax wings.

5 (Before)
The Black Bishop

The day wanted something. It had been waiting and listening, holding its breath.

Sylvanie, Maisie and Finch were sat on the swings in the children's play area on the green at Exford, having spent most of the morning together, walking and chatting, mostly downstream along the Exe. They had cycled and left their bikes leaning against the railings opposite the Post Office. The mist, which had appeared at times almost impenetrable, had provided the friends with a haunted sense of isolation and intimacy. It had been damp all day without actually raining. Everything was wet: the grass, the swings and slide, the trees. An autumnal musk of turned soil, muck-spreading, wet leaves and woodsmoke pervaded the sodden November air.

"The mist doesn't creep me out, exactly," Maisie said, "but, like now when there's tiny droplets on all the millions of cobwebs on the grass, you get to see what's actually out there all the time and we don't realize it. It's fantastically magical. And totally weird."

"Me and my mum and dad were on Woolacombe beach once, and the rockpools were crammed with spider crabs, mating," Finch said. "Thousands of them."

"Eugh!" The reaction from Maisie and Sylvanie was of uniform distaste.

"It was like the planet was being attacked, like in one of those ancient black-and-white movies where people don't understand that the Earth's under threat and they just carry on with their normal ignorant lives."

Sylvanie attacked Finch with spider crab hands. He huddled into himself.

"I had nightmares about it for years," he said. "I somehow got it into my head that my mum and dad changed into spider crabs at night, and I wouldn't go to sleep without my nightlight on. I was only a kid. I thought I could hear their long, spindly claws scratching on the door downstairs." He shuddered and hugged himself.

"Horrible," Maisie said. "Poor you. But it was a long time ago."

"It was last night," Sylvanie said. "He still sleeps with his Thomas the Tank lamp on."

"Oh my God," Maisie shrieked. "How would you know?"

"Because his psychotherapist phones me every night with all the embarrassing details," Sylvanie explained, improvising effortlessly. "She's got to talk to somebody. She's close to a nervous breakdown because of him being such a total freak. She's quitting the profession she's always loved and going to live in this super-creepy Gothic asylum on an island where they tested atomic weapons on psychotic prisoners, because of *him*." She pointed at Finch.

He buried his head in his hands. "I loved her. And she will become a crazy zombie lady like all my previous girlfriends."

"That's where the story falls apart," Maisie said.

"Where?" Finch asked.

"The bit about you having previous girlfriends," Sylvanie told him.

A schoolfriend and her mother passed by on a pair of well-groomed chestnut mares, heading along the lane at the side of the green toward the mist-obscured pub and primary school. Everybody waved. The two riders looked smart, their mounts proud and elegant, but insubstantial, ethereal. People had been appearing and disappearing all day; materializing out of the mist and then dissolving again.

"There's this fantastic old bloke me and Mum know," Sylvanie said. "He was her art teacher when she was at school. On his living room wall he's got the most beautiful carousel horse in the world. You can't sit on her because she's fixed up with big metal hook things. When I was little I fell in love with that white horse and I used to dream about rescuing her from the wall. I called her 'Jess'.

"In my dreams her legs never moved. We rode everywhere by magic. Jess leapt right across the sky with me on her back, holding her mane tight in my fists. I used to ride round and round and round in great big circles in the sky and over the hills and far away. I could reach out my hand and touch the whitewashed wall. If I looked to the right I could see people going by, and everything around them was painted white. They looked like they were carved out of wood and painted white, like clunky, wooden, puppet-ghosts."

"Cool," Maisie said.

"I drew that dream horse about a thousand times," Sylvanie said.

They sat in relaxed silence until Maisie got a message from Danny. He was beating for a pheasant shoot near Dulverton with his dad and uncle, and sent pictures of Boots and Shoes, his spaniels, licking his face. Finch and Maisie scrolled through photographs of dead birds: fifteen or so brace of pheasant in rows on red soil in a stubbly field, a pair of woodcock and a solitary, demolished snipe.

"That poor thing looks like some dipshit tried to make a puppet out of twigs and a few feathers," Finch said, "and failed miserably."

There was no one else on the green now except a portly gentleman in a long, black raincoat with a shih-tzu on a retractable lead. He wore an unusual, brimless, black hat. Maisie watched him. His coat was so long she couldn't see his legs or even his shoes, and she wondered if he had little wheels, like castors, instead of feet. She thought the stranger looked like a chessman: a black bishop. He was scarcely of this world, dragging tendrils of the mist shroud as he moved. Maisie thought she could make out another, smaller figure beyond him: a child, perhaps a boy. There he was: a sullen kid. She nudged Sylvanie's swing with hers and turned to say something, but when she looked back the sinister trinity had disappeared.

6 (After)
The Dispossessed

Sylvanie watched her mother closely: Hannah was arranging a generic bouquet of garage-forecourt flowers in a green glass vase. She looked neither happy nor unhappy, as if her thoughts were elsewhere. Sylvanie thought her mother's movements were too slow, too deliberate.

The Watch insisted on flowers, hoping to break up the monotony of the interminable chain of days spent in the 'safe house' apartment.

"So," the woman said, "Hannah, Syl, my darlings, I'm your Watch until midday on Thursday. If there's anything at all you need me to do, or anything you want from the shops, just let me know. If it's within my powers to do it, consider it done." This woman – bright and breezy, always upbeat and affable – wore a black, snub-nosed revolver in a shiny leather holster on her right hip.

"Find us somewhere in the country to live," Hannah said. "Somewhere where the sky isn't piss-yellow at night. Somewhere where we can go outside, walk in the woods, on the beach. Somewhere remote. Or find us a city where we can walk anonymously in the park or stroll to the shops on our own."

"I will pass on your requests, as ever, Hannah, to the powers that be," the Watch replied, frowning sympathetically.

Hannah was wearing Sylvanie's light-brown sleeveless dress with the white daisy print. Sylvanie adored it. The rigidity of the ironed cotton made her feel relaxed as soon as she put it on. She thought that the dress made her mum look younger, and that cheered Sylvanie.

The Watch took a sandwich and a mug of instant black coffee to her room.

Hannah was leaning over the kitchen sink, appearing slightly overbalanced, as if straining to look through the window to see something or someone on the pavement, three storeys below. An elderly woman, bent almost double with the weight of her shopping, reminded Hannah of Mrs Slee. It puzzled her that Mrs Slee and her companion should seem so central to this chronic mess. Why would they have been in a position to play a part in any of it? She wondered how Mrs Slee and Lilian had coped with all the turmoil. Were those extraordinary ladies refugees now, too?

"You look nice, Mum," Sylvanie told her mother. "We should have a hippy chick sort of afternoon. We could read poetry to each other. Or listen to music. Take it in turns to choose tracks?"

"I wish you would try to understand other people's pain, and their godforsaken, unremitting anguish," Hannah said, without turning from the window. "I wish you would take on board the awful sense of loss that some people are feeling. You seem ... *callous* sometimes, Sylvanie."

Her mother's voice, Sylvanie thought, sounded hot. As if her words had been spooned from a saucepan of boiling water.

"I feel guilty, Syl. I feel guilty sometimes, and ashamed that I've got you, and they've lost—" Hannah stopped herself. "I don't mean it, Syl." There was a note of panic in Hannah's voice. She didn't turn.

"I heard from Maisie's dad two days ago. It was early. You got up and went straight into the shower. He had to arrange the call in advance with the Watch, and they had to clear it with me. I was going to tell you, but I felt scared. I could hardly make sense of some of the stuff he was trying to tell me. I wondered at first if he'd been drinking. I realize he mostly wanted to tell himself things. He sounded so desperate. He broke down and it all became very uncomfortable. He was outdoors. He had taken the phone outside where they were. I don't have any idea where in the world they are, or how many times they've been relocated. It was raining. I could hear it. It sounded like he was standing under some kind of awning. He was crying, Sylvanie, all the way through the conversation. Not that it actually was a conversation at all. He said that he had no idea what to say when Maisie's little brothers asked when she was coming back, or even where she'd gone."

"You should have called me, Mum. You should have let me talk to him."

"I didn't *talk* to him. You're not listening to me. For Christ's sodding sake, Syl; the world has descended into chaos and we just happen to be right in the middle of it."

"Mum, I don't see it that way. There's always been loads of chaos everywhere and people waiting to grab the opportunity to exploit it. What happened with us and the Barrow Ship has forced people all over the world to have a radical rethink about a lot of things they've always taken for granted, or even been scared of thinking about at all. It just feels more dramatic, Mum, because it's all focussed on us. It feels sometimes like you want me to apologise. Many things are going to happen, but that's not one of them."

"I watched a woman on the news, Syl – she'd been on a talk show thing in America – telling everyone you were a witch. A *demonic* witch. Then there was a young guy in the Netherlands saying that he thought you were the new Messiah, the female incarnation of the second coming of Jesus. How do you feel about that? When he said that, all the young people he was with cheered and clapped. They all had pictures of you on their T-shirts. And another woman said that you were all predatory aliens planted on Earth to grow amongst us human beings. She said that Finch, Maisie and Danny were going to bring back awful creatures to harvest us all."

"They're not talking about me or the others when they come out with that sort of crap." Sylvanie said calmly.

"If it's not you, then why – in the name of every-damned-thing that we used to call sane or normal – are we here? Why are we stuck up here in this grey flat in this grey town that we're not even supposed to know the name of?"

Hannah was still in the same position, not focussing on anything beyond the window pane, tipped slightly forward over the empty sink. Her knuckles, turned back in the direction of Sylvanie as she gripped the stainless steel rim, were rigid and white. She had, for several minutes, completely forgotten her physical self.

"Trust me, Mum. *Please*. It'll all be OK in the end. I don't honestly know what the end will be, but I know it will be totally amazing, and actually just the beginning. Please relax. Just think of it like they've all gone on a school trip."

Hannah spun round, her eyes wild. The suddenness of the movement made Sylvanie jump.

"I just know how I'd feel if you'd gone off in a flying saucer."

An explosive laugh erupted from Sylvanie's chest. After a moment they were in each other's arms, neither able to tell whether the other was laughing or crying.

That night, alone in her wholly characterless room, Sylvanie wrote: *Am I possessed? There is someone inside me who is stronger than me. More determined than me. I am her.*

7 (Before)
A Cartographical Discrepancy

Finch and Sylvanie were sat facing each other on the wooden slats along the concrete bench in the bus shelter. They had their knees pulled up and their chins on folded arms.

It had been drizzling for half an hour, but now it was raining harder, forming a curtain between them and the rest of the world as it ran off the gutterless roof. The temperature had fallen and the interior of the shelter had darkened. There was a dusty fragrance washed from the tarmac and shaken from the gardens and hedgerows along the roadside.

"If Pony Chalice sees us," Finch said, "he always stops for a chat. I guess he's on his own most of the day. He has to shout over the noise of his tractor. He's a complete nutter, but he makes me laugh."

People had always called Derek Chalice "Pony". As a boy, he rode to school in the village every day, rain or shine, on his Exmoor pony: bareback, always. At the school gates he'd dismount with the aplomb of a circus performer, slap his pony on the rump and send her off with a gentle "Get on home, Moonie."

"Everybody likes Pony," Sylvanie said. "So what?"

"Last week we pulled in to let him pass, knowing he'd want to stop and have something to say about something. Mum wound down her window and Pony opened the door of his tractor and leaned so far over the wheel it looked like he was going to fall out. He'd been up on the moor since the crack of dawn and was heading home for what he called 'a nice bit of bread and scrape'. He told us he'd pull back on some of his homemade cider to wash it down. He said he'd been working in the cover he's got near Rowbarrow, at the far side of Worthy Airfield. His rusty old trailer was hitched up behind the tractor, full of long, straight hazel sticks to split to make hurdles to keep the wind off Lady Jeffers' veg. He'd kept a brushwood fire stacked up all day. He told us that the air had been still and the flames had risen straight into the sky. He said the copse was full of bluebells, 'like the sky had laid itself down to walk on'. Mum told him that he was lucky to have such a beautiful office to work in. He said, 'It might be a bliddy lovely office, maid, but my desk be still covered in bliddy bills, just like anybody else's.'"

Sylvanie had closed her eyes. Finch liked looking at Sylvanie's face when her eyes were closed, not just because he could look at her face for longer than he otherwise might, and less self-consciously, but because he could make a real effort to fix the memory.

"Pony took the piss out of me for being too tall," Finch said, "or growing too fast or something; he always says pretty much the same thing. He told Mum she must have been putting too much horseshit in my wellies, but he could find a use for me as a fishing rod or a beanpole. They started talking about the standing stones and barrows up near the woods where he'd been working, and he told us about this missing barrow on the moor, over from Dunkery Beacon. It was the closest one to Pony's copse of a row of three. He said it had been used as target practice by American and British tanks and artillery in the Second World War, and they'd blown it completely to oblivion, Syl, not giving a toss that it was an important ancient site that Pony reckons hadn't ever been excavated. When we got home I went through those flat black-and-white maps that Mum got from the vicar before the one at the vicarage now. I found a sheet of that area of Exmoor, dated 1908. It clearly shows a sequence of *three* barrows, not two. When I checked their position against our modern walking map, I could only find two."

"Right," Sylvanie said. "So, when the map was updated, it wasn't put on, because it wasn't there anymore."

"Ancient history blown to bits."

"So you want to organize a massive international expedition up onto the desolate moor to retrieve the priceless contents of that incredibly important, long-lost ancient burial site?"

8 (After)
The Still Point of the Turning World

Sylvanie and Hannah had roasted a chicken and made two salads. One of the salads was a favourite of theirs, consisting of grated carrots, runny honey, bashed cardamom pods, fresh coriander leaves, black pepper and lime juice. The morning had been pleasant and uneventful; they had both spent time on the exercise bike and rowing machine, chatting to the Watch and sharing their lunch with her. Afterwards, when the washing-up had been done and coffee had been made, the Watch went through to the living room to watch football on television.

Something had risen to the surface in Hannah's mind. Sylvanie, cross-legged on the kitchen chair in her patched jeans and plain white T-shirt, was waiting.

"When you were a baby," Hannah said, "you used to cry and cry sometimes, even after being fed. You wouldn't be screaming, but you'd seem like you were unsatisfied, and you wouldn't be comforted. I was out with you in the garden one day, hanging out some washing on the rotary drier. I'd plonked you down in the shade of the Bramley tree on the big brown-and-pink blanket. You'd only just learned to sit up;

you were surrounded by toys, as well as bees and birds, butterflies and flowers, but you were howling.

"I was doing a little dance for you, making a puppet out of a white cotton blouse, when I saw Mrs Slee ambling up the path. 'Hello, dears,' she said, as she came toward us, focussing, really, on you. 'Please forgive the intrusion. But, was there something you craved when you were expecting?'

"She was wearing her raincoat, of course, even though the weather was utterly gorgeous. You had gone quiet, watching her every move. I told her raw carrots had been the thing. She sent me inside to fetch a whole, peeled carrot, and when I came back out, she was trundling off down the path to the track with her shopping bag thing on wheels. 'Try your little angel on that, dear,' she called. I remember incredibly clearly: you had your hands on your little bare knees, sat up, watching the shiny blue clockwork woman depart. As soon as I gave it to you, you stopped crying and started gnawing away at it. And from that day on you've loved raw carrot. If it wasn't for Mrs Slee's guidance, you might have been a perpetually discontented kid, instead of a perennially happy one."

"I know you'll hate me for saying this, Mum, but I'm as happy now as I've ever been in my entire life. And I can see really well in the dark."

"How can I hate you for telling me that you're happy? But what have we got to compare this to? Who in the world has any point of reference for any of this, for what's happened to you and your friends, to everyone we know?"

Hannah opened a cupboard door and closed it again. "I feel like a stranger in my own sodding existence, in my own body. Worst of all, I feel like an outsider when I'm with you,

Syl. And who else have I got to be with? We're at individual still points while our worlds spin out of control around us. It feels like I'm standing in the eye of a storm. Maybe I'll wake up in Kansas."

"I'll make us some lemon tea."

Hannah continued to talk, raising her voice as Sylvanie filled the kettle.

"You're waiting for your friends to come back and tell you all about everything, or waiting to go wherever it is they've gone. Everyone is either waiting for their wildest dreams to come true or their worst nightmares to be confirmed."

"Do you think that people know enough about their dreams or nightmares to know what to hope for?" Sylvanie asked as the white plastic kettle switched itself off with a dull clunk. She returned to the table, carrying a large aluminium tray, upon which was a pale pink teapot, two mugs with football team insignia on, a saucer with slices of lemon, and a small jar of honey.

"I hate that teapot almost as much as I hate you for being happy," Hannah told Sylvanie.

Sylvanie smiled. "We've known people who spent their whole lives waiting to die and go to Heaven, Mum. I'm just waiting for Finch to come back with my entire universe in his hands."

That night, sat up in bed with her journal propped up on her knees, Sylvanie wrote: I can see my mouth moving. I can see myself mouthing words. I can see myself on the other side of the mirror. But I can't hear what I'm saying. How am I supposed to answer myself when I can't hear myself ask myself the question?

9 (Before)
A Timetable

Maisie and Sylvanie were sitting at opposite ends of the long refectory table that Maisie's dad had made. The house was peaceful, and the two friends were luxuriating in the hush. Maisie had made more coffee, the doors leading out onto the paved courtyard were wide open, and a nuthatch was hammering away at the peanut dispenser, upside down, like an inverted bandit. Maisie and Sylvanie had spent the morning revising conscientiously; geography mostly, but also some chemistry and maths. Danny had sent some pictures of his newly-hatched quail. For almost half an hour the two friends had been sending imaginary culinary delights sliding back and forth along the table for each other's delectation.

"I send you a soft-boiled cuckoo's egg, tattooed with beetroot juice, accompanied by a candied elver on a bed of cabbage sog with caterpillar syrup drizzle," Sylvanie said, miming the dispatch of the delicacy.

Maisie halted the invisible foodstuffs at her end of the table, cut the top off the egg with a knife, seasoned the morsel and consumed the first tiny mouthful. She then licked the imaginary teaspoon, placed it on the table, gulped air several times and burped loudly.

"I had an awesome dream about getting a tattoo."

"Tell me about it," Sylvanie demanded, pretending to sweep plates, cutlery, glasses and condiments crashing to the floor with her forearm.

Maisie placed both hands flat upon the table, as if attending a séance. Sylvanie sat bolt upright, her arms folded.

"What do you call those massive places," Maisie asked, "like giant domes with trillions of lights that are supposed to be stars in the ceiling?"

"Planetarium."

"Yeah. I was carried into it on my back on a hard stretcher kind of thing. I knew it was you guys who were carrying me. My eyes were open. I looked at them. All the stars and the moon above me were reflected in my eyes."

Sylvanie felt as though Maisie was looking through her, to somewhere far beyond.

"I floated above myself," Maisie said, "like a mirror image of me, looking down. My clothes, my hands and my face were covered with dots of light. It felt like maps had been inked onto my skin and stitched into my clothes."

"Wow! That is quite cool, actually."

"Then the moon was just a white disc on a white piece of paper. I folded it up and put it in my pocket."

"Is it still there?"

Maisie felt in the pocket of her jeans. "Here it is." She mimed unfolding the non-existent sheet.

"It's a map of all the places we can go in the holidays," Sylvanie said.

"No. It's a timetable, really, of everything to do and when to do it. It's a horoscope."

"You're going on a long journey," Sylvanie said. "You'll meet a dark stranger."

10 (Before)
The Jewel

"Oh, just look at him," Mrs Slee's friend, Lilian, exclaimed. "What a proud creature."

She had been gazing out of the window of the bus, watching the warm Somerset countryside roll by, and had spotted the stag in a field of ripe wheat. Lilian tugged at the sleeve of Mrs Slee's raincoat and pushed back as far as she could to give her a better view through the grubby window. The old single-decker was stifling. Lilian felt as though she was melting. She wondered how Mrs Slee was surviving in her plastic raincoat.

"It's an omen," Mrs Slee said excitedly. One or two fellow passengers turned to look.

"Is it?" Lilian asked. "Why is it, old girl?"

"He sees us. He knows exactly where we're going and why, dear."

Mrs Slee watched the statuesque animal until the course of the bus made it impossible.

When they arrived at the seafront, the fragrant air and the heat of the day filled their heads. The pavement felt warm and soft. There were mature pines and there was concrete, and a grey wooden hut where Lilian could buy ice creams. They sat on a bench and watched seagulls, jackdaws, dogs, ships and holidaymakers swimming in the hazy liquescent flux of land, sea and sky.

Mrs Slee did not find the walk along the beach easy. She held Lilian's arm as they made their way in an easterly direction until they reached the foot of the crumbling cliffs. Lilian thought her elderly friend looked like a piece of plastic flotsam, an alien body among the pebbles and big grey boulders. Mrs Slee's coat was the colour the sea had been in postcards when Lilian was a girl.

"It's all as I remember it," Mrs Slee said, hands on hips. She was smiling and squinting skyward, her head tilted onto her shoulder.

"I hope we don't have to do any climbing."

"We can concentrate our search at the base of the cliffs, amongst the broken rocks that have fallen recently, and hopefully find what we've come for."

"Isn't that going to be somewhat dangerous, old girl?"

"I am no stranger to danger, dear," Mrs Slee responded, clutching her friend's arm tightly.

The beach at the foot of the crumbling cliffs was littered with fresh rockfalls. Several times they heard splinters of stone clatter onto the beach.

Less than an hour later, Mrs Slee was holding a pale pink rock resembling a hailstone suffused with blood. She held her hand out for Lilian to inspect the treasure.

Lilian slowly raised her eyebrows. "Good God! Old girl, that is truly gorgeous. It looks for all the world like fossilized candyfloss."

"Indeed, dear," Mrs Slee said, slipping the rock into the frayed pocket of her raincoat. "Our delightful quest has been a success."

On the way home, Mrs Slee, without looking up from her lap, said, "Sometimes I feel like a stone and sometimes ... I feel like a jewel."

11 (Before)
The Hare Amulet

Mrs Slee was standing beside the phone box in the village, waiting for Sylvanie to descend to the lane from the footpath. She had placed four Hare figures on the metal shelf beside the telephone. One was ceramic, one wooden, one plastic and one lead. They made an enigmatic group, holding council on the thin ledge, two with their long ears pointing straight up and two with their ears laid lengthways. Mrs Slee found it difficult to look up at them through the panelled door. She heard Sylvanie singing. The footpath sign had been broken years ago by Pony Chalice, who cut hedges around the village with the arm on the back of his tractor. A third of the sign had been smashed off. It now read: PUBLIC FOO.

Sylvanie smiled in greeting. "I hope you're not waiting for a call. I can't remember when it was last working."

Sylvanie carried a long hazel switch, with which she proceeded to whip the corner of the decommissioned call box.

"I have been decorating the shelf in there. It is now a magical kingdom where Hares rule."

Sylvanie shielded her eyes from the sun and peered through a cracked glass panel. "Wow! They're really amazing. Why did you put them in there?"

"My cottage is bursting at the seams. Things are beginning to spill out. And I thought they might enjoy a little outing."

"I saw a hare earlier on this afternoon," Sylvanie told Mrs Slee. "It didn't take much notice of me. It lolloped away, not in any hurry. It was scruffy, and actually massive."

"My goodness, dear. What a wonderful thing to see. There are not so many about as when I was a girl. You were lucky. But we make our own luck as we wander along life's highways and byways."

"I would have taken a picture of it," Sylvanie said, tapping her phone in the back pocket of her jeans, "and then I could have shown you. But the stupid technology didn't want to cooperate."

"Sometimes it is better simply to recollect something, and share the memory." Mrs Slee put her hand into the pocket of her raincoat and withdrew a necklace in the form of a seated Hare. The jewel was threaded onto a leather cord through the fine silver ring that pierced its upright ears. It swung in slow circles like a dowser's pendulum.

"I made this. If you like it, Sylvanie, you can have it."

Sylvanie looked at the exquisite object, the cord hanging loosely between the elderly woman's heavily-lined fingers. She could not believe her eyes.

"You didn't make that! I mean, it's just that it's so incredibly beautiful. Did you really make it? I can't believe how truly awesome and beautiful it is."

"Well, it's yours if you want it. I so much wish you would have it. I carved it with my penknife and polished it myself."

Mrs Slee was smiling, her sky-blue eyes shining like speedwell, like raincoats.

Then the amulet was being lowered onto Sylvanie's open palm.

12 (Before)
A Little Black Tin

"Do you believe in—" Lilian began.

"Yes, dear," Mrs Slee told her. "I do."

"You didn't let me finish."

"No, dear. You can't always be waiting for things to be concluded before taking action, you know. Sometimes interruptions are necessary. Anyway, I *do* believe in whatever it was you were going to ask me if I believed in."

There was, Lilian recognized, a delightfully seductive warmth in Mrs Slee's voice.

"God, then? Fairies? Reincarnation? What about aliens? Humanity? Justice? The afterlife?" Lilian heard a note of exasperation in her own voice, and not for the first time in conversation with her companion.

"Yes. There are many fissures in ordinary existence for somebody unbelievable to stick her or his inquisitive snout through. If you meet the Devil face-to-face, disbelief won't get you very far. By the time you've changed your mind, you're in his arms, dancing the 'Lobster Quadrille' at the Tower Ballroom."

"Old girl, you do my head in sometimes."

The two women were seated side by side at the edge of the ancient trackway leading from Hawkridge down to the River Barle, drinking tea from Lilian's tartan flask and eating bruised bananas. So heavily rutted was the track, so deeply had it scarred the green skin of the field, that they sat upon its bankside with their feet dangling, scuffing the exposed stones and dusty soil.

They could see open fields grazed by sheep, horses and cattle. And marching lines of slate-grey beeches, their vast wind-sculpted canopies holding all the passing skies aloft. Beyond was oak woodland, where the centuries-old giant trees supported entire ecosystems along their muscular limbs. Then high moorland, cloaked with heather and scribbled with haggard thorn trees.

"I have some information," Mrs Slee said.

"Well," Lilian prompted, "I shared my bananas."

"It is intelligence pertaining to the bigger picture."

"Naturally."

"The youngsters harvest their dreamscapes. It is a way of sorting the wheat from the chaff without everyday clutter clouding the issue, and communicating findings – to significant others as well as to themselves – without drawing undue attention to their endeavours."

"Did you say communicating things to others?" Lilian leaned forward and twisted to look up into her friend's eyes. "How do you know that Sylvanie and the others have been dreaming?"

"There are connections between people that act much like your beloved ley lines do between important ancient sites. And I am an important ancient site."

Lilian laughed and poured more tea. "It's a bit like spying, though, isn't it? I mean, listening and looking in on people's dreams?"

"It is like listening. It is like looking. What arcs across the spaces that divide us – often when we are least conscious of such connections – can empower, inform and unite us."

"It seems to me that we do an awful lot of things without really knowing what we're doing, or why. Obviously, I speak for myself."

"Of course, dear," Mrs Slee said. "It is essential."

"Why is it?"

"Because people cannot bear too much reality. If some of those involved caught more than a glimpse of the larger situation at hand, they might be too frightened to act."

Mrs Slee's words, it seemed to Lilian, had been pulled out of pockets, emptied from diaries and purses, and blown to her on the burgeoning breeze.

"I'm confused. I seem to spend half my life in this state."

"Good," Mrs Slee said. "That is precisely as it should be."

"Oh?"

"Confusion is the starting point for enlightenment."

Mrs Slee pointed her arthritic fists at the grass beside her and leaned on her straightened arms. Lilian thought she looked like a fledgling cloaked in sky.

"Thoughts can travel great distances if they don't happen upon a willing recipient," Mrs Slee continued. "Nightmares can rest dormant, like a virus sleeping in a major organ, for seemingly interminable periods, waiting to wrest control when defences are low. Information is like dust, spores: we breathe it in and we breathe it out." She breathed in deeply through her nose and exhaled slowly through her mouth. "The Hares in the telephone box will keep our little troupe focussed. There is an old line to each of their homes."

Lilian fitted the yellow plastic beaker back on the top of her flask. She looked at the back of her hand, at her elegant fingers, and saw liver spots mottling her skin. "I'm not terribly sure, old girl, that I'm comfortable breaking and entering people's subconscious."

Leaning toward her like a heron, Mrs Slee tapped the back of Lilian's right hand with one finger. "We must. If *we* don't, then the next man will. The next man who *will*, will anyway. But at least he won't know more than we do."

Mrs Slee rose and bimbled off down the track toward the gate into the woodland, leaving Lilian to pick up the banana skins and stow the flask. Lilian noticed a pair of buzzards wheeling high on a thermal in the turquoise above the church.

"Are you going to tell me about your dream?" Lilian enquired when she'd caught up. The two women walked arm in arm.

Mrs Slee looked mostly at her feet as she spoke. "Finch's mother and Sylvanie's mother were sat to either side of me on the bench where you and I often sit by the grave-flower tap in the churchyard. I could hear the jackdaws conversing with their echoes, with previous selves, in the tower. Finch's mother passed me a little black tin, of the sort your father would have bought his pipe tobacco in upon some other day in history. Speaking precisely as one, she and Hannah said, 'Open it.' I did as they bid me. The old tin had four tiny birds in it, each about the size of my little finger. I thought they must be dead, but the two women blew some whispered incantation gently over the poor creatures and they began to shake themselves into life. I looked at the women in turn and they were smiling, their eyes bright with wonder. When I looked down into the tin, it was empty, the shiny interior reflecting the rolling sky above."

13 (After)
Sacrifice

The landline phone rang.

Sylvanie was sitting with a blanket around her on one of two massive off-white settees in their new safe house apartment. Having been the source of all the distressing news coverage, the radio was now silent. That morning, Hannah, Sylvanie and the Watch had sat at the table in the kitchen and listened to a woman newsreader describe how three Chilean children, chosen through some bizarre form of lottery involving their ages and astrological signs, had been killed in a rush to get past them into a painted wooden version of the Barrow Ship that a cult leader and his followers had built high on a mountainside.

Sylvanie was deep in thought, having spent the best part of three hours crying. Hannah, who had been asleep for more than an hour, did not wake. Although Sylvanie was not asleep, and although she was shaken by the noise, the phone rang seven or eight times before she was able to claw her way upwards through a mire of fatigue and despair to answer.

The phone never rang without Sylvanie and Hannah having been informed of some prior arrangement. This cold call was unprecedented, and Sylvanie expected the Watch to come racing into the room. She felt herself stop breathing. She had the sensation of being at the bottom of their pool in the river, looking desperately into the gloom, waiting for a face to emerge.

"Hello, dear."

The kindness and solicitude contained in Mrs Slee's voice was so thick that Sylvanie felt she could have cut herself a fat slice of it and saved it for later.

"Oh, my God. Mrs Slee, how are you? Was it difficult to arrange the call? Oh, God. Where are you calling from? Are you at home?"

Sylvanie could have asked a thousand questions, but she stopped and tried to think if anything she'd said had made sense.

"I am near home, dear, in the telephone box in the village. And I am quite well, thank you."

"I didn't think it was working. I mean, I didn't think it would ever be used again."

"Well, it seems to be functioning perfectly well this eventide."

"Gosh. How does the village look?" It seemed to Sylvanie as though the question had been pulled from her mouth like bunting on a ribbon. "Is the village even still there? What about the cottage? Our cottage, Mrs Slee; is it damaged? I mean, I imagine it's been boarded up." Sylvanie felt herself beginning to well up.

"It is raining softly just at the minute, on slugs and lettuces alike, and the village is most certainly still here. Your cottage is fine. There are roadblocks at either end of the village these days, and very few people who don't actually live here are allowed through. It started raining about twenty minutes ago, though it's been threatening all day. The rain has washed and burnished the lane. I am glad I decided to wear my raincoat when I left home."

A smile flickered across Sylvanie's lips. Nobody had ever seen Mrs Slee without her blue plastic raincoat.

"Rain has burnished the lane," Sylvanie repeated. She felt euphoric and devastated at the same time.

"How are you and your mother, dear?" Mrs Slee had caught what she thought were two muffled sobs.

"Well, I think today surely qualifies as one of the worst days of a lot of people's lives. I am brought to my knees by the deaths of those children in Chile. So is Mum. Did you hear about it? We've had some diabolical crap perpetrated in our name, but nothing to compare with this. I wonder if we can live through it. I wonder if we even should."

Mrs Slee was armed and ready. "People have murdered each other in the name of God, in the name of justice, righteousness, honour, and even in the name of love, for centuries and millennia. We cannot ever allow ourselves to stop loving, caring, and believing in what is real, right and good because some people's lives crumble into madness and badness. It is an unimaginably awful thing, this accident, this tragedy, Sylvanie. The only answer is to be sad while at the same time believing that we don't have to be sad forever. It is called grief. Grief is despair and love in equal measure, you see. It sticks you right where you are, glues you in the time you're in, until it's right to carry on. Sylvanie, you have to find the balance yourself when something like this happens. You, dear, I promise, will not be broken by this. It is the saddest thing, but it is not where happiness ends."

Sylvanie was silent. She let her tears fall.

"Routinely, love is hard to give away, if the truth were told. Not everyone wants it. I am here if you need me."

"It's not the same."

"It isn't," Mrs Slee admitted. "You're right."

"Do you think they'll come back?" Sylvanie asked, her voice trembling.

"I do, indeed. I *know* it."

There was a weighty pause in the conversation.

"Are you crying?" Sylvanie asked.

"I am."

The wind, which pulled and shoved the gorse and the twisted hawthorns, came between them.

"Are you still there?" Sylvanie asked.

"I am."

"I've been thinking about how everything is connected, about how things have been made to fit together to make other things happen. I feel like me and Finch and Danny and Maze have been puppets, and I'm beginning to wonder if there was or is any part of our stupid little lives that was or is actually ours to live."

The evening sky had thickened above the apartments and office blocks opposite. Sylvanie had not switched on any lights. She sat on the floor, hunched over the phone, feeling like she had been talking to Mrs Slee for a lifetime, and visualizing the old woman with her foot in the phone box door, inviting in the wind that made its way down Snowdrop Valley from the moor.

"Do you still wear the Hare, dear?"

"I do. I couldn't live without its coolness against my skin." Sylvanie paused to take stock of what she had heard herself say. "Why did you make it for me?"

"The Hare will speak to you when the time is right."

"Who are you?" Sylvanie felt the impertinent directness of the question ache in the centre of her chest, right where the alabaster jewel lay.

"I am an old lady who cares more than is good for her, knows more than is good for her, and has the vanity to imagine she might have a part to play in all of this."

"You've been part of a quiet conspiracy to make all sorts of weird things happen."

"I do hope so, dear."

Sylvanie had risen and was standing at the window. Light cast by streetlamps below was yellow, and those shops that remained illuminated appeared full of the same coagulating light. Perhaps, she thought, the whole world – everything beyond that mercilessly ordinary room in the safe house – was silent.

"I'm sorry," she said. But Mrs Slee had gone. The line was dead.

For a long while Sylvanie stood motionless, watching the lights of the city traffic pushing shadows away, only to see darknesses scurrying back as soon as vehicles had passed.

When she eventually went to her room, Sylvanie turned on her lamp and sat cross-legged on her bed, leaning over her open notebook.

With a sharp pencil, she wrote: I watched the girl dancing. She had been pulled free of the mirror. She was dressed in grey. I watched her lips moving quickly as if film of her speaking had been sped up. She was flying with her arms outstretched, looking down. I said how do I know when I close my eyes that you still exist?

Sylvanie took her eraser out of her pencil case and proceeded to take back from the page every leaden word that had fallen there.

14 (Before)
The Third Barrow

"Do you love that trials bike, kid?" Sylvanie asked. "I mean, are you *in* love with it?"

"I *do*. I *am*," Finch replied, deep-voiced and without hesitation, as though standing at an altar.

"Sometimes, do you read poetry to it? Hmm? Do you? Do you love it *that* much?" Sylvanie's bright eyes were as sly as her crooked grin. "Do you sing love songs to it?"

"I love this motorbike so much that I *write* poetry for it. *And* I sing to it." Finch understood what he was setting himself up for, and smiled inwardly as he tried desperately to think ahead.

"Recite some of that amorous verse right now," Sylvanie demanded, biting her lower lip.

Dropping to one knee, Finch turned to his 1970s Montesa 250 trials bike.

"Oh Motorbike, from where I kneels
I see your wheels, the wheels I love.
I would adore nothing more
than to ride across the moor, just like before.
You and me and Syl-vay-nee."

Sylvanie applauded with gusto. "Bravo! You are truly a great poet. Your abnormal romance is a very moving and beautiful thing to behold."

Pretending to well up, Sylvanie bit her knuckles. She took a step toward Finch, helped him up, then punched him hard on the shoulder. Grabbing the handlebars of his motorbike, she pulled the slim machine from the hedgerow, threw her leg over, kicking his helmet to the ground, and sat astride the saddle.

"I'm in charge, poetic freak," she informed Finch, before jumping hard on the kick-start. "You're pillion. Forget your helmet. Forget your fears."

The vintage Montesa growled into life on her second attempt, and Sylvanie gave the throttle a couple of sharp twists before looking round at Finch. She had to shunt up to the petrol tank to allow him space to perch behind her. She had ridden his motorbike many times, but never with him on the back. She was uncomfortable, but in control. Finch was clinging to her, his legs stuck out to keep his feet clear of the ground. Sylvanie pulled the clutch in, clunked into first gear, and up the path they roared, Sylvanie leaning over the handlebars as far as she dared.

"Scream if you want to go faster," she cried.

They had arranged to meet up with Danny and Maisie at the cattle-grid at Dunkery Gate. Within sight of the head of the combe Finch fell off the back of the motorbike, coming down hard on the base of his spine. Sylvanie stopped and waited for him to get back on. Very red in the face, and rubbing his lower back hard, Finch remounted the Montesa behind her.

"She dumped you, matey," Danny shouted when they reached the truck. "She was only after your shit old bike all along." Danny was clapping and laughing and slapping his thighs. He and Maisie had witnessed the fall from grace. Finch was still rubbing his lower back and buttocks.

Picnickers and walkers parked near the cattle-grid were giving them black looks. They were teenagers, shouting and laughing; they had a motorbike, but no helmets; they had the muddiest vehicle on the planet. The thickness of the mud on his pickup was a source of immense pride for Danny.

"That truck has never seen a single drop of water that didn't fall dreckly from the sky," he had once boasted to Finch.

Danny had his spaniels, Boots and Shoes, and Maisie had brought Royston Quantock. The fox and dogs had been caged together on the journey, and Royston Quantock had nervously deposited a small, dark and seriously malodorous turd on a matted old blanket. Maisie had gone to the stream to wash it out. She was tying the wet blanket to the bars behind the cab of Danny's pickup when the motorbike came into earshot. The animals were running rings around each other, the fox nipping hard when he felt threatened, and the trio were causing quite a stir amongst the walkers and holidaymakers.

Royston Quantock had been a present from Danny, who had handed the bedraggled cub to Maisie, on her doorstep one very wet evening, swaddled in an oily square of ripped tarpaulin. "Little bugger didn't want to die," he had said simply. Although she had adored the animal from the very first second, she would later remove his collar, as she had many times before, and let him choose between her and the wild.

Finch pulled a roughly folded map out of his back pocket and gestured for them to gather round.

Danny had other ideas. "You can't lock your bike, matey," he shouted over his shoulder. "So someone's got to risk riding it. No one's going to want to be pushing it up that bliddy hill." He pointed his thumb at Dunkery Beacon.

Danny bump-started the Montesa on the slope, then rode straight through the stream and roared off across the moor, pulling sustained wheelies with the engine steaming. Maisie was left holding Royston Quantock on his lead in one hand and Boots and Shoes on their lengths of bailer cord in the other.

"We're here," Finch said, pointing to Dunkery Gate and then the beacon on the old map. "We should just go straight up the path to the cairn and then follow the line of barrows across, counting them off against the ones on the map until we get to roughly where we think the missing one used to be."

It was a chilly day, but moistly bright. From the cairn they could see northwards across the Vale of Porlock to Hurlstone Point. The Welsh coastline appeared incredibly close and more sunlit than much of Somerset. To the east, the islands of Flat Holm and Steep Holm were clearly visible in the Bristol Channel, along with the brutal geometry of the nuclear power station at Hinkley Point. To the south-west, beyond a vast, undulating patchwork of farmland, Dartmoor sat darkly on the horizon.

They walked in a westerly direction from Dunkery Beacon, over Little Rowbarrow and Great Rowbarrow. When they got to the approximate area where the third barrow was marked on the monochrome sheet, Danny was lying in the damp heather. Boots and Shoes went crazy for him. Royston Quantock kept his distance.

"What took you so long, suckers?" Danny asked.

"You belting off into the distance with our transport might have something to do with it," Maisie told him.

Danny was lying on his back, juggling spaniels. He ignored Maisie.

"You're out of juice," Danny informed Finch. "So, unless you want to piss in the tank again, you'll be pushing this death-trap wee wee wee all the way home."

"You'll be pushing it, or I'll be pushing you," Finch told him.

Danny's grin broadened.

"Danny has agreed to push Finch's motorbike back to the cattle-grid when we've completed our mission," Sylvanie said. "So let's just *get on* with it, shall we?"

Finch looked at Danny. Danny looked at Finch.

"I think we're here," Danny said, pointing straight down at the ground. "I've got the X-factor and I mark the spot. I reckon this is where the thing you wanted to come up here and look for used to be. The big question is: so effin' what?" He had closed his eyes. Boots and Shoes, frantic for attention, were licking his face and hands.

Sylvanie sat in the heather and felt the damp of the waterlogged moor reaching up to her. In her mind's eye there were four Hare ornaments arranged on a mound of peaty earth on the shelf in the phone box in the village.

"I feel weird," Maisie said.

"Do you feel as weird as you look?" Danny asked without looking.

"I feel sort of spaced-out, like I'm a bit drunk," Maisie said.

"I feel it too," Finch said.

"Maybe it's altitude sickness," Danny suggested, getting up and staggering through the heather like an intoxicated morris dancer.

"*Attitude* sickness is what you've got," Finch offered. "It's a degenerative disease and there's absolutely no cure. You are one sick individual. Medical science will be very interested in you, matey."

Sylvanie stood up and looked around at her friends. She felt dizzy for a moment. Finch, Danny and Maisie seemed too far away. The way they were grouped gave the impression that they were standing in a glass box, looking out. For a moment there was silence. It seemed as though the world was waiting with bated breath for something to happen. To them.

"I don't know exactly what it is we're supposed to be looking for," Sylvanie said, "but I think we've found it."

And the world exhaled, and once again began to turn.

15 (Before)
A Big Holiday

"What's your favourite subject at school now?" Sylvanie's grandfather asked the faintest ghost of his reflection in the car window beside him. He didn't appear to be holding the steering-wheel. "I remember when it was all about dressing-up, and ballet dancing and dollies with you, and now it's probably all blessed screens and computers."

"Sylvanie never did any ballet at all," Hannah said. "Or had 'dollies', for that matter."

"I did have one doll for a while. Sleepy, she was called. Her eyes closed when you laid her down." Sylvanie looked at the left side of her mother's head. "Do you remember? I used to think she was a little version of me. I mean, she wasn't like a baby. I lost her somewhere in the woods."

"Yes, of course," Hannah said. "I remember Sleepy. She lived in a box some knee-length boots of mine came in. She was always asleep when you took the lid off. You always told me to be quiet, because you wanted to be the one to take off the lid and wake her up gently. You loved the woods, and you said it would be like a big holiday for her. You didn't cry."

16 (Before)
Art Homework

Hannah dropped Sylvanie off at the top of the steep lane leading to the beach. There to catch up on some art homework to do with weather and nature, she would be ahead of what needed to be done if she produced four or five decent sketches. She stopped at the loo, then headed for the seaward slope of the dunes, watery hot chocolate from the café in hand.

The tide was a long way out and the vast area of flat, wet sand perfectly reflected a sky crowded with sculptural cloud figures muscling in over the Atlantic. Two hundred yards away, a family group was playing Frisbee, a lively mongrel leaping into the air every time the disc left someone's hand. People were running and jumping on a mirror image of the sky, bruises appearing as water was displaced from the sand where they landed, then rapidly glossing over as the reflection healed itself. It was almost impossible to distinguish land from sky.

On the first clean page of her notebook, Sylvanie wrote: *Where does it begin? Where does it end? One moment and the next? Sometime and some other time? One place and the next? We try to tie ourselves to these moments and we drown like voices in the wind.*

Sitting with the dunes at her back, she opened her sketchpad, removed the lid of her water jar and began making marks with water-soluble coloured pencils, smudging and overdrawing repeatedly, washing over the work with a paintbrush. After two or three attempts, she slowed down, working more knowingly and deliberately.

She pulled off her boots and socks and pushed her toes through the dry surface into the cool, damp sand beneath.

Sylvanie had been on the beach for about an hour and a half when she looked up and saw a young man in the same year as Danny walking slowly toward her, surfboard under his arm. She looked down at her work, then straight back up. Sylvanie then made five or six wonderfully fluid marks, putting the young man in her beachscape. He stood in front of her, planting his surfboard – black with a big silver skull – upright at his side.

"What are you doing?" the young man asked.

"Homework."

"What kind of freakin' homework you doing on the beach?"

"Art." And without hesitation, she showed him.

"Cool. I knew you were an arty-farty type."

"Cheers. It's more than just homework, though. I don't need much of an excuse to draw or paint. Or write, for that matter. What are you doing?"

Sylvanie sensed that she was losing her grip on what she was saying.

The young man turned slowly, smiled, and pointed at his surfboard. "Extreme ironing. So ... You coming in?"

"What? In the sky?" Sylvanie replied, and immediately wished she hadn't.

"Some other time, then," he said, shrugging his shoulders. "Keep up the Picasso shit. You're not bad."

He moved off along the line of the dunes without looking back. Sylvanie watched him walk barefoot up the sandy concrete toward the shops and showers.

She dug a hole and buried her feet, sprinkling dry sand, pebbles and shells around her ankles, then stood. She imagined being an ancient sculpture of a goddess stuck in the sand, forgotten for thousands of years, not able to live, not able to pull free and run away as the breathless tide raced in.

On the way home in the car, intoning each word to Hannah, who listened intently, Sylvanie wrote: People move differently when they can see the marks they're making on the world, when they turn and see their footprints in the sand. Flattened grass stands up. To show that there is life. Afterlife. People run through cornfields just to see that they've been there. That they've existed. They write important declarations before the hungry waves, knowing that the faithful tide will come and erase it all. Then what was written, and consumed by the ocean, becomes encrypted in a million grains of sand. The sand takes custody of the secrets. The knowledge. Kids fill their buckets and build their castles.

17 (Before)
First Pieces

Everything around them was familiar, perfect: the overwintered whortleberry stems, the scrubby gorse with its patches of rich yellow flowers, and the black twigs of burned heather; the wind blowing in over Lundy from the Atlantic, wrapping standing stones and pounding on the hunched backs of bone-hard hawthorn; the musk of the moorland, richly peaty, sodden and faintly fungal, moving among them.

"That is strange," Sylvanie said, looking down at the thing she'd stepped back from.

Finch stooped and touched the exposed surface. "It's glass – or maybe stone." He rubbed it with the ends of his fingers. "It's hard."

"It's just useless concrete, matey," Danny said, and immediately doubted himself. "Cast from a mould. If it's not concrete … It looks more like a chunk of glass poured on the floor. It won't have nothing to do with your blown-up burial chambers."

"But it would be *very* interesting if it was," Finch replied, striking a Sherlock Holmes pose, stroking his chin.

The material, Sylvanie thought, seemed to be taking in light, then holding it, like a breath.

They began digging at the edges of the object with sticks, attempting to gain leverage. Maisie and Finch managed to get their fingers under one side and tilt it free of the ground. Ants, woodlice and millipedes fled as the roof was lifted from their world. Seven or eight centimeters thick, their find resembled a section of shell or crab carapace, or part of a broken engine casing.

"It's weird," Finch said, holding the textured, slightly dished object out for someone else to take, to feel, "but it's actually as light as a feather. Here." He passed it to Sylvanie and Maisie, who held out their hands for it.

"God, it's so much lighter than you'd think it would be for the size of it," Maisie said. "It's plastic, isn't it? If it was something important, I don't think it would be so light. I don't even think it would still be here."

"Somebody dumped it here ages ago," Danny said. "It's got to be a man-made thing; I mean, part of something … something bust. It must have come out of your ancient, long-lost barrow, bird-boy – *Not*."

"It's like a fossil," Sylvanie offered. "A bit of fossilized sea-bed or plant stems, maybe."

"It looks more like a lump of cow's innards, if you ask me," Danny said. "It won't be worth a bleedin' penny, I can tell you that. You couldn't even weigh it in."

"Yeah. But who cares?" Finch asked. "We came up here and we found something that might have come out of the barrow," he said, turning to include the others in his statement. They saw the excitement in his eyes.

"There's loads more of it," Maisie said. "There's some there, look," she pointed into the bracken to her left. "And a much bigger bit behind Syl."

They soon had eight or nine more lumps of lichen-mottled material, muddied and discoloured, but looking like quartz or etched glass. The smallest were no bigger than a thumb, and the largest about a quarter of the size of a dustbin lid. They made a rough pile of pieces in the heather.

Danny and Finch sat side by side on the motorbike. Maisie stood facing them.

"Are we going to take it all home?" Sylvanie asked nobody in particular. "Because if we are, I think we should wash it off in the stream first."

"Definitely, we've got to take it all back with us," Finch said. "We're going to find out what it is and where the hell it came from."

They all felt the spots of rain and looked at the sky.

There had been one or two fleeting patches of blue – gone in an instant – as though queueing clouds had desperately bandaged wounds.

"It's going to piss down," Danny said.

Maisie looked at Danny, at his full, brown face. Anywhere he went on Exmoor, she thought, he seemed part of the landscape. He could have been planted on the moor, rooted and grown there, or some farmer had hammered him into the ground to use as a gatepost or waymark in the snow.

Boots and Shoes had been bounding about in the chestnut-coloured bracken, following scent tracks, leaping on each other and yelping wildly. For more than half an hour, no one had given a thought to Royston Quantock. Maisie had removed his collar and lead and looped them round her neck. The empty collar caught Danny's eye and he scanned the moorland and horizon. Maisie's fox was nowhere to be seen.

"Where's your fox?" Danny asked. "I can't see him."

Maisie froze, as if waiting for her thoughts to settle and clarify, then stood and looked out across the moor.

"Roy, come back! Royston Quantock, come back," she shouted, loudly, sharply, turning her face into the strengthening wind only for it to throw her words back at her.

"Give me the collar." Danny called his dogs and held the collar for them to sniff. "Where is he? Where is he? Eh? Go find him. Get on. Get on!"

Boots and Shoes took off across the wind toward the boundary between the copse and the airfield – noses in the air, then to the ground, threading in tight circles on the way – while Danny and Maisie followed as fast as the rough terrain would allow.

"We'll stay here until you guys get back," Finch called. "If we see him, we'll yell." He was happy to sit and wait with Sylvanie. She rose to her feet and watched the spaniels leap the high-banked hedgerow and disappear into the grey wood.

"I reckon Maze's been dreaming of Royston going back to the wild," she said. "Coming back to say hello now and again, turning up just in time to fight off the blood-sucking freaks and zombies that are always lurking about in the woods."

"I can see that fox ripping out the throat of some American college-kid vampire who was just over here for a quiet little vacation in a cabin in the woods," Finch said.

"But," Sylvanie said, "if a vampire was attacking Maze, and Royston Quantock did rip out his jugular, with tons of blood spurting out all over the shop, then Royston Quantock would turn into a vampire too. Then Maze and Red Roy would roam the woods at night seeking victims who were abroad at ungodly hours. Maze wouldn't mind running around in the deep, deep, dark, dark forest at night in her cape and her hood, with her ferocious sidekick, slaughtering innocent American college kids who blubbed loads and shone their torches up under their chins all the time."

The daylight was dying in a blaze of glory when Danny and Maisie emerged from Pony Chalice's copse. They had not found the fox. Maisie had obviously been crying.

"He's gone," she said. "None of us thought it was supposed to be forever. Little sod never really wanted to be a pet, but I think he gave it his best shot."

Danny bowed his head and folded his hands at his waist. He looked like he was about to say a prayer.

To everyone's astonishment, he put his arm around Maisie's shoulder and pulled her briefly to him.

Finch and Maisie took the largest piece to the stream and held it under the cold flow. The shard of material was transformed. When they held it in the beam of Danny's headlight, everyone gasped. It looked like a slab of clear stone crystal, a prismatic shell-like sheet, casting a myriad tiny rainbows on the sheep-bitten turf.

18 (Before)
Tuesday's Child

"I bumped into Mrs Slee," Sylvanie told Hannah, "in the aisle with all the magazines and notepaper and cards."

"Stationery."

"No, actually she was moving at the speed of light."

"Oh, shut up," Hannah said in mock exasperation. "Little Miss Witty Knickers."

"Love that, Mother. I'm going to get a T-shirt printed. I might even change my name by deed poll."

Hannah smiled and checked the shopping list.

"She was trying to find a birthday card for an old friend who lives in Maidstone," Sylvanie said. "Wherever that is."

"In Kent. It's where I went to college. Was she with Lilian?"

"I think Lilian was in the loo. I waited a bit, but she didn't materialize."

"Was she wearing that ridiculous coat?"

"It's boiling in here, Mum. Of course she was wearing her lovely coat."

"What did the old witch have to say for herself, then?"

"Witch? I'll be a witch just like her one day, if all goes according to my cunning plan. When I was young, you told me that being like her was something to aspire to, because she's strong and independent."

"That's right. She's a strong and independent witch. And you're still young."

"She said she thought I must be 'Tuesday's child'. Whatever that's supposed to mean."

"God," Hannah said, stopping the trolley. "Yes. It's been ages since I've heard it. It's a line from a traditional nursery rhyme. Wednesday's child is full of woe, or … something, something … far to go. I think it's meant to be like a fortune-telling thing. I don't remember what Tuesday's child did, sorry. I'll bet it's been at least three decades since I heard it last. It'll drive me crazy trying to think of it. Have a look."

"I'm on it." A moment later, Sylvanie read the rhyme from her phone.

"Monday's child is fair of face
Tuesday's child is full of grace
Wednesday's child is full of woe
Thursday's child has far to go
Friday's child is loving and giving
Saturday's child works hard for a living
The child that's born on the Sabbath day
Is bonny, blithe, good and gay.

"Why would she think I was full of grace? What exactly is grace anyway?"

"I think she was just trying to be nice, trying to say something pleasant and kind in an old-fashioned way."

"But what does it mean? Does she mean 'graceful'?"

"It's just her way of saying you're lovely. It's the sort of thing elderly people say."

They turned left past clothing and headed into wines and spirits. Hannah came across a teaching colleague she'd met on a supply job, and they joked about meeting in the booze aisle. Sylvanie slipped away to find Mrs Slee again, and Lilian.

They were in the aisle with all the biscuits and crackers. They saw her coming and waved.

"We were debating the pros and cons of hard-baked water biscuits, the larger and the smaller varieties," Lilian informed Sylvanie.

"I see," Sylvanie said, eyeing the contents of the women's trolley.

"I like Stilton, the richer and riper the better, and I like it for supper," Mrs Slee stated gleefully.

"Doesn't it give you nightmares if you eat it late at night?"

"Yes indeed, dear. But the shadow beneath a tree is as important as the tree that casts it. There are shades we don't know exist until we roll away the stone that harbours them. Nightmares are as essential as any other form of dream."

"That's a little abstruse, old girl," Lilian told her friend. "Do tell Sylvanie and I – in lay person's terms, please – what you mean."

"I expect you mean that without the line of darkness cast by its gnomon, a sundial might as well be a birdbath," Sylvanie volunteered, smiling broadly. "Are we singing from the same hymn sheet?"

Mrs Slee and Lilian were holding onto their trolley together, leaning so far over in Sylvanie's direction that they would certainly have toppled had it not been there to support them.

"Your teachers must be very pleased with you, I'm sure," Lilian said.

"I looked up 'Tuesday's child' on my phone, and it said 'full of grace'. I suppose it sounds like a nice enough thing, but I'm not really sure what grace is meant to be."

Lilian looked bemused.

"Well, dear," Mrs Slee said, "let's say it's a real happiness deep inside you, shall we? You carry it with you and it gives you strength when you need it."

"Wow. I like that. OK. I'd better go and find Mum."

Hannah was still talking with the other teacher, who spoke briefly with Sylvanie and then went off to find ice cream for after her yoga.

"Deep inner happiness." Sylvanie folded her arms and smiled smugly.

"Nice. Do you want to get a tin of tuna for a sandwich for one of your packed lunches?"

"Yeah. Yummy, Mummy."

At the checkout, Sylvanie was researching birth days and dates on her phone, while half-heartedly loading loo rolls, soap and fire lighters onto the belt.

"I knew it. I knew she'd be right. Mum, do you remember what day of the week I was born on?"

"I honestly can't say that I do. Sorry, love. I suppose it's something I ought to know. You're going to tell me it was a Tuesday."

"Oh my God." Sylvanie did a breathy laugh with her mouth open wide, as though amused and incredulous in equal measure. "How would Mrs Slee know?"

Sylvanie felt chilly in the car park. She loaded the shopping into the boot of the car and ran back with the trolley. The sky was low and dense.

It was dark by the time they drove through North Molton, the glow from Sylvanie's phone cocooned her in the passenger seat. It was drizzling, and the wipers were beating a steady rhythm.

"You were born on a Friday, Mum. Did you know that?"

"I didn't. So what am I then?"

Sylvanie had to refer to the rhyme. "'Loving and giving'. Which is, I would say, pretty much on the money, dearest, darling matriarch."

"Creep. Although I do feel that I have always been both of those things to you, dearest, darling offspring."

"Maisie was born on a Thursday, so she has 'far to go'."

Sylvanie was certain that she'd got Maisie's date of birth correct. She messaged Danny and Finch. Danny replied as they were driving down the hill toward Simonsbath. She did the research.

"Danny was born on a Thursday, too. Danny and Maisie – both born on Thursdays."

Sylvanie seemed to wait ages for Finch's reply. He responded just as they were pulling up outside the cottage. Sylvanie sat in the car while Hannah unloaded the shopping as far as the porch.

"Thursday," Sylvanie told Hannah, walking along the glistening path, trying to avoid the journeying slugs and snails, showing her mum the information displayed on her phone. "All three of them have 'far to go'."

19 (Before)
An Unbreakable Bond

Finch was sat in bed, headphones on, watching videos on his tablet. On the wall beside him, glossed by the cool light from the screen, was a black and white photograph of Sylvanie's cat, Kinky, asleep within the protective curve of Eccles Cake Thief, now deceased. Eccles was a rescued whippet: always shivering, nervous, and dotingly affectionate. Kinky and Eccles were soulmates. Sylvanie's young cat had been bitten at the base of her spine by another cat, putting a permanent bend in her tail. In Finch's photograph, large smears were visible across the cat's jet-black fur where the dog had given her big, wet licks.

Finch's phone lit up. He paused the film of insane downhill mountain bike stunts in Brazil, and removed his headphones. He could hear muffled television sounds from downstairs.

Maisie had sent the same message to Sylvanie and Danny. It read: 'Call me now'.

Finch's digital clock read 22:42. He called Sylvanie, who answered after two rings.

"Hi. What do you want? Hang on kiddo; let me dry my ears."

Finch heard a muffled whump as Sylvanie threw her phone onto her bed. Ten seconds later, she had the phone to her ear again.

"Hello, Mr Finch, you complete stalker. What's all this about?"

"I got a text from Maisie. I felt like speaking to you first."

"I've been in the bath, listening to one of Mum's poetry CDs. It was truly deadly; some guy who's been dead fifty years, reading his poetry. I guess it was recorded before he died. I'll check my phone. Hang on. Putting you momentarily on hold, sir."

The line went quiet. Finch waited. His mum and dad were pottering about in the kitchen before going to bed. He heard a spoonful of laughter, light as thistledown, from his mum.

A second later the living room door opened and his father called upstairs, "I'm making cocoa. Want some?"

"I'm good, thanks," Finch called down. "Night."

"Hi." Sylvanie was back. "Crazy Maisie did message me. I'll ring her now if you want."

"No. It's OK. I'll ring her."

"Why did you ring me, then? Why didn't you just reply?"

"It's late. Maybe it's got something to do with losing Royston Quantock."

"So, I'll ring her. No worries, kid."

"I'm happy to call her," Finch said. "It was kind of an epic day."

"It was," Sylvanie agreed. "I felt pretty windswept."

"OK. Later, then."

Sylvanie adopted an American accent. "Thank you for calling the twenty-four-hour customer helpline," she said brightly, and hung up.

Finch called Maisie, who answered immediately, giving the impression that she had been waiting for a response since sending the original message.

"Sorry it took me so long, Maze. I was watching movie trailers and bike stunts with my headphones on."

"You know the lumps of stuff from the moor?" Maisie launched in. "Well, I thought three of the pieces I brought home looked like they might fit together, and now it's like they've been permanently glued, like they're the strongest magnets in the universe."

"OK. Were they, sort of, interlocking pieces?"

"Not really. Two of the faces that stuck together were pretty flat. Now there's no way they're ever coming apart."

"OK."

"It's not just that," Maisie continued, "if I turn my bedroom lights off, I can still see them."

"You mean they glow in the dark?"

"Not exactly. It's just that I can see they're still there. They're like ghosts. And I'll tell you something else as well: if you hold them up to the light, you can't see anything like a crack or a join where they fitted together; there's no sign that they were ever broken apart."

"Does it look like something, now? I mean, something recognizable?"

"No. Just bigger, I guess. But the pieces look as if they should be loads heavier than they actually are."

"They look like glass," Finch said, picking up one of the splinters he'd brought home. "But, if that's what they were, then they'd be so much heavier. I know what you're saying."

Maisie yawned. It sounded like the yawn had taken her by surprise. "I'd better go."

"We should get together tomorrow, all of us. See if we can fit more pieces together."

"What do you think it was?"

Finch took too long to answer.

"Finch?"

"I suppose it could be something perfectly ordinary, something there's a boring explanation for."

"Yeah. Is that what you think it will turn out to be?"

"Nope."

20 (Before)
I Am the Door

Mrs Slee and Lilian were seated to the right-hand side of the central entrance of the bus shelter. There were low walls on either side of the entrance, over which anyone seated could see the road. A neighbour was standing just inside the entrance, her umbrella at the ready. It was drizzling, but there had been heavier showers throughout the morning. Mrs Slee and Lilian had chatted to the woman about the use of unwaxed lemons in the production of elderflower cordial until the arrival of the 10:20 to Minehead. The neighbour bade them a cheerful goodbye and boarded the bus. Mrs Slee and Lilian waved as it pulled away, its tyres hissing on the wet tarmac, sounding like an inflatable version of itself deflating.

"The Door in the churchyard wall again," Mrs Slee informed Lilian, her tone conspiratorial.

In the churchyard, three-quarters of the way along the perimeter wall on the school side, was the black-painted, heavy, wooden door to which Mrs Slee referred, its jamb set deep into the rosy sandstone masonry. It appeared entirely sealed with paint, though a large, forged-iron latch could be moved upward quite easily, falling back into place with a weighty clunk. Above the latch were two heavy-duty padlocks, rusty and firmly locked. On the lintel above was a hand-painted wooden plaque, which read: 'I Am the Door'.

"Had you been knocking, old girl?" Lilian asked. It wasn't the first time Mrs Slee had recounted a version of this recurring dream.

"I had. Undaunted, I kept stepping up to the Door, knocking loudly, then stepping back, as is polite, awaiting an answer. I could hear someone moving about, shuffling and whispering; perhaps two people, sounding secretive. One of the voices was that of a man."

Lilian opened a packet of sugar ring doughnuts, picked one between her forefinger and thumb and took a bite. She placed the others on the bench between them.

"Did he sound like anyone we might know?" Lilian asked, licking her sugary lips. "Did you recognize either of the voices?"

"Perhaps, dear, but I couldn't be sure."

"Who do you think they were?"

"I think they were people trying to tell us something. Perhaps attempting to convey intelligence without being discovered, hoping to deliver a message from some elsewhere, some other point in time. People don't always know where they're supposed to be, which side of the Door they're supposed to be on. Now and then, people get stuck in the 'now' or the 'then'."

"You don't think it was *him*?"

"Certainly, he was at their backs."

"Then what happened?" Lilian asked with her mouth full. She had taken a substantial bite because her doughnut had begun to fall apart.

"The churchyard grew darker. I walked backwards, and didn't stop until I got to the path, its cobblestones squirming like a serpent's scales. I was motionless for an eternity, isolated. I pleaded with myself not to wake. I heard someone in tears. A man was attempting to console – or cajole – a child. I watched myself from a distance, hammering on the black Door. I hurt my hands and my wrists. The crying dissolved, and *he* stepped out among the gravestones and the yew trees."

Without even glancing at the packet, Mrs Slee picked out a doughnut.

"What did he look like?" Lilian asked, rubbing her fingers together to allow crumbs and sugar to fall where three or four reddish ants were foraging on the concrete between her brown, ankle-length, rubber boots.

"He wore his Astrakhan karakul. He was little more than a silhouette. Little more than a shadow."

"What on earth is an astral-can carry-cool, when it's at home, old girl?"

"A Jinnah cap, if you like: a furry pillbox hat. They have no brim, so they'll keep the sun off your head, but not out of your eyes. They sit on people's heads like hilltop fortifications."

Lilian closed her eyes to better envision the scene. "Well, you learn something every day."

"If only that were true, dear. Our worlds, our lives, our histories and futures would be so very different."

"I dare say. What did he do, the apparition sporting the exotic millinery?"

"He made a beeline for me. He looked straight at me, but his eyes were unseeing, as though I wasn't there. There was a child with him. And then no child. He had a little dog on one of those ubiquitous recoiling leads all dog owners seem to have these days. It barked and barked at me. But soundlessly."

Rather than consuming the sweet crumbs themselves, Lilian noted, the ants were transporting them back to the nest.

21 (After)
The Silver Pupil of the Darkest Eye

After twenty-five minutes on the exercise bike, Sylvanie had retreated to her room. She wanted to see particular thoughts take shape on paper. Hannah was in the lounge area doing a crossword while listening to the radio. It was rare for any news programme not to contain a reference to the Barrow Ship or its repercussions. The last item Hannah and Sylvanie had listened to related to a majority vote in the House of Commons to increase expenditure on research concerning communication with extra-terrestrials. Sylvanie was in no mood for more of the same.

Something had happened outside the building at about midday; there had been an altercation, raised voices in the street below, the slamming of car doors and the screeching of tyres. The Watch had told them it had been about someone scratching someone else's car while trying to get out of a tight parking spot. Nothing more than that.

Sylvanie's room was small. She had begun to put artwork on the walls: sketches from memory of hedgerows, lanes and wind-sculpted thorn trees.

She opened her journal.

She wrote: Lady Jeffers allowed me to go into the Manor gardens to draw anytime I wanted. I could go in at night and sit on the terrace between the strawberry trees, watching the moon in the pond. Once I watched it from the time it arrived at the edge of the circle to the time its silver rim left at the other side. Bats flew around me so close I could hear the whirr of their wings. I was always alone and I loved it.

Me and Mum were talking about the way I tapped myself to sleep when I was a kid. I pretended I knew Morse code. My bedroom had a fireplace at one time, ages before we moved in. It was boarded up and painted over. My little bed was pushed sideways against it. If I tapped the board with my fingernails it sounded hollow. I was totally obsessed with the idea of something happening if I got the code exactly right. My whole world would turn upside down in a brilliant way. Maybe a scary way. I didn't care.

One night something on the other side tapped back. I pulled my bed right out into the room and knelt down beside the covered up fireplace. It sounded like someone with long fingernails scraping on the other side. I fetched a big flat screwdriver and a hammer from the toolbox under the kitchen sink. Mum called out, but I went straight back up. The board didn't break, it peeled away gradually in one massive sheet.

It was a raven. It looked like a lump of darkness burned to charcoal. When it flew out at me I howled. Mum says I screamed again as she rushed into my room. It crashed into the paper lampshade, the walls, shelves and wardrobe, and into us. There was soot everywhere. I could feel it in the back of my throat. Mum turned off the light, opened the windows and the raven flew out into the night.

Sylvanie leaned back, her notebook in her lap. After two or three minutes she sat upright and sharpened her pencil into her coffee mug.

I'm trying to make it make some sense. There's always more. More than meets the eye. I am a Russian doll.

On the day we cycled all the way over to Bossington I was the only one who didn't go through the headland at Hurlstone Point onto Selworthy Sands. When it's low tide you can do it. It was Finch's idea. Someone had told him about the cave going all the way through. We left our bikes in a line at the top of the beach. Maze, Finch and Danny climbed up from the pebbles and went in. They didn't try to persuade me to go with them. Danny did a bit. Finch knew I didn't want to go. It was weird because the hill just swallowed them up.

Two enormous tankers went across the horizon really slowly. I found one of those dogfish egg cases that Mum calls mermaid's purses and loads of interesting driftwood. Two groups of people with dogs came and went but no one spoke to me. The dogs came up to me but the people didn't. I walked for ages along the beach toward Porlock as far as a Second World War pillbox. I went up to it, but I didn't go in. It was rammed with darkness and reeked of piss. I turned and saw Maze

78

waving from the cliff. I waved back. I ran all the way, waving and shouting like a lunatic.

They crashed down onto the grey pebble slope. Finch was the last one to jump from the ledge.

He gave me a pebble. He didn't say anything and no one saw him give it to me. I put it in my pocket. Actually I put my hand in my pocket with its coolness in the middle of my palm.

Sylvanie opened her right fist and looked at her dark grey pebble. It was as much a part of her being as the Hare amulet.

22 (After)
The Alabaster Child

Lottie, their friendliest Watch, was sat beside Sylvanie at the breakfast bar. Hannah was on the kitchen side, facing out. The woman unclipped her snub-nosed revolver in its holster from the belt beneath her denim jacket and slid it to her right, on the counter. She then placed her phone on top of the black gun, as if to hide it, or at least soften its brutality.

Hannah had spent the best part of an hour talking to Danny's stepmother, Sue, on the phone.

"It was a ridiculous conversation. She kept asking the same questions that people constantly ask on TV. She wanted to know if I thought they were ever coming back. I told her how positive *you* invariably were, Syl. I told her I couldn't always share your hopefulness. She said that Danny's parents were talking about changing their names, selling the farm, getting new identities, and going to live somewhere like Spain."

"Christ," Sylvanie said with a sigh. "What kind of a plan is that? So, when Dan the Man returns, his beloved family won't exist? Or worse, they'll all be lying on sun loungers on some stupid beach somewhere *pretending* they don't exist. We hide away because we're forced to. It's not going to be forever. We're not sleeping in glass coffins in the deep, deep, dark, dark wood."

"I feel utterly powerless, Syl, every time something like this happens, mostly because it takes us back to times and places and people that are lost to us now. Everything I thought was mine to think about and remember has been mashed up and moulded into some kind of mythology for sharing with strangers. I've lost my place on the page. I've lost the kids in my class with their sparkly plastic unicorns, their stickers and farts and bogies." Hannah smiled. "There were things that let us know where our realities ended, and gave us the props we needed to carry on mining the mediocre little lives we imagined were so special."

"They *were* special. They *are* special, Mum. Did Sue seem very upset?"

"Not especially. We were both floundering. Going under, really. Drowning in useless days and distance."

"Sue's my friend Danny's stepmum," Sylvanie told Lottie, whose eyes had been darting between mother and daughter. "Sue's alright. No one knows how she puts up with Danny's dad."

"One bizarre thing happened, though." Hannah said.
"What?"

"We both just about dissolved in hysterics."

"It must have been when I was in the shower, I guess. I didn't hear any of that."

"Sue told me about when Danny was a little kid, when she first moved in at the farm, how he used to run away from home in his Batman suit if he'd been told off. She laughed so much. She said he wore it so people could easily

find him. I laughed too. But then she couldn't stop. I …
What's the point in being angry about any of it?"

Hannah fetched the biscuit tin.

"I almost told Sue about a dream. I'm glad I didn't."
Hannah was looking straight into Sylvanie's eyes. "I would
have ended up feeling pathetic and exposed."

"What dream?" Sylvanie's tone was level and persuasive.

"You two talk about dreams a heck of a lot," Lottie said.

"Well," Hannah said, "being prisoners in this place
makes us a bit more introspective than we might otherwise
be. Anyway, if you don't talk about dreams and try to
understand them, they're like letters left unopened and
unread."

"Tell me, Mum."

"Do you want me to leave you two to it?" Lottie asked.
"Is this something private?"

"It doesn't matter," Sylvanie told her. "Stay, if you want.
We've forgotten what 'private' means."

Hannah leaned across the breakfast bar and touched
Sylvanie's hand.

"It felt like *I* had run away from home, like I had run
backwards in time. I was in a place in Cornwall I used to go
on holiday with Granny and Grandad. You weren't actually
born then, Syl, but in the dream you were. There was an
enormous cast-iron bath there, and I was washing you in a
little, white, plastic bath in it. The window in the bathroom
was crystal clear in the daytime: you couldn't see even the
merest ghost of a picture on the glass. But at night, when it
was dark outside and the light was on in the bathroom, the
faintest image of a woman, all in blue and white, appeared
on the surface of the pane. I kept looking over at the

window and back down at you, like I was trying to make the dream make sense. You were made of pink alabaster: an immaculate stone sculpture of yourself. The woman in the window looked exactly like Mrs Slee."

Lottie got up and went to the canvas shoulder bag she'd left on the coat hooks in the entrance. She returned to the breakfast bar with a ballpoint pen and a small spiral-bound notebook. She put her forefinger to her lips.

She wrote: 'DO NOT REACT TO ANYTHING I WRITE'.

"I'll make us another drink," she said. "And maybe a sandwich?"

She wrote: 'EVERYTHING IS RECORDED'.

Lottie looked at Hannah and Sylvanie.

"Fancy a game of swearword Scrabble?" Hannah asked through gritted teeth. "Just for a bloody giggle?"

Sylvanie marvelled at her mother's composure.

She and Hannah leaned forward to see what Lottie was writing.

'THE APARTMENT IS BUGGED'.

They never saw her again.

23 (Before)
Phantastic Mysteries

The friends rapidly amassed more than two thousand crystalline fragments – ranging in size enormously – from the area of rough moorland around the missing barrow. There were pieces in carrier bags hidden in drawers; shards in shoeboxes, rucksacks and suitcases, pushed under beds and on top of wardrobes; substantial chunks in containers and crates in garages and stables, and bigger lumps under piles of hay and feed bags in sheds and barns. They also had hundreds of considerably larger sections hidden under bracken and brushwood over the bank in the copse beside Worthy Airfield.

Although they varied their routes to and from the site, their activities did not go unnoticed. Andrew Snell – the ruddy-faced farmer whose motley flock grazed the moorland adjacent to the airfield – had seen them on several occasions.

"It's all about their field studies assignments for geography," Danny told the farmer, improvising, when he and Finch bumped into the man in the shop at the garage in Wheddon Cross. "I had to do it last year; I had to go up there with the Tucker twins and the red-haired girl who hacks up there all the time on her fat little skewbald. You remember seeing them up there with me?" He was making it up as he went along. It was a side of Danny that Finch barely recognized.

Farmer Snell said he did remember. He smiled all the time. He dyed his grey hair orangey brown. He had a plastic fertilizer bag tied around his right leg.

"I'm buggered if I know where you get all yer energy from," he said, having watched them through his binoculars. "Aren't you lot supposed to be in school?"

They had woven untruths around revision time and illness to parents and teachers alike.

"It's all about boggy land and where rivers start," Finch told him, affecting an earnest academic tone.

Farmer Snell drove off in the white David Brown tractor he had owned for almost five decades. He waved his pasty and the plastic wrapper blew off. He didn't question them again.

The search slowed. Pieces were getting harder to find – buried deeper, and further afield. The friends learned that if they spread out wide in a rough rectangle, then turned and walked toward each other, there would invariably be one or more beautiful shards waiting to be found at the point where they met. Often they would have to dig – cold, dark water flooding their excavations, cloaking the object that lay within. The largest section to date was almost three metres in length by sixty centimetres at its widest part. This dazzling, glass-like splinter weighed no more than polystyrene.

"It looks like a giant broken spanner, or a piston," Danny said.

"But swollen, or kind of grown out of itself," Maisie added.

The myriad smaller pieces were equally enigmatic. Rinsed in the stream, they looked like cut diamonds.

"It's like ice," Sylvanie said. "Some bits are more geometric, but some are like icicles twisted round, like solidified intestines. Maybe that's why they stick together so strongly: they melt a bit and then reset. Like, weld together. I don't mean it actually *is* ice," she added, before Danny had a chance to shoot her down.

"Ice – like snowflake patterns, and when it forms on windows – can be geometric, anyway," Finch added. "And Giant's Causeway … and quartz crystals "

When several pieces were discovered in close proximity, they were rinsed and offered up to fit together. Once the pieces were reunited, they would not be parted. Many larger sections had to be kept apart, because of the size they would be once joined. Frequently they found pieces that didn't want to go together. They exuded a force that felt like trying to join two same-poled magnets.

"Maybe," Sylvanie said, "it was a vast, ancient building that just got trashed when they blew everything up in the war.

"Or it's a spaceship." Finch was scanning the brooding sky.

"Yeah," Danny said. "Most likely looking for you, matey. Come to take you home. Do you remember your first day on Earth? How you bawled when they chucked you out of the mothership in a bin bag, and told you that you wouldn't be picked up until I'd taught you everything I know?"

"He'd have been beamed straight back up five seconds later," Maisie said.

"As long as that?" Sylvanie asked. "How long does it take to say, 'Shoot stuff and talk bullshit'?"

"If it is a UFO, I want to be the first to get in it and blast off," Finch said, his smile wide and his eyes alight.

Danny, Sylvanie and Maisie grabbed him and attempted to launch him into the bracken, but he proved too strong and too wriggly.

Finch took a natural lead when it came to fitting pieces together, and in the organization of sections that might go with pieces they had hidden at home.

"How come you're so good at working out what goes where?" Maisie asked him.

"I learned about it all from a book."

"*Phantastic Mysteries*," Sylvanie interjected before Finch could say another word. "Am I right?"

"Yeah."

"He was obsessed with it when he was a kid. Weren't you, obsessive kid?"

Finch closed his eyes. "Yeah," he said again, watching words and pictures scroll past behind his eyelids. "I loved that crap book." He opened his eyes. "I saw lots of books like it, on the same wacky subjects, but I wasn't interested. It got completely under my skin for years. Like Syl said, it was called *Phantastic Mysteries*. It was one of those books about so-called unexplained stuff all over the world, from different times in history. It was really about things that have rational explanations, and *have* been explained, written for the sort of people who want to pretend things *haven't* been explained."

"It sounds pants," Danny said, and Maisie nodded in agreement.

"Right. But I loved it. It had an intense smell; I used to think it was the smell of the unexplained." Finch threw back his head and laughed. "It had sections on ghosts, and haunted castles and pubs; and stuff about ancient civilizations and mummies; and a chapter on markings in the desert, with drawings and symbols so huge they can only be properly seen from the sky. The stuff about spontaneous combustion used to really creep me out, though."

"Tell them about the missing page, kiddo." Sylvanie said.

"I got the book from Mrs Slee, originally. Mum was going to give it away before I even saw it, because she thought I might be a bit too young for some of it, but she let me have it anyway. Pages 147 and 148 had been ripped out. I got fixated. I needed to know what earth-shattering information I was missing out on. I used to drive Mum and Dad crazy. I know I used to bore the shit out of everyone over it."

"No change there, then," Danny said, faking a cavernous yawn.

"Ages after I got the book, a friend of Mum's bought an identical one in South Molton market and gave it to me. I didn't read the missing pages straight away; I cut them out of the new book with a—"

"Hang on a minute," Maisie interrupted. "You cut the page out of the replacement book, when you could have just chucked the old, missing-page book in the bin?"

"Because I wanted the puzzle to be solved. My book: my puzzle. I stuck the new page in and it felt great. I made a card for Mum's friend, to say thanks, and copied a flying saucer out of *Phantastic Mysteries* to go on the front."

"What exactly are you on about, matey-boy?" Danny asked. "Where's any of this fairy tale supposed to be heading?"

"Pages 147 and 148 were all about incredible patterns in nature. In plant cell structures, honeycombs and dragonflies' wings; patterns that are geometrical, mathematical – and totally natural. And patterns you don't see until you join the dots up all over a map."

"What bliddy map?" Danny asked.

"Maybe this one," Sylvanie said, taking their roughly folded black-and-white sheet from her back pocket. "Maybe we're the dots, and we're joining everything up."

"So?" Danny asked. "What's his idiot book got to do with any of this?"

"So, that's exactly how come he knows how all these chunks of whatever-it-is fit together," Sylvanie said. "Isn't that right, puzzling kid?"

"Yeah. I suppose it is."

24 (After)
Necropolis

The windows in the latest safe house – a bungalow this time – had mechanisms to ensure they could not be opened wide enough to allow anyone to enter or exit. The only exception was the one in the separate toilet, presumably considered too small for a human being to squeeze through. Sylvanie broke off the upright metal pin of the window stay – it stuck up enough that it would hinder her exit. She hit it with the end of a rolling-pin she'd found at the back of a drawer in the kitchen. Three or four seconds later, their current Watch on duty was at the other side of the toilet door, knocking vigorously.

"What was that?" The question was like steel, sharp as a knife. This officious woman was more gaoler than housemate.

"Oh, bloody hell. I dropped the bloody loo seat, for Christ's sake. It slammed down. It was an accident, alright? *Alright?* Leave me alone."

Sylvanie listened hard as the Watch retreated. She sat on the lid of the toilet seat and waited. Through the frosted glass of the little window, Sylvanie could see dark laurels, dense and high. She pushed the rolling-pin back up the baggy sleeve of her jumper, flushed the toilet and went through the motions of washing her hands.

In the early hours of the following morning Sylvanie stealthily re-entered the toilet and fed herself head-first through the narrow aperture, folding her body over the wooden crosspiece that divided the window. She lowered herself onto the lid of a wheelie bin covered with beads of rainwater, slid to the path and headed for the bushes engulfing the summer house. A vixen, ragged and sodden, sloped away beneath adjacent decking. From the neighbouring garden, access to the street was direct and without obstacle.

Sylvanie's unplanned route took her out of the bowl in the landscape that cradled the metropolis. As dawn began to bleed into the eastern horizon, like bleach gnawing at a sheet of carbon paper, the rain eased and the temperature began to fall. Sylvanie caught her reflection in the window of a shop with a dark interior; she was wet through, her hair lank and her sweater heavy with moisture.

The street met the wider thoroughfare that followed the contour of the hill. Facing her, immense cast-iron gates opened onto an area of hillside flooded with inky darkness and bristling with ethereal stone tombs, crosses and statues. Three hundred metres to the west, in an arena of butter-coloured electric light, a murder of crows was dancing and singing, feasting on something recently deceased.

Sylvanie crossed the road.

She walked in among the gritstone vaults and graves with their sphinxes, saints and lions materializing coldly in the timid dawn. She breathed into her hands and pushed them in her pockets. She looked up into the face of a marble angel whose once benign countenance had been uglified by pollution and erosion.

"Good morning, Miss Hart."

Sylvanie leapt sideways from the voice. A man stepped out from the pitch-black mouth of a Victorian family crypt. As shock propelled her, Sylvanie felt the moment slide past her face and hands and through her saturated hair and clothing; she felt time begin to congeal around her. She could run, though the man showed no sign of preparing to give chase. A little dog, its lead in the man's hand and its head cocked quizzically to one side, watched her every move.

"Welcome once again to a real world, Miss Hart. Your so-called protectors have kept you prisoner for so long."

Sylvanie took two very measured steps further away.

There was an awful coldness in the man's voice. He, Sylvanie thought, fitted perfectly in this forlorn place. He had been smoking a disgusting cigar. It stank, even though it was dead now, between his fingers.

"What are you waiting for, Miss Hart? I can take you to your friends in the blink of an eye. A nominal fee may be incurred: standard terms and conditions apply, et cetera, et cetera." He smiled. He sounded almost jovial.

Sylvanie looked carefully at the man.

He had the sinister kind of smile, she thought, that could easily change into something else. Was he a nutter from one of those stupid Barrow Ship cults on TV? One of those 'devotees', 'followers' she'd never met and never wanted to? But there was something oddly familiar about him. Why had he been there, waiting?

Why wasn't she running away?

"Time is of the essence, Miss Hart. Time … is … *always* … money."

His words rolled like spilt marbles through the clarifying morning.

"How long will you wait? Your friends are a mere stone's throw away."

The man put the stale cigar stub between his lips, and in an informal, easy-going gesture, held out his hand.

Sylvanie recoiled.

He was wearing an odd hat: brimless, black. Was it animal pelt? His long, black raincoat hung loosely from rounded shoulders, tucked back on his left hip behind the bright, mother-of-pearl handle of an antique Remington six-shooter revolver cradled in its elegant leather holster.

Sylvanie sensed that they were being watched. Not by the blind eyes of saints and angels, but by some occult being cloaked by shadow. Was it a child, dressed in darkness?

"Give me your hand," the man said, his voice strangely compelling.

Sylvanie turned and ran like hell.

25 (Before)
Doug Valentine's Present

"The clock in the kitchen's stopped," Sylvanie called.

Hannah didn't hear. She was in her workroom, pulling out files and worksheets for a short-notice supply teaching job. Sylvanie went upstairs to find her and they met as Hannah was coming out of her little office with an armful of folders and books.

"The clock in the kitchen's stopped. I took it down and cleaned it, but I can't find any batteries."

"I'm coming down right now, love. You make the drinks and I'll make the sandwiches. There are some batteries in the second drawer down next to the fridge, but I haven't got a clue if they're the right size or not."

The clock in question had been a plate, through which a hole had been drilled to allow hands and mechanism to be fitted, with numbers painted by hand. The cobalt-blue image was of a tall ship, all sails billowing roundly, charging across the rich, white glaze to some romantic shore. No sea was depicted, no waves and no horizon. The vessel was nameless.

Sylvanie replaced the battery in the clock, corrected the time and returned it to its hook on the wall. Mother and daughter sat at the kitchen table and ate their lunch.

"When I was at college in Maidstone," Hannah said, "I rented an amazing room in a truly magical place called Moor Court. I had two housemates: one bloke and one crazy chick. Doug Valentine, our landlord, lived there too. He gave the clock to me when I left, because I'd liked it so much."

"I think you've spoken about him before."

"He had a white English bull terrier called Chuggypig who slept in a deckchair in the courtyard. Doug always wore corduroy: trousers, waistcoat and jacket. And he always wore brown suede winkle-pickers."

"Oh my God. Are you serious? He sounds so cool."

"I am. He was. Everybody loved Doug. I loved him." Hannah listened to the renewed ticking from the moon-coloured clock. "Moor Court was a jumble of peachy-red, brick-built buildings, three storeys high in most places, all of which opened onto, or looked out over, the courtyard. A noble and ancient quince tree grew in a triangular bed in the middle. The tree was easily twice my height. I saw quince the size of grapefruit on it each year, weighing its lower branches down to the ground. It was beautiful and ugly beyond reason and had birds in it every time you walked past, like they'd come along especially to decorate it."

"Wow."

"There was always a feeling of complete serenity, as if time kept sailing by out there along the pavements and the streets, but wasn't bothered about that serene little backwater. If it wasn't raining, Doug would be stood at his easel, painting that enchanted tree, surrounded by tubes of oil paint, rags, turpentine, and stoneware jars stuffed with a thousand paintbrushes. He worked on four gigantic canvasses in rotation, scraping and repainting, measuring and marking the brick walls beyond the tree as the fruits swelled and bent the branches. He picked his canvas according to the weather, and seemed to move around and around the tree with the seasons. The walls of the courtyard had thousands of white paint-marks all over them."

"You can imagine," Sylvanie said, "if you hammered a nail into the walls at every paint mark, then tied a thread across the courtyard between every permutation of every pair of nails, you'd weave yourself another quince tree."

"Absolutely. We students had rooms in the tower. I had the top room, accessible only via an exterior, cast-iron staircase from the balcony deck below. There was a massive square skylight in the middle of my room that rose to a wooden tower with a weathervane on top that was a fox chasing a hare over a hill."

"It does sound fantastically romantic, Mum."

"It truly was. But if I needed a pee in the middle of the night I had to use an old galvanized bucket with a wire handle." Hannah pushed her plate away and leaned forward on her elbows. "I used to find butterfly wings on my bed, Syl. I had a sumptuous old counterpane covering my double bed. Sometimes when I came in there'd be as many as six or seven pairs of wings. On my bed."

Sylvanie sat up very straight on her chair. "That's insane. Who was putting them there?"

"There were never any bodies, just wings, on the counterpane and on my pillows. When I told Doug about it, he came up to investigate. He just stood in silence in the middle of my room, at the foot of my bed, under the skylight, waiting. I sat in the battered leather armchair. He watched the room and I watched him. It was like he forgot I was there."

"How long did you wait? What was he even waiting for?"

"More than an hour. He told me that if you wanted to see something amazing, all you had to do was stand and wait until the amazing thing that was due to happen there took place."

Hannah started to clear the table.

"Mum! So what the hell happened?"

"We heard a bird fluttering about above us. A moment later, the wings of a small tortoiseshell butterfly came spiralling down. 'It's a flycatcher,' Doug said, 'threshing its prey up there in the gods.'"

26 (After)
Believe and Leave

"Miss Hart," Mr Tagore said, "you've been running. Away."

Mr Tagore was not a government man, but he answered to officials who valiantly pretended to understand the answers he supplied. People associated with the Watch, by necessity, dwelt beyond the confines of other people's power and control. For some time, Sylvanie had been annoyed with herself for not disliking him.

Outside the iron gates of the sprawling Victorian necropolis, at the curb of the broad flagstone pavement, Mr Tagore was holding open the rear door of a limousine the colour of dried blood. The driver, a dark-haired woman in her early forties with an olive complexion, turned and smiled as Sylvanie came aboard. The woman had no left arm; the sleeve of her jacket was folded and pinned neatly just below her shoulder. She had a prominent aquiline nose and eyes as black as bitumen.

"You could have caught your death, Miss Hart," Mr Tagore said, as he followed her into the vehicle's palatial interior.

"How did you know I'd gone?" Sylvanie asked, working on getting her breath back as the car pulled silently away. "I mean, left that stupid bungalow?"

"Your implant allows us to track you wherever you go. It is there solely for your safety. It woke everyone up when you broke through the prescribed electronic perimeter in the small hours of this very morning, and we've been nearby since then."

"I should have known." Sylvanie practically spat the words out. "I did bloody know."

Mr Tagore seemed unaffected by her anger.

"Where is it?" she hissed. "I can't feel it. Is it under my skin?"

"No. Actually, you drank it. Its coating was digested and its tiny barbs hold it in place. Only a surgeon could remove it. I am sincerely sorry it has to be this way."

"When did you give me the drink?" Sylvanie could hear feral thoughts nipping at the heels of her words.

The driver turned to give Mr Tagore a look.

"Some while ago, actually; before the Barrow Ship," Mr Tagore replied. "On a science trip."

"I beg your pardon?" Sylvanie felt the heat of outrage and disbelief rising in her eyes. "What?"

"Before you and your friends decided to embark upon your remarkable quest." Mr Tagore was looking directly at her.

"I don't believe you," she told him. But she did believe him. "You're lying."

"I'm afraid not, Miss Hart," the driver said, keeping her eyes on the road. "Mr Tagore is a man who has no appetite for deceit."

"You people manipulated me, and, it feels like, everything I've ever done. And not for the first time. Everything *we* ever did." Something was materializing in her brain. "You put a tracker thing in Finch?"

"Miss Mead and Mr Barton-Webber also," Mr Tagore informed her.

"Right. So, where the hell are they?"

Mr Tagore took a moment. "We lost all signals at the point when your friends entered the Barrow Ship. Unfortunately, we are unable to pinpoint their precise whereabouts at the present time."

"You're not in control after all."

Mr Tagore placed the ends of two fingers against his temple. Sylvanie thought he was going to mime shooting himself.

"Some creep in the cemetery jumped out at me. He freaked me out. Why would he be there, anyway, waiting? He knew my name. How could he have known I was going to be there? I thought maybe he was part of your organization. He was coming out with loads of deluded crap. I was legging it when I ran into you."

"Stop the car, please, Georgia," Mr Tagore ordered. The driver pulled into a long lay-by with an overflowing litter bin that had attracted the attention of a trio of juvenile magpies.

Mr Tagore listened while Sylvanie described what the man had been wearing and what he had said.

"He had a gun, but he didn't look like he was out and about poaching pheasants. He didn't threaten me with it."

"What sort of gun?" Georgia, the driver, asked.

"Like a cowboy gun, I guess. It was in a long, leather holster on his belt. His coat was tucked behind the handle, like he was ready to use it. He had a stinking cigar butt that had gone out. Revolting. And he had a little dog."

"Was there anyone with him?" Mr Tagore asked.

"No," Sylvanie said. But the question did make her wonder. "Though I got the feeling that there was somebody else lurking in the shadows behind him. All of his other mates must have got left behind at the fancy-dress party."

Mr Tagore disembarked, made a brief call out of earshot, and returned to the vehicle. Traffic was getting heavier. The rain had stopped, and the cold light of day was reluctantly approaching. The three young magpies were waiting in the wings on an adjacent telegraph pole.

One for sorrow, two for joy, Sylvanie thought. *Three for a girl. That's me.* "I'm starving."

"Fortunately, Georgia and I passed a bakery that had been open – would you believe it – since before five this morning. Georgia bought you a rather special cream cake."

Taking her hand from the steering-wheel, the driver passed back a pink-and-white-striped paper bag.

"It's a Barrow Ship bun," Mr Tagore informed Sylvanie, opening the bag and showing her. "They are delicious, and all the rage. Lots of places do them now, don't they, Georgia?"

"Most places, it would seem," the woman said, her voice soft and rich. "As I was turning to leave the shop, the girl who served me made the Barrow Ship sign and said, 'Believe and Leave.'"

Georgia reached across her chest and over her left shoulder to meet up with Mr Tagore's left hand to form the other half of the sign. When their fingertips and thumbtips came together, a roughly barrow-shaped space was created. The leather-clad steering-wheel remained precisely as the driver's hand had left it, as though the woman was controlling the vehicle telepathically.

"They're eclairs, basically, Miss Hart," Mr Tagore explained. "The choux pastry is supposed to be the barrow; the chocolatey icing the moorland terrain; but, inside the cream filling there is a surprise: a light framework of brittle sugar representing the Barrow Ship itself."

"I'm not hungry. Just the thought of it makes me feel sick."

"Eat it on the way, then. Or later, perhaps."

"Or, if you like, not at all," Georgia said. "I just thought it might be a bit of a treat."

"What do you mean, 'on the way?'" Sylvanie asked, ignoring Georgia. "We can't be more than a couple of minutes from that godforsaken bungalow."

"In approximately forty-five minutes," Georgia said, "we'll be transferring you to the vehicle currently conveying your mother. We'll say goodbye at that point. Hannah knows you're with us, Sylvanie, and that you're safe."

"The two of you will then be driven to a stunning location high on the North York Moors," Mr Tagore told her.

"Wow. I'll shake all the gold doubloons from my magic piggy bank, and we'll all live happily ever after. If we haven't already."

"We're hoping you'll like it," Mr Tagore continued. "It's a handsome stone-built dwelling set in wonderfully natural wooded grounds. It comes with acres and acres of its own . . . well . . . countryside."

"You sound like an estate agent."

She saw a herd of Guernseys. She saw rose bay willow herb and marguerites in profusion.

"Maybe it will be OK," she said.

They passed an unprepossessing gritstone church, outside which a printed banner, tugging dejectedly at its moorings on the railings, read: 'SEEING IS BELIEVING AND BELIEVING IS LEAVING'.

"I've got a pizza delivery for the pavement."

"A what?" Mr Tagore asked, puzzled.

"I'm going to puke," Sylvanie told them.

"Please, not in the car. Please, Miss Hart, I beg you not to be sick in the car. Pull over, Georgia. Now."

Sylvanie stepped out onto a grey suburban pavement, placed both hands on a low stone wall and retched violently three or four times. Georgia was soon at her side. She laid her hand lightly between Sylvanie's shoulder blades.

"Are you prone to travel sickness?"

"No."

Mr Tagore remained inside the vehicle. He was on his phone again. A noisy articulated lorry waited for an opportunity to go around them.

Sylvanie was drooling long gouts of viscous liquid, but not actually vomiting. She retched violently six or seven more times, and coughed, almost growling.

Mr Tagore wound down his window. "We need to go," he called, one hand over his phone.

Sylvanie straightened up, took her hands off the top of the garden wall and placed them on her hips.

"Not so bad, after all." Georgia lifted her hand from Sylvanie's back. "There's mineral water in the car."

Very red in the face, Sylvanie coughed again, but less aggressively. Then, with the forefinger and thumb of her left hand, she picked a tiny silver capsule from her tongue.

"Shit!" exclaimed Georgia.

"Your shit," Sylvanie told her, flicking the diminutive electronic device into the rhododendrons.

27 (Before)
Candlelit Supper

Lilian watched Mrs Slee's eyes shining in the soft light. On the uneven planks of the kitchen table stood a porcelain candlestick in which a curved candle was burning, its warm glow – yellow, physical – being the only light in Mrs Slee's humble home, flooding the space between the two women and reaching out across the kitchen to coax shadows and reflections from artefacts attendant on the periphery. Mrs Slee's draughty cottage made the little flame dance.

Lilian looked at her hands folded at the edge of the table, picked them up and placed them in her lap. She thought for a moment that they might not belong to her. She rubbed her right thumb lightly over her left, and renewed her sense of ownership. She was accustomed to prolonged bouts of talklessness, often simply waiting for Mrs Slee to say the next important thing. She looked around, from one object to another, from one figure of shuddering darkness to the next.

Lilian wanted to ask Mrs Slee why she had so many clocks that didn't work; in the kitchen alone she counted nine, their hands rigid over pale faces. Some of her friend's timepieces ticked and tocked, some even made a vague effort to whirr and chime periodically, but most were silent. Some sounds, Lilian thought, added depth and substance to quietude.

It had been light outside when they had begun their simple supper. Lilian tried to remember Mrs Slee lighting the bowed candle, but she could not; nor could she recall the point when darkness had invited itself in around them.

"You know what they say about stopped clocks."

"What, dear?" Mrs Slee asked.

"Well, you know, that at least they're right twice a day."

"Some of these clocks are correct but once in a blue moon," Mrs Slee said, sounding wistful, almost mournful. "When I die, strangers will traipse in here and take all these loyal chronometers, cast them away or put them 'right', set them up like metronomes to keep the beat of marching hours and days. They will carelessly unhook the delicate pendulums, overwind them and let time slip through the fingers of their blued and plated hands."

Lilian had never heard Mrs Slee sound so melancholy. Never so mortal.

"I won't let them do that, old girl."

Mrs Slee smiled. "They all tell the right time when the time is right to tell it. I like to give myself time to think."

Lilian looked at a dessert spoon on the table beside a jar of pear and mustard chutney. The bowl of the spoon was worn down on the right-hand side and thinned by use. She saw how this ordinary object had taken on the humanity and humility of its owner.

"What is it, dear?" Mrs Slee asked, straining her neck and back to look up and out across the table.

"What is what?" Lilian asked. Mrs Slee's face was obscured by the flame's glow.

"You had an important question perched upon the tip of your tongue, dear. I saw it about to fledge and take flight." Mrs Slee's words emanated from the light.

"What happens," Lilian could feel her lips shaping the words, muscular and deliberate, "when you die? Not you, necessarily, but when someone, anyone, dies?"

Lilian realized that the blue of her companion's plastic raincoat was the colour of the robes worn by the Virgin Mary in any depiction she had ever seen.

"Let me make us some cocoa, dear," Mrs Slee suggested. "Then I will try, as best I can, to answer your question."

Mrs Slee took the little flame with her. At one point, as she turned briefly toward the table, Mrs Slee's head was surrounded by a halo of rich golden light.

Lilian was aware of movement at the edges of the room: reflections and thrown shadows, small and dense, were migrating alongside Mrs Slee over the surfaces of pieces of china, framed pictures, ornaments and clocks. A bronze figure of a young girl skipping, the overhead arc of her rope missing from her outstretched arms, and a porcelain shepherd holding a lamb in the crook of each arm, were both particularly animated.

"I'll show you, dear," Mrs Slee told Lilian when she returned to the table with the hot drinks. "I'll show you exactly what happens when you die."

Mrs Slee removed her raincoat and placed it over the back of the chapel chair upon which she had been seated. She was wearing a man's white, collarless shirt, clean and stiff and bright.

Shuffling to her left, she pulled open the drawer at the end of the table and withdrew a part-burned, bottle-green candle. She came and sat opposite Lilian once more. Holding her candle close to the one alight in the centre of the table, Mrs Slee bent her body backwards and sideways in order to look directly into her friend's silver-grey eyes.

"Lean into the light, dear, and blow softly and evenly to extinguish the flame that has been our most amenable companion this eventide."

Lilian did exactly as requested. Like a wind-blown handkerchief, the flame reached toward the waiting wick of Mrs Slee's green candle. It stepped from one wick to the other: same flame, different candle.

Mrs Slee relit the original candle and extinguished the one from the drawer with a sharp exhalation. Licking her forefinger and thumb, she pinched the glowing and smoking wick before placing the candle on a crack in the table to stop it rolling away.

"Thank you, old girl. I'll finish my cocoa. And then I really ought to be wending my way homeward. What time is it, do you think?"

"Let's see," Mrs Slee said, rising and pushing back her chair. She crossed the room and lifted a timepiece from a shelf beside the range, moved the hands and pushed a lever at the back with her index finger. She put the clock back on the dusty shelf.

It chimed laboriously: *Deng ... Deng ... Deng ...* Lilian counted to eleven.

"It is the eleventh hour," Mrs Slee said, her words laying themselves in the open arms of the patient shadows.

28 (Before)
Hangar Three

Finch looked at his watch as Danny pushed the nose of the pickup against the rusty gates of Worthy Airfield. Six thirty-one. Maisie jumped out with two keys on a long wooden tag and kicked her door shut. The sun was burgeoning in the east, beyond the hangars, flooding the airfield with clarity and colour. To the right of the gates a shambolic group of brick and block buildings flanked a low conning tower, and seven or eight light aircraft in various states of disrepair were huddled on the concrete.

Boots and Shoes were barking and scratching frantically in the mesh-fronted box in the back of the truck.

Danny backed up to allow Maisie access to the padlock and chain binding the tubular framework of the unwieldy gates. They drove to the furthest of three enormous, arched, corrugated-iron hangars. The ends were flat, vertical, but the roofs curved all the way down to the ground at the sides. There was a metre-wide brown margin of desiccated vegetation where Danny's uncle, Des, had repeatedly sprayed herbicide over the years.

"Flog the lot, if you want, or burn it." Des had told Danny. "I was going to sell it, but woodworm have gone through the whole lot of it like a dose of salts over the years. An antique dealer from Kent wanted all the storage he could get, back in the day. If you burn all his rubbish, then the place is yours for as long as I don't want it. You'll have to burn it on the grass, though, not on the concrete – 'cause you'll crack it. Don't make the fire too big, or too close to the hangar, and don't do anything you wouldn't want me to catch sight of you doing."

Boots and Shoes were off on the scent of rabbits. Maisie went in first, making Danny wait. As he entered the hangar, Danny could just make Maisie out, standing in the gloom with her hand on a big switch.

"Ready?" she called.

"Get on with it."

There was a split-second delay between each of the twelve strip lights as they went on in succession, and the contents of the hangar seemed to shudder with surprise at the coming of light. Danny and Maisie scanned a forest of dusty brown furniture, stacked two or three items high, with aisles to the left and right of a dense central row.

"I've got matches," Danny said, "and there's newspaper for the dogs' box. This is going to be the biggest bliddy bonfire in history."

"We'll have it blazing by the time the others get up here," Maisie said. "We don't want to have to drag all this stuff too far. Some of it looks pretty heavy. I can't wait to get all this junk out of the way, and start building 'the thing'." Maisie looked straight at Danny.

"What?" He looked straight back.

"It's exciting." Maisie had tucked her thumbs inside her fists.

"We've got shedloads of the thing everywhere, and now we've got a bliddy shed that's big enough to chuck it all in."

"I'm worried that people will see us coming and going up here. I reckon we should say we're rehearsing a play or something, so they don't get suspicious."

"People would laugh their bollocks off if you told them I was going to be in some sort of effin' theatricals. We'll just say we're sorting something out for my Uncle Des. Anyway, it's freezing. Let's have ourselves a little burn-up."

An hour later Sylvanie and Finch rode up on his Montesa. A vast pyre was consuming worm-eaten furniture as fast as it could be hurled into the ravenous flames. Danny saw the two of them first, looping the chain back round the gate. When they set off again, Sylvanie was standing over Finch, one foot on the back of the little saddle and one foot on the tank, arms outstretched like a stunt rider. Danny watched them for a second, then went back inside the hangar for another stack of chairs. When Finch and Sylvanie got to the hangar, she ducked and they rode right in. Sylvanie jumped off the bike, and stood with her hands on her hips, surveying mountains of old furniture.

"This place is awesome," she exclaimed. "Fantastic place for a party. We could all live in here. And the fire's unbelievable. Finch was going to do a stunt jump right through the middle of the flaming-hot flames, but he chickened out. Didn't you, oven-ready kid?"

"How long have you guys been up here?" Finch asked, as Danny plodded past dragging a double wardrobe, wire hangers chiming inside.

"Long enough to get tired of waiting for you half-arsed part-timers," Danny replied. "You going to get your hands dirty anytime this week?"

Planting his left boot firmly on the dusty concrete, Finch leaned the Montesa over, revved wildly and let out the clutch, allowing the bike to turn two full circles around him before he rode back outside, leaving the air in the entrance of the hangar thick with dust and exhaust fumes. He leaned the bike against the slope of the galvanized building, threw his jacket and sweater over the handlebars, and strode back inside, picking up business cards from the ground as he went. They had fallen out of drawers in a paint-spattered desk that Maisie had pulled to the fire. They were all the same: '*L. Everet, Timeless Treasures, Moor Court, Maidstone*'. Behind the text was a blue-and-white image of a clock face without hands.

Each hangar had an outside tap, with water that was drinkable once it had run clear. They found a heavy reel of hosepipe to wash out the hangar once they had cleared it. At least a quarter of the contents of the hangar had been burned.

"We don't have to empty the entire hangar, though, do we?" Maisie asked. "There's still hundreds more lumps of what antique people must have affectionately called complete shite."

"The deal with my uncle is to clear the place," Danny said.

"We'll need the whole space, Maze," Finch said. "We'll need to lay all our pieces out across the floor, so we can work out what we're doing."

"Christ! Look at the fire now." Sylvanie stood, hands behind her head, gazing in awe at the blaze. "It's so intense. It's like looking into a volcano. It must be hot enough to melt the metal bits of the furniture."

"The alloy bits, at least," Danny said, pulling his T-shirt up to wipe the sweat off his face. He seemed to be bathing in the heat. "There'll be puddles of aluminium in the ash when it's all cooled. It'll take three or four days for the heat to go."

The furniture was so dry that the fire was almost smokeless. A fat column of flame, heat and sparks rose thirty metres into the daytime sky. When the blush of the setting sun flooded the horizon, the giant hangar was empty.

They watched the immense disc of embers darken like a fallen sun. Finch and Maisie sat with their backs against the flaking paint of the hangar's wide-open door. Sylvanie was perched on the tailgate of Danny's pickup, hugging a two-litre plastic bottle of tap water.

"Do you guys remember," she asked, "when we were at Danny's birthday party, and we spent ages mucking about in the woods? He cut hazel spears for everybody with his penknife."

Danny moved closer, his back to the waning glow.

"I do," Finch said. "Bat Boy here was eight."

"But, do you remember how Danny put lethal points on all our spears?"

"I know what you're going to say," Finch said.

"I think maybe I do, too," Maisie said.

"You," Sylvanie said, indicating Finch with an upward thrust of her chin, "threw your spear really hard at a massive beech tree, but you missed the tree as Danny stepped out from behind it. You didn't know he was there. Your spear was heading straight for him. Right for his head, actually. It slowed down as it sailed through the air, giving him just enough time to jerk his head back out of the way. I watched it fly past his nose and bury itself in a bank of brambles. I guess it would have killed him. I know what I saw; I don't know why we've never said anything about it."

"Maybe," Maisie said, "we didn't talk about it because we didn't want to think about what could have happened."

Danny remained silent.

"Yeah, maybe," Finch said. "Or perhaps we didn't believe it happened."

"Well," Sylvanie said, "we believe it now, don't we?"

"I definitely do," Maisie said, watching streams of firefly motes spiralling heavenward.

Finch lay on his back on the cool concrete.

"We're all wiped out," Maisie said. "I feel totally knackered, but I feel strong, like I'm reinforced. It's like there's wires pulling me, threaded right through me. It's like I'm being born all over again."

Finch lifted his head. "Yeah, I absolutely know what you mean, Maze. I'll tell you something else, too: when I close my eyes, the dark, the dark inside me, is … *full*. I don't feel anything's missing when I close my eyes. It's like I haven't shut them at all."

29 (Before)
The Imaginary Friend

After talking for almost three hours, their voices had softened and darkened. Sylvanie felt her words reverberate through her body and dissolve in the incoming ink of night. She and Finch, and her cat, Kinky, were curled up on her little cast-iron bed. A confident breeze pushed the curtains in rolling and falling body-shapes; ghosts tumbled over the sill and into the room. A moment after the moonlight failed, it began to rain. Sylvanie lit a candle. The steady downpour fell as an audible hush upon the apple tree outside her bedroom window, and the candleflame danced until Sylvanie placed the glass chimney from an old paraffin lamp over it. When she sat back down, Kinky was snoring.

"The owl has stopped," Finch said. "Owls can't hunt in the rain. Are you going to close the windows?"

"No. The rain can't come in. It hardly ever even blows in, because the thatched roof overhangs the windows so far. It's my dream that one day a swallow or a robin will nest in here with me, and I'll be able to hear the chicks chirping all the time, and I won't care if I can't ever close the windows."

"I had a dream a couple of weeks ago, and I can remember absolutely everything about it."

"Everybody's having them all the time," Sylvanie said. "It's like we're all drinking from a well of dreams."

"If you shook this room – turned it upside down with us in it – it would be like we were in one of those globe things, and our dreams would fall like snow all over us."

"How cool would that be? Tell me about your dream, kid."

"It seemed like it was delivering something. When I woke up, I felt I'd understood something. Now I'm certain I don't understand a single bloody thing about it. It was weird. I'm not sure you'll think it was worth hearing."

"I'll be the judge of that, dreamchild," Sylvanie said, looking down her nose with theatrical sternness. "If you think *your* dream was weird, I'll tell you something properly shocking when you've finished, something that will freak you right out."

"Is it a competition?"

"Yes. It's a weird-off."

They heard Hannah coming up the stairs. She put her head around the door.

"Please don't let the candle burn all the way down. I'm off to collect a few more zeds for my Sleepy-Time Alphabet Sticker Book. Kinky's litter tray is in, and everything's turned off. Oh, and I've done all the washing-up that you two said you were going to do. Night. Love you *both*."

"Mother!"

"Night," Finch said. "Thanks for the yummy stew. Love you too."

"Jesus," Sylvanie groaned.

Hannah was gone.

"I'd better be on my way," Finch said.

"Tell me your dream, right now, kiddo."

"You're my dream."

"I can't take much more of this. Don't be utterly pathetic. Tell me your dream."

"I was at Lady Jeffers' place. It was night-time, and I was there on my own. There were no lights on at all, anywhere. When I looked at the house, it looked *full* of empty rooms."

"Interesting," Sylvanie said. "Gothic."

"Everything looked like it had been painted with ten coats of moonlight. The slate paths and the leaves on the roses and the fig tree were all silver. The pond looked like it was full of mercury."

"I've seen it like that. I've seen the pond full of sky, silver and black."

"I was standing there, looking for something in my pockets. I could hear birds singing, even though it was the dead of night. I kept putting my hands into my pockets, searching them, but they got deeper and deeper. I started to feel anxious, and frustrated, and I kept looking behind me. But each time I turned around there was only blackness."

He paused a little too long. "Pray continue," Sylvanie prompted.

"I turned my pockets inside out, practically. In the dream it didn't matter that I didn't know what I was looking for, just that I was looking for it. I realized my pockets were changing and swapping around; my clothes felt like a puzzle. But then I found it. It had been in the back pocket of my jeans the whole time."

"What'd you been looking for?"

"The pebble. I mean *your* pebble; the one I gave you when we went to Bossington. I went to the pond and threw it in. When it hit the surface, it didn't go straight through. The circle went dark for a moment and then filled back up with clouds and stars and the moon. I could barely stand up. The stars in the sky in the water made me feel like I was falling. Falling upward. And I closed my eyes, Syl, and woke up."

"I like your dream. Even though, by rights, it should have been *my* dream about *my* pebble. As the Official Inspector of All-Your-Dreams, I am happy to grade it as a QSD."

"What's a QSD?"

"Quite Splendid Dream. Don't you actually know anything at all?"

"What about yours, then?" Finch asked, happy to have shared his dream, but secretly hoping Sylvanie wouldn't want to analyse it.

"What do you think it meant?" she asked. "That you're in urgent need of experimental surgery that'll leave you physically and mentally scarred for the rest of your numbered days?"

"I do. I'll have to go and live in a jar where no one can hear my embarrassing bawling. Thanks ever-so-much for listening. Cheers for caring. Now tell me about *your* dream."

"I never said it was a dream. You're not paying attention."

"Tell me anyway, even though I'm not listening."

"What do you think of Mrs Slee?" Sylvanie asked. "I mean, what do you really make of her?"

"Danny says she smells."

"Well, he's right, isn't he? But she doesn't smell bad, does she? I mean, she doesn't smell of pee?"

"She smells of old people's belongings."

"That's right. She smells of ink and wax, cardboard, blackcurrants and soap, books and biscuits. I like her. Lilian, too, obviously. They could tell us a lot, kiddo."

"About history and stuff, and their lives, and all that?"

"About us."

"What could they tell us about us? They're constantly chuntering away like a couple of witches. If we don't listen to a word they say, then we won't get pulled in."

"Too late. We're already snared," Sylvanie whispered. "Want to know about the weird thing?"

"Fill your boots. The little red and gold ones that the elves made for you while you were napping in the enchanted forest."

Sylvanie went and sat cross-legged on the magic carpet in the middle of her room.

"I saw Mrs Slee in the woods. She'd been up to Wheddon Cross to get some shopping from the garage. Naturally, she was wearing her plastic coat, and she was pulling that tartan shopping trolley thing bumping along behind her. I was supposed to be drawing, and collecting stuff to draw, but I was mostly daydreaming. I was way off the path, but she spotted me. I showed her some sketches of fungi and lichen."

"When was this?" Finch asked, folding his arms across his chest as if lying in state.

"Maybe late August. It was dark under the trees, but I was sitting in a pool of sunlight. There was an evil bunch of horseflies stalking me, and bumblebees buzzing about. There were butterflies following Mrs Slee like they thought she was a big flower; like she was getting married and they were her veil. She asked me if I liked being on my own, and I told her I loved it. She said she had no brothers or sisters, so she'd spent loads of her childhood playing by herself in the woods where she grew up."

Sylvanie noticed the rain had stopped. Finch and Kinky were motionless. "Are you two actually alive?"

"I'm pretty sure kinky is. She's snoring."

"Mrs Slee told me that when she was a girl she had an imaginary friend. A girl. She told me the girl's name was Sylvanie."

"What?" Finch rose – without disturbing the cat – and sat on the edge of Sylvanie's bed. "She must have been trying to wind you up for some reason."

"She said she'd given the girl that name because she came from the woods. 'You're the only person I've ever told about Sylvanie, Sylvanie,' she said."

"She made it up." Finch yawned expansively.

"Maybe she made *me* up."

"You're *my* imaginary friend."

"Dream on, kid."

30 (Before)
The Home Guard

Pony was clearly energized by the ride, his eyes were wide and bright, and his handsome horse was shining with sweat. He wore an ancient-looking pair of black, steel-toe-capped work boots, patched jeans, and a T-shirt that was a souvenir of someone else's Red Sea scuba-diving holiday at least twenty years previously. Fresh scratches on his forearms bore testimony to his woodland gallop. He dismounted with a flourish, opened Mrs Slee's gate and, with a gentle hand beneath his young horse's jaw, guided the animal a short way up the garden path. Pony had ridden the whole way bareback.

"You wait here." He closed the gate and strode up the path. "And don't go eating herself's roses."

Lilian opened the top half of the door just as Pony was about to knock.

"You're not raising your hand to me, are you, Pony Chalice?"

"I would raise a smile or a glass to thee, maid, but never in a whole month of Sundays would I raise a hand."

"I wouldn't want to have to use these on you." Lilian held up her hands in what she imagined to be a martial arts style. "They're deadly weapons, Mr Chalice."

"I can see that, maid, but I come in peace, seeking only knowledge and understanding."

"Knowledge? There's plenty of that about. We're simply awash with it. But *understanding*, Pony Chalice, might well be a very different matter."

"That's why I'm here, to see the two of you, to pick your brains."

Lilian turned her head away from him. "We have a visitor, old girl," she called. "A solitary gentleman. A lone traveller charging pell-mell along the stony path to enlightenment, no less. He rides a dark horse."

Lilian disappeared into the cottage leaving both halves of the door wide open and Pony left standing just beyond the low flagstone step. The smell of baking wafted from the interior.

"Come in, Pony, dear." It was Mrs Slee's voice, growing from deep shade toward the light of day. "Bring your mount, by all means."

That made Pony smile. He walked confidently into the narrow hallway, closing the lower half of the door behind him. Stepping into the kitchen, he found Lilian and Mrs Slee sitting at a small table set with tea and cake. There was a tumbling posy of honeysuckle and knapweed in a stoneware bowl, and a white, porcelain candlestick with the puddled remains of a bottle-green candle. A dead moth was stuck in the solidified wax.

"Please sit down, Mr Chalice." Mrs Slee spoke without looking up. "We have made a Victoria sponge especially."

"But you didn't know I was coming."

"Oh, but we did. Please, Mr Chalice, join us. Take a pew, do." Mrs Slee gestured to a chair.

As he moved to sit, Pony pulled a rolled-up, black-and-white magazine from the back pocket of his jeans. He unrolled the tatty periodical and flattened it out on the table. It was a copy of *Riding* magazine from September 1941. The cover bore a photograph of twenty-or-so men – some partly in uniform, others in tweeds and Sunday best, and all with some form of weapon, be it a shotgun or a pitchfork – riding across the bridge in North Molton. Beneath the photograph, the caption read: 'The Home Guard in The West Country'.

"I've brought this picture on this here paper from back in the Second World War. I've identified everybody except for one chap; no one has the foggiest who the bugger is. I've got them all named: the Snell brothers; the Webbers, uncle and nephew." Pony indicated these people with a tap of his forefinger. "The nephew, though, he was the one who got killed in the combine harvester. Fell backwards in. That was a terrible sad job; the top of his head was cut clean off. And that's old Arthur Westcott who used to do the delivering over Exmoor in his van, rain or shine, hell or high-water. There's plenty still about who remember him. Every single chap in this picture has had a name put to him, except one."

Lilian poured the tea, milk first. She watched Pony dig four heaped spoonfuls of sugar out of the bowl and give his tea a vigorous stir. Lilian and Mrs Slee looked down at the wartime magazine from where they stood to either side of the man. Pony was poised, but the women beat him to it, their fingers meeting like divining rods.

"Him."

They spoke and pointed in unison to a heavy-set man astride a horse at the forefront of the motley posse. He wore a long and stiff-looking dark overcoat, buttoned and belted over his belly. His coat was tucked back on his left-hand side to reveal a long and elegant revolver in a leather holster at his hip. He wore knee-length hunting boots, as did several of the other mounted gentlemen. All in the photograph were wearing hats: mostly flat caps, but bowlers and trilbies too. The man in question wore a crow-black karakul.

"Well, yes," Pony said, his thunder having been resoundingly stolen. "That'll be the chap. No one has a clue. Don't tell me you know who he is. I should have come here first. It would have saved me a whole bliddy basinful of time and effort."

"Temple is his name, Pony," Lilian said, topping up their teas. "Evil is his game."

"Temple, is it? It seems odd he's the one stranger in a gang of local chaps."

"Temple is a stranger everywhere he goes, dear," Mrs Slee said.

Their guest rattled his delicate teacup into its saucer. Both women had moved off to the sides of the table once more, and Mrs Slee, her head leaned almost parallel to the table top, was cutting the cake, whipped cream bulging from each slice.

"Temple is a bad man, Mr Chalice," Mrs Slee said, looking sideways into his eyes.

"Temple is *the* bad man," Lilian added. "He is really the worst sort of bad man there could possibly be. Temple is a villain. And he has found the means to perpetrate his immoral endeavours in perpetuity."

"Oh. Right. What's he done, then, that's so awful bad?"

"He brings back people's loved ones from the dead," Lilian told Pony, as if he'd asked what sort of car Temple drove, or whether he preferred holidaying in Spain or Florida. "Temple is the paradigm of evil."

"Well, *was*. He'll be long dead by now, ladies. He looks like he's in his mid-fifties in the picture. And he don't exactly look like no fitness freak to me."

"He looks the same now as he did back then," Mrs Slee said, still fixing Pony's widening gaze. "Although it would be wrong of me to suggest I'd seen him recently. He buys time. Sells it. He's a merchant. He's a killer. Time, human life, eternal life – they're mere commodities to him."

Mrs Slee allowed her words to sink in.

"We all know things we wish we could unknow," she said, sighing. "We have all seen things we wish we could unsee. Cake?"

The fat slice of homemade Victoria sponge looked gorgeous. But Pony had to focus. His eyes narrowed.

"He can't be alive, though, can he, this Temple chappie? If he was, wouldn't he be over a hundred and twenty years old?"

"Mathematics won't help, I'm afraid, where metamathematics struggles, Pony, dear," Mrs Slee told him. "I'm afraid he'll live until he's broken the fragile heart of this beautiful world and ground it all to dust. Just like the next world."

Pony watched as Mrs Slee tucked fine strands of grey hair behind her ears.

Lilian rose, stood behind Mrs Slee and placed her hands lightly upon her friend's shoulders.

"You two are beginning to worry me," Pony said, looking up and down between the faces of the women. "I don't know what to say to it all. I'm not joking. Perhaps I should whisper a travelling spell into my little colt's lugholes?"

"Knowledge and *understanding*, Mr Chalice. If you leave now, you'll be going home with only half of what you came for," Lilian said.

"I was always told that a little knowledge can be a dangerous thing," Pony replied.

"This particular little bit of knowledge was probably the one they were trying to warn you about," Mrs Slee slurred, with her mouth full of cake, and cream on the downy hairs on her top lip.

"Maybe you two know more than I care to."

"We certainly know more than *we* want to know," Lilian replied.

"And that has been the case for as long as I care to remember," Mrs Slee added. "And we seem miserably unable to stop people foisting their unwanted information upon us."

Lilian and Mrs Slee laughed.

"We must look as if we don't have enough information, old girl. Mustn't we?" Lilian asked, chuckling.

"We are all in the same little lifeboat. I know it sometimes feels as though we are aimlessly adrift." Mrs Slee folded her arms across her chest. "We will have strong coffee and brandy now."

Lilian left the table and wandered off to locate the alcohol.

"Nicholas Temple's motives centre on the idea that everything has a price," Mrs Slee informed Pony. "It sounds simple, doesn't it? Most people have an idea of the price of an apple, don't they? But what price the tree, the potent pip? What price the garden, or the serpent?"

"You've lost me, I'm afraid, maid."

"What price destiny? What price freedom? How much is the life of a human being worth? Does the value vary from person to person? How do you begin to value eternal life?"

Lilian returned to the table. She thought Pony looked like a stook of wheat with the grain threshed out of it. She held a tray of piping-hot alcoholic beverages balanced on one hand.

"I wouldn't have a clue about very much of it," Pony told them. "I mean, I don't think I'd be sure where to start."

"But you know the price of a horse," Mrs Slee said, "and have a good idea how much an acre of hazel copse is worth. Estate agents in this area value tracts of beautiful countryside every working day. What would someone have to pay you for that enchanted glade of yours? Do you suppose a poor person would be more readily tempted by financial gain, whereas an elderly person might favour payment in years?"

"Here we are, then," Lilian said, setting down delicate china coffee cans, the sugar bowl and a silver teaspoon on the table. "This should shake us up."

"I've been shaken up plenty," Pony said. "You two have said enough to give me a bliddy headache."

Mrs Slee clutched her drink between the arthritic fingers of both hands.

"Temple engineered the heavy shelling of the missing barrow in the Second World War," she told Pony. "He also brought about its expurgation from maps published subsequently. He will simply have bribed someone in the military to facilitate the placement of targets for heavy artillery on the barrow and blow it all to kingdom come."

"It makes even less sense now, doesn't it?" Lilian said. "But it will surely provide you with something to ponder as you canter homeward through the darkling woods. You haven't touched your coffee and brandy."

"Please do drink it while it's hot, dear," Mrs Slee insisted. "Medicinal purposes only, of course."

Pony did as he was told, downing the potent draught in one. His eyes widened and his eyebrows raised involuntarily. He exhaled forcefully.

"Yeah. Just the bliddy ticket, that is. Proper."

"How old are you, Pony?" Mrs Slee asked. "Do please forgive the impertinence."

"Forty-seven."

"Then open the magazine you brought – if you will – to page forty-seven. Be so kind as to humour me briefly."

In the upper left-hand quarter of the page in question was a monochrome photograph of a silver trophy, destined to be awarded – so the caption read – to the best young horse in show each year.

The engraving on the cup was clearly legible: 'The Pony Chalice'.

31 (Before)
An Underground River

Finch was standing with his hands on his head, pivoting at the hip, surveying serpentine rows of found pieces.

"Can you fetch the hosepipe, Maze? And bring me all the bigger sections I point to."

Without waiting for a response, he marched off across the hangar, indicating various crystalline fragments as he went.

Danny had been ferrying Sylvanie back and forth between the village and the airfield, happy to make as many runs in his truck as necessary, to collect all the pieces she had taken home and hidden in her room, below the workbenches in the shed, and in their derelict garage with the buckled door.

It was Finch's idea that all pieces should be lined up along the walls inside the hangar. He repeatedly strode the length of the building until drawn to one seemingly random piece or another. Over a nine-hour period, Finch oversaw the construction of one singularly extraordinary segment, bringing together more than thirty partially-assembled sections to be rinsed under the hosepipe and then united.

The element that they had constructed was beautiful, massive, and clearly part of something considerably larger.

Sylvanie and Danny had not been inside hangar three for nearly four hours, having made sure that they had retrieved all of Sylvanie's hoard. They backed up to the front of the hangar as Maisie came out to greet them, and Boots and Shoes came careering across the airfield.

"This is going to blow your minds," Maisie said, standing to one side of the hangar door and ushering them through.

A few paces in, Danny and Sylvanie came to a halt. Danny's arms fell to his sides. He took a step backward and bumped into Maisie. She held his shoulders.

Finch was standing in front of the object, with his back to them. They watched him gently push, with both palms flat on its surface, and they saw it begin to rotate. It was barely touching the concrete.

"It's like a glass tree with a shell over it, like armour." Finch's words were slow and breathy. "It's like looking into the heart of some giant creature."

"Wait," Maisie said. She walked over to the hangar door and slammed it, crossed to the switch for the lights and turned them off.

The object – bigger than an estate car balanced on its rear bumper – held light, made light, and light pulsed along arterial courses inside it. There were ribbons of light connecting the four of them to each other and to it.

Maisie pulled the heavy switch back down.

"How can anything even begin to be that beautiful?" Sylvanie asked, conscious that she was trembling.

Finch turned to face the others. "I knew it was going to be awesome."

"It's like one of those incredible deep-sea creatures that live miles and miles down and nobody even knows exist," Maisie said, without taking a breath. "And it's alive."

"It can't be alive," Danny said, then looked in the air around him for the words he seemed to have lost.

"It's impossibly beautiful," Sylvanie said, approaching the object and placing both hands flat on its surface as Finch had.

"Maybe we don't want other people seeing it," Finch said. "I'm not sure what anybody else would make of it."

"We don't even know what *we* make of it, matey," Danny said, without taking his eyes off the structure. "I mean, what the bliddy hell is it supposed to be?"

"We've asked that question over and over since we found the first pieces," Maisie said. "Since we saw how it wanted to be whole again. We all want to know what, exactly, it is, so we'll have to keep fitting all these lumps together until we find out. It chose *us* to build it, anyway."

"What?" Danny asked, still staring at the object with his mouth open.

"What do you mean?" Sylvanie asked Maisie.

"You know exactly what I mean."

"This is just one bit of it," Danny said, slowly walking forward. "It's going to be massive when we get all the really big lumps out of Pony's copse."

"Everybody come here," Finch said.

Maisie and Danny went to stand shoulder to shoulder with Finch and Sylvanie.

"Just touch it," Finch told them.

"It feels like something moving a very long way away," Maisie said, "and we can feel the vibrations. It feels like a river that was asleep, deep underground. And we've woken it up."

32 (Before)
Another Self

There were few weekends or evenings when they weren't all together at the hangar or making trips to their caches of pieces. Whenever they left home they carried schoolbags loaded with books, and whenever friends or family asked where they were going, 'to revise with mates' was the stock answer.

Danny was often on his own in the hangar, scrubbing and rinsing sections, with Boots and Shoes to keep him company. College hours could be manipulated easily, but he had almost given up on any pretence of coursework. He spent four full days digging and scraping on the moor, walking in circles with the dogs, then standing and contemplating where to begin. In the deeper holes, water was often a problem; like cider from a press it seeped from the peat to swamp his excavations. He used a yellow plastic seaside bucket to bail out the holes. His aunt had bought him the bucket and spade at Westward Ho! when he was four, and he had kept it and used it as a feed-scoop. From one particularly deep and waterlogged pit he extracted two pieces of crystal that he thought looked like his arms. He wrapped them carefully in his ancient wax jacket and lay the bundle on the front seat of the pickup.

Halfway across the airfield Danny took his foot off the accelerator, depressed the clutch, and allowed the truck to coast to a halt. He unfolded his jacket and looked at the long, bone-like objects. He felt as if he might have found pieces of himself that had been lost. Or, perhaps, pieces of another self from another time and place.

Development was rapid over the course of the following weeks. Finch, Maisie and Sylvanie made repeated trips to the moor and the copse with Danny's quadbike and trailer, returning with the larger splinters and segments. They threw an old tarpaulin over each load, tying it down with bailer cord and bungees. People sometimes viewed them from afar, but only twice did they have to respond to any serious questions about what they were doing. Both sets of inquisitive walkers were told that they were involved in 'The Big Exmoor Clean-up', part of a team of young volunteers removing lumps of concrete left behind from the Second World War.

Light aircraft came and went, but no pilots or passengers showed the slightest interest in them or their endeavours. They saw Danny's Uncle Des sporadically, usually through the window of his shabby little office as they went by. One especially clear morning he stood at the top of his concrete steps and beckoned Sylvanie and Danny over.

"I've got two planes scheduled to land this afternoon, so you lot will have to make sure to stay off the runway. They're good as gold. One's an aerial photographer. She says she's got eight or nine farms and some other properties to do. The other's a plastic surgeon. He's flying the family in for a picnic on the moor. They won't bother you if you don't bother them. You're so bloody busy, anyway, you lot, I can't keep track of all your comings and goings. I'll scoot over later on and see what you've been up to. I've been meaning to stick my head round the hangar door for ages."

"No way, Des," Danny told his uncle, quick as a flash, and with a wide smile. "Nobody gets to clap eyes on the project until we're ready. And we won't be anywhere near ready for a while yet. Then everyone can see it, and laugh all they like."

"It's a bit of fun, really, Des," Sylvanie promptly added. "That's all. But we've put a lot into it."

"It's a float," Danny's uncle guessed. "For the carnival. Don't go breaking into a bloody sweat, will you? No one wants to see bloody teenagers breaking into a bloody sweat." Des laughed and opened the door to his office, throwing the cold dregs of his coffee into the nettles as he went. Danny and Sylvanie took the long way round, driving on the grass at the boundary of the airfield.

There were now nineteen breathtakingly beautiful sections resting on the dusty concrete floor inside hangar three, each at least as big as Danny's pickup. The lights in the hangar were off. Not only did the massive structures appear to be lit from within, but they were humming. They moved almost imperceptibly when Sylvanie and Danny walked among them.

Maisie and Finch watched their friends.

"They look like icebergs," Sylvanie said. "They are the most beautiful things I've ever seen in my life."

"They make noises now, like music," Maisie said.

"And," Finch said, "they change colour when they're happy with where we put them."

"I can't see us being able to move them now," Danny said. "I mean, they've grown every time we come back in here. They're massive now. They won't even go through the bliddy door now."

"They let us know," Finch said. "We can move them because they want to be moved. Tomorrow we can start to bring them all together."

"I don't like the idea of these things in here all night, lit up like Christmas trees," Danny said. "People will start sticking their beaks in."

"When we leave the hangar," Finch said, "they fade out."

"How would you even know that, matey?" Danny asked him.

"I've seen them do it," Finch said.

"How can these things know when we're not here?" Danny asked. "Stop and think about it for a minute. They're lumps of rock."

"How are we supposed to know anything about any of it?" Maisie asked. "Every time we think we know something, what we thought we knew has changed. So, watch this."

Maisie moved closer to the nearest illuminated structure and placed the palm of her hand flat upon its surface. There was a change in the tone of the noise it made; it moved from a low, melodic hum to what sounded more like a sung note. She then lifted her hand from the giant jewel, pointed it directly at the surface and leaned slowly forward. Her hand began to change, to become transparent and crystalline. The ends of her fingers did not make contact with the surface, but simply passed through it. As her forearm became light and liquid, Sylvanie, Finch and Danny saw the intense brightness in her eyes and heard the rhythm of her heart pulsing through the clear stone.

Maisie slowly withdrew her hand. "How about that for a party trick, then?" she asked, with light still dancing in her eyes.

"Most of the pieces have got a sort of finished side now, underneath or behind, like a skin," Finch said. "I reckon those parts will form the outer shell of the thing. And you can tell … pretty much, what it's going to look like."

"What's it going to look like, then?" Danny asked.

"Exactly like a UFO," Maisie said.

"A flying saucer?" Danny had wanted to sound scornful, but failed.

"It's going to be more like two flying saucers stuck together, actually," Finch said. "Maybe, end-to-end."

"I want to go somewhere in it," Maisie said. "I have done ever since I thought I had some kind of idea what we were building. I'm not frightened of it."

"I think we're *supposed* to go somewhere in it, Maze," Finch said.

33 (Before)
A Prospective Buyer

The next time they saw Danny's Uncle Des he appeared incredibly animated, clapping his hands firmly and rubbing them together. Danny and Finch got out of the truck to speak to him.

"Hey, big fella. Hey, Finch." Des's eyes were as grey and wild as the sky above Dunkery. He was grinning.

"Hey," they said.

"It won't change me."

Finch looked at Danny for guidance.

"What won't change you?" Danny asked his uncle.

"The money."

"OK. What money, for Christ's sake?" Danny asked.

"Have you won the lottery or something?" Finch asked.

"Look," Des said, making a point of looking around as if someone might be spying on them, "this is strictly between us, right?"

Danny and Finch shared brief blank looks.

"I met this chap – Temple – snooping around by the gate a couple of months back. He'd parked down by the cattle-grid and had walked up here with his dozy little mongrel. He was chatty, and eventually got round to telling me he was interested in buying this whole poxy place – lock, stock and barrel. I didn't think he was serious at first. I don't know the bloke from Adam. Turns out it wasn't bullshit. I had no idea how deadly serious he was." Des stuffed his hands into his pockets and leaned backward. He looked smug. He looked drunk with smug. "Of course I could have said no, and stayed here for the rest of my days, watching those planes rot, and thousands more pissing dandelions sprout through the cracks in the concrete."

Danny and Finch looked at each other.

"Are you actually considering selling up, then?" Finch asked, growing pale.

"It was a no-brainer. My new best friend Mr Temple told me to think of an *obscene* amount of money. So I did. Then he told me to double it. So I did that too. And the rest, as they say, is history." Des clapped again and rubbed his hands together vigorously.

"So … what have you sold, exactly?" Danny couldn't have been more direct.

"Everything. The airfield, the crap sheds, the leaking fuel tanks, the rusty tools, the hangars and contents – even my little brick shithouse."

"Well then how long have we got?" Finch spat the question out.

"Any day now. I had another call from my solicitor first thing this morning. But you lot don't have anything to worry about. He's in no hurry to turf you lot out. He said tell you that he can give you all the time in the world."

34 (After)
Sleeplessness

Mr Tagore held a wry smile.

It was dark. And the darkness was as molasses.

"Are you smiling?" Georgia asked, using a voice made from dust shaken from the wings of moths.

"Indeed, I am," he replied, so slowly his words seemed to unwind.

"I could feel your smile. It made this delicious darkness quiver."

"Hah!" His exclamation was like a distant footfall in fresh snow. "We lie here, in this Tudor vault, like Victorian vampires, trading words as if they were beads or bonbons. My sweet goddess, fruit of my dreams, where are you?"

"I am here, Satyajit. Did you think I might not be?"

"I thought you might not be. I foolishly allowed myself to imagine I might not only be alone, but I might be all there is of the world, and my thoughts of isolation and desolation might be all there is of me. Hold my hand." He let his arm unfold and fall to the brick floor between his straw-filled mattress and hers. She found his hand and intertwined her fingers with his.

"If ..." Georgia began.

Mr Tagore sensed the question's energy accumulating in the unfathomable blackness, stiffening her arm and tightening her grip on his hand.

" … if you had the wherewithal and the opportunity … to *kill* Temple … would you? *Could* you do it?"

The question sounded childlike, and painfully honest.

"I would kill him. I would fire a silver bullet into him – and then I would fire some more. And when I was satisfied he was dead, I would acknowledge, with the appropriate measure of sadness, that another such creature would come along, in the course of some new, vast and sprawling history, to replace him."

"And then would you reach within the intimacy of the dead man's pockets and remove the disc and the little black book? And when you held those potent artefacts – knowing all you do about all they can do – what would you then do?"

Mr Tagore was enjoying the ache of the cold of the floor on their locked fingers, and the shared sleeplessness.

"What would you suggest?" he asked.

"Would you hold them in your beautiful fingers long enough for the potential of their power to register? Would you hold them until they no longer felt like the bunch of keys to all eternal damnations?"

"We will each have the strength to do what is required of us. Bringing about an opportunity to do the right thing has been the journey we have both been on for the longest time. Nicholas Temple is the slipperiest of customers."

Mr Tagore became aware again of the invasive cold beneath their hands; it was the kind of stone-coldness that overtook the bodies of human beings and left them for dead.

"If we did manage to kill the man in cold blood," he asked, "would all the peoples of the Spheres miss having someone at whom they could direct all their righteous hatreds? Would we all miss the undeniably unifying sense of purpose and direction?"

"He is the magnet of bias for every roll of every dice that ever led to a wrong decision."

"Do you think it is time to bring everyone together?" Mr Tagore asked.

"We are together, all of us, always, twinned and grafted and melded and woven."

"Doug Valentine told me that we should never fall into the deadly trap of seeing Temple as Satan or Devil. He said Temple is – and I quote – an 'extraordinary example of humanity'. If we label him, we see 'the label, not the man', and our attention is diverted. Our prejudices are our worst enemies."

"Temple procures and purveys our darkest fears and our most incandescent hopes," Georgia said. "He is a trafficker of souls. We see his footprints in the sand. We hear his footsteps in the dark. How close he has been. And now?"

"He will be closer soon enough, or all our winding and watching will have been in vain. We will remain patient and vigilant. We will bide our time, as he will buy his."

"Let go of my hand. Be brave, Satyajit."

He disentangled his fingers from hers, and placed his arms at his sides on the rough ticking.

"I am here," she told him, her voice honeyed and deep. "Have faith, Satyajit."

Mr Tagore was floating upon an ocean of dark thoughts.

"Mrs Slee gripped my hand very tight when she read my palm," he said. "She drank four cups of strong tea, bless her. You've read the report?"

"I have. All two hundred and forty-something pages of it. She hardly stopped talking for three-and-a-quarter hours. And, apparently, often speaking in tongues."

"Who would dare suggest otherwise? It has been said that she was channelling first-hand experiences from the histories of both Spheres. She carries everything from everywhere, everywhere she goes. I watched her become almost completely transparent."

"Were you unnerved, Satyajit?"

"I was. Fortunately, I've always relished being unnerved."

"You once told me that having a conversation with Mrs Slee is like holding a glass to a wall and listening to gods chatting in the room next door."

"Indeed. She is perfectly here and perfectly not. Perfectly there and perfectly not. And we're in the room next door."

"Can we really hope to catch Temple, when we find travel between this world and the next infuriatingly impossible."

"Things are set to become significantly more practicable. I remain eternally hopeful."

"Now you sound like you're mentally reconfiguring a bus timetable, my darling man. Mrs Slee would have us tear up our hopes and cast them into the flames of practicality."

"The Barrow Ship is a magical old bus. It amuses Temple to stand back and observe our risible endeavours.

And I can't shake off the feeling that he's the one selling tickets for the ride."

"Doubt is a very useful weapon, protecting us against arrogance and complacency."

"Doug Valentine said that when Temple threatened him on some historic day at Moor's Court, Temple asked him to choose between two bullets, held out upon his greasy little palm like a bus fare. Temple told Doug that the lead bullet would take away his life in this Sphere. The silver bullet would erase all record of his eternal soul."

"Remind me what our man Valentine did then," Georgia said.

"Doug told me that it was like being paid a visit by a door-to-door vacuum salesman."

"Nature abhors a vacuum salesman," Georgia said.

Mr Tagore laughed. "Temple held the same vapid smile the whole time they were face-to-face. Doug's dog was howling and growling fiercely. He had to keep telling Chuggypig to calm down. I think he was afraid his dog was going to eat Temple's dog."

"Tell me how it ended."

"Doug put his hand over Temple's hand, closing the man's cold fingers over the proffered ordnance, and slowly intoned, 'There's nothing for you here'. There was a big commotion. Hannah and the other tenants came bursting into the courtyard, making their usual fuss of Doug's great big ugly pooch. Temple walked out as they came in, Hannah holding the door for him and his dog."

35 (Before)
A Leap of Faith

"I love it when it's like this," Sylvanie told Finch.

He looked into the shining darkness of her eyes. He closed his eyes, and tried to understand what he thought he had seen. Deep within the liquid of Sylvanie's eyes, several funeral-black rooks had flown by. Remarkable. Unnervingly beautiful. Perhaps they had been mere reflections of charcoal ravens drawn across the sky. He opened his eyes and looked up. There was no sky.

"What?" Sylvanie asked, tilting her head.

"Sometimes I don't want to stop," Finch said. "I don't want to arrive. I want to go sailing past where I thought I was going. I love it when it's like this too."

Sylvanie had ridden pillion, her arms around Finch, her cheek between his shoulder blades. The mist, heavy enough in the coombe, had grown steadily denser as they gained height.

"Things get a taste of isolation when it's this heavy," Sylvanie said, pushing open the airfield gate. "Whatever you come across, you see in isolation. It doesn't matter if it's a tree, a deer, a building or a person. You have to relate to it alone, like you and it were the *only* ones – the *last* ones."

No 'No Trespassing' signs. No 'For Sale' or 'Sold' signs. Finch revved and rode through.

"I'm going to walk to the hangar," Sylvanie told him. "It's magical."

She wrapped the chain tight, and clunked the padlock shut.

She watched Finch disappear, involuntarily going with him a short distance. He created a portal as he rode off, a corridor the mist seemed desperate to swirl in and occupy in his wake. The sound of his bike came to nothing. In order to orientate herself, Sylvanie turned to the gate, but it had vanished. She put her arms out and walked forward. She hooked her fingers through the cold grey wire.

Then, a man's voice. Sylvanie stood completely still and listened hard. She thought it was coming from the moor, not the road. The mist unrolled the voice, offering tattered fragments of something called out, almost chanted. She held her breath.

… ost? Where are you? Mirror, mirror …

Then laughter. Sylvanie didn't like it. It sounded forced, like someone was pretending to laugh. To taunt her. To frighten her.

… through the looking-glass. She can't see …

Sylvanie had no idea how near he might be. Was it one person? She heard a small dog barking. The man's voice sounded like a recording being played back.

… be afraid of your own …

… see her again. I can take …

… n't open the Door. Open the mirr …

The words sounded stretched, strung out across the untrustworthy distance. None of it made sense. The dog was yapping. Nearer, this time. Clearer.

... e can't hear you. Tell her not to ...

... ink she's dead. There's no one there to hold ...

Sylvanie could feel fear taking hold, clutching at her ankles and wrists as if to bind them.

... pen the box. Open the ...

... ing for you here. There's nothing fo ...

Somebody was fooling about. Out on the moor. But she didn't like it.

... ost, little girl?

Sylvanie froze. The voice was so close that she felt like someone had touched her, pushed her. Her knuckles were white, her fingers tight around the galvanized wire. She turned around, pushed her back to the fence, and searched desperately for the shape of a building. There was only thick, white fog.

But ... something else.

There were looser patches, less dense, as if someone had disappeared there, as Finch had, and swirls of mist were again rounding in, desperate to occupy the void.

She must be facing in the direction of hangar three. If it still existed. She couldn't even see the corner of Des's office.

To let go of the wire would require a leap of faith.

36 (Before)
Shipbuilding

Sylvanie ran as fast as she could across the airfield, looking at the ground for reassurance, counting the lines of grass grown through the cracks between the concrete slabs of the runway. She was running through the sky, watching countries fly by beneath her feet. She developed a stitch, but didn't stop. By the time the grey mass of hanger three loomed into view, she had begun to seriously doubt her sense of direction. She ran straight to the door, locked from the inside, and kicked and thumped it with as much force as she could muster.

A plaintive voice, somewhere behind her. At a distance. Calling.

… ere have they gone? Where are …

Was someone trying to mimic her?

"Syl?" It was Maisie.

"Let me in, for Christ's sake," Sylvanie growled, her ribs and abdomen aching wildly.

Maisie slid a big metal bolt and stood aside as Sylvanie pushed the door.

"Me and Danny put that on." Maisie indicated the stout new fastening as Sylvanie staggered in. She re-bolted the door. "You've been running."

Sylvanie was awestruck. She stopped breathing, and had to tell herself to start again, staggering, heaving lungfuls of air. She heard her own voice telling her not to fall.

"You won't believe," Maisie said, feeling Sylvanie's hand on her shoulder, "how many pieces have gone together. Now we've got to figure out how all these glass mountains link up. Finch can do it. Why has it taken you so long? Finch has been here ages. He was about to go back out and find you."

Danny and Finch were rotating one enormous, glacial section of the structure, which did not appear to be touching the hangar floor. Danny went to turn the hosepipe on.

"What have we done?" Sylvanie asked in an almost breathless whisper. "What is it?" Her lips were moving, but there was little sound. She stood, her dark eyes wide. "It is a magical thing."

Danny aimed a steady jet of clear water onto the structure, but none was passing through or running off. Sylvanie's hand was clasped as tight as a falcon's talon on Maisie's shoulder.

"It's like the pieces brought themselves together," Maisie said. "They move when there's one of us close. It seems to needs us."

Sylvanie watched Finch and saw how focussed he was. Light arced between his body and the object he was touching. It was the size of the school minibus.

"It's *one* thing," Sylvanie said. "Finch is going to fit it all together."

"Yeah, well, there's not much point in trying to stand in his way."

"It is becoming." Sylvanie marvelled as giant segments reacted to her proximity. "It's a beautiful thing, isn't it, Maze?"

"It just gets stronger and lovelier the bigger it gets. It makes us happy."

"It makes us happy," Sylvanie repeated. "And we get stronger with it."

The strip lights were off. All the light in the building was emanating from the pieces. Maisie took hold of Sylvanie's hand and moved closer to Finch and Danny.

"What took you so long?" Finch asked, turning one immense section ninety degrees with no apparent effort.

Sylvanie saw water coursing through the muscular interior of the structure. "The water's like glue. It's like blood."

"They've been slowly filling up," Danny said. "Thousands of litres. Takes ages."

Finch slapped both hands hard upon the surface of a vast piece shaped like a broken wine glass bowl. "OK, we're going to lift this one to about waist height, then see what happens, what kind of reception we get from that one." He gestured toward a neighbouring piece at least half as big again.

Maisie turned the hosepipe off.

"It sounds like a machine," Sylvanie said. "Like a tractor or a combine working miles away across the fields."

They placed their hands on and under the curves and edges of the chosen object. It seemed impossible to believe that they could lift such a massive piece of crystal. The adjacent section responded immediately, rising from the concrete, and rotating to allow the location of the cradled piece. The humming grew deeper and louder.

"It sounds like it's alive," Sylvanie said.

"There are pathways, like living veins, everywhere inside each piece," Finch said. "They all seem to want to connect."

"There are patterns growing inside each of them," Maisie said. "I've seen them too. Growing like trees when their roots need to get around or through something."

Danny moved and stood beside Maisie. She turned and saw a myriad of tiny lights reflected in his eyes. Then they watched Danny do something impossibly wonderful.

He stepped up to the shimmering object closest to them, and leaned his head and shoulders slowly through its glassy surface. They all witnessed the upper third of Danny's body become as one with the structure.

Sylvanie thought he might overbalance and fall forward. She tensed involuntarily, reaching out, prepared to grab him and pull him back.

To their astonishment, Danny rapped against the outer shell of the object with the knuckles of his right hand, while his head and upper torso became increasingly transparent within the object.

"Oh my God," Maisie breathed, only slightly more in awe than fear.

Sylvanie and Maisie clutched at Danny's belt and hoodie and tried to pull him free. Nothing happened. Danny remained, head and shoulders locked in the singing, ringing stone.

Five or six seconds later, with his hands flat on the surface of the structure, he withdrew. He did not breathe, but swayed as the dizzying firefly lights in his wide eyes went out one by one. At last he exhaled, then drew in a deep, unhurried breath and broadened his sublime grin.

The others, who had also been holding their breaths, exhaled as one.

"It's like water," Finch said. "You can slap it hard with the flat of your hand and it feels pretty solid, like if you do a belly flop in the river. Or you move your hand slowly, and there's no problem."

"I want to do it," Maisie said. "I'm going to do it. What happens? What does it feel like?"

"It's liquid in there," Danny said, unemotionally. "Sort of. I had my eyes open. Stuff moves around; bits of light and shadows and shapes swim past. You don't feel in any big hurry to breathe in. It's as thick as blood, but you can keep your eyes open and you can see through it. It's like you're down at the bottom of the pool in the river, watching everything in the world going by."

"You're not wet, though," Sylvanie said. "You're as dry as a bo—"

There was thunderous banging on the door of the hangar.

They froze.

Then aggressive hammering on the corrugated iron at both sides of the building.

37 (Before)
Authorities from the Real World

"Open up, immediately!" A woman's voice. "This is the police."

Danny went straight to the door. "What do you want?"

"Either you open this door, young man, or we'll break this door clean off its hinges, young man. Clear? Get a move on." A man's voice this time. He banged insistently. "You youngsters are a danger to yourselves, and we're here to put a stop to it."

"Danny, it's me." It was Des. "Open the goddamned door now, big fella. I don't want this lot smashing down the door. I don't want nothing jeopardizing the deal. They've been told you've got Second World War bombs up here, mate. They say you could blow yourselves and everything else to kingdom come." There was more banging and kicking on the door and at the sides of the hangar. "It's for your own safety, you lot."

"Come on. Open up, now. Open the door." Two official-sounding voices shouting – a man's and a woman's – deliberately gruff.

Sylvanie, Maisie and Finch were now beside Danny at the door.

"They haven't got a stupid clue," Sylvanie whispered. "It's not a bomb."

"What do we do?" Danny asked.

They turned as the warm glow from the structures waned to nothing, leaving them in absolute darkness. The temperature began to fall.

"Open the door." Danny answered his own question. "We don't have a choice."

"He's right. Open it," Finch said. "They'll see there's no problem and leave us alone."

"I don't think it'll work like that," Sylvanie said. "But it is Des's place, and they're only going to break it down if we don't open it."

"Lights on, lights off: doesn't make a blind bit of difference." The police officer's voice sounded urgent and irritated. "The longer you keep us standing out here freezing our testimonials off, the more pissed off we'll be when you finally decide to do as you're told, like good boys and girls. You're not fooling anyone. Get this damn door open."

Danny slid back the bolt. The sound of it surprised him. It sounded like surrender. It wasn't a sound with which he was at all familiar.

Des pushed the door and stepped in. The day had disappeared. It was a crow-black night. Des shone a big torch into their faces. There were three uniformed officers; one woman and two men, each holding torches or phones. Des barged in, swearing under his breath as his heavy torch began to falter, and made his way to the light switch in the corner. He pushed it down, but nothing happened. The police officers' torches all faded and failed. They shook them violently, banged them against the palms of their hands, against the door jamb; all to no avail.

"What the hell?" one of the male officers exclaimed. "Why in the name of sweet sanity would that happen?"

"Spin the patrol car and get the headlights pointing straight in here," the female officer ordered.

The driver went to do as instructed, but was unable to start the vehicle.

"Battery's dead as a bloody dodo," he shouted.

They tried the police radio in the car, but that wasn't working either. Phones were useless. Equipment they routinely relied upon was failing them.

"Try the landline up there," Des suggested, jerking his thumb toward his office in the low conning tower.

"Right," the female officer replied, clearly annoyed at being thwarted. "We'll come back in daylight, when we can see what it is we're supposed to be dealing with."

The four friends remained silent. Des and the police appeared to have seen nothing of the wonderous structures within the hangar.

"You could try pushing the jam sandwich down that way toward the fence," Des suggested. "The runway slopes a bit. Maybe you could bump it?"

"Lock this godforsaken place up, and let's get out of here," the female officer said, livid with frustration and embarrassment. "Jesus only knows what's been going on in the real world while we've been farting around up here, off-grid. Do as the man says. I don't care if you have to push me all the way back to the station. I've had a bellyful of this."

Danny's uncle put the padlock on the door of hangar three.

"We'll be back up here in the morning," the officer continued. "I'll expect some answers to this wild goose chase. You lot stay clear until then. Do you understand?"

Danny sauntered to his truck, which fired up first turn.

38 (After)
Pandora

Mrs Slee lifted the receiver, but said nothing.

"Pandora?" A man's voice. Beautiful. Soft and low, but with hesitancy and a touch of frailty. It was the voice of an elderly man, an artist, in a corduroy suit.

Mrs Slee knew who it was. She luxuriated in the recognition.

"When you told me, all those years ago, Douglas, that you would one day give me a ring – this, I have to say, was not quite what I was hoping for. My darling man, it has been far too long a time."

"Time? Time – as I've told you a thousand, thousand times, Pandora, my darling girl – is a tower of scraps of paper upon which we can scribble our experiences, jot findings, make field notes ... before they all blow away in the breeze."

"Douglas, you incorrigible old reprobate, every drawer and every cupboard in every room of my potted existence is stuffed with files and ledgers and tins and bags of such fallen leaves. And where has it got me?"

"Georgia and Satyajit tell me that all our journals, all our letters and notes have been archived side by side for ease of reference."

"Isn't that simply divine, dear, having all our most desperate notions hermetically sealed in some museum library together? All our dreams and desires buried in a lonely crypt, side by side."

"Someday, perhaps, people will want to look back at our endeavours and see how things were brought laboriously and meticulously to fruition, Pandora."

"It is precisely that sort of vanity that might undo us. I would burn it all – honestly – if I could throw the disc and the little black book onto the same pyre."

"Our young friends have been gone a while. I trust you have not begun to lose hope?"

"My resolve is akin to my spine: bent as a stricken Exmoor hawthorn, but stoically supporting little old me. Hope can be an obstacle sitting obstinately in the path of what needs to be done. I left hope far behind in some long-lost lifetime."

"Fortunately, your Sylvanie has all the hope and conviction we cynics feel it is the gross misfortune of others to require."

"It was not cynicism brought me to this place," Mrs Slee replied, looking around the interior of the old telephone box. No one had moved the Hares. No one had dared interfere with their charmed lives. She picked one up, rubbed it with her crooked thumb and replaced it atop the mound of now bone-dry soil.

"What, then?"

"Oh, you know: dogged determination to be eternally vigilant in the face of the most avid and insidious evil."

"Duly noted, Pandora. But they have been gone—"

"Time flies, Douglas; it crawls, and it pirouettes upon a moonshiny silver sixpence."

"We can wait it out, though time waits forever for no man. Or woman."

"Fortunately, not even Old Nick. For he is but a man."

"A man who is nonetheless forever a hop, skip and jump ahead of anyone courageous, unfortunate or foolhardy enough to find themselves at his shuffling heels. Many times we have unwittingly danced to his tune. Perhaps he holds all the tickets to all the waltzes, jigs and reels we've not yet learned?"

"But you are right, we do have Sylvanie, now, Douglas. We have Finch, Danny and Maisie. They – with just a little help – are the ones to redress the balance."

"If they arrived. Even if they survived. If they were well-met by moonlight. If they return."

"We must have Sylvanie's resolve."

"Love drives that girl."

"Yes, Douglas." Mrs Slee smiled into the receiver.

"Why doesn't Temple simply murder us all? I know that on many occasions his patience has been sorely tested. Why doesn't he have all our candles cursorily snuffed?"

"He sees us as caged birds singing," she said. "He is no sportsman, though he considers us all fair game. I have always been afraid he might find it amusing to kill two birds with one stone if we shared a cage. He'll shoot us in our cages anyway, if our songs annoy him sufficiently. Mostly we divert and amuse him. He does not always know

156

precisely where we are and what we're thinking and doing, but he does know where we *want* to be, what we *want* to think, and what we *want* to do. The more threatened he perceives us to be, the more laughable he finds our intent. Perhaps he sees his fate in us? His own mortality? His *only* potential mortality? Perhaps, Douglas, he fears us, and that fear is part of what motivates him? Does he cling to that vaguest suspicion of fear because it makes him feel *real*, makes him feel *alive*?"

"He fears us and we motivate him. We're doing a really fine job, aren't we? How are you getting along with Lilian?"

"Magnificently. You picked the perfect acolyte. She thinks about ley lines, tumuli, barrows, wells, cairns and standing stone alignments as frequently as others think of breakfast, lunch or supper. Her research helps determine the safest and most timeless locations. Her maps of ley lines are amongst the most dizzying images I've ever seen. She is as dogged with her lines as you are with your paintings. She makes me smile. And I amuse her. She thinks I'm funny peculiar. She says I turn every conversation into a séance."

"We can trap Temple. I do believe it's possible. Between here and there. Between now and then." Doug Valentine's voice was as cool as mountain meltwater.

"We'll one day sing from the same hymn sheet, at the same funeral service."

"Is Sylvanie safe? And Hannah?"

"No. None of us are. Safety is always out of reach. Sylvanie is our Alabaster Child, waiting upon the skin of the lake. Georgia and Satyajit know when to bide their time and when to step back into the mill-race."

"And what of our young Mr Chalice? Do you and he communicate with any frequency?"

"Yes, on many frequencies. He gallops by on the wind, coming and going like the tide, his old shirt billowing as if it was the mainsail of some fabled vessel. He joins the dots. He is also out of his depth. We are all in this way over our heads. Take a deep breath, Douglas."

Mrs Slee smiled a crooked smile and looked sideways at Lilian drawing a diagram in the dust at the bottom of the footpath with a spiky blackthorn wand.

"Look at me, Douglas, dear."

"Would that I could."

"Close your eyes and look at me." Then, like an old-time music-hall hypnotist, she said, "Look into my eyes."

"I see you. You look like my most beautiful friend."

"It's time to go," Mrs Slee said, preparing herself for the struggle with the cast-iron door. "I want to see what Lilian is drawing. Oh! And I meant to ask you about your artwork, Douglas, about your beautiful paintings."

"The quince tree responds to every brushstroke, and its responses only make my task more challenging. It is an entirely joyous journey. Art is never about arrival, and perfection is the enemy of creativity."

"Fail again. Fail better."

"I wonder, before we part ..." Doug Valentine's words seemed to coagulate, and fall away.

"What is it?"

"I wondered if you might consider sending me some dreams? I am not short of them, exactly; it's merely that they make less and less sense. Like memories, actually. My memories have evolved and metamorphosed, and so I question them. They shift their shapes. You will be at least as familiar with my dreams as I. I am so alone now. Forgive me. I wondered if you might have a dream or two to spare, to share."

"I see. Why don't you try to forgive *me*? There have been so many distractions. All my dreams, Douglas, old flame, I will happily share with you."

"Will you marry me, my dearly beloved, my childhood sweetheart, my eternal only one?"

"Yes, Douglas."

39 (Before)
A Souvenir

The police inspector sat behind her desk with her back to a long window overlooking a tidal section of river, beyond which straggled a shambolic row of warehouses and assorted wharf-side buildings.

There was an aspect of the institutional ordinariness in the police station, Hannah realized, that she found repellent: the grubbiness, perhaps, at the edges and corners of everything. Hannah had never been in a situation that made her feel so out of place and uncomfortable. This room and this officer were supposed to serve a particular purpose. Hannah didn't think that she and her daughter were that particular purpose.

There were heavy footsteps before the knock on the door.

"Yes," the inspector called.

Two men entered; one in police uniform, the other military.

"Morning, Ma'am," the police officer said as he sat and prepared himself for note-taking. The soldier withdrew a long, brown envelope from the inside breast pocket of his jacket and opened it. He fumbled, and Sylvanie noticed that his hands were shaking. He also sat, almost as an afterthought.

"OK, then," the police inspector said, taking a tape recorder out of a drawer in her desk. "There's a wild goose up there on the moors that taxpayers are apparently happy to see us chase."

Sylvanie and Hannah slid each other a look.

"Let's get started," said the inspector, pressing the 'play' and 'record' buttons simultaneously. She named everyone present and gave the time, date and location before nodding to the soldier to proceed.

The soldier did not introduce himself. "What does hangar number three at Worthy Airfield contain?"

Sylvanie stood, strode the five paces to the window, and responded without turning. "I can only tell you what I know. It is a beautiful, good and wonderful thing. It was supposed to happen. However difficult you find that, that's too bad. We shoved everything we were supposed to be doing aside; all revision and exams and normal-life stuff. It all started to feel unimportant. Any attempt to stop us finding answers to the million questions that lie in those living stones is totally futile. You'll have to live with that. As will we."

"Repeat the question, please," the inspector told the soldier. "Answer the question, please, and sit down," she told Sylvanie.

Sylvanie did not sit.

The young soldier looked across at Sylvanie silhouetted against bright sunlight. "What does hangar number three at Worthy Airfield contain?"

"I know my friends are all here in this stupid grey building. I can sense it. They're all being asked the same idiotic questions." Sylvanie turned sideways to the police inspector and her tape recorder. "I'm sure they'll all give you the same answers. Not because we've sorted out what to say, but because there's nothing else to say. If you want to ignore what we tell you, it's your call. We'll let you know what it's all been about when we've finished."

Sylvanie turned again to the window. Two trucks had parked in front of a derelict warehouse across the river. She watched scaffolding poles being slid onto the tarmac. There was a fraction of a second delay between the sight of the end of each pole hitting the ground, and the clanging sound it made.

The soldier looked down at his list and read the next question. "What is the origin of the objects in hangar number three at Worthy Airfield?" He allowed the stiff paper to refold itself in his hands.

Sylvanie turned to look directly at her mother. "The pieces are all from one area on Exmoor where there was an ancient barrow. Someone told us it got blown to bits in the Second World War. We found all the fragments and splinters and put them back together like a great big jigsaw. Nearly. There's just the final stage to complete, then everyone gets to see what it's all been about. That's when all the innocent bystanders, stargazers, boffins and generals will start scratching each other's heads as well as their own."

Sylvanie crossed the room and sat down. Hannah immediately took hold of her daughter's hand. The dynamic in the room had shifted; it seemed less formal, but with a very focussed teenage girl completely in command.

"You can do your exams later on, can't you?" Hannah asked. "All of you can. It's not the end of the world."

Sylvanie looked at her mum and smiled. "We can. It's definitely not the end of the world."

"I'm supposed ..." The young military man glanced at the tape recorder. "Please answer the questions. What are the objects in hangar number three at Worthy Airfield made of?"

Sylvanie also looked at the tape recorder on the inspector's desk. She stared at it. Two flat buttons at the front of the machine popped up. Off.

"Damn." The inspector leaned forward to push them back down. They clicked up immediately. She caught Sylvanie's eye. With two fingers she again pushed down the 'record' and 'play' buttons. Sylvanie looked at the buttons. They came back up. Off.

"Right. We seem to be experiencing some technical difficulties," the inspector said, without looking at Sylvanie this time. "Not a problem. We'll carry on. You continue taking notes," she instructed her colleague. "I'll do the same."

"We've no idea what it's made of," Sylvanie said, "but it looks like glass or some sort of natural crystal. You can see things if you stare into it. If you want to find out what it is and what it's for, then you'll have to let us get on with the job of building it. We can't make any progress until we're allowed back up there to get on with it."

The soldier read the next question on his sheet. "What is the duration of your involvement with the contents of hangar number three at Worthy Airfield?"

"All you had to do was ask Danny's uncle. We started in the early spring, and it's just got bigger and crazier ever since. It's taken over our lives. As I already told you, we worked in school- and college-time as well. And we'd be working on it right now, if we weren't here, wasting your very precious time."

Sylvanie had her eye on something on the police inspector's desk. It was one of the few personal things in the room: a souvenir mug from the Olympics. Sylvanie stood, took two steps to the desk and picked up the mug. It was empty, but held the stain of coffee.

"Please put that down," the police inspector said. "My daughter gave that to me. She's a gymnast. She brought it back." Clearly, she imagined her daughter's gift being dropped, or thrown and broken.

Sylvanie held the mug out in her right hand, as if to make a show of letting it go.

"Syl, do not even think about dropping that mug," Hannah told her.

The inspector was on her feet.

"You have to try to get your heads around how powerful this experience has been for us," Sylvanie said. "And how empowering."

Sylvanie let go of the mug.

Everyone in the office gasped.

The mug fell approximately forty centimetres before coming to a halt in mid-air.

40 (Before)
Authorized Personnel

Hannah and Sylvanie were collected in a black Range Rover, a vehicle that made them both feel ill at ease. It was raining hard. Hannah looked angry and lost.

"Why have I known literally nothing about this?" Hannah had been talking to herself sporadically for hours. "Have I chosen to keep myself in the dark? That's what parents do, isn't it? When they can't deal with actually knowing about something? I've never even been to Worthy Airfield. What the hell have you and your truanting friends been doing that's been worth lying about to everyone who cares about you?"

Sylvanie watched a heavy, wet world go by. She listened to the sweep of the windscreen wipers. As the car drew up to the airfield – which now had four armed soldiers at the gates – she turned to her mother. "I suppose we didn't speak about it, because we didn't want anything to go wrong, or anyone to get in the way. We wouldn't even have known which words to use to talk about it. To ourselves. Let alone anyone else."

Sylvanie read the notice on the gates as soldiers waved them through:

'M.O.D. TRAINING IN PROGRESS
DANGER! KEEP OUT!
NO UNAUTHORIZED PERSONNEL'

"I've never been an 'authorized personnel' before," Sylvanie said, looking sideways at her mother again, and smiling hopefully.

"Is that what you think you are?" Hannah asked. "Think again."

"This is a whole other level of authorization, Mum. Me and Finch and the others – we're the ones with clearance, not them. Trust me."

As the Range Rover moved across the end of the runway, Sylvanie and Hannah began to take stock of the number and variety of vehicles parked in rows with military precision.

Their driver was eyes-front and silent the whole way. She aimed for a vast, brown tent, pitched on the grass beyond hangar three. After picking up a little speed, she depressed the clutch, turned off the engine and rolled silently into an allocated parking space. It was a practised manoeuvre. A soldier who had been standing in the rain at the entrance to the tent ran forward to open the door at Hannah's side.

Sylvanie noticed that hangar three was also under guard. "Christ all-bloody-mighty," she exclaimed as she stepped out into the rain. "Isn't this a bit, kind of, overkill? You people are making this as full-on obvious as you possibly can, aren't you?"

"They're waiting for you inside," the young soldier said. He looked miserably wet despite his hooded waterproof cape.

Sylvanie turned west toward the centre of the airfield and stood looking up at the sky. Raindrops struck her eyelids. She opened her mouth and raindrops fell onto her tongue. She didn't want to be comfortable in the big tent, and she didn't want the officials inside to feel comfortable about her. If they were all dry in there, then she wanted to be wet. If they were all seated, then she would be the one standing. And they could wait.

"Sylvanie," Hannah called desperately. Sylvanie didn't turn. Hannah got back in the car and slammed the door. The driver didn't move.

"You've got to go inside, miss," the soldier shouted, spitting rainwater with his words.

Sylvanie looked down at the wet concrete and shook her head wildly. She strode to the car and opened the back door. "Come on. Let's go in. The others will be in there waiting for us."

After a moment's hesitation, Hannah got out and stood beside her daughter on the runway. "You're completely wet through. Why did you go and get so wet?"

"You're getting wet now."

"Should we go home for dry clothes? How long will this take?"

"There's no time for that, Mum. But don't worry; this won't take long."

The soldier marched ahead and pulled aside the heavy canvas door. He remained outside in the rain as Sylvanie and Hannah went in. The military marquee was full of people and warm, damp air. It wasn't dark. There were four bare electric light bulbs strung up. Sylvanie scanned the assembly as she went forward. Of the sixty or seventy people in the tent, more than half were in uniform. Finch and the others were all there; most mums and dads too. Maisie and Finch were nearest. They were looking straight at her, as was everyone else. She walked over to Maisie and Finch and hugged them as they rose to greet her. She moved to Danny. He stood. He hugged her. He slapped her on the back, and blushed.

Eight large wooden tables had been placed together to form a conference space in the centre of the tent, and everyone was seated around it. Some people had documents and files in front of them, others had laptops, phones and other devices, all closed, all dead. Sylvanie became aware of the sound of a generator grumbling somewhere beyond the sagging walls. She recognized almost all the civilians.

"Sit down, please." A brigadier, positioned at what could be seen as the head of the table, issued the order.

"No," Sylvanie said, without looking at him.

The air in the marquee seemed clogged. There was the sound of persistent rain on canvas, partially muffling the noise of the generator. All eyes were on Sylvanie.

"Look," she said, standing very upright with her hands clasped behind her back. "Understand this: everything that needs to be done can only be done by the four of us. You've all discussed it in your homes, in your offices and your secret underground bunkers. Nothing you fear might happen, or dream might happen, can happen without us. Some of you will understand that by now. We're not sorry about any of it. It will be mind-blowing. You can't do anything. You've tried, and you can't make anything work or move. You can't lift anything; you can't scan or electronically analyse anything; you can't take any nice holiday pics to show your superiors, to try to make them believe what you yourselves can't believe you've seen. And you really ain't seen nothing yet."

Sylvanie paused and drew a deep breath. The brigadier insisted that she sit. Again, she ignored him.

"Put up your hand," she said, raising her own hand to show them all how, "if you know what the thing in hangar three is." No response. "OK. Put up your hand if you think you're any the wiser about any of this than you were when you got here or first heard about any of it."

No hands went up. One or two people coughed. All eyes were still fixed on Sylvanie. She wasn't finished.

"This awesome puzzle is locked." She looked at Maisie, Danny and Finch. "We four are the keys needed to unlock it."

The brigadier stood. "You have a very great deal to say for yourself, young lady; which is fine, because you and your friends have a lot of serious questions to answer, not only to the many officials gathered here, but to your families also."

Sylvanie made eye contact with Maisie's mum. She looked pale, worried, confused. Sylvanie couldn't make up her mind whether Danny's dad, his ancient tweed jacket darkened with rain across the shoulders, looked anxious or furious. Perhaps both.

"I'd like my friends to join me at the door. We'll need someone to open the hangar, please. If that's not too much trouble."

The brigadier – very red-faced now – beat the table hard with his baton as Danny, Maisie and Finch pushed their chairs backwards over the groundsheet.

"They will certainly do no such thing," he ordered, observing Sylvanie's progress toward the exit. "You will all be seated immediately. You will all remain inside."

They paid him no heed. He was too late.

As the four friends left the enormous khaki tent, the generator fell silent, and the bare light bulbs were extinguished one by one.

41 (After)
Levitation

Georgia had hardly said a word. Sylvanie thought she seemed subdued, distracted. She thought about Georgia being just a woman, just a person, like herself and her mother, in this vast, insane situation, and recognized that morning that Georgia and Mr Tagore were treading water, just like her and her mother, caught in the same slow-motion whirlpool of events, over which they had as little control.

"It might be pleasant to retire to the drawing room," Mr Tagore said, standing with his back to the kitchen window, watching Sylvanie make a pot of tea.

"Yeah. Well, we were going to head that way," Sylvanie said. "It's the nicest room in this big, beautiful, decaying house."

Hannah had made ginger biscuits, five of which Sylvanie placed on a plate with a bold 1970s design of an owl with green, brown and orange plumage.

"You are such a wonderful cook, Hannah," Mr Tagore said as he entered the drawing room with the tea and biscuits on a large wooden tray. "We should come to this café more often." He laughed to himself.

Sylvanie saw him look at Georgia, who was staring into the distance through the drawing room window.

"Is there something troubling you, Georgia?" he asked, setting out cups and saucers. "You seem far away."

"Something is going to happen," Georgia said. "I have no idea what, when or where. I am also fully aware that something is about to happen all the time, everywhere."

"Everyone here is safe," Mr Tagore told her.

The Watch looked in on them and asked if they needed anything. She then went about her business, which might have seemed like housework.

"Now is a good time," Georgia quietly suggested to Mr Tagore.

"Now is the very best of times, I would say," he responded.

Georgia took out her phone and placed it in the centre of the Persian rug that lay in front of the monumental stone fireplace. She then removed a small canister from the pocket of her jacket and sprayed two bursts of fine mist into the air above her phone.

It was three months since their last hologram. It had been from Finch's mum and had turned out to be unrelentingly disturbing and distressing. Hannah and Sylvanie had sat at a distance from each other and wept.

This time it was Doug Valentine who had recorded a message. Georgia closed the heavy curtains across both bay windows as the hologram began to play.

The man stood silent and still in the room before them, his hands folded in front of him, a benign and patient smile shaping his mouth and wrinkling his eyes. The recording was high-resolution. Hannah had not expected this. Doug Valentine looked more real than she felt. It was a shock.

He was not as Sylvanie had imagined him; her version had been infinitely more resistible and less charismatic.

"Are we ready?" Mr Valentine asked, and was presumably answered in the affirmative by the crew operating the booth. Sylvanie thought he sounded and looked like a man who was perfectly comfortable with his age, physical self, intellect, and his faded corduroy suit.

"My dear Hannah. Lovely Hannah. Long-lost Hannah. Greetings to you."

Sylvanie's mother began to cry. Large tears rolled down her cheeks. She let them fall.

"A hearty hello to Sylvanie too, about whom I have heard so many positive things. Hello to Satyajit and Georgia, of course: dear, trusted friends. I know you two will be adding your invaluable support. But, Hannah and Sylvanie, this message is to the two of you. I hope this strange ethereal epistle finds you both happy and healthy." He paused and smiled.

If the kindly gentleman in the room had been real, Hannah would have leapt to her feet and thrown her arms around him.

"I want you to know," Douglas Valentine continued, "how much I have felt for you all this time. If we were to weigh all the time that has flooded our lives and flowed over our heads since the departure of the Barrow Ship, it would surely crush us. Just when we thought we had perfected the art of waiting, we find there to be yet more waiting awaiting. For no *end* at all, of course, but the kind of beginnings we imagine only when our hearts are full to bursting and our eyes are tight shut."

Sylvanie and Hannah had moved to the edges of their seats and were leaning forwards.

"When did he record this?" Hannah asked, without looking away.

"Thursday morning," Georgia replied. "He insisted no one see it before you."

"We know of so few," Doug Valentine said, "who have passed between the Spheres without having had their tickets punched." He took hold of his lapels. "Your friends, Sylvanie, are part of a particularly select coterie."

All the colour had drained from Hannah's face. She had stopped crying. Mr Tagore was aware of the effect the apparition was having on her.

"Shall we pause the recording? Would you like to take a break?"

Hannah didn't answer. She was pushing the sides of her head with her hands. Georgia picked up her phone and the bright vision of Douglas Valentine fell to nothing.

"We'll take five," Georgia said, and put her hand lightly upon Hannah's shoulder. With considerable force, Hannah shrugged Georgia's hand away. She put her head in her hands and wept.

"Mum, I'm so sorry," Sylvanie said. "You don't have to listen … I mean, you don't have to see …"

Hannah stood up with a suddenness that surprised everyone.

"I'm going to wash my face and have a pee. I want to see the rest of it when I come back down. How can Doug look exactly the same as he did when I was a student?

174

There's no way he recorded that two days ago." She pointed at the teapot. "Make another, Syl, will you. I'll be down before it's brewed."

Sylvanie followed her mother from the drawing room. She met the Watch in the kitchen. Five minutes later they reconvened. The Watch chose to stand. Everyone else was seated.

"Will you be mother?" Georgia asked the Watch, who responded without hesitation and began pouring cups of tea. She was wearing her revolver. Sylvanie was briefly amused at the thought of them having an armed waitress. The Watch caught her smile.

"Start it from the beginning," Hannah said.

Georgia once more sprayed the mist and set Mr Valentine's recording to play. A little after the point where they had taken the break he appeared to turn to face Sylvanie.

"You found a transcendent craft," Douglas Valentine said, looking directly at her, "shattered and scattered like chaff upon the wind. Every far-flung splinter, every broken jewel, you retrieved and reclaimed. Nicholas Temple, arch iconoclast and cruel architect of miserable chaos, destroyed it. You and your friends rebuilt the dream."

Doug Valentine paused and looked down at his pointed suede boots and stood more at ease.

"Hannah and Sylvanie, we are deadly serious about bringing an end to the sorrowful furrow Temple has chosen to plough, sowing corruption and harvesting despair wherever he goes. But you may rest assured that it is of at least equal importance to all concerned to bring your lovely friends safely home."

Doug Valentine unfolded his hands and looked again at his feet, perhaps conscious of a mark he'd been asked to keep. He coughed. His eyes shone.

"The house wherein you currently reside, was built almost two hundred years ago at the confluence of fourteen spectacularly clear and charged ley lines connecting wells, sites of ancient ritual and miracle, wonderfully majestic trees and standing stone alignments. It is a location where the hounds of time go howling by almost entirely unheard and unheeded."

Right on cue there was heavy barking inside the booth.

"Chuggypig!" Hannah exclaimed.

Doug Valentine made a gesture with his hand and the barking immediately ceased.

"None of the other families are in quite the same position. You are of paramount importance to the Spheres. If you have questions, please direct them to Georgia and Satyajit. They are most loyal keepers of friendship. You can trust them with your lives." The holographic Mr Valentine sighed. "Mrs Slee and Lilian send their love. Mrs Slee, bless her winged soul, takes it all very personally indeed. You must continue, Sylvanie, to come to terms with your special strengths and abilities, and build on them."

Sylvanie saw the twinkle in Doug Valentine's eye.

"The sun is shining. I am signing off. All my love to all you remarkable people."

Doug Valentine waved, and the recording was terminated.

Mr Tagore rose to open the curtains.

"That cannot have been recorded when you say. It's not possible." Hannah's words sounded as though she'd rushed to get them from a cupboard in another room. "I don't believe any of it. And I don't trust you – either of you." She glared fiercely at Mr Tagore and Georgia. "I ..." She faltered. "I don't even trust myself anymore. I've never been brave, like Syl. I've never been strong. I don't give a shit what anyone wants me to be. I feel like I live my life, now, levitating. My feet never quite touch the ground."

42 (After)
A Bell-Jar

Although the first sequence of shots sounded like a snare drum being beaten by an enthusiastic child, Hannah and Sylvanie recognized the sound of gunfire.

The Watch was drinking a mug of strong instant coffee at the kitchen table at the time of the assault, a little over three hours off completion of a two-week shift. Watches invariably involved an hour swap-over time when shifts changed. The current Watch ushered Sylvanie and Hannah to the walk-in pantry beside the kitchen. Georgia switched on the single light bulb in the cold, windowless room, then closed the door on Sylvanie and her mother. Mr Tagore and Georgia – both now armed – remained on guard at either end of the long tiled hallway.

It was particularly bad timing on the part of the two amateur killers, since the relief Watch saw them crossing open ground as she took a call in her car before going inside. She attempted to warn the Watch on duty by phone, but abandoned the idea in favour of putting herself between the house and the attackers. The ensuing exchange of gunfire was warning enough. The Watch on duty exited the house via the front door, ran along a line of substantial trees and shrubs bordering the sloping lawn to the rear of the building and surprised the assailants from their most exposed side. Between them, the Watches fired seven shots, killing both intruders.

When the gunfire had ceased, a profound silence enveloped the house and grounds, sitting over the location like a bell-jar. No shooting, no desperate yelling of urgent instruction, no screaming and no birdsong. Only a sickening stillness remained.

43 (Before)
The Nature of Knowing

Things had tightened up. There was a cordon around the village; no tape or fences, but roadblocks with camouflaged Land Rovers, barriers, and soldiers standing about joking. The police had distanced themselves as the army set up the pretence of control.

Talk of first-hand experiences, second-hand rumours and wacky conspiracy theories ricocheted between local people. There was a sense of something going on, and of people not having any real idea what it might be. Personnel from the police and the army, in their reports to higher-ranking officers and government officials, had immense difficulty explaining what they had witnessed. No one wanted to appear foolish. No one wanted to file an earnest report on something that later turned out to be a risible hoax. Several times, when more excitable officers and soldiers had made ill-judged calls, they were laughed at. The official response to the on-going situation at Worthy Airfield was slow, because no one wanted to take responsibility for putting into words what they believed they had seen or what they imagined was taking place.

Mrs Slee called a secret meeting at her cottage. Lilian told Maisie, who informed the others, and they made their way there separately after dark. Mrs Slee's cottage was of no interest to the army, and no sentries, patrols or other obstacles were encountered in the moonlight. Lilian was at her friend's back door when Danny and Finch bowled up with their arms around each other's shoulders. Sylvanie and Maisie were already ensconced within.

Mrs Slee and Lilian had laid on a feast and seemed almost giddy. Mrs Slee was wearing her plastic raincoat, but Lilian was dressed in garments she'd tailored herself. Beneath her plum-coloured skirt she wore baggy burgundy trousers; over her midnight-blue waistcoat she wore a dark-green frock-coat that changed tone with every flicker of a candle. Her frock-coat was embroidered with stars and moons, dates, times and places, lines, numbers and names and a range of weird symbols and hieroglyphs. She wore black velvet slippers, noiseless on the stone tiles of the kitchen floor.

"You look awesome," Maisie told her.

"Why thank you, kind miss," Lilian replied, clasping her hands and rolling her eyes heavenward while curtseying. "I wanted to dress for the occasion."

The four friends felt at ease in the homely cottage, but were amazed by the clocks on the walls, cupboards, shelves and ledges. And there were at least as many lit candles as there were timepieces. Sylvanie felt her heartbeat slow to the languid rhythm of the clocks.

The two women had spent all day making salads and sandwiches, and baking pies, sausage rolls and little quiches. Homemade delicacies were arrayed upon an assortment of small tables that formed a roughly level linen-covered surface around which they could all be seated.

After three-quarters of an hour or so of pleasantries the conversation took a more meaningful turn.

"You must watch the skies, now, each night, paying special attention to the moon and stars, Maisie and Sylvanie," Mrs Slee told them.

"Think of the sky as a great big clock," Lilian added, "and you'll know when the time is right. Look to every memory and every dream you've ever had about the night-time heavens, and things will fall into place for you all."

"Never had ... dream ... like that," Danny slurred, his mouth stuffed with Scotch egg.

"I think we can do that," Maisie said, kicking Danny under the table as he took his seventh pork-and-apple chipolata. She watched him push two sausage rolls into his mouth at once. He didn't flinch when Maisie kicked him again.

"We're going somewhere, aren't we?" Finch asked. "In the thing we're making. I call it the 'Barrow Ship'." He was looking at Mrs Slee.

Everyone looked at Finch.

Lilian replenished his glass with lemonade she had made that morning.

" The Barrow Ship," Mrs Slee intoned. "It has a ring to it. And yes, you are going somewhere. Although I have not visited there myself in such a very long time, I do have some knowledge of your destination."

"It's where she comes from," Lilian informed them, a note of reverence in her voice. She had been waiting for this. This was, after all, what she had dressed up for.

"What ... you talkin' ... 'bout?" Danny asked, his mouth bulging with curried chicken. "Why aren't ... you two goin' ... then?"

This time, Sylvanie kicked Danny under the table. Everyone saw it.

"I *want* us to go," Finch said, sparks of excitement in his eyes. "We're *supposed* to. We've known it all along."

"Excuse me, but – what did you mean when you said something about knowing our destination?" Sylvanie asked Mrs Slee. She then turned to Lilian. "And you said, 'It's where she's from'."

"The other Sphere," Lilian replied.

Mrs Slee placed her hand over Sylvanie's.

There were greyish blotches on the back of Mrs Slee's hand, like lichen on sandstone, and veins, pale blue, like cartographical watercourses. Sylvanie noticed that the cuff of Mrs Slee's coat was worn away, and there were now two separate frayed edges.

"We're going there, then, are we? It's decided?" Sylvanie asked. "Where is it we're going?" She laughed at her question. "How long will we be gone? It's impossible. Everything about the last few months is properly, insanely mad."

"We've all been places without really knowing where we're going," Finch said.

"And without knowing for certain that we'd actually ever arrive," Maisie said. She looked down at her plate. It had a motif of running hares around the edge. For a second, in the flickering candlelight, the hares became animated.

"Thank you *so* much for going to all this trouble," Sylvanie said. "Thanks for making all these lovely and delicious things."

"Yes, it's mega kind of you," Maisie added. "Is there a special reason for getting us all together?"

Mrs Slee and Lilian nodded their heads.

"The *more* it all makes sense, the *less* it makes sense," Sylvanie said. "Perhaps there'll be a time when we'll think we understand everything and end up understanding that we understand nothing."

Mrs Slee laughed.

"That's how it is with understanding, dear," Mrs Slee said. "The more you know of a subject, the more that subject expands. It is the nature of knowing."

"Right," Sylvanie said.

"What *do* we know, then?" Danny asked, reaching across Lilian for pickled onions. "You two seem to know quite a bit. Quite a bit about us. We've all gone along with it, right from the start, but we haven't got a clue why. Or what bliddy for."

"Because we're part of it," Maisie said, looking very serious.

"It is all as nothing without all of you," Mrs Slee said. "There is no starting again. This is my last shot at redemption."

"To be honest," Maisie continued, "I've felt sometimes like I've been walking away from everything I was and everything that people expected me to be and do."

"One should always travel light," Mrs Slee said, smiling.

"The thing you call the Barrow Ship," Lilian said, looking at Finch, Maisie and Danny in turn, "you have to get in it." She paused. "But Sylvanie must remain here."

"I …" Sylvanie was attempting to catch up with what Lilian had said. "I stay here? Wait, why am I even asking that stupid question? This is just mad."

"You have to stay," Lilian told Sylvanie. "If you don't, the others may never find their way home. You will act like a beacon for their return."

"I don't want to go any-bloody-where without you," Finch told Sylvanie.

"It is of paramount importance, dear, that you *do* go," Mrs Slee told Finch, leaning back and twisting around in her chair. "And imperative that Sylvanie remain."

"Where did you say we're supposed to be going?" Maisie asked.

"To the other Sphere," Mrs Slee replied. "To the other side."

"What if we decide – even if it's true, this whole nut-job idea – that we're not going anywhere, any of us?" Danny asked, his eyes defiant.

"The choice is yours," Mrs Slee told him. "It always has been. Fate has struggled to wrestle us this far. You are all strong-willed individuals."

"You're trying to persuade us—" Danny began.

"To see things as they truly are," Lilian interjected. "To trust your feelings."

"We're all amazed by the thing up there," Finch said. "The Barrow Ship. We've all been under a spell since we found the very first piece."

"Does it feel," Lilian asked, "like a hex that has been with you all your life now has a purpose?"

"Yes. I don't know. I give up. Why do they have to go?" Sylvanie was holding back hot tears.

Maisie shunted her chair up to Sylvanie's and they put their arms around each other.

"Well, they need to see some people and places," Lilian said. It's really all about bringing a very bad man to justice."

"Bliddy cloud-bliddy-cuckoo-land," Danny said, folding his arms indignantly. "Bliddy fairyland." He looked at Mrs Slee. He looked at Lilian, and then back at Mrs Slee. "Why the hell are you two supposed to know anything about it? Why the bliddy hell are we supposed to trust you, and go along with all the witches' horseshit you come out with?"

"I am from the Hereafter," Mrs Slee said.

"She knows what she's talking about," Lilian intoned sombrely.

The multitude of candleflames in the little kitchen brightened, and the clocks throughout the cottage struck eleven with a cacophony of bells and chimes.

"Home time," Mrs Slee said. "Keep your eyes fixed upon the firmament, and your feet firmly upon the water."

44 (Before)
Interstellar Voyaging

Sylvanie had been in the garden all night, sitting on two white-painted metal chairs, swaddled in her duvet. She had come in at dawn, made herself a hot chocolate and gone upstairs to drink it in bed, not realizing how damp the duvet had become overnight.

She picked up her notebook and pen, and wrote: Me and Maze have been staring at the sky for the last three nights completely non-stop. It felt like I was on a little boat adrift in the sky. Maze said she was waiting for all the stars to fall on her. I didn't have a clue what I was supposed to be waiting for. I just kept looking up as it all went by. Sometime before it started to get light the moon seemed to cover a space in the sky that had been waiting for it. It was like the pond at the Manor waiting for the moon to glide over it and cover all the cold dark water with silver light. I know I saw what I was supposed to see. The moon was a hole in the sky. It was a tunnel you could pass through into the light.

Sylvanie finished her drink and called Maisie. She hung her duvet over her bedroom door to air and left the cottage without waking Hannah.

Less than an hour later they were all in Danny's pickup, its bull-bars touching the red and white barrier of the road-block at the bottom of the hill. Maisie was in the cab with Danny; Sylvanie and Finch were perched on the sides of the open back. The dog cage was empty.

"Can't let you through, kiddiewinks," said a young soldier with a shaved head as he stepped up to the open window on the driver's side.

Another soldier was leaning against the bonnet of a green and brown Land Rover, an automatic rifle slung round his neck.

"What are you going to do if I back up and plough straight through? Shoot us?" Danny asked. "Raise the barrier, or you'll have to fetch a dustpan and brush for the splinters," he said.

"You'll have to drive over me, mate," the soldier at the barrier said, gripping his gun and standing bolt upright.

"Just make a call, please," Sylvanie said. "Phone your boss and ask what you should do. We're on our way up to the airfield. We're not going to flee the country." She smiled to herself. "Not all of us, anyway," she added, under her breath.

The soldier sneered, turned away from the truck and made the call, moving along the lane out of earshot to speak. The other soldier joined him.

When the call was terminated, the soldiers conferred briefly, then marched over to Danny's pickup.

"You lot have got to follow him up the hill to the airfield," the one with the shaved head ordered. "Keep up, but not too close. You will stay behind the escort vehicle all the way to the gates of the airfield, then turn off your engine and wait for clearance. Got it?"

"Right you are, Mister General," Danny said, saluting.

The shaven-headed soldier pushed the barrier's counterweight down as his comrade pulled the Land Rover into the lane. The driver turned on his headlights and hazards and started up the hill.

They didn't have to wait at the airfield; the gate was swung open for them, and the Land Rover pulled over to let Danny's filthy truck through. Soldiers at the gate shouted and waved for them to stop, but Danny ignored them.

"Aren't we forgetting something?" Maisie asked Danny.

"What?" Danny asked, accelerating.

"Everything. Packed lunches, raincoats, flasks …"

Danny traced an arc around the perimeter of the airfield, skirting approximately a hundred vehicles. They were mostly military, but there were unmarked vans and cars, as well as ambulances and fire appliances.

" … shampoo, lippy, phones, exams, mummies and daddies, a change of clothes, toothbrushes … our entire previous lives."

People were pointing and shouting. Personnel were mobilizing.

Danny stopped the truck at the far end of the concrete runway and turned off the engine. People were moving about between vehicles and what was now a pair of enormous brown tents. There were five sky-blue shipping containers, brought in to house useless electronic equipment. Maisie thought that the people in civvies, scurrying about with clipboards and armfuls of numb technology, were probably scientists. The big white H on the disc of tarmac to the right of the runway had been repainted, and a Chinook roosted there like a dragonfly on a lily pad. Soldiers were hurrying in and out of Danny's uncle's office trying to look purposeful.

"Why have you stopped?" Sylvanie asked, leaning around to address Danny through the driver's window.

Danny ignored her.

Sylvanie banged on the cab roof. Danny got out and leant on his open door. "Does anyone want to bail out?" he asked. "Does anyone want to take this opportunity to piss off home?"

"Drive on, chap," Finch told him.

As Danny restarted the truck they saw a knot of four uniformed men gather outside the marquees. The soldiers moved as one when they realized the pickup was heading directly for hangar three.

Sylvanie jumped down as Danny pulled up. She walked confidently toward the group of military officials. "We've come about the interstellar voyaging," she told them, smiling innocently. "We thought we'd better get in quick before you actually advertised the vacancies worldwide."

45 (Before)
The Point of Absolute Surrender

"Strictly no access," one of the soldiers ordered.

Finch, Maisie and Danny came to stand shoulder to shoulder with Sylvanie.

"So what the hell did you let us in here for, then, please, Major General, Mister Colonel, Sir?" Danny asked.

"You have to report to the Field HQ now," the same soldier barked into Danny's face.

Sylvanie stepped sideways and marched to the unlocked door of hangar three. Finch, Danny and Maisie followed. Sylvanie had half expected to see scientists in white lab coats holding clipboards, shuffling about pretending to measure and calculate. There weren't even any lights on. The hangar was filled with solid-looking greyness. No attempt was made to bar their entry.

"Nobody's been able to work in here at all, have they?" she asked the soldiers who followed them inside. "I can understand how you must feel. I would be well hacked-off if I was in your oh-so-shiny-you-can-see-your-face-in-them boots. You all got frustrated and angry, and now you're getting puzzled and nervous. Am I right?"

The soldiers glanced sheepishly at each other.

Finch walked over to the big switch and turned the lights on, flooding the interior of the hangar with light for the first time since the police and Des had come knocking.

As Finch, Maisie, Danny and Sylvanie moved among them, the massive sections responded with a joyous humming and pulsed with light. Danny wasted no time getting the hose going. Finch got to work, ignoring the officials who entered the hangar, standing close to each other and the exit, clearly taken aback by the fact that the lights were now fully functional and the incredible structures were not only visible, but audible.

"Do you kind of hope that our families don't find their way up here?" Maisie asked Finch.

"Yeah. If they even got let in. But it's all too late for everything else. It's unstoppable, Maze."

"Finch?" Maisie was talking across his shoulder, into his left ear.

"Mm?" He saw that Danny was watching them.

"Are we going away ... *to* somewhere? To the other place that Mrs Slee was talking about??"

Finch looked at Danny and Sylvanie. They appeared to be made of liquid light.

"No doubt," he said.

People by the door attempted to use their phones. They gave up, but held their devices for comfort. They wanted photographs. Proof. Evidence. Records they imagined might be more trustworthy than their overloaded senses and unreliable memories.

Maisie closed her eyes and saw every particle of the world fall away.

A man was shouting, "It's a miracle! It's a miracle!" There was the sound of his round laughter, insistent and insidious, but unreal. The same man was clapping enthusiastically.

Maisie opened her eyes to see Finch and Sylvanie pushing two worlds together.

Finch felt the structures drawing his earthliness from him. He saw that the people around the walls near the entrance were fixed by the light and held at bay.

The friends slowly brought the giant sections to meet. The immense object sang. The sound travelled to the marrow of their bones. Sylvanie watched people cover their ears. Soldiers and civilians alike ran from the hangar. The light from the Barrow Ship suffused every molecule in that fragile enclosure.

Danny dropped the hosepipe. He watched the dark water creep across the concrete. He looked up and saw Maisie dissolving in light.

Sylvanie's lips moved, but no sound came out. This was the point of absolute surrender. She looked at the light flowing through her fingers like blood.

Finch touched her shoulder.

He was underwater. Breathing.

He held her.

They felt the light and the music spinning through their arms, their heads, their hearts.

He felt the light taking hold of him. Taking him.

He looked up through the river.

She could see his beautiful face.

His lips touched the surface of the air as her lips touched the surface of the water.

46 (After)
Wooden Feet

They had been relocated three times since the attack. Always at night. Not to anywhere as interesting, isolated or as palatial. Not to anywhere with a garden, let alone grounds. This place was distanced and separate, on the top floor of a high-rise block overlooking a grey cityscape. The apartment had a balcony wide enough for a deckchair, a little round table, some woody geraniums, and a bird-feeding station that clipped onto the corner of the handrail. Hannah replenished the feeders daily.

Georgia and Mr Tagore visited regularly, and their open, friendly discussions helped keep them all sane, but Sylvanie knew that there were some things better kept in reserve.

She had been sitting outside on her own for most of the afternoon. She suddenly sat forward in the deckchair, planting her feet firmly on either side and startling the small group of goldfinches and sparrows busy at the peanuts and sunflower hearts. She opened her journal on her knees, closed her eyes and visualized throwing the book into the air and watching it flap to the ground like a falling squab. Leaning over her book, her shadow colluded with the waiting pages.

She wrote: Something has happened.

Tides of rotted hope and almost hopelessness. I haven't been standing outside of everything. I'm flesh and blood. We're just human beings.

The Hare on my necklace is warm. It's always been cool. I know its coolness like I know my own skin. I've never taken it off. Not once. I was scared of losing it.

The ache of my love for Finch has kept everything real as all these ridiculous years have crawled past. I haven't cried too much. But today I've been doing quite a lot of proper sobbing. I've been sitting here on the balcony in the middle of the air and everybody has kept their distance. I think they might have run out of places for us to hide away. We're fairly high up here and you can see for miles and miles. If I close my eyes I can imagine I'm being carried along on the wind to where Finch and the others went. Georgia told me that people on TV have been talking about them being dead. That's really nothing new. But it feels now like people want it to be true. Tears have been running down my face like rain down our apple tree. My tears are entitled to their freedom.

I love the others. But I've never before let myself understand how much I love Finch. Now he's coming back. I know he is because the Hare that Mrs Slee made for me is warm. It's that simple and ridiculously insane. And it's all I have.

Time has passed me and Mum by. Like it passes Mrs Slee and Lilian by, and Mr Tagore and Georgia. Somehow it takes ages to race by. Seasons have come and gone like days. Sixteen years have passed. I haven't changed. Neither has Mum. We haven't got older but the world has. Mum thinks it's not natural. Georgia says it's just a different sort of natural. Sometimes I can reason with Mum when I can't reason with myself.

Mr Tagore and Georgia bring in their machinery to test the flow of time. They're obsessed with the perfect way to wait. They bring their chronometers and sit there watching the hands moving backwards and forwards over little enamel moons and they look at me and Mum with concern or even pity in their eyes. We just don't get any older. Or wiser. Maybe we've all had to wise up a bit. I will hold Finch's hand when he comes back and never let it go again.

Georgia and Mr Tagore are like weird family to us now. Mr Tagore is sweet. He doesn't play the government man so much anymore and if he does Georgia shouts at him. But he was never a government man anyway. I used to be so rude to him. Both of them. I don't recommend trying to be too rational about any of it. It will get me about as far as feeling sorry for myself.

We'll be alright. No one has tried to shoot us lately. Which is nice.

There are coins now called Silver Sylvanies. It's like a whole other currency. They've got my head on one side and the Barrow Ship on the other. Georgia showed us Golden Harts and Half Harts. We can't go anywhere so we can't spend any money. We ask for things sometimes and we mostly get them. I got a fantastic old leather jacket that's a bit too big for me. I want Finch to say he likes it and then I can just give it to him. They get books and films and music for us all the time. I read loads but Mum reads more than me. It's part of how we get by. Georgia likes dancing. Sometimes when me and Mum and Georgia are dancing I reach out for Georgia's missing hand and it's not there. I reach out for Finch's hand and it's not there every day.

I haven't told anyone about Mrs Slee's Alabaster Hare. Yesterday afternoon we were sitting in the kitchen area. Mum and Mr Tagore were pretty quiet. Georgia said some things to me that obviously startled him. I don't think it was because he didn't already know the things she said. He was shocked because she wasn't playing by the rules. He didn't think we needed to know the things she told us. Mum started crying and pushed her chair over as she got up to leave the room. It clattered really loudly on the kitchen floor. I'm pretty sure that no one lives below us. Sometimes I hear things but they don't sound like real-life things.

Georgia said that Mrs Slee has wooden feet. Really amazing prosthetic wooden boot things with beautiful carved feet and toes.

I stood the chair that Mum had knocked over back up before Mr Tagore could get to it. He can't handle that kind of drama and he hates stuff being out of place or disturbed. I didn't move. I didn't touch it. I looked at it and stood it back up.

47 (Before)
The Skin of the Sky

Sylvanie walked out of hangar three.

Civilians and official personnel alike stood transfixed in awe or crouched in fear among the vehicles out on the airfield.

With irresistible force, the Barrow Ship broke free of the hangar. Bolts sheared and popped as the corrugated-iron roof buckled and slid away; concrete supports groaned and bust and toppled. There was the screaming of diamond scraping concrete and steel; and, as the cage collapsed, whirling figures of dust fled and fell to nothingness upon a trembling world.

Sylvanie was without fear. The Barrow Ship rose like the sun. She strode backward.

People were running, stumbling. People seemed to be turned to alabaster in the howling light.

Rain blew down from the grey that swept the moor, and sunlight flooded through fields of blue moored above the copse and the coombe. The Barrow Ship sailed out over the concrete and grass, and rain-washed vehicles shone like pebbles in the tide as it passed over.

A magnificent rainbow, broad and bright – one end stood upon the crow-black circle where all the world's possessions had been incinerated, and the other upon the clearing in the woodland where Pony Chalice had his brushwood fires – arced over the airfield, holding the crystal vessel in an inverted cradle.

And the world turned upside down.

Sylvanie saw the great jewel – a mirror one moment, transparent the next – press against the sky's skin. It lay like a skimmed stone upon the surface of a lake of sky.

And Sylvanie was to have faith.

She was to be strong.

The pebble fell through the mirror and was gone.

Sylvanie watched the ripples move out across the shuddering sky.

Part Two:

Here and There

1 (There)
The Hall of the Handless Clock

Danny had opened his eyes and seen the Hares, and heard them talking together on the mound.

He had seen the window. The window was everything.

He did not move; his body slowly materialized from the stream of dreams that flowed through the window, through his head. His eyes closed and he slept for three more hours.

He dreamed of being himself, of standing firm with his arms folded, looking at the Hares, trying to believe in them. He could hear them speaking, but could make no sense of what they said. Jackdaws came to his pillow to whisper words into his ears. While sound asleep, Danny listened.

You are the Alabaster Children. Go. Seek. Believe. Amen. Understanding will fall upon you like rain from the sky. Wait. This world has been waiting for you. Follow your destinies and see for yourselves. Your sun rises in the west. You have crossed over to your rightful home. You are your rightful selves. We have given her the path. What you seek will find you. What you seek will go with you. Amen. The key to the Door will offer itself to you. Look into your eyes. The window is everything. Everything is falling at your feet. The Hall will turn. Tides will turn. Change will come. Amen.

Now, when he opened his eyes, the Hares were gone and the low mound of soil was bare. Danny pushed the starchy cotton sheet off and sat on the edge of the old metal bed. He shook his head and rubbed his face hard. Beside him, in a pair of similarly utilitarian, hospital-style beds and uniform pyjamas, Maisie and Finch were almost motionless in soft, warm sleep. Their clothes – washed, dried and all neatly folded – were piled on simple wooden chairs at the ends of their beds. Trainers and boots were there too, cleaned and polished. Danny looked at Maisie's hair rolling and flowing over her pillow like a riverside willow's roots.

A group of five heavy workhorses, and two spindly-legged foals with their heads side by side, stood in the immense pool of coloured lights cast by the window, snorting, bringing a warm musk to the air in the great room.

At the opposite end of the hall, ten or twelve strides in from the arched doorway, with its doors wide back against the walls, an industrious group of people were busy at long beech tables – talking and singing happily while they worked – with what looked to be flour and dough, fresh herbs and fruit, baskets of eggs and stoneware flagons of water. There was a large white clock above the doorway. Only the enamel face with black numbers. No hands.

A tall woman – strong-looking, with long straw-gold plaits – was pushing brushwood bundles into an oven in the wall with a pitchfork. The smoke smelled like incense. Danny watched as spiny branches of gorse, heather and bundled withies were fed to the hungry flames. The woman at the mouth of the oven, all in grey like her colleagues, was wearing wooden clogs. They clopped on the floor as she went about her work, underpinning every step.

Danny became aware of hundreds of small birds, twittering and singing among the roof timbers above him, attending nests in the walls and circling the glow of the candleflames within the two smoked-glass spheres hanging side by side in the centre of the room.

Laughter, light and spontaneous, rose from the folk at the big tables.

Danny turned. They were not looking at him.

He stood and thought about shaking Maisie and Finch awake, but decided that he wanted, more than anything, to be in his own clothes. He changed quickly, wondering whether it was rosemary or lavender that his freshly-laundered clothes smelled of. Someone had used ox blood polish to put an incredible shine on his derelict dealer boots. Like his truck, they had never been cleaned – let alone polished – since the day he bought them.

"Stupid shit-for-brains," he mumbled, under his breath.

As he stamped into his boots, Maisie and Finch stirred, but didn't wake. Wherever he was, Danny thought, he would be here on his own terms, in his own crummy-but-comfortable clothes and knackered boots with split soles that let in water every time it rained.

He saw the woman sat with her back against the wall, mostly in shadow. She had pulled off a pair of beaten-up, dusty, leather cowgirl boots to air her feet. He wondered how long she had been sitting there on the floor with her broad-brimmed, sweat-stained hat tilted over her eyes, and her toes wriggling in the shaft of thick, yellow sunlight that poured onto the floor through the narrow glassless window.

Danny stood at the foot of his bed, remembering a picture book he'd owned about a boy who flew off to all sorts of exotic places on his magic bed. His mother had read it over and over, until one night his father had thrown it into the fire. He turned his back to the far tables and walked toward the towering window, the seated woman away to his right showing no interest in his movements. He heard a horse stomp and draw an iron shoe over one of the tree-wide elm floorboards, and he realized that the floor in the vast hall was not remotely level, but undulating, rising as he approached the window. There were areas of flagstones, and cobbles set in swirling patterns, making the floor read like a map, with courses to follow, currents, winds, streams and routes.

He looked over at the woman by the wall as he passed, and noticed her gun, big and heavy-looking, resting in the shadow beside her. Even in a space this size, Danny thought, that thing would go off with a bang big enough to wake the dead and make the living jump out of their skins. The woman wasn't paying him any attention. She was licking her thumb and rubbing between her toes.

It would have been easy to draw too close to the window; it seemed as big and wild and clear as the night sky over Exmoor. Danny stood with his arms folded, hands tucked in his armpits, gazing in awe at thousands of individual panes of midnight-blue stained glass.

The foals came to him. He unfolded his arms and they nuzzled his open hands.

In a myriad panels, objects and symbols floated, drifted. There were moons waxing and waning, waves breaking, foxes slinking and bright eyes blinking, keys jangling, stars and ships and boats floating and sinking, Doors opening and Hares and horses talking, lit faces and flames dancing, hills and trees, birds and bees, lakes, lanes and serpentine rivers. Everything was constantly changing places within the dazzling firmament, shifting position, rotating, sliding and relocating like the tiles of an infinite puzzle. Danny could hear them clicking and clacking, ticking and tocking as they slid and slotted.

The effect was dizzying. He looked down to see that the floor had darkened with watery shadows. He could not say how deep the floor now was; like a moorland reservoir, achingly cold.

His knees began to buckle. He was going.

The window, the sky – with all the objects and artefacts – began to fall over the surface of the water upon which Danny stood. The stars and moons and birds and boats and keys and eyes fell into the water. He heard them blip like young trout leaping for newly-hatched mayflies.

The woman from beside the wall was behind him when he went. She caught him and laid him effortlessly down.

2 (Here)
A Buyer's Market

Mrs Slee was waiting in the old telephone box. She was bent so far over that there wasn't room for Lilian.

Lilian was disgruntled. Not because she felt left out. It was something else. And she felt she should have known better. It just felt like an impossible situation; weird, even by Mrs Slee's standards. Lilian had turned her back on the old red phone box and was waiting to see if whatever busy little creature was making the dead leaves in the bottom of the hedgerow rustle would show its face. Wan autumn sunlight warmed the nape of her neck. She looked at the trees on the hillside below the road and saw that the world was getting ready to shed its skin again, play dead again, and be born again.

Lilian was annoyed with herself. Only with herself. Hadn't she long since given up doubting Mrs Slee? Hadn't Mrs Slee taught her never to give up doubting? She had to draw the line somewhere. She smiled. *No pun intended.* She drew lines everywhere.

Mrs Slee had been reluctant to say from whom the expected call might come.

The thick black cable to the receiver hung down. This was the source of Lilian's discontent. It was disconnected. Useless – in a phone box that hadn't been in operation for years. Somebody had pulled the receiver off the end of its wire, and then replaced it in its little metal cradle.

Lilian was disappointed in herself for allowing the question to form and fester.

Then the telephone rang. Of course. Loudly. Lilian heard it. She shook her head and laughed. She should not have doubted it for a moment.

Mrs Slee turned sideways and upwards to look at Lilian, then rotated her whole body and lifted the heavy receiver.

The Hares were gone from the shelf and the mound of dry earth was bare.

"Nicholas," Mrs Slee said, cradling the disconnected receiver tenderly in both hands.

"Pandora. How truly delightful it is to hear your beautiful voice after so much dark water has flowed beneath so many flaming bridges."

"You know nothing of truth, delight or beauty. What do you want, Nicholas?"

"Forgive me—"

"No. I will not be so weak. I would have no right to begin to forgive the heartless havoc you have wreaked wherever you have chanced to go. Death is the closest you will ever come to forgiveness." Her voice was bone-hard, cold as the tomb, dry as ash.

"You have been most patient, Pandora, and I admire you for that. But it has got you precisely nowhere. Your followers must despair."

"No living creature requires your admiration," Mrs Slee replied, leaning on the panelled side of the phone box. "And none admire you."

"Well, I fervently admire the way you have so very ruthlessly used the young people of your village as bait to lure me toward some pathetic, imaginary denouement. You have put them in harm's way. I am harm. And they are in my way."

"How wrong you are, Nicholas. How strong they are." Mrs Slee started to cry. Silently. Covering the mouthpiece with her cupped arthritic hand and unintentionally adding a seashell whisper to the exchange.

"You're crying. Don't do it just to make me happy." He laughed. "I could bathe in your tears. It would be like floating in the Dead Sea." His laughter sounded hollow.

"You are complacent. You are a narcissist. And you are wrong. You are everything that is wrong."

"I went through a bleak phase, some time ago, Pandora, of despising myself. I would take great pleasure in something unconscionably evil, and then feel genuinely bad. It was all part of the journey. I no longer hate myself. I am perfect. I am remorseless. I take the weight of the guilt that those who wish to judge me project upon me, and I crush them with it. It is an art. I have honed my skills. Now I am perfect. 'Let he who is without sin cast the first stone'. Do you have a stone for me, Pandora?"

"No," Mrs Slee told him. *But*, she thought, *I know someone who does.* "I am coming for you, Nicholas."

"Yes. I know. It has been like watching a child throw pebbles into the ocean in the hope of building a bridge. Take all the stones out of the pockets of that ridiculous coat,

Pandora, and you can use them to cobble the winding pathway to your timely demise."

"Why did you call?"

"To tell you that I am coming for *you*. I will wind up, on the way, what remains of your Watches, friends, acolytes, and those innocents you have used to build and bait your traps. I will erase them all. It will be your legacy, Pandora."

"My only wish is for you to see yourself as others see you."

"I really must go, Pandora. My coffee has arrived and I have a queue of people waiting to sell their souls. It's a buyer's market, you know." And, with that, he was gone.

Mrs Slee replaced the handset.

A daddy-long-legs was struggling against the glass panes of the phone box, falling and rising again. Mrs Slee cupped the insect gently in both hands and backed through the heavy door. She let it go. It danced over damp grasses and dark-red docks on the verge and then flew off, past Lilian, along the lane.

Lilian turned slowly. "Who was it, old girl?"

"Do you fancy walking up to the pub for lunch, dear? I need to bring you up to speed on one or two matters. My treat."

3 (There)
Eleftheria Mutt

Maisie screamed. When she got to Danny there was blood bubbling from his nose. The woman stepped back.

"He'll live," she told Maisie. "I'd stake my worthless span of days on it." She padded barefoot to the wall to retrieve her hat, boots and the unwieldy fifty-calibre firearm. "It's a nosebleed, nothing more."

Everyone at the big worktables stopped what they were doing, but waited to see how matters progressed without them. Finch knelt at Maisie's side. Her scream had woken him. She was cradling Danny's head. It felt heavy on her fingers against the wooden floor. She looked at the thin, snotty blood in Danny's nostrils. Without thinking, she nipped it away with her forefinger and thumb and wiped it on the leg of her grey flannel pyjamas.

"What happened?" Finch asked, reeling, slowly waking. "Did he faint? Is he OK?"

"We should get him over to the beds," Maisie said, adrenalin pushing her toward sense and action. But Danny was coming round.

"Did she hit him?" Finch asked, jerking his head toward the woman, perched on her adjacent windowsill, pulling on her dusty boots.

The woman threw her head back and laughed. "If I'd hit him, it would be the middle of next week already. Something hit him, for sure, but it was not I. Perhaps it was enlightenment struck him. Like a bolt from the blue."

"Where are we?" Finch asked, looking back at the woman, then down at Danny.

Danny sat up, clasped Maisie's shoulder and rose to his feet. "Who is she?" he asked, rubbing his eyes with his knuckles.

"I think maybe you passed out, dude," Finch said.

"You were lucky that lady was there to catch you," Maisie said.

"There was a shedload of Hares in here earlier on," Danny told them, wondering where his voice was coming from. "Over there." He pointed to the mound. "Really big bastards, scruffy and scarred. I could hear them talking for ages." He really wished he hadn't said the last thing. He looked down at his unnervingly glossy boots. "I was looking at the big window. Nothing would stay bliddy still, and I started spinning right out."

They all looked at the window.

The window was everything. And everything was in a state of flux. It was like looking in a mirror and seeing the whole universe just behind you, waiting for you to turn around and bare the reality of its magnificent entirety.

A man from the tables at the other end of the hall was heading their way. They turned when they heard his clogs. A horse coughed; jackdaws debated and sang dirges, and finches and sparrows stitched those voices with filaments of bright music. There were sounds from outside the room: someone calling a child; horses' hooves clattering on stone; barrels being rolled; doves and pigeons cooing and calling. No engines, no motors. A distant bell, and the dull ringing of a blacksmith's hammer on hot iron.

The envoy from the table had long ginger plaits. He was the freckliest man any of them had ever seen. His freckles looked as though they'd been freshly painted. He had flour on his hands and in his glossy copper beard.

"If you would like to wash and dress, you can then come outside and eat with everyone else." He looked to the woman with the unfeasibly large handgun. "Half an hour?"

"Ten days ago would have been better. I can't remember my last strip of jerky. My teeth have forgotten how to chew; my stomach's forgotten how to churn a measly morsel, and my sorry arse has forgotten how to shit."

Maisie, Finch and Danny looked at her. She was smiling. Finch noticed that she had prominent canines. Her eyes were smiling. Her lips were dry and cracked. Danny saw that the butt of her gun was pointing forward from its holster on her right hip. That meant that she was left-handed. And quick on the draw.

"Victuals," the woman said, with considerable glee. "You need to jump into your strides. Look sharp. Don't waste time with ablutions – it's going to rain in September, so the toilers of the soil tell me, and the soap they give you here makes you reek like a sheep."

"How long have we been here?" Finch asked her, struggling to make sense of anything she had said.

"Outside or in?"

"Outside or in what?"

"This place: the Hall of the Handless Clock."

The man with the ginger hair went back to work.

"I don't know," Finch responded. "What difference would it make?"

"Time ... moves ... very ... slowly ... in ... here," she told him, looking around at the walls and the horses and the birds. "They say it moves twelve times faster outside. When you look out of the window, you see that everything is happening at the same speed and the same time as it is in here, because your brain makes a connection that balances the different time speeds. It's the most basic way human beings have of controlling time. Most people do it without thinking, without knowing, but there are some who can think it and do it. Every time a little birdie flies in or out of this place, a brief connection is made and a parity occurs. If it didn't happen that way, then everything would rapidly spiral out of control. These people working in here have to do very long shifts. They don't get paid. They do it for the love of it, because their mothers and fathers did it and their grandmothers and grandfathers before them. Some people are born stupid, and others inherit their idiocy when their elders and betters think they're up to the challenge."

"That means you can time travel just by going in and out of the door," Maisie said, staring at the open door beyond the people working at the tables.

"You have all sorts of time zones in the Therebefore too. Where you come from. Rivers of time in full spate and quiet eddies and backwaters."

"So, how long have we been *in* here?" Finch asked the woman. "Or just *here*, in this place?"

"They tell me you've been in here – mostly asleep, sleepwalking a bit – for three days. You walked out of the Dreamboat and keeled over. The nurses tucked you all in. The

Dreamboat was put to bed too, hidden from view in a place that's been waiting for it since some dawn of some time. It'll be there when you need it, when you've enough souvenirs." She tapped the side of her head. "When you've been struck by enough bolts of enlightening." Then she looked sternly at them. "I'm hungry," she said, clapping her hands and ushering them toward their beds.

Danny started to move, then stopped, very deliberately looking the woman up and down. "Do you mean the Barrow Ship? What's it got to do with you? What have you got to do with us? Who are you?"

"Eleftheria Mutt. I'll be your guide for the duration of your stay in the Hereafter. I represent Shit Creek Tours. I trust you brought your own paddles, like it said in the small print. If you didn't read the seventeen volumes of small print, then you don't stand a cat in hell's chance. The Hereafter is your oyster. You can do whatever you like, as long as it's whatever I tell you. If you have any more questions, please don't hesitate to ask someone who you think might feel that giving a sweet goddamn will win them a coconut."

Eleftheria Mutt strode through the centre of the vast room in the direction of the open doorway. The horses turned their heads to watch her pass.

"We have to get dressed," Maisie said. "We should follow her, I guess, and see what's out there."

Maisie went to the bowl by her bedside and found it full of crystal-clear water. On the surface of the water she saw the oak rafters high above her, the illuminated spheres and all the birds. She splashed her face with those images.

4 (Here)
The Moonskin

As Pony's horse moved, the moonshadow it cast flexed and shrugged as if being formed from clay by a sculptor's hands. Mrs Slee and Lilian had not seen this creature before. An ex-police horse, standing eighteen hands, that went by the name of Valentine. The name made Mrs Slee smile.

Mrs Slee and Pony, then Lilian and Valentine, were making their way along the lane that led past the entrance to the Manor. Pony's horse wore no bridle, reins or harness of any description, he simply walked beside them in the moonlight. They had encountered no other travellers in the dead of this heavenly night, but they had heard the coarse screams of foxes and seen a barn owl working a recent plantation of saplings. Pony had strapped short leather boots over Valentine's hooves.

"I hope Lady Jeffers is alright about these night-time shenanigans," Pony said, smiling to himself.

"We did ask her," Mrs Slee told him. "We bumped into her up at Webber's Post, sitting in her car, doing the crossword in *The Telegraph*, drinking coffee from a flask like Lilian's and admiring the wonderous panorama. We were out picking whortleberries, and she had been waiting patiently for us without the faintest idea what or who she had been waiting for, poor dear."

"She was fine about it," Lilian added. "She said she takes a sleeping pill most nights before retiring, so she'll be blissfully unaware of our nocturnal mission."

"You haven't even told me yet what our mission – should we choose to accept it – might bliddy-well be."

"How many horses do you have, Pony, dear?" Mrs Slee asked.

"Seven to call my own, but I livery another four that no other bugger is daft enough to throw a bliddy leg over, and at least another score that'll come off the moor if I so much as wink at 'em. That's my whole family, that is."

He turned to Lilian. "You can ride up on this one if you wish, maid. He's a master gentle soul."

"No, thank you, Pony," Lilian replied, a little taken aback by the suggestion.

"May *I*, dear?" Mrs Slee asked, turning her whole body around and her head upwards and sideways.

Pony stopped and Mrs Slee stopped with him. Valentine and Lilian came to a halt and the horse began tugging at the lane-side vegetation.

"If you're serious, maid, there's Thorney's old churn-stand just up ahead. If we can get you up on that, we'll get you on this boy's back in a jiffy." Pony pointed to a slate-topped, stone-built corner, where the track for Thorne Farm turned off.

"I am serious."

Lilian was holding her head in both hands. "Old girl, are you sure?"

"I am."

"Stand," Pony told Valentine as they drew alongside the old platform. He then gently ushered the immense animal sideways to be closer to the improvised mounting-block. Together, Lilian and Pony lifted Mrs Slee to a standing position atop the mossy corner. Moving once again to Valentine's lane-side flank, Pony reached up and slapped the palms of both hands on his steed's back. In one fluid movement he jumped up, pushed down hard as if vaulting a pommel horse and swung his right leg over Valentine's rump.

"Give me both hands," Pony told Mrs Slee, reaching over as far as he could with his hand. Mrs Slee fell forward onto the horse, with Lilian holding onto her plastic raincoat. Once he had a firm grip, Pony hoisted the old lady high in the air and swung her over Valentine's bowed neck in front of him. The horse lifted his head, allowing Mrs Slee to bury her fingers in his thick mane. Pony dismounted, leaving Mrs Slee balanced on the horse's broad back.

"Alright, you can walk on," Pony told Valentine, and the horse ambled steadily on toward the gates of the Manor.

Pony stood and watched Valentine plodding along the lane with Mrs Slee bent doll-like over his neck.

"How're you doing up there, old girl?" Lilian asked, holding both arms up in case of a fall.

"Fine and dandy, dear," Mrs Slee replied as they turned in between the Manor's stately sandstone gateposts.

To their left, a good two acres of ancient apple trees in various states of decrepitude. To their right, running alongside the driveway, a long line of pollarded beeches guarded the boundary. After sixty or so paces the tarmac curved to the left in front of a fine tulip tree. To the right, a rough track led steeply upward to a field the Jeffers family had always called the Polo Lawn.

Pony spoke softly to Valentine, head-to-head with his horse. "You can abide here and munch as much of herself's sweet clover as takes your fancy."

The horse nodded so enthusiastically that Mrs Slee lost her grip on his mane and started to fall. In an instant, Pony rolled beneath the horse's belly and caught her. He sat down with Mrs Slee clutched to his chest, feeling how light she was, weighing little more than a partridge. Though her long, lace-up boots seemed oddly heavy.

"I feel like a falling star, Mr Chalice," Mrs Slee confided, looking up into the man's shining eyes.

"Put her in your pocket," Lilian sang. "Never let her fade away."

Lilian pulled Mrs Slee to her feet, then offered Pony her hand.

"That was wonderful, dear," Mrs Slee told Pony, patting Valentine's neck as he nuzzled and ripped the grass. "We must cross now and go through the hedge. We'll come out on the upper terrace, from where we can find our way down between the strawberry trees to the Study Garden. Then we can get ourselves into position beside the pond."

"Are you at any point going to let us in on why you've brought us here?" Lilian asked, taking Mrs Slee's arm.

"All will be revealed," Mrs Slee said, looking at the moon-silvered terraces descending with formal elegance toward the house.

All the Manor's south-facing windows mirrored the moon.

Mrs Slee unhooked Lilian's arm and led the way past a trio of date palms to the corner of the lower terrace. Two magnificent topiary Hares – one with its ears pointing at the moon, the other with them laid along its back – stood sentinel at the top of the steps leading down into the sunken Study Garden. The night air within the walled space was thick with the heady scent of roses and ripening figs. Lilian and Pony breathed in deeply and looked up. Above their heads sailed a brilliant moon and billions of stars, with several bats attempting to join all the dizzying dots. They followed Mrs Slee through the maze of rose beds to the edge of the circle of water.

Pony leaned a little too far over the pond and staggered back.

"Be careful, Pony, dear," Mrs Slee warned him. "It will be as cold and dark as the grave in there."

From where they stood at the water's edge, Lilian and Pony could not see their elderly companion's reflection. Pony dipped the toe of his boot in the water, sending the shimmer of a ripple across the surface.

"In a while," Mrs Slee said, "the moon will fill the pond. It will lay itself perfectly over the disc of water, leaving no room whatsoever for the edge of darkness. At that precise point in time the two of you will need to be standing exactly here." She pointed to the flagstones at her feet. "I will be standing opposite you, around the circle. Please await further instructions."

"I won't be going in there for a bliddy swim if I can help it," Pony told Lilian under his breath. "It looks colder'n March mercury."

"All we have to do now is wait," Lilian said, watching the creeping silver light. "Then do as we're told."

The moon had plated five-sixths of the surface. Pony and Lilian saw it moving. It would fit exactly. And they would be there when it did.

"Wait please," Mrs Slee told them.

"What for?" Pony asked Lilian in a whisper.

"Now, grasp the edge of the moonskin," Mrs Slee said, her voice skimming the surface of the pond like a silver sixpence. "Pick it up in both hands, the two of you, and pull it slowly up, across and off the water."

Lilian dropped to her knees and, looking her reflection directly in the eye, slipped her fingers into the cold water at the very edge of the circle. She could feel the slippery surface of the liquid between her fingers and thumbs. Pony swiftly followed suit, unable to believe what was happening. They were drawing the entire burnished skin of the pond to them.

Mrs Slee came to join them. "If you lift it now, every ounce of its weight will run away with the water," she said, reaching down to pull at a crease in the silken mirror.

"What incredible magic have you woven, old girl?" Lilian asked breathlessly. "We could wrap ourselves up in it completely."

"And never be seen again, dear."

Pony and Lilian proceeded to shake and drain the skin, with Mrs Slee pulling and plucking as best she could, until the treasure they had harvested was as insubstantial as gossamer on gorse. When Mrs Slee was satisfied with their labours, they folded the silver circle and she pushed the bundle into the pocket of her raincoat.

"What of the pond?" Pony asked, looking down into what was now a fathomless black hole.

"Throw a stone in," Mrs Slee said.

Lilian picked a reddish, walnut-sized rock from the nearest rose bed and cast it in.

It made no sound at all.

Mrs Slee set off for the slate steps to the topiary Hares.

Lilian caught Pony's arm and leaned over the abyss.

Still no sound.

"It's bliddy bottomless," Pony said.

They caught up with Mrs Slee halfway up the steps in the corner of the sunken garden.

"It will, over the course of the night, heal itself," She said. "Just don't fall in before sunrise."

5 (There)
A Movable Feast

The girl stroked the dark hairs on Finch's forearm. Her other hand was holding a bread roll with a doorstep-sized chunk of crumbly white cheese and slices of red onion pushed into it. Two bites had been taken. She was chewing, both cheeks bulging.

Finch looked at her and smiled. "I'm real enough," he said, and the girl stepped back into the river of people from whence she had emerged. Finch looked at the flowing crowd; they weren't all looking at him.

The circular, sun-bleached, wooden tables sat on top of cog-shaped platforms that were turned like roundabouts as people pushed and pulled them. Finch noticed that the cogs didn't mesh; there was room enough for people to shuffle between them without being crushed, but the effect was of a rough clockwork mechanism encircling the building. Finch couldn't see the stained-glass window. He could see lots of other windows, all glassless, with birds flitting and swooping constantly in and out. He couldn't see Maisie, Danny or Eleftheria Mutt. He had waved to Danny half an hour ago, six or seven tables away. Danny, who had been munching a whole chicken leg, stopped and waved two fingers in response.

Finch saw that there were oak beams projecting from the walls of the building, all at the same level: higher than head-height. Three or four metres long, they protruded from the stonework all the way round, reaching over the deep groove of a pathway that had been trodden for centuries. At the end of each pole there was what looked like a stitched leather collar for a heavy horse. Finch couldn't work it out; there appeared to be a shadowed gap between the ground and the entire structure.

People rose with their plates, cups and cutlery, allowing the next folks to take their places. Several times, Finch followed instructions to step across to another cog and sit at a different table. Tables turned, people changed and were gone. People talked to him about horses, rivers, wells, soil, tomatoes, shoes, and about where he had come from. They asked him about the Barrow Ship. They called it the Dreamboat, but he knew what they meant. There were questions about salt, water, leather, and about his hands. They asked him about work, school, his friends, his family, and about Eleftheria Mutt. A boy sang a song about waiting for miracles to happen, and an old woman joined in with the chorus about miracles not being for sale. People stopped eating and listened. No one cheered or clapped when the song ended; they blew kisses. It made Finch smile. He blew kisses too. He closed his eyes and blew one to Sylvanie. Wherever she was. From wherever he was.

Maisie couldn't see Danny or Finch. She had been seated right next to Eleftheria at one point, but Eleftheria had ceded her place to a frail old man, and then been washed away in a tide of people. The man had held a lump of seeded bread in his hand, rested his elbow on the edge of the table, pointed his bony index finger, and waited for a scruffy sparrow to perch upon it. Maisie watched the bird, its beak full of bread, take off and fly in through one of the windows in the wall of the Hall of the Handless Clock. The building was like a mountain; there were trees growing out of it, and ferns, toadflax and valerian. Ravens were circling and barking. Jackdaws came to the tables, all suited and booted, swaggering between goblets, jugs and plates. But the ravens remained aloft, aloof, high and mighty.

The old man ate nothing. Rising from his seat, he pointed to a shallow stoneware bowl piled high with pomegranates. A middle-aged man, dressed in a black suit, shiny with work and wear, picked a ripe pomegranate from the bowl and rolled it across the table. The old man sliced the brick-red fruit with a silver penknife, placed one half on Maisie's plate and the other in the freshly-scrubbed wooden bowl of a young boy who had come to the table. The boy, whose eyes were bluer than robins' eggs, sat down beside Maisie. She broke him a hunk of bread and passed him grapes, walnuts and a small bowl of yoghurt and cucumber with paprika sprinkled on it.

"I wish I was coming with you," the boy said, dipping a spring onion into some pinkish-brown rock salt.

"I wish I knew whether you were right to wish that," Maisie told him. She held out her cup to a woman offering water from a leather pouch slung over her shoulder.

"I think you've got all the answers," the boy said, cracking two walnuts together in his tough, brown hands. "You don't know it. Now you've got to go and find all the questions."

6 (There)
Horsepower

"She's probably buggered off to the pub," Danny said, standing in one of the windows at the side of the Hall of the Handless Clock, looking out at the assortment of dilapidated or derelict civic buildings before him. "If there even is a pub. If people drink here." He was holding onto the stonework at the sides of the window and leaning out. He saw a peregrine falcon being taunted by pigeons on a castellated parapet. The six-storey building directly opposite had, at some point in the dim and distant past, been painted sky-blue, but was now peeling to reveal cloud-formations of whiteish distemper.

"She said we should get some kip," Maisie said. "We're going somewhere in the morning." She and Finch were sat on the sill in the alcove of the window, behind Danny. "I don't know where. I guess we just go with her."

"I feel pretty knackered," Finch said. "It's been a long and properly bizarre day. Somebody – a girl of about seven, actually – asked me if I was dead. I told her I wasn't. But she didn't seem all that convinced. Because even to me it sounded like empty words."

"You'll be dead when you get home and mummy and daddy get you indoors, matey," Danny told him. "You're not usually allowed out so late. It's way past your bedtime. I don't even know how many bedtimes you've passed. Maze'll tuck you in. Won't you, Maze?"

"Of course I will. And I'll read you a nice story, too," she told Finch, smiling and patting his knee. "You're such a twat, Danny."

"There's loads of horses coming through the town," Danny said, jamming his left fist in a crack in the wall and letting go with his right hand so that he could lean further out.

Maisie stood up. "Are people riding them?" She went with Finch to the next window and leaned out over the rough, green stonework mottled with algae, lichen and bird shit.

There were a lot of large work horses making their way along streets and pathways toward the centre of town. People were dragging and rolling the last of the tables and platforms away.

"There's a hell of a lot of big horses heading this way," Maisie said, counting eleven in one street. No one was riding them or even walking with them. People greeted them and patted them as they passed. Maisie looked to her right and saw Danny waving at her. She looked down. It was a long way to fall. She looked at the beams sticking out all around the building, and the hard flagstones beneath. She knew that if she told Danny to be careful, he would only do something reckless.

The horses knew where they were going. They each walked to the end of a great beam, squared themselves to shoulder the task, and pushed their heads into the hanging collars. All around the immense building they were nose-to-tail. The hall shuddered. Danny yelled, grabbed at the stonework on both sides of the window and jumped hurriedly back down to the floor. The whole building was rumbling, turning. Danny joined Maisie and Finch and watched half the town sail slowly by their window.

"We're turning," Maisie exclaimed. "The horses are doing it."

"They've done it before," Finch said. "I mean, I think I felt it before, but slept through it."

"It takes a lot of horses to move this place," Danny said, picking up the courage to lean out of the window again. "There's people bringing stuff for them to eat. Looks like hay and alfalfa. And they've got buckets of oats and carrots."

Pigeons and jackdaws had taken to the air, their wings clapping. Finch and Maisie clasped each other's hands and arms to steady themselves. Danny held onto the windowsill. Their side of the Hall of the Handless Clock now felt the full honey-coloured richness of the lowering sun.

When the building came to a halt, it felt as though it locked into place against some giant buffer, and the whole structure shuddered again.

"Look," Finch said, walking toward the stained-glass window end of the hall. "They've turned the building so that the *setting* sun shines through the big window." He walked toward the lake of coloured patterns on the floor. "It shines through the window each morning when it's facing that way, and then the building is turned so that it catches the sun as it goes down."

"West in the morning," Danny said. "East in the evening." He knew the Hares had told him. "Amen," he said, under his breath.

Finch walked forward among thousands of shafts of coloured light.

Danny looked up at the window. It was everything. Another everything.

Maisie caught his hand and pulled him with her into the waterfall of colours.

7 (Here)
The Window's Aurora

When Sylvanie woke, the darkness that enveloped her was absolute. There was no light at all beneath the door or behind the curtains, and the darkness was thick with silences. She switched on the bedside lamp, pushed the duvet off and sat on the edge of the bed, allowing her mind to settle.

There was a short pull-cord under one of the units in the kitchen area; Sylvanie made it that far without turning on any other lights. The red switch on the wall by the cooker went down with a heavy clunk. Sylvanie took a saucepan from the cupboard and milk from the fridge. She poured milk into the pan, then changed her mind. She switched off the cooker, poured the milk into a glass and went back to her room.

She opened the curtains and windows. At once she felt the real night flood her room with dreams and nightmares. She pulled on a big yellow-ochre sweater that Hannah had knitted long ago and got back into bed. Propping her journal on her knees, Sylvanie took a drink of cold milk and picked up her 2B pencil.

She wrote: I've just woken up from the most incredible lucid dream. I knew I was having it all the time and I let it happen and it was beautiful. I woke up when the building – I mean this whole block we live in – started to shake. My bed was spinning. I swam out of the dream and it let me go. It was all colourful and everything in the dream was clicking all the time and made of bright glass or painted stone or wood. Danny was painted white. He was made of sticks and feathers and yet he was completely real. He was talking to me all the time but I couldn't really make out what he was supposed to be telling me. There were wooden fish like articulated little carvings swimming in the coloured water with us. Lilian and Pony were riding massive horses. And Mrs Slee was riding a hare. And the hare was talking to Danny and there were lots of little birds flying around his head all the time saying things to him. There were clocks with people's real hands pointing and showing us trees and guns and books and wolves and doors.

Sylvanie stopped writing. She felt as though she hadn't breathed. The night brought eager distances from different times and places. She lay down her pencil in the centre of her journal and took a long drink of milk. When she started writing again, it felt less urgent and more measured, but no less intense.

She wrote: I saw Maze's brown arms all covered in tattoos of everything. Loads of things I remember from when we were just little kids together. There were jackdaws and rooks and Exmoor ponies and Royston Quantock and heather and cotton grass all on her arms. And there were primroses and buttercups and dandelions floating up off her skin. There was music as well, but you couldn't hear. But you could feel it. And then there were butterfly wings falling like rose petals and you could smell the sea in the air.

8 (Here)
Cosmic Dancer

Sylvanie pushed her invisible self away in front of her with both hands. She stood like that; shoulders hunched up, arms outstretched and palms facing forward, waiting – on tiptoes, like the girl in the mirror – to take her cue from Marc Bolan singing 'Cosmic Dancer'.

She had taped her big 'Do Not Disturb' notice on the door, pushed the rowing machine and exercise bike over to the wall, and pulled the free-standing, full-length mirror out from the corner. The mirror had been her dance partner countless times before.

The sliding aluminium windows were wide open; pigeons, starlings, parakeets and gulls, like flaws in a clouded sapphire, flashed past, catching and trailing ribbons of light and darkness across the wide cityscape.

Sylvanie was preparing to dance herself whole again. Into existence again. Finch would hold her hands as they span round and round and became indistinguishable. She would lose everything. She would throw it all away.

She looked at her reflection. She and the other her, she thought, were almost identical. As near as made no difference.

When the music started, Sylvanie bowed and shook her hair wildly.

'I was dancing when I was twelve ...'

And the years began to fall away.

'I was dancing when I was eight ...'

And Sylvanie searched the mirror to try to catch a glimpse of her other self as she flew by.

'I danced myself right out of the womb ...'

9 (There)
Useless Riches

"I can't feel my arse anymore," Danny groaned, standing in the stirrups and waving his backside in the air.

"It's gone," Maisie informed him. It was their third day on horseback, the weather had been great, and she was in her element. "It must have fallen off somewhere back along the way. It's not the first time you've lost it. It seems a bit careless. Or was it your elbow you lost last time? You weren't sure."

"No, no. I saw it," Finch said. "Down beside the track. Miles back. I thought it was your face, dude. Either way, I didn't think it'd be missed."

Danny took a big swipe with his right arm as Finch drew level. Finch had only to lean to his right in the saddle to escape the predicted blow.

"It's seems unfair that your bottom has to be the butt of so many millions of jokes," Maisie told him.

"But it's such an easy target," Finch said. "You could shoot an arrow in any direction and you'd be bound to hit it."

"He's right," Eleftheria added over her shoulder. "I saw it shining bright up in the sky last night."

Danny laughed. He looked at her. She laughed.

They slowed to a stop. Their horses grazed the wayside flora.

Finch noticed that Eleftheria had put her hand on her gun, as if laughter – hers or anyone else's – made her feel vulnerable. He wondered who had given her this job, the job of being their guide and … was she their guardian? And he wondered if she was ever going to tell them where they were going.

"Are we nearly there yet?" Finch asked, smiling and looking directly at her.

"Yes you are," Eleftheria told him. "You've been nearly there all your lives and you didn't even know it. Sometimes you've been closer to being there than you could possibly imagine." She nudged her horse with her heels, clicked her tongue, and before the others could tighten their reins and raise their horses' heads, she had gained the scrubby ridge ahead.

They had passed working villages and abandoned towns, isolated dwellings and farming communities; they had ridden through mile after mile of landscape that looked like it had once been something else – agricultural or urban or industrial. Nature was swallowing whatever vestiges of human habitation and endeavour had been visible. Mother Nature – in the form of briar, bindweed, nettle and knotweed – was desperate. They had also met and crossed extruded lines of refugees heading in one direction or another.

"What's happened to them?" Maisie had asked. "Where are they going? Where are they coming from?" She watched as they waited for the line to break. She saw parents carrying their children, and children carrying their parents. And she saw and felt the sort of hunger and hopelessness that she had only previously glimpsed on television.

"It's the same everywhere," Eleftheria had said, "in every time and every place. If you think you own something, somebody will think they can buy it or steal it. And if they don't want it, they know a man who does. And so it goes. And so it goes into 'Old Nick' Temple's pockets, purses, banks. All the useless riches paying for all the wasted lives. And people are ground to dust between the grindstones of the Spheres. To give us this day his daily bread."

"Money can't buy you love, though," Maisie said.

"There are many forms of currency," Eleftheria said, "and money and love are but two of the most common."

10 (There)
His Favourite Trick

The following part of their journey on horseback – from the point where their rough track met the coast road to the entrance to the walled city – had been difficult. The old, metalled main road was cracked; every few hundred metres, deep fissures broke their path. Some were narrow and shallow, others were dark and wide. To their left, rocky terrain rose steeply; to their right, precipitous cliffs fell away to a colourful sea.

Eleftheria insisted that they dismount and walk the horses around each hazard rather than making any attempt to step or jump over.

"It would give me no pleasure to have to make you shoot a horse with a broken leg," she said solemnly. "And as for having to put one of *you* down – well, just remember, these big ugly bullets cost me a pretty penny."

She told them that there had been a devastating earthquake six months previously.

"I only heard about it. I've never been here. Not alone, or when I was on my travels with Mr Temple."

"With Temple?" Danny asked, before anyone else could. They were leading their horses along a lengthy crack in the broken skin of the world. "What do you mean, *with him*?"

"It was him gave me my name: Mutt. Maybe because of my teeth. I gave myself Eleftheria. Means liberty. Freedom. I am a free dog. And my bite is much worse than my bark." She smiled broadly and showed her prominent canines.

Eleftheria looked out across the sea: emerald and burgundy and cobalt blue. Perched upon the horizon they saw a vessel large enough to be a container ship or tanker, plying its trade between continents.

"You were with him against your will," Finch said.

"There are people going to him all the time to beg for help, to pray at his feet for mercy or murder. And there have always been people who seek him out and stay in his company completely of their own free will. Because there are always perks. But he quickly tires of sycophantic sorts; they make it all too easy for him. I was his prisoner. I knew no better. I knew no different. I could certainly remember nothing before that time that was better or different. Difficult to say if I was there against my will, because, as far as I knew then, I had none."

"But you do now," Maisie called out, trying to hold on to her stumbling horse.

"I do now, right enough. What free will I have right now, he beat into me."

"He beat you?" Danny asked, reluctant to get back on his horse, looking at the whitening knuckles of his fist holding the reins beneath his horse's jaw, the colour rising in his cheeks.

"I was bought and paid for. As was he, in some previous life. His favourite trick was lifting me up by my hair …"

Eleftheria's voice travelled away from her. She raised her head as if to watch her fleeing words. " … and hitting me with whatever was to hand."

"I'm sorry," Danny told her. He looked at Maisie and then back at Eleftheria Mutt. "It was when you were a little kid." It was a statement, not a question.

Maisie felt that Danny seemed strangely at home in this conversation.

"That is correct," Eleftheria said. "Sometimes he beat me just because he found something interesting to beat me with. If I wriggled; if I fought, it only pulled my hair and hurt my head more."

"If I ever meet this …" Danny began, but Eleftheria had nudged her horse and moved off in the direction of two old women, all dressed in black, tending little terraced gardens at the foot of the cliffs on the landward side of the road.

Maisie, Danny and Finch watched her go.

"It sounded a bit like she'd never said anything like that to anyone before," Finch said.

"Let's try to keep up," Maisie said.

They followed Eleftheria to where the women were working small triangles of soil behind low retaining walls in the arid escarpment. They were tending and watering tomatoes, dwarf beans, basil and potatoes. They must have carried the water a long way. Some of their plots were no larger than a milk pail, but the soil was rich and loamy. Eleftheria was respectful. She dismounted, and the women handed her four ripe plum tomatoes. Maisie had never tasted anything so good.

They saw other people as they made their way along the once-busy coastal route – collecting twigs for cooking-fires, climbing rope ladders from hidden coves with driftwood tied to their backs, bulging hessian bags hung around their necks. The going became easier thanks to more frequently trodden pathways and makeshift bridges. Folks waved and lifted their hats in greeting. Eleftheria had a way of waving that looked like a salute. People called out in greeting as they passed by.

They came across a small orchard set back from the road. There was no fence; it was a communal resource. A boy threw a small brown-and-red apple to Finch, who caught it to the left of his head. He closed his eyes and snuffed deeply. The apple smelled like home. He offered it to Maisie, who shook her head.

"You have it," she said.

"I'll have it if you buggers are just going to sniff at the bliddy thing," Danny told them.

"I know you will," Finch told him, smelling the blushed russet again before pushing it into one of the stained leather pouches that hung behind his saddle. He waved to the boy, who was loading apples into wicker panniers on the back of a donkey.

"It doesn't feel," Maisie said, "exactly like people know us – I mean ... why would they? – but it feels like they know something about us that we don't know yet."

"There it is," Eleftheria said, pulling up her horse to allow the others to draw abreast at the brow of the hill. "I don't have a disc like Temple's to calculate times, or his little black book stuffed with places and names, but I got you here. Let's hope it's worth the trouble."

11 (There)
The Four Mirrors

Nothing could have prepared them for the sight that greeted them upon entering the walled city. The facades of every building that faced into the main square had fallen away to reveal each poor living space and plain bedroom, every staircase, every meagre detail of all the occupants' lives: their pictures, cupboards, wardrobes, beds and tables and chairs. The buildings looked like dolls' houses with their hinged fronts torn off, like theatre sets where every stage was unsafe to tread.

"They can't go back in anywhere," Danny said, looking around with his eyes wide and his mouth open, "to get their stuff, because everything's unstable. The earthquake must've shaken all the fronts down."

"Get off your horses," Eleftheria told them. "We'll lead them through the rubble."

"It's so sad," Maisie said, dismounting. "They can't get back to their lives. They can't even get their belongings out."

Some of the masonry from the taller buildings had been thrown a long way across the square, but there were pathways through it, and people had even set up produce stalls on some of the larger clumps of stonework.

They saw that some of the carved stones had been numbered and, in some places, wooden scaffolding had been erected.

"They've started to put it all back together," Finch said, looking at rough piles of masonry with the remnants of plaster, paper and paint.

"Bloody hell," Maisie said, under her breath. "It's like the barrier between home and chaos is only as thick as a bit of flowery wallpaper." Her horse was nibbling and tugging at the sleeve of her jacket. Maisie followed Eleftheria and Danny, who had picked a pathway through the rubble toward a steep, paved street that led to an imposing municipal building at the highest point of the town.

There were swifts and jackdaws in the calm air above the square; pigeons had begun to occupy the exposed strata, and martins and swallows were nesting in the corners of abandoned rooms.

Pictures hung at odd angles on walls. Maisie noticed a table, set with plates and cups and cutlery, waiting to fall. She noticed a picture of a group of angels, all with tall, creamy-white wings, all seemingly looking into a box. And she tilted her head to look at another painting; it was on a wall above a bed that only had three legs on the floor. A moorland scene; it reminded her of Exmoor. More than that, she thought: it looked like Dunkery Beacon.

People started to applaud. Adults first, then children. More people were coming out of their homes, walking down streets apparently unaffected by the terrible earthquake. There were dogs barking. The noise of the applause was washing into all the unsafe, exposed rooms in the buildings in the square, and chiming off china and glassware and cutlery.

"What are they all clapping for?" Danny asked Eleftheria.

"Maybe because we finally made it. Maybe they've been waiting for us. Maybe they've been waiting a very long time for *you*."

"What are you talking about? I don't know anybody here. There's nobody here who knows anything about any of us lot." He sounded adamant. Indignant.

"How do you know they don't know you?" Eleftheria asked. "Maybe they knew another you."

"What are you talking about? I haven't got a clue what you're even bliddy talking about."

"Listen, my friend. You get in the Dreamboat … and you wake out of it another you. You go through a Door, and you're another you. You are another you in your dreams. Close your eyes. Open them. You're born again."

That shut him up.

More people exited assorted buildings and houses to stare and applaud.

A very elderly woman came out into the street to greet them. She was dressed from head to foot in black and walked with the aid of a gnarled blackthorn stick.

She looked at Finch. "You have something for me, I believe, young man?" she said, smiling. Her heavily-lined face reminded him of Mrs Slee. Her voice was coarse and small. She held her throat as if squeezing her windpipe when she spoke.

Without a second thought, he moved around his horse, bowing beneath its head, and took his little apple out of the saddlebag. He presented it to the old woman. Her cupped hand seemed made to clasp it. The apple was the colour of Exmoor, and she was the colour of peat.

She lifted her bent walking stick and pointed at the troubled sky. This made the horses nervous. The clapping ceased, and the old woman lowered her staff.

"They're in what was the library," she said, pointing up the hill to the grand building at the top. "There are no books in there anymore; they're long gone. The place was ransacked. Precious books were stolen, sold. Burned. The mirrors were moved in there after the earthquake. They're safe. Valueless, since we cannot keep our reflections here. Go there first, then you can eat. They'll give you water up there. The keepers will take you in. Leave your mounts to be liveried here."

The old woman stepped aside as the horses were led away.

"Thank you kindly," Eleftheria said, smiling and lifting her hat.

Danny hoped never to see his horse, or any creature remotely like it, ever again.

The entire population of the city followed them at a distance as they plodded up the hill.

Four women, all with long plaits, plain, olive-green dresses and big wooden clogs, came out onto the steps of the old library to meet them.

"Why do these people always have plaits?" Maisie asked Eleftheria, trying to keep up with her loping stride as they climbed the steps.

"They're symbolic. An offering. They're supposed to represent all they own. They're easy enough to hack off with a knife. People will slice off their own plaits and throw them in the dirt. That's how it's supposed to work."

"Why haven't you got them, then?"

"Maybe I bartered mine for a meaty firearm," Eleftheria tapped the handle of her gun.

"I guess," Maisie said, as they reached the top of the steps, "that there could be times when that might be more useful than plaits."

"Every single day of all my worthless lives," Eleftheria Mutt said, turning to show her big white teeth to the attendants. "We'll need to piss and wash before we do anything else."

They followed the uniformed women into what appeared to be a disused office. On the floor were grey enamelled buckets, and, on a long pitch pine table, stoneware bowls of crystal-clear water. They took turns in the room. Danny first. He peed for the longest time, then plunged his face into a bowl of water.

"Why does everybody know we're coming?" he asked Finch as Maisie went in. He saw the crowd that was amassing.

"I don't think they know *when*, exactly. But it does seem like we've been expected. Who knows how long they've been waiting. And I really don't know why."

People had been flooding up the granite steps and through a vast revolving door at the end of the marble-floored vestibule. They were bustling, remaining just on the polite side of pushing and shoving. The old door squealed wildly as it turned.

It was a shock to walk into the main hall of what must once have been an important library and see only vacancy and ruin where knowledge and wisdom had once been stored. There were high, empty shelves on every wall and shelving systems that had been pushed, skewed and toppled. In the centre of the hall, an arena had been created around four floor-standing, full-length mirrors. At the outer perimeter of this space, more than a thousand people stood facing the centre. More were entering the library all the time, some out of breath from running.

If Eleftheria Mutt had not been with them, Finch, Danny and Maisie might have turned tail and fled.

An ungainly silence shuffled into place within the building. Maisie thought that the people encircling the mirrors looked like a choir, and half expected them to burst into song. Danny, Maisie and Finch felt unnerved: by the crowds of onlookers – who seemed now to be holding their breath – by the desolate, broken sadness of the empty building and by the fact that all eyes were once again upon them.

The four officials wanted Finch first. They beckoned him. He looked at Danny and Maisie. He saw in their eyes the bewilderment he felt.

"I think they want you to stand in front of one of the mirrors," Eleftheria Mutt told him, placing a hand on his shoulder and pushing him.

Finch stepped forward. The women took his hands and led him to the first mirror. It was heavily pitted, mottled behind the tall, bevelled glass. He stood before it and saw himself.

There was a unified gasp from gathered townsfolk. They could see his reflection in the looking-glass. They clapped and cheered.

Something wasn't right.

It took Finch a moment. He hadn't seen the attendants reflected in his mirror. The crowd behind him was not reflected. He was alone in the mirror.

He stepped back. There was an almost imperceptible delay. He saw himself wait. He saw himself step back. He was sure he saw the Finch in the mirror wait to take his cue from the Finch he actually was. He went and stood in front of Maisie.

She held his hands. Danny watched Finch close his eyes and close his grip on Maisie's hands.

"Your turn next," Eleftheria told Danny.

He was ushered before the second mirror and saw himself alone. He felt unbalanced. He felt the women's hands on his arms as he swayed, but they were not reflected in his mirror. Nor the people stood behind him.

Maisie was taken to her mirror. She saw herself. She waved self-consciously and her reflection waved back. She started to cry and the Maisie beyond the glass cried too. Danny stepped forward and took her in his arms.

The keepers wanted the three of them to go to the fourth mirror together. The crowd became silent again.

"In for a bliddy penny," Danny said softly into Maisie's hair as he released her from his embrace.

There was a sharp intake of breath from the people within earshot, then a murmur of disapproval.

Finch held Maisie's hand. Danny put his arm across Finch's shoulders and they moved as one to the fourth long mirror.

They did not see themselves.

They saw Sylvanie.

The crowd gasped. Tears flooded Finch's eyes.

Sylvanie pushed something invisible away in front of her with both hands. She stood on tiptoes, arched her back and shook her hair wildly.

'I danced myself right out of the womb ...'

12 (Here)
Angel

They were sat out on the balcony: Sylvanie in her faded deckchair, Georgia on a more upright and far less comfortable folding wooden garden chair. Surrounded by the tomatoes, geraniums and herbs that Hannah and Sylvanie were nurturing, the two women were almost completely hidden from view. When they looked out, they saw only dazzling white clouds against blue-slate grey.

Hannah and Mr Tagore were out. Out. In the big wide world. Their intention had been to walk alongside the canal in the countryside for a few miles and then go shopping in the city centre mall. It was a relatively new thing. Sylvanie had been out with Mr Tagore too, and Georgia, on separate occasions. It had been heavenly. Sylvanie growing her hair had helped. It had taken years. But Hannah and her daughter could never go out of the apartment together; as a pair, it was felt that they were simply too recognizable. It had been Georgia's idea, and – as long as the Watch was doubled whenever one pair or another were out – Mr Tagore was happy enough to go along with it. The last time Sylvanie had been anywhere, it was with Mr Tagore, who had insisted upon setting off early in order to meet as few people as possible. Those folks they had met – a farmer with at least four collies in the back of his Land Rover and a man preparing to go fishing on a windswept reservoir – had regarded them quizzically.

Georgia and Sylvanie had been out on the balcony for more than an hour, both wearing jumpers and hats. Georgia had a matted woollen blanket around her legs and a fat paperback book about palaeontology open upside down on her knee.

"You told me," Sylvanie said, "ages and ages ago, that Mrs Slee had wooden feet. And I've been thinking about what you said and why you said it. I've been meaning to ask you about it ever since. Why did you tell me that? Is it even true? How do you ... How did she lose her real feet?"

"Satyajit had a real go at me for telling you about that. I like it when he feels he has to tell me off, because it always ends in smiles, no matter how serious or stupid the subject. All I have to do is look pathetically penitent. It never fails."

Georgia gave Sylvanie a look of doe-eyed supplication, and they laughed.

"Unforgivable. Tell me what happened to Mrs Slee's feet."

"Nicholas Temple cut them off. *Had* them cut off, I suppose."

Sylvanie covered her face with her hands. She felt her insides freeze.

"He brought some people to hold her down. And he brought somebody else to saw both her feet off at the ankles. She subsequently made herself a pair of wooden feet. She carved them. They're like boots that strap to her legs below the knee, hinged at the ankle." Georgia looked out at the mountains of wrestling clouds and called them home into her lovely big eyes. " 'If you're really an angel,' Temple said, 'you won't be needing those.' "

13 (Here)
The White Hart

Lilian counted eleven dogs. One was a Great Dane, asleep right in front of the bar, wagging its heavy tail against a stool and shuddering excitedly in its dreams. Two cats. The tabby was asleep in the kindling basket beside the roaring fire, and the Siamese was curled up between her and Mrs Slee on the sofa, flicking its ears occasionally. The Hart was packed with people, lots of whom said hello to the two women. Mrs Slee and Lilian were seated facing the open hearth. When their meals came, they were placed on a low, copper-topped table. Mrs Slee unbuttoned her blue plastic raincoat, but kept it on. They had both ordered the Sunday roasts; Lilian had plumped for the pork, Mrs Slee the beef. Lilian helped Mrs Slee to put her plate on her knee on top of a green velvet cushion with a white deer embroidered on it.

When Pony Chalice came out of the skittle alley on his way to the bar, he made a friendly detour to greet them. He stood directly in front of them with his back to the fire, leaned over their table and held their hands.

"We need more cider to make the boards in this bliddy alley less warped," he told them. "They're terrible bad. You take potluck when you roll one of them wonky balls. It's going to take a lot of cider, I can tell 'ee. They old wood balls looks like they bin chewed on by bliddy hounds."

Lilian and Mrs Slee wished him all the luck in the world.

He put two hefty birch logs on the fire before leaving. He glanced at their half-empty glasses of ale, then swayed his way to the bar to order them two more pints along with his round for the skittle team.

"I know who you talked to on the phone in the village," Lilian told her friend, looking around to see if anyone might be listening. "It was Temple, wasn't it, old girl?"

"It was indeed *he*, dear. I had a feeling that after all these years he might think it necessary to reconnect and reacquaint."

"What did he say? I can't believe that you would even talk to him, I mean … after everything."

"Let's eat," Mrs Slee said, as the beer that Pony had ordered for them was brought to their table.

"How is everything?" the waitress asked.

"Delicious, dear," Mrs Slee told her.

"Divine, thanks," Lilian added.

"He said that he's coming for me," Mrs Slee said. "He's going to finish me off. He's going to kill everyone that stands in his way. He's going to kill our young heroes who have helped us. He's going to kill anyone linked in any way to me."

Lilian thought for a moment. "We've put ourselves and all those lovely people directly in harm's way."

"That's what *he* said," Mrs Slee replied, loading her fork with beef and carrots, before dipping the tip of her knife in the horseradish sauce at the side of her plate. "I wish I could be confident that we have done the right thing, dear."

"Are they safe, wherever they are?"

"Two very unsafe Spheres. Forever rolling, around and around, and around and around each other. One – you might say – goes clockwise, the other anticlockwise. Because they touch, they are unable to rotate in the same direction. What goes around, as they say, comes around. Safety very rarely visits."

Mrs Slee lifted their beers from their circular mats. She slid the two pieces of cardboard together, touching. As she turned one in a clockwise direction with her finger, Lilian watched the other move anticlockwise.

"We know how to step out of time," Mrs Slee continued. "You have seen how that is possible. But Temple uses one flow of time to act against the other. Sometimes there is very little separating one Sphere from the other; people hear what they might call 'ghosts' moving about, calling out from the 'other side'. Other times it's like tunnelling through a mountain. Unless you've got a Dreamboat, a Barrow Ship. Or Nicholas Temple's disc of times and his little black book of names and locations.

"Maisie, Finch and Danny are no more safe than Sylvanie, Georgia and Satyajit," Mrs Slee said quietly. "No more safe than we are. You've always known that, dear."

"I think that they are, in truth, infinitely *less* safe." Lilian looked into the fire. "Because Temple will want you to know that they are dead." She put down her knife and fork. "I am afraid that that might be something that would please him. And it makes me feel sick."

Mrs Slee had finished her meal and started on her second glass of ale.

"Give up hope, dear, and start believing," she said, with a foam moustache. "Finch and the others are in the sister Sphere. When they return, Temple will follow. They will lead him to us. And we will be waiting."

14 (Here)
In the Middle of Nowhere

By 11:30 a.m. Sylvanie and Georgia had left the balcony and had gone inside to make fresh coffee, an indistinct note of concern having crept into their conversation.

Georgia tried Satyajit's phone at midday, to no avail.

"Are you sure he took it with him?" Sylvanie asked, vaguely looking under cushions and on work surfaces.

"I am. It's a rule. He's not allowed to go anywhere without it if he goes without me. It just goes to answer each time I call. Anyway, if he'd left it here, we'd hear it."

Georgia received and made several short calls, and twice more left messages on her lover's phone.

They ate the two sandwiches that Sylvanie made. Because they thought they ought to, perhaps in order to sustain them through whatever might happen next.

At 3:20 p.m. Georgia received a protracted and official-sounding call. She had been through it all in less detail during previous conversations: times, the vehicle, intentions, destinations, estimated duration, etc.

When that call ended, Georgia tried Satyajit's phone again. This time it was dead. She spoke his name many times, over and over, breathily, like a mantra.

"Something's gone really wrong, hasn't it?" Sylvanie asked.

"Yes."

For a long while they moved around inside the apartment, around furniture, around each other.

The final call came at 7:09 p.m. The sunset was wild and bright and crimson. Sylvanie and Georgia had not switched on any lights. The apartment was swimming in blood-red light.

Sylvanie answered Georgia's phone. Georgia was in the bathroom. Sylvanie did not want to miss the call. The polite but morose man would not speak to her. He said he would wait until Georgia was available. Sylvanie and Georgia were both shaking as Sylvanie handed over the phone.

Georgia took the call standing, with Sylvanie at her side, able to hear every word.

"Yes."

"Georgia?"

"Yes."

"Georgia, this is Stephen."

"Yes."

"Georgia, I must give you terrible news ... Everybody here, Georgia, is distraught ... I don't know—"

"Say it, please, Stephen."

"Hannah and Satyajit are dead."

Sylvanie felt the blood in her veins turn to ice.

"Tell me everything, Stephen. All of it at once. Now."

"There was some kind of trap, we think. It looks like some people were pretending to have broken down at the roadside, out in the countryside. It seems that Satyajit and Hannah made the decision to pull over and offer help.

Georgia ... We all would have done the same thing. Georgia—"

"How were they killed?"

Sylvanie had turned to stone.

"With knives, Georgia. They were stabbed to death. We think that Satyajit was unarmed. Obviously, Hannah was unarmed. The police think he had been trying to protect her. I ..."

"Yes, Stephen?"

"I am told that his arms and his hands were lacerated. It took almost four hours before we could get clearance to get any information at all from the emergency services personnel at the scene. The road – it's little more than a country lane in the middle of nowhere, really – is still closed."

"In the middle of nowhere ..." Georgia took the phone away from her ear. "The arms he used to hold me ... The hands he used to touch me ..."

Sylvanie took the phone from Georgia's hand.

"Thank you, Stephen," she said, and terminated the call.

15 (Neither Here nor There)
An Ungrateful Little Brat

The boy had fallen again, and Temple had dragged him to his feet by the scruff of his neck.

"Walk. Keep up, or lie there in that foul dirt for all eternity with the filthy boots of the dead trampling every bubble of breath from your living corpse."

The boy had cried out all his tears. His besmirched cheeks and chin were streaked with their tracks. His little body was now empty of tears.

There had been a moment when the boy had been so terrified by the passing of the dead along their route that he had run to Temple's side. Against all innate sense of judgement, the boy had sought the refuge of Temple's coat tails.

The boy had no shoes on. He had lost them, back along, in the blackest mud. His feet and his hands were filthy. He began another bout of tearless blubbering.

Temple stopped dead in his tracks. The shih-tzu started whining. Temple stooped to remove his pet's collar.

The boy's head was bowed. Temple grabbed the boy's hair and yanked his head back. The boy could feel Temple's rage vibrating through every strand of hair.

"Remain here forever," Temple snarled, his face overshadowing the boy's, "or we shall go together to your dear mother. Choose."

Holding a handful of hair tight in his grasp, Temple shook the boy's head remorselessly.

"Choose, you ungrateful little brat."

Temple had hurt the boy's neck and pulled hair from his scalp.

"I want my muh ... muh ..." the boy stuttered as Temple shook him.

"There you are. You want your mummy." Temple growled into the boy's ear. "Of course you do. It's only right."

Temple relinquished his grip on the boy's hair, wound the dog's collar around his little neck and buckled it tight.

"Heel, mutt. Good dog."

He patted and stroked the back of the boy's head.

"Let's see if we can find you a stick."

16 (There)
The Singing Ringing Tree

"I don't understand," Finch said, "why Nicholas Temple hasn't come here and just destroyed this ... whatever-it-is, if it's such an important thing."

"They tell me it's a tree," Eleftheria Mutt said. "Maybe Temple hasn't destroyed it because he thinks it's part of something else, that's all: part of a bigger picture that he doesn't understand, and can't assess its true value. I guess he knows better than to destroy something priceless. He's made mistakes in the past, and it could be that leaving this thing alone is one of his mistakes. Perhaps he thinks it will provide some leverage or distraction at some point in the future? Who knows? He's the spider. We're the flies."

"We're the flies in his soup," Maisie said, tying her horse to a spindly branch of hawthorn, its berries the colour of dried blood. "We are the flies in his ointment."

"I might not have your innocent confidence and optimism, but I've got a really big gun," Eleftheria said.

Danny tied his horse to Maisie's. He had refused to ride the animal, walking or jogging beside it for the last six days. The soles of his old boots were all but worn through, and his socks were matted with blood and burst blisters.

"How can there be a tree inside there if there's a bliddy roof on it?" Danny asked, pulling a canteen from one of his saddlebags and pouring water over his head. "How's it supposed to grow?"

"Let's find out," Finch said. "We've come a long way to see this ... tree."

"Some people pray to really special old trees in some countries, don't they?" Maisie asked. "Or at least go to them to pray."

"I won't be doing any praying at any trees," Danny told her.

Maisie shrugged.

"I'll go in first," Eleftheria told them, handing the reins of her horse to Finch.

The windowless building, with its mud-brick walls and domed, green copper roof, was silent.

Eleftheria's six-gun made a barely discernible choke sound as she slid it from its stiff leather holster. She let the firearm hang alongside her left thigh. They watched her every move.

Eleftheria pulled up the wooden latch, placed her fingers in the hole that served as handle and pulled the weathered door toward her. Stepping inside the building, she was immediately dissolved in a cool darkness shot through with fine lines of light. The old door clattered shut behind her.

Maisie raised her canteen and drank. "We should go in after her," she said, wiping her mouth on the back of her hand and lifting off her broad-brimmed hat. She had stuck four white goose feathers into the band; they stood proud like the sails of a tall ship.

"Let's get out of this heat," Danny said.

Finch opened the sun-bleached door.

Once inside, they had to wait for their eyes and brains to get used to the strange darkness and beauty. There were thousands of tiny holes in the walls, through which thin strands of sunlight penetrated the dense brown gloom. At the centre of the building, at the confluence of the myriad threads of coloured light, an incandescent crystal quince tree stood.

They were drawn in. As they walked through, musical notes played. Every line held a sound, in perfect harmony with its neighbours, waiting to be plucked or struck, as if thousands of tiny glass hammers chimed the singing ringing tree as they moved through the room.

Through a narrow gap above the door, a pair of swallows entered the building. Before finding their way to their nest and hungry offspring, the two birds circled the tree, playing the room..

Eleftheria was standing near the tree, apparently beginning to dematerialize. Finch went to her. He lifted the hand with the gun and guided the weapon to its holster on her belt.

They saw fruit, ripe with light and colour, bending the branches of the magical tree.

"I've seen too many beautiful things," Finch said, almost inaudibly. "I don't know if I can bear it." He felt like he wanted to sit down, to give up, but his body felt too light, as if he was swimming to the surface of a sea of sunlight.

When Maisie and Danny came to them, the music increased in volume.

"It's like the Barrow Ship," Maisie said. "It's the same kind of magic."

"I am supposed to tell you," Eleftheria said quietly, as if in a trance, "that this is the work of an artist called Douglas Valentine."

The name meant nothing to Danny, Maisie or Finch.

Eleftheria hooked her thumbs behind the brass buckle of her belt. She seemed almost transparent. "They were childhood sweethearts," she said, her mouth motionless as the words came out.

"Who?" Finch asked, feeling that he had sung rather than spoken.

"Douglas Valentine and Pandora Slee," Eleftheria whispered. "Sweethearts, artists, magicians, dreamers."

Maisie opened her mouth to let the music out. Danny caught her wrist before she had a chance to say what she was thinking.

"Look at that," he said. "There's an axe."

They all saw it. An incredibly elegant glass felling axe with a fine long shaft, leaned against the trunk of Douglas Valentine's artwork.

"Please don't touch it," Maisie cried, hearing her words turn to music.

Danny was swaying. The music was coursing through his bones, through his teeth, his eyes.

"It's mine," he said, losing his physical self increasingly to the tree. "I'm going to take it."

"Please don't. What are you going to do with it?" She saw the light pouring from his eyes.

Danny stepped forward to claim his dazzling prize.

17 (There)
A Balance of Payments

The boy had slept soundly for almost eleven hours. His mother and father had been summoned.

Nicholas Temple was taking a late breakfast in the shade of an ancient olive tree. Its tiny pale-yellow flowers were falling onto the white cotton tablecloth, shaken free by the fragrant breeze. Temple was dressed in a long, plain white kaftan. He was shaved, and his thin hair had been oiled and scraped across his head. There was no sign of his karakul, his enormous overcoat or his gun.

A maid was throwing a red rubber ball for the shih-tzu. Once or twice the ball skittered on the paving slabs and bounced into the pool. Without hesitation the dog leapt into the powder-blue water.

"I like it when his little wet paws make pretty patterns on the path," Temple said.

The maid smiled and threw the ball into the pool. The dog's footprints were drying quickly in the mid-morning sun.

Temple ate smoked haddock and poached eggs. He buttered chunks of crusty white bread and dipped them into his eggs. He ground aromatic peppers from a wooden mill and sea salt flakes between his forefinger and thumb. A cigar was smouldering in an enamel ashtray the whole while. He liked his orange juice roughly squeezed, with flesh and pips alike. He liked his coffee from beans freshly-roasted and slowly percolated.

There were six or seven newspapers in a pile beside him. He loved the obituaries, and had circled several with a red pencil.

He whistled for his dog and gave it a few flakes of the haddock fillet. The dog stood on its hind legs and growled softly with delight before shaking itself all over the tablecloth and all over Temple. Temple smiled and showed the dog empty hands. The maid called the dog away.

"Fetch the child," Temple told her. "Bathe him and give him something special from the wardrobe. I want him looking the part."

The maid nodded, threw the ball once more for the dog and left.

A while later she returned with the boy. Temple was smoking the fat, greenish cigar, and there were newspapers spread across the table, spilling onto the ground. The boy was clothed in what appeared to be the dress uniform of a late nineteenth-century Russian prince.

"Splendid," Temple exclaimed, and applauded. "We will have the table reset and you can eat, my child." He looked at the maid, who had already started to fold newspapers and stack dishes.

"It's on its way now," she said. "Everything a hungry boy might dream of."

Two more maids brought a clean tablecloth, iced water with slices of lime and lemon and sprigs of mint, fresh juices and coffee, fried eggs, toast, blood sausage and devilled lamb's kidneys.

Temple bid the boy sit opposite him. The boy had never felt such all-consuming hunger.

Temple blew a vast smoke ring. It seemed to stand still above the table. It looked like a hoop through which the boy might be expected to jump.

"What do you want to start with?" the first maid asked the boy, holding a pair of large silver spoons.

"What about him?" the boy asked, not looking at Temple.

"How kind, child," Temple responded. "How endearingly thoughtful. But I have already partaken in an ample sufficiency."

"That's never stopped him before," the maid stage-whispered into the boy's ear.

Temple grinned with his cigar clamped between nicotine-stained teeth.

"I want a big sandwich," the boy told the maid, pointing to the fried eggs, crispy rashers of bacon and black pudding.

The maid created an enormous sandwich and cut it into triangular quarters so that the boy could manage it. She gave him a starchy napkin, unfolding it onto his lap. The boy ate noisily. Temple watched. The maid sat sideways on a cane sun lounger and the dog jumped up to sit beside her. The shade beneath the old olive tree had darkened as the sun had strengthened.

"In the blink of an eye," Nicholas Temple informed the boy, "your mother and father will be here."

The child immediately stopped eating and put down his sandwich. He looked plaintively at Temple.

"I am a man of my word. My word is my bond." He poured himself another black coffee and slowly lowered a large white sugar cube into it on a golden spoon. "You do not have to hurry your repast. They are not here yet. Take your time, young man."

The boy consumed the sandwich, then drank two glasses of milk.

"Wipe your mouth on the napkin provided," Temple told the boy. "Do you like coffee?"

The maid clapped her hands and a manservant came to clear the table.

The maid placed a hand lightly on the boy's shoulder. "Answer Mr Temple, please."

"No. I hate coffee. And I hate that smoke."

"Tea, then?" Temple asked.

"I think he was happy with his milk," the maid replied, ruffling the boy's hair.

"Fine," Temple said, puffing heartily on his cigar. Something moving in the blue water at a far corner of the pool had caught his eye.

"What's that?" he asked, pointing with his cigar. "Go and see."

The maid strolled along the paved poolside as a hoopoe swooped across the terrace in her wake. She attempted to shield her eyes from the sun and the dancing glare upon the water.

"It's a hedgehog," she called, kneeling at the poolside.

"Fish it out," Temple called back. "Before the poor thing drowns. Use the leaf net."

Temple clapped, and the manservant ran to fetch the net. He and the maid rescued the exhausted creature and took it to the shade of a massive pink granite boulder.

"It's panting," the maid called. "I think it's going to live."

"Now bring out this young man's long-lost mummy and daddy. And fresh coffee for all who might require it. And brandy."

The boy rose, left his chair and stood on the flagstones next to the table. Bolt upright in his counterfeit uniform, his pale face distrustful and anxious, he waited.

"I told you, my child, that I would reunite you with your dear parents. You called me a *liar*. You said you *hated* me." Temple sounded sad, as if his feelings had been hurt.

"Let the entertainment begin," he said, under his breath, as the boy's mother and father walked out onto the palatial terrace, flanked by the first maid and a female colleague.

As soon as the woman saw her son she ran to him, grabbing the boy before collapsing with him in her arms. She went down hard on her knees on the stone. She wept. She wailed.

The boy's father stood alone in the heat of the sun.

"I'm sorry, my love," the boy's mother said, between sobs, between kisses. "I had to leave you. I should never have left you. I should never have given up. At the hospital, I ... I lost all my strength. I lost everything." She brushed her hair from her face. She brushed her son's hair from his eyes, across his forehead. She wiped away the tears from his cheeks. "The kind man brought you here? It has taken so long. So long. But I never gave up hope."

She stood with the boy in her arms. She looked at Temple, a blur through a tide of tears.

"Thank you. My son means the world to me."

Temple smiled as the woman put the boy down.

The child turned away from his mother to look directly at Nicholas Temple.

"I hate him," the boy growled. "He's a liar. He hurt me and hurt me. He's cruel. He's the cruellest man there could ever be. He's a monster."

"Please don't say those things about the kind gentleman," the boy's mother pleaded. She was trembling.

Her husband stepped forward and took hold of her shoulders.

"He isn't kind at all," the boy screamed, pushing away from his parents. "He hit me. He hit me and hit me."

Temple, his fat cigar smouldering between his purple lips, folded his hands across his belly.

"Let us gather our wits over coffee," he said, as the manservant poured first for his master. Temple was also presented with iced water and brandy. Everything they needed was on the tray the manservant had brought to Temple's side of the table: coffee pot and little china cans, cream, milk, sugar, biscuits and wafers and freshly-cracked walnuts. And Temple's antique revolver: the one with the carved mother-of-pearl handle. There was also a little bowl of bullets. They looked oddly like sweets.

"Sit. Drink," Temple said, his words directed at the boy's mother, "and tell me how you plan to deliver the balance of payments."

"It's not possible," the weeping woman told him. "There must be another way. I …"

"No other way. You made a deal with me."

"I don't understand," the boy's father said. But he did understand. "What have you done?" he screamed into the woman's face. But he knew what she had done. And he knew the part he had played.

They watched Nicholas Temple lift his antique pistol from the circular silver tray, load it with the six bullets from the bowl, and spin the magazine with his thumb.

"You can't take my son," the woman howled. "Not now. Give us ... Not now. You can't take his father. He's my husband. We need ... You can't ..."

She swept her son up in her arms and turned her back on Temple.

"Take me," the boy's father cried. "I will go. Don't take him. Don't take her. I'll do whatever it takes. I beg you to take me. I beg you. I beg you."

Temple smiled at the man. "It must come from her, for it was with her that the deal was struck."

"Take him," the woman screamed, pointing at her husband and running with her child in her arms.

The first maid relit Temple's cigar. It had a red and gold paper band around it, concealed for the most part by Temple's chubby fingers. He inhaled the foul smoke deeply.

Temple shot the man in the chest. The shih-tzu yelped and ran away.

The man had his back to the pool. He staggered, but didn't make the water.

Temple took aim and fired again. This time the bullet took much longer to reach its almost motionless victim. The man was helpless, cruciform, turning, with his shoes barely touching the pale stonework.

The man watched and waited. He saw the bright silver bullet tunnelling through the scented air. He felt the bullet touch the bridge of his nose. He felt the remarkable pain. The blackness came from nowhere and grew in volume, like ink spreading across a sheet of blotting paper.

"You've made a lot of mess again," the maid said. "I'll have the pool drained and the terrace scrubbed."

"No. Leave it awhile." Temple poured himself more coffee. "Go and see how our spiny little friend is doing."

By the time Temple's sugar lump had disintegrated in the bowl of his spoon the maid had returned.

"Recovering fast. He's wheezy, though. And very snuffly."

18 (There)
Roulette

"I want to go home," Finch said.

He didn't care if it sounded petulant or desperate. He resisted the urge to tell Eleftheria that it was Sylvanie Maud Hart that he wanted to go home to. All that day he had been burdened with the sense that he had lost his heart.

"Is it my cooking?" Eleftheria asked. Her laugh didn't quite materialize. She hated cooking. "Two days ago we had eggs. What more do you want? And you've had all the bread and field beans a growing boy could wish for. The wretched weevils come free with every stale loaf and dry biscuit."

They were surrounded by open prairie: long, silver-green grass as far as the eye could see. The horses, each hobbled with a fore and back leg tied, were on a sliding tether between two stakes. It was a system that Eleftheria had used many times; the animals could wander along the line to graze. They were all stood, noses away from the remnants of the fire, looking westward to what seemed to Finch like solid darkness where the horizon lay. Maisie and Danny were asleep. Danny was snoring. The sound made Finch think of his motorbike. Only a thin woollen blanket separated each of them from the earth. Maisie slept to

Danny's right; his translucent axe lay on the ground to his left. The bizarre object, almost the length of its young owner, was absorbing light from the stars and the sharp crescent moon. The vast sky, with the entire Milky Way a cloud of diamond dust, was spread like a shawl above their heads.

"It's not the food," Finch said. "No offence. No one loves a frugal diet of completely flavourless dried beans more than me, and no one loves catering for a party of guests more than you."

"I enjoy making the fire, at least. I like the scent of the lichen and birch bark makings in the tinder pouch, the smell of the spark arcing from the flint struck off the back of my knife and the musk from the woodsmoke in my clothes and hair. But you're right about the cooking part. Raw's good. Do you want some chocolate or some cake?"

Finch knew her well enough. "You haven't got any."

"No, but it's not like I never had some of it. Temple gave me big lumps of chocolate sometimes. I think he thought of it as an act of kindness. I never threw it back in his face. I told myself that it might give me the strength I needed to break free. Sometimes he'd give things to people to throw them off guard. I saw him do it. He was good at that; getting people to drop their defences and tell themselves that he wasn't as bad as the reputation that ran breathlessly before him. All too often a lie is all some people have got; it's the last solid thing they can cling to. Sometimes he'd give people real riches and then walk away. I mean, he would randomly make people richer than they could have ever dreamed and ask nothing in return, until maybe years later, when the time was right. Then he would laugh when they screamed the walls down and begged for mercy. He would smile and watch them tear themselves apart."

Eleftheria looked up at the sky. "Mercy was always pricey. It was like he was spinning a kind of insane roulette wheel in his head."

"What are we actually supposed to do about it?"

"You're supposed to stop him. That's all I know. All any of us know. It's your job. For all I know it's been that way since before you and me were born."

Finch felt queasy. He closed his eyes and turned toward the embers. He could see their glow through his eyelids. He tried to picture Sylvanie's face, but he couldn't. He saw her sitting on a chair, her back to him, alone in a room full of shadows.

"We're all part of the plan," Eleftheria continued. "You know that. You've met important people without having any idea how important they have been to you. People I'll never get to meet. You three were sent here to find out if you *could* get here. And if you can jump back in the Dreamboat and head on home. A lot of work has gone into it over what seems like forever. I am but a cog in a rusty old machine that might just be falling apart. You'll be like shadow puppets that slipped out from behind the screen. It doesn't make sense. We're all just figures in this endless, inhospitable landscape. Our time will—"

Two of the horses whinnied and snorted. Eleftheria froze. Finch looked at her, then into the infinite darkness.

"Wake the others," she told Finch. "Then follow my lead with the horses."

Finch leapt to his feet. There was something out there. He heard a thin, wild sound in the darkness. He shook

Maisie, who woke immediately. Danny had to winch himself up from a deep well of sleep.

Eleftheria had pulled up the metal spike at one end of the horses' tether and was leading the nearest horse around to the other side of the fire. The four animals were clearly spooked.

"Grab the next horse along the line and lead him round. Maisie and Danny, you hold on to the other two until I can get to them."

Danny had been forced to have a horse – not least because of the state of his feet and boots – but he still spent more time trudging beside it than in the saddle.

When Finch arrived with the second horse, Eleftheria lashed them nose-to-nose to the spike and brought them quickly to their knees. Maisie and Danny led the other two horses to the opposite side of the fire and forced them head-to-head as Eleftheria hammered another spike deep into the ground with a shaftless hammerhead from her saddlebag.

"Sticks on the fire, now," she told them.

Danny leapt to the task, throwing an armful of dry brushwood onto the mound of embers.

They saw that Eleftheria was using the horses to barricade them against whatever marauding presence was out there. She had hauled her firearm from its holster.

"Get your hat and fan the fire," she told Maisie. "Keep four or five good lengths of firewood out of the flames. We might need them. Finch, you can feed me with lead. Always keep six bullets in your hand, and load when I'm ready."

Danny watched Eleftheria empty the magazine of the silver bullets and refill the chambers with lead bullets from a goatskin pouch in her saddlebag. She handed the pouch to

Finch and stared into the distance, buttoning the half dozen silver bullets into her waistcoat pocket. As the sticks on the fire caught, the blackness closed ranks around them.

"We'll need the fire, but don't look at it anymore. Keep your eyes on the dark and tell me if you see anything."

Maisie, clutching a bundle of longer sticks, crouched down with her back to Eleftheria's horse. "What is it?" she asked.

"Wolves," Eleftheria told her. "Too many to count even if we had the daylight to do it."

Danny picked up his axe and stood with the fire to his back. "I can see some of them. They're shifting backwards and forwards and some are looking straight at us. I can see their eyes." He lay the head of his axe on his shoulder and ran his hand down the glass shaft.

"Get down," Maisie told him. "For God's sake, Danny."

Danny looked down at her beautiful round face, mottled with the pink and orange of the firelight, then returned his gaze to the dark distance.

Eleftheria came to stand beside Danny. Clasping her gun in both hands, she fired. The report was like thunder. The horses panicked, snorting and screaming, but unable to pull up from the stakes.

"You got it." Danny had seen a hunched wolf collapse.

Eleftheria fired again. Danny watched the burst of sparks and flame from the barrel of the pistol as it jumped with the recoil. Finch wanted to cover his ears with his hands, but was afraid of dropping the ammunition.

A wolf was hit, but not killed. It leapt into the air, fell on its feet and was howling as it ran in circles, like a dog chasing its tail. Eleftheria did not shoot it again. Danny wondered how many bullets she had. She went to the other side of the fire and loosed two more shots into the rippling night.

"How many are there?" Maisie asked Danny.

"Enough. They'd still be hungry if they ate us and the horses."

When Maisie stood up, the wolves began to howl. It sounded like the whole night – all the unseen and unknown creatures therein – was calling. The music was both mournful and aggressive. It came from everywhere.

Maisie dropped her sticks and stood at Danny's shoulder. She watched the coloured lights of the flames travelling the length of his crystal axe.

Finch replaced the four spent shells in Eleftheria's revolver, then counted four more from the bag into his palm. He could see at least another six pairs of eyes staring out of the crow-black dark.

Two more shots ringing in Finch's ears. Then three more in rapid succession. Reloading, then hurrying with Eleftheria to the other side of the fire.

Maisie pointed to a single wolf trotting along the outskirts of eyesight. Eleftheria shot it. Danny thought she got it in the neck or shoulder. The impact of the bullet sent the animal spinning and yowling. It died gnashing its teeth, as if gnawing a bone the night had thrown it.

"Two more," Danny said, as Finch reloaded.

As Eleftheria shot one animal dead, the other ran directly toward them. The wolf – a young male – was no more than eight metres away when Eleftheria killed it. Danny instinctively stepped sideways to put himself between Maisie and the oncoming threat. The animal somersaulted four or five times before slamming into the flank of one of the horses. Maisie felt spots of blood on her forehead and ear. She wiped them away with her sleeve.

Eleftheria tipped out the contents of both her saddlebags to find a shirt, twine and a small bottle of yellowish liquid. She grabbed her gun and stood with her back to the fire again. "Tear the shirt into strips, tie them onto the ends of the longer sticks we've got left and pour the liquid onto them," Eleftheria demanded. Maisie went to work.

Finch was pointing and reloading. Danny and Eleftheria were shouting and shooting.

But the ammunition was getting low. Finch had six shells in his hand and three in the pouch. As he counted, Eleftheria fired three more times. He shouted in her ear, "Have you got more bullets?"

"I have six of silver," she yelled, patting her waistcoat pocket.

"There!" Danny grabbed Eleftheria's arm and pointed to a line of four wolves looking directly at them.

"And there," Maisie called frantically, almost stumbling backward into the fire. Two more large adult females were facing the firelit tableau, their eyes shining.

Eleftheria used five bullets to dispatch three more wolves. She unbuttoned the pocket of her waistcoat.

"Light the torches and pass them out. On my shout, throw them as far and as high as you can. Make sure we're all facing out and away."

By Danny's reckoning, Eleftheria had another six or seven bullets.

"Now," Eleftheria shouted, and the four of them threw their torches. The fiery missiles went further than any of them had expected, illuminating eight pairs of unflinching eyes.

Danny picked up his axe again.

Eleftheria shot six wolves with her remaining bullets.

"I'm out," she said, letting her arms fall.

"What the Hell are we going to do now?" Finch asked, picking up the two remaining torches, igniting them in the fire and passing one to Maisie.

As one terrified horse managed to get its rear end in the air, Danny pushed Maisie to the ground. Two panic-stricken horses pulled their stake from the ground and began to rise to their hobbled feet.

Two wolves hit the horses' backs together, gaining height dramatically, coming down hard.

Danny brought his axe up with all his strength. Maisie watched the weapon hit one vaulting wolf in the middle of its chest. The blade sliced through the animal's ribcage, neck and head. Its split carcass fell to the ground as a thousand round yellow sparks, cold and gone in an instant, leaving no trace.

The other wolf knocked Eleftheria to the ground. She was on her back, desperately wrestling the ferocious animal, clutching its throat, holding its jaws from her face. Finch caught hold of the thick fur on its back and pulled with all his might.

"Let go," Danny screamed, swinging his axe and striding forward.

Eleftheria released her grip. Finch recoiled just in time, pulling his arms away from the animal, his fists full of silver fur.

The blade of Danny's axe struck the wolf's head sideways on, just above the jawline, and the animal shattered. The body of the wolf disintegrated. A thousand round, yellow sparks fell on Eleftheria Mutt. They were cold and they were gone.

Danny put the axe to his ear.

He knew it.

It was singing.

19 (There)
Some Wingless Thing

"What are you going to do with that?" Maisie asked, watching Eleftheria dragging a dead wolf toward the fire.

The last of their sticks and logs had gone on the fire. It was little more than a mound of embers now.

"I'm going to skin it," Eleftheria answered, taking her antler-handled knife from its sheath.

"Why?"

Finch and Danny were re-tethering the horses. The animals were beginning to settle down once more. There was a brushstroke of pale fuchsia on the western horizon. As dawn approached, the temperature was descending rapidly. Danny left Finch to finish dealing with the horses. He went and stood beside Maisie.

Eleftheria slit the pale skin on the wolf's belly without spilling its guts. She turned the animal on its back and worked its pelt free of its flanks down to its back legs. She then peeled the skin free down to its feet.

"What are you doing that for?" Maisie asked as Eleftheria did the same thing with the front legs and severed all four at the carcass.

There was little blood. The sweet odour of the meat lodged in Maisie's nostrils. The animal, with only the twisted pelt of its legs, looked pitiful, like some wingless thing fallen from the heavens or finless creature cast out of a desperate sea.

"There's one each," Eleftheria said as she tossed the four skinless legs haunch-end first onto the embers.

"I've never had wolf for breakfast." Danny rubbed his hands together as Finch arrived at his side.

"Or lunch," Finch said, his voice wavering and his eyes dark and wide. "Or even supper."

"I'm not going to eat that," Maisie exclaimed in disgust.

"Why not?" Eleftheria asked. "It would have eaten you, as sure as eggs is eggs."

"I'll have yours," Danny said, grinning, as the smoke from the barbequing wolf legs drifted between them.

"We'll save yours in case you change your mind," Eleftheria told Maisie, who had turned her back on the others and was rolling her blanket and packing her saddlebags.

"When the wolves came," Finch said, "I thought it was Temple, or somebody he'd hired, scaring the horses, come to try kill us or take us prisoner."

Eleftheria turned the legs over. They were black and they were smoking. The lower part of each leg down to the paw remained almost raw. Eleftheria licked her fingers.

"It's *always* him," she said, striding to the carcass of the beast she had butchered. She felt both its ears, then cut one off.

She handed the severed ear to Finch, who received it reluctantly. There was something alien, hard and metallic, pinned like an earring through the thinnest and least furry area.

Maisie joined them. Finch passed the ear to Danny.

"What is it?" Maisie asked.

"There's some kind of device in it," Finch replied.

"It receives a signal," Eleftheria said, laying the cooked wolf shanks down on flattened grass. "A 'kill' signal. Only Temple can bring that sort of science here. If not for that they'd have all turned tail and bolted for cover at the sound of the first shot."

She took out her knife again, wiped it on a hank of pulled grass and began to hack into a charred leg.

"Breakfast is served."

20 (Here)
Spontaneous Combustion

There was a familiar knock at the door. Certainly it was the Watch. Both their current Watches, who occupied adjacent apartments on the same floor, used the same jaunty rat-a-tat-tat code. The door was locked. Always locked. Invariably, Watches waited on the landing out of politeness to be let in, even though they possessed keys.

Sylvanie had been reading on the balcony since a little after daybreak. Georgia had been shortening the straps on some dungaree culottes while waiting for her luxurious mane of black hair to dry. She worried about Sylvanie out on the balcony, so high above the concrete below. Since the death of Satyajit, Georgia had taken to worrying about spontaneous combustion. About it happening to her. Sometimes her grief would turn to anger, shaking itself into what felt like flames inside her. Sylvanie kept her sane. Or, at least, their insanities were shared. And, therefore, halved. They both needed to be needed, so that it wasn't gravity alone that kept their feet touching the ground. Georgia thought about how high above the ground they led their lives.

Sylvanie didn't hear the knocking. Georgia went to the door in the silk pyjamas Satyajit had had made for her in India.

Georgia opened the door and stood face-to-face with Nicholas Temple. He smiled. He winked. He shot her twice in the abdomen; then in rapid succession fired the remaining four bullets in the revolving magazine. If he hadn't run out of bullets he wouldn't have stopped shooting.

Even out on the balcony the sound of gunfire was deafening and terrifying.

Sylvanie leapt to her feet, pushing the little round table away. She turned to see the man from the necropolis walking toward her across the living room, reloading his antique firearm. It had been a very long time, but she recognized him.

She saw Georgia. Torn up. Bloody. Dead.

Sylvanie turned away from the man, placed both hands on the balcony handrail and jumped up onto the narrow strip of metal. She rose to her full height and leaned forward, out into the air.

I would rather die.

She looked like a diver rising from the edge of the highest platform; like Danny, pushing up from the river, bringing with him a pair of crystal wings. Her arms outstretched behind her, Sylvanie was taking flight.

And there she remained, held in stasis, waiting for the air, for gravity, for time, to come into being or to pass away.

Nicholas Temple grunted as he lowered himself into Sylvanie's faded deckchair.

"Now, Miss Hart, you must choose very carefully between certain death and a very uncertain life. Luckily for you, child, I am on hand to assist and advise."

From the breast pocket of his coat he extracted an odd disc: really a set of darkly-tinted but transparent discs pinned at the centre. There were words and numbers, places and dates. The discs were scuffed and scratched. Nonetheless, Temple was reading them, consulting and deploying them.

Sylvanie could feel what he was doing: winding time backwards at the same speed as it wanted to progress. She could see time hanging above the city, going nowhere, struggling with all the clouds, birds and sounds that were pinned to the sky like paper notices to a board.

There she was, in Temple's grasp, without him having laid a finger on her. He held her life in one hand and her death in the other. Georgia, her new big sister, lay slain somewhere behind her and an entire stationary cityscape lay before and beneath her. It was a long way down. She wondered if Temple would want her to look her death in the face as she fell. She wondered if he had the power to prolong the thought of the impact of her body on the concrete. Of course he did. She began to feel her death-wish ebbing. She could feel the ground, the concrete, pulling at the frayed strands of her being.

Yet she remained motionless. Ready to fall. Ready to be saved.

"I will be your saviour," Temple told her, sliding the disc back into his coat and interlocking his chubby pink fingers over his belly. "You've chosen a rather melodramatic way of giving up the ghost. Let me make the unenviable process of having to choose between life and death a little easier for you, Miss Hart. I will take hold of you. I will support you so that you cannot fall unless I allow you to do so, then I will ask the question once again."

In the sickening weight and patina of Temple's words Sylvanie heard the well-worn gravitas of a thousand previous statements of requirement and ultimate power.

Temple rose and stood behind Sylvanie. He caught hold of her arms just above the elbows. He rocked her to illustrate the control he had over her. The cityscape rocked. And the sky. She felt sick. She felt vertiginous. Now she was in trouble. This felt like more trouble than death.

She did not want to die. Even though her mother was dead. Even though Satyajit and Georgia were dead.

She did not want to die. Because Finch was alive.

I am alive, she thought. *I have waited long enough. And it has come to this.*

How grateful she was to Mr Temple for holding her. For giving her this choice. For erasing the dreadful mistake she had made. For plucking her from the jaws of death.

She felt sick.

"So, Miss Hart, what will it be? I can only be your saviour if you desire to be saved. I can, as I have told you before, take you to your boy, Mr Finch, and to your friends. They are within spitting distance. They are but a stone's throw away. You might want to dally a while along the way, perhaps to take time out to pick the flowers of the wayside to present to your beau. You can tell me all about your friends, and about your relationship with my beloved friend Pandora. Slee, P. was stitched on the label of her little green satchel at school. That's why we, her classmates, called her 'Sleepy'. I could tell you some things that would help to set

289

the record straight, then you can make up your own mind about me. How about that? That's all. You can be my judge. That is the bargain into which you and I shall enter. That is the deal we will have to make if you want to see your beloved Mr Finch and the others again. Do you understand?"

He shook her again. As if trying to shake the idea of dying out of her head. It was working. She was losing the battle. She felt the weight of her body, her life, in his hands. She was losing the will to die.

"What will it be? Life or death?"

He shook her again. Her eyes closed.

He shook her again. Her eyes opened.

She was alone in the woods. There was a fox. She was having a long holiday all by herself. She would not cry. She would not be afraid. She wanted to run after the little red fox.

"Life. I choose life."

But not for you. For you, you disgusting devil, I choose death.

"Let me live." *And you shall surely die.*

21 (There)
The Hexemore Hares

There were three Hares. Through the trees, down by the stream. They looked to be in animated conversation. One of them was standing on its hind legs.

"It feels like we've come full circle," Finch said. "This is the most beautiful place I've ever—"

"I know I've been here before," Danny said, cutting Finch off. "And seen *them* before too." He nodded in the direction of the tawny trinity on the low mound at the bottom of the slope.

"You're supposed to listen to them, that's all," Eleftheria said. "I'm told they can be cantankerous creatures. They know important things that they've been waiting a long time to tell you, so you should just stand there and listen to what they have to say. Speak when you're spoken to. They don't suffer fools gladly."

"Are you suggesting he stays here?" Maisie asked, turning and stopping Danny dead in his tracks.

"No," Eleftheria said, smiling. "Somebody's got to carry that axe."

Everywhere there were primroses and celandines, pretty, short-stemmed daffodils and ramsons with buds about to burst. They made their way between giant granite boulders covered in mosses and ferns, ducking under the boughs of ancient oaks that seemed to link arms and dance down the combe with them.

Danny went ahead as everyone else slowed down. Maisie clutched at his sleeve, but he shrugged her off. He came to a halt and let the shaft of his axe slide through his fingers, guiding it so that the head came to rest between his newly-repaired boots. He had hardly let go of it; it was as much part of him now as his right arm. He sometimes walked or even rode with it across his shoulders, hanging his hands loosely over the shaft. He looked like a warrior. It had rained heavily the previous night and they had slept out in the open – hungry, cold and wet. Throughout the hours of rumbling darkness, Danny had listened to the music of raindrops falling on his axe. When he touched the crystalline weapon, notes travelled along his arm to the core of his being.

The Hares' eyes were dark and wild, brimming with wisdom, speckled with birds and unspoken words, scudding clouds and flooding sunlight, scarred with magic and atrocity in equal measure. Danny felt he could see the history of everything – including his Exmoor, his childhood – in those eyes. He faced them. He looked them in the eye.

Eleftheria came to stand beside him at the foot of the mound. Finch and Maisie too. They could hear the music from his axe. Danny turned to them as if to show them his changed eyes. He bowed his head and looked at his boots.

Eleftheria had had his boots repaired at a cobbler's shop in a brick- and concrete-built town through which they had passed. Finch, Maisie and Eleftheria sat on a bench outside the shop while the work was being carried out. When the cobbler saw the state of Danny's feet she made a scalding-hot camomile infusion. He sat in her shop with his feet in a wooden pail, wriggling his toes in the steaming liquid, listening to the woman sing, watching her stitch and glue dense felt and rubber soles to his beloved dealer boots. Both repairs – to boots and feet – were successful. Danny had no further problems with blisters.

Eleftheria bought bullets in the same town, replenishing her stock of lead and silver. She also bought bread, cheese, apples, as well as carrots and oats for the horses. Her money was either gold or silver and the coins were tiny and almost paper-thin. Danny shoved three stubby carrots in the pocket of his jacket for later.

He had seen the Hares in the Hall of the Handless Clock. Hadn't he? Doubt was another thing you had to stuff deep into your pockets for later. These great animals were at least the size of the chocolate Labrador his Auntie Brenda used for picking up pheasants at shoots.

He straightened his back and lifted his head. The Hares were looking at him. *They were waiting for us. They are old,* He thought. *Older than everything. They were waiting for me.*

Those creatures are majestic and magnificent, Maisie thought. *They are beautiful and wonderful. They look very wise and very tough.* She felt like she hadn't breathed since seeing the Hares.

The sun was coming out, delivering to them a rainbow that began in another world and ended amongst the Hares. Their coats were of oak-browns, bracken-browns, milk-white, rook-black and bullet-silver. They had yellow teeth and they had long claws. One Hare was scratching and preening, pulling at its claws with its teeth, licking its front legs and washing its long ears.

They are gods, Finch thought, his feet feeling like they were going to part company with the leaf-strewn woodland floor. *Where is Sylvanie? If I can't share this, I am lost. How can I see this if I can't see her?* He was becoming aware of little birds, more and more of them, landing in the trees around them, twittering, flitting from branch to branch and threading light through every opening leaf.

Too many miracles, Finch thought.

"Too many miracles," the Hexemore Hares said in unison.

Maisie bowed her head. *Help us to open our eyes.*

Finch felt tears rising in his eyes. *Amen*, he wanted to say.

"Amen," the Hares said as one.

"The two old women," Danny said, telling it to the Hares, wanting to show that he understood what all this was about. "The two old women and Sylvanie. I mean, they must go back to them." He gestured at Maisie and Finch with his thumb.

"Yes," Finch said. "They'll be waiting for us."

"Everything has changed," the Hares said. "Nothing has changed. They will be waiting for you. Go to the blind girl first. Tell her she can go. Tell her she can see. She is the guardian of the Little Black Tin. It belonged to Pandora. It has remained unopened since she left. Tell the pale girl that you accept ownership of the contents and that she can go out and see the world."

"Pandora is the last of the angels," the Hares said. "No wings with which to fly, or feet with which to run. The bloodline ends with her. She has almost outlived her reflection and outwitted time. Temple knows where the flaws and fissures lie. She must outlive him and then the Spheres can unite, and life and death can walk hand in hand in their newfound freedom."

"Are we dead?" Danny asked. "I think that's what's happened. We're all dead."

"Only the dead can be here," the Hares replied. "And those Nicholas Temple drags by their hair. And you, who travel in Pandora's Dreamboat."

"The Barrow Ship?" Finch asked.

"Indeed," the Hares said. "Pandora Slee slept in the waters of the Hexe. She swam to the bottom of the deepest pool, where she hid and dreamed of escaping from Temple. We know it. The river held her breath and kept her secret. That is how the story goes. She dreamed the craft that took her to you and brought you here. That is how the story goes. It will take you back. We know it."

"So, we *are* dead?" Danny asked.

"Go to the Hexe. Lay yourself upon the bank and look at the running sky, at the river of dreams. If you can see yourself, then you do not number among the dead."

Danny strode to the riverbank and threw himself on the grass. He saw himself with a beard, looking thinner. There was Finch too. And Maisie leaning over him.

And Sylvanie.

He pushed himself up. "I am alive!" he shouted, looking skyward in amazement.

Maisie laughed and threw her arms around him. "I knew it." She kissed the side of his head. "Even if you don't always show it."

"Upon the riverbed Pandora wove the Dreamboat," the Hares said. "It carried her and Douglas Valentine away from harm. It is the feather that falls from the sky. It is the pebble that rests upon the skin of the ocean. It is a mere teardrop. Pandora has been a refugee for as long as any dream of any lifetime, but you will soon return to your families."

"I don't have a bliddy family," Danny said, telling the Hares. "Uncle Des is alright. My dad hits me with the same plastic pipe he whacks the bullocks with. He did, anyway, before I ran away from home. Before I escaped in the Barrow Ship. Mrs Slee dreamed it all up like I dream myself up. I dream I get my dogs back; Maisie gets her fox and we all live happily ever after."

Danny started to cry.

"When did you last shed such tears?" the Hares asked him.

Danny could not answer. A tide of grief and anger rose in him. He was shaking.

"I don't think he ever has," Maisie said, taking hold of his hand.

"Amen," the Hares said, shaking.

22 (Here)
Wednesday's Child

Sylvanie was coldly infuriated. She could identify feelings of grief, repulsion, hatred, powerlessness and impatience long since turned to exasperated rage. And she was going along with the man who was the root of all the misery.

Earlier that morning, Temple had requested that his driver – an utterly silent man in his early twenties with his long blonde hair in plaits – pull the Range Rover into the grey car park of a nondescript out-of-town garden centre.

They sat in silence for several minutes. Sylvanie looked at the side of the driver's head. Temple, she thought, had a different kind of power over him: the young man's compliance was almost robotic.

"I put my dog down on Wednesday," Temple said with a sigh. "Perhaps you remember him, Miss Hart? I was born on a Wednesday. One of life's minor coincidences."

Sylvanie thought that she did remember his dog, from that night long ago in the Victorian graveyard. She tried to recall the rhyme that Mrs Slee had referenced in the supermarket and the qualities attributed to Wednesday's child. She shivered and pulled the sleeves of her jumper down over her hands and into tight knots in her fists.

This was the man who killed her mother.

"He was a faithful companion of many dog-years," Temple continued. "But I'm certain I shall find myself another obedient mutt sometime soon."

Sylvanie slid across the back seat to sit behind the driver. That little distance from Temple felt important.

Temple pushed the button to lower his window.

The garden centre was busy. People were walking by with trolleys full of bags of compost and assorted plants, shrubs and equipment.

It was, Sylvanie thought, a little like ordinary life. And here she was, in this horrible car, with all connections between her and ordinary life severed. "Are we getting out here?" she asked, her voice like mud in her mouth.

A middle-aged woman walked by carrying a pair of shears wrapped and in a plastic carrier-bag. She looked at the big, white vehicle and made inadvertent eye contact with Temple for the briefest of moments. Her face fell and she stumbled on the way to her car.

"You can get out if you wish, child. You can get out whenever you wish. I know how you must feel. And I want you to understand that I can take you back to your balcony at any time and you will be at liberty to plummet to the petty finale of your entirely unfulfilled existence. You are not here, in my company, against your will."

Sylvanie felt caged. Bound. Chained.

"You are a prisoner only of the choice you made to live."

Sylvanie unclipped her seat-belt again, moved over to the middle of the back seat and leaned forward. Temple smelled of cigars and some sort of perfume.

She looked at the electric window-button. It rocked back on its central axis. Temple's window whirred and rose until completely closed.

"*You* are the prisoner," she told him. "Only of the choice you made to allow me the choice I made to live."

Temple turned to show Sylvanie the full extent of his repugnant grin.

"Your mother would be so proud."

23 (Here)
A Minor Diversion

Temple turned on the radio as they pulled out of the garden centre car park. It was tuned to a classical music station. A vigorous Paganini violin concerto.

The driver did not require directions.

"I have a business meeting this evening," Temple said. "We are wending our merry way homeward, Miss Hart, over the next few days, but I want you to bear witness to a brief transaction on the way. It will delay my promise to you very little and you might learn something of my methods and motives. It will be but a very minor diversion. Then a few short days on the Continent before heading back to your beloved Exmoor."

He turned the radio up, but Sylvanie slept for more than four hours straight. She woke with a stiff neck as the car came to a halt.

"They don't put pictures of places like this on chocolate boxes anymore," Temple said. "Such a shame. Images of rural idylls were all the rage in the 1950s and '60s."

They had pulled up on a patch of dusty gravel in front of a picturesque, thatched cottage. The wrought-iron gate led through a garden full of hollyhocks, dahlias, foxgloves, delphiniums and a hundred varieties of rose.

"I could very happily retire to such a perfect little retreat," Temple said wistfully, chortling deep in the folds of his throat. "I'm sure that in time the neighbours and villagers would warm to me. But I'm long past that sort of age."

He looked at his wristwatch. "Time is of the essence. Time is money."

He got out of the car without his hat and opened Sylvanie's door.

"I keep expecting my dog to try to jump out. He could be quite naughty."

He held the door for Sylvanie. She saw his gun.

"Get out. I want to share this with you. I hope you'll find what takes place here to be of interest. It will provide you, Miss Hart, with most privileged insights into what exactly it is that I do."

Sylvanie went with him. She surprised herself by walking beside him, not following in his footsteps. It felt like walking through a lucid nightmare.

A low and narrow porch stood out from the doorway, with roses winding through the latticed woodwork and a slim seat on the right-hand side piled with birch and ash logs. Temple leaned in and used the Wellington boot-shaped knocker.

"Does it remind you somewhat of home?"

"No," Sylvanie lied.

There was the sound of a large dog – more than one, perhaps – barking deeply. The barking faded, as though the dogs had been shut away, and a man and a woman came to the door. The couple looked as though they had been crying all their lives.

"I am Nicholas Temple," Temple informed them, smiling broadly and showing his stained teeth. His lips looked ridiculously purple.

"This is Miss Sylvanie Hart, here for the purpose of experience and enlightenment." He gestured toward Sylvanie and checked his wristwatch again. The couple gasped in recognition of Sylvanie.

They were ushered into a bright but impersonal living room, which opened onto a small dining area and in turn led through to a conservatory. There were faded prints of hunting scenes, gamebirds and dogs on the walls. There were various photographs of a young girl in school uniform.

"Why has it taken you so long?" the woman asked. "It's been nearly two months. We almost gave up hope. We've been so desperate."

"I am a frightfully busy man. And what's more," Temple said, gesturing upwards, "one must wait for the favourable stars to align."

"Please forgive my wife," the man said. "We've hardly slept in all that time. And we put all our faith in you. The hope that you would come has put all our grieving, I suppose ... on hold."

"Are you *the* Sylvanie Hart?" the woman asked.

"Yes," Sylvanie replied. "I am *her*."

"Would you like a cup of tea or coffee before ... before we start what has to be done?" the man asked. He was trembling.

"Two small, fresh, strong coffees," Temple told him, and the man disappeared into the kitchen.

Temple lowered himself into one of the armchairs beside the wood-burning stove.

Sylvanie stood by the window. A bunch of flowers from the garden had been roughly arranged in a moss-green ceramic vase. It stood in the middle of the window ledge. Sylvanie watched an earwig burrowing into a drooped foxglove flower. A tiny amount of yellow pollen fell.

"I smoke," Temple said, taking a plump, dark-brown cigar from a tortoiseshell case in the breast pocket of his jacket. He began searching and patting his pockets for matches or a lighter, but without result.

"I don't seem to have a light," Temple told the woman, who appeared unable to decide whether he or Sylvanie was the more frightening or fascinating.

She picked up a gas-fuelled fire-lighter from a log pile beside the stove and pulled the spark-trigger six or seven times before getting ignition. Temple drew deeply on his cigar and the woman coughed.

"Sometimes," Temple said, turning to address Sylvanie, "time moves so slowly in a place that it seems to thicken up and turn to jelly. When you've been in this game as long as I have, you get a feel for it. Time moves especially slowly here; it's like the difference between swimming in the Red Sea and the Dead Sea."

Sylvanie perched on the windowsill beside the flowers. She noticed a ladybird tending aphids on a rosebud.

"Would you like to take a seat?" Temple asked.

"No," she replied.

"Would you like to take notes?" Temple asked.

"No," Sylvanie replied.

When the man came from the kitchen with the coffees, Temple asked him how many dogs they had.

"Two. Golden retrievers. They've both been brilliant working dogs. Good as gold, picking up at the shoots. I had a lurcher called Lucifer for the hare-coursing. He was like a streak of lightning, he was: a finely-tuned killing machine. We lost him a couple of years back. I mean, we had to have him put down."

"I see. Do you by any chance have sugar lumps? I am rather partial to them."

"No, I'm afraid not," the woman said. "We've just got ordinary white sugar."

"Two sugars, then, and we can proceed with the matter in hand."

"You can have all the money we have," the man said. "You can take it all. We've withdrawn every single penny from the banks and borrowed more from friends and family."

He tipped at least thirty bundles of used banknotes from a cardboard box onto the rug in front of the stove.

"There's over sixty thousand pounds there," he informed Temple. "Sixty-two thousand four hundred to be exact."

Temple turned to Sylvanie. "Do you think that's a lot of money? Would it, perchance, buy me the pretty little pendant that hangs around your neck?"

"No." It made her feel sick to know that Temple was aware of her precious Alabaster Hare.

"We're hoping that the money will cover what you need for this … exchange," the woman told Temple.

"I don't think my associate made any mention of money," Temple said, turning his attention slowly back to the woman. "He informed me that you would 'give anything' to get your precious daughter back. You begged for the possibility to exchange your own lives for hers. It was also noted that you wished with all your hearts that the lives of the other three teenagers in the vehicle with your daughter that fateful evening could be swapped for her most treasured life. Did you not?" He waited. "Did you not?"

"We desperately hoped that this money might go some way …" the man said. "But we will sell the cottage if you want, and you can have everything that's left after the mortgage has been paid off."

"Where are the three teenagers now?" Temple asked.

"The gentleman warned us that something like this might happen," the woman said.

Sylvanie stood. She felt as though mercury was being poured into her veins. She wanted to open her mouth to let some words spill out, but she could not.

"Where are those youngsters now?" Temple repeated.

Silence. Neither the man nor the woman could find the strength to form the words.

"Are they here?"

There was something palpably wrong with the time in the room. Sylvanie recognized the experience. Time was beginning to weigh unendurably heavily on the hapless couple.

Temple looked at his watch.

Sylvanie was unable to move her eyes. She could not even move the thoughts inside her head.

"Burn the money," Temple said, relighting his cigar with the gas taper.

"Burn it?" the man asked. His mouth remained open.

"Indeed. Yes. Stuff it all into the stove and light it," Temple ordered.

"I ... I ..." the man stuttered.

The woman stepped forward and opened the stove's double doors. She threw the money in, two or three bundles at a time. Temple passed her the lighter. She clicked the ignition several times, lit the money and closed the doors.

The woman started to cry. She fell to her knees at Temple's feet.

"What is your daughter's name?" Temple asked her, softly. He leaned forward and stroked her hair.

"Becky," the man said. He too began to cry. "Short for Ruh ... Ruh ... becca. Her friends call her Buh ... Bex."

"Is there anything you would not do, would not give or give up, to have her back?" Temple asked, taking his little black book and thin disc device from the pocket with his cigar case.

"No. Nothing." The woman was rocking to and fro.

"Nothing," her husband echoed. He folded his arms, then unfolded them and held them rigidly at his sides.

The money was blazing in the stove. Banknotes were peeling away from the bundles and flaring in bright bursts of green and orange.

"Nothing," Temple repeated. "I do hope Miss Hart is making mental notes." Temple smiled at Sylvanie. He leered at her for too long.

Sylvanie wanted to scream.

Temple was in perfect control.

"Where are the three teenagers who were in the car that night with Rebecca?"

The woman and the man seemed to be having trouble breathing.

Sylvanie couldn't feel herself breathing at all.

"In the barn," the man said, clutching his throat.

Temple allowed him to speak.

"We ... We turned it into a sort of club for them, about two years ago," the man said.

"They're waiting for you," the woman told Temple. "We told them that you were a spiritualist medium, coming to give them messages from Becky. We said it would help them. We said it would help us." The woman dissolved into tears again.

"I don't understand the difference between right and wrong," the man said. "We lied to them."

"They've been in there for hours and hours each day," the woman said. "Every day for weeks and weeks. They've got a pool table. They know it's been on the cards for you to come."

"You lied to those young people," Temple said, "because my associate gave you prior warning of what might come to pass?"

"Yes," they told him.

The dogs started barking in another room.

Sylvanie's rage solidified. She could feel her nails digging into her palms. She could hear the dogs' claws on the door of the further room.

Temple stood, deliberately tucking back his jacket to reveal his gun.

The man and the woman saw it. As they lifted their hands to cover their faces, Temple froze them both at the precise moment when they understood the consequences of their thoughts, words and deeds.

Temple left the room.

There were five young people in the barn, not three. He calmly asked those who had been in the car crash to identify themselves. When they raised their hands, he shot them. He left the other two screaming and scrabbling in the dust and straw for cover.

On the way back to the cottage, Temple picked a rosy-hued apple. When he bit into its hard, crisp flesh, it turned out to be unripe. He spat, and let the fruit roll from his fingers into the grass.

A little knowledge can be a dangerous thing, he thought, and smiled.

As he strolled back through the conservatory and dining room, Rebecca burst through the front door. She appeared to be in good health, if a little out of breath.

"Sorry I'm late," she said, throwing down her bag and pulling off her shoes. "I'm starving. Did you pick up my message?" She saw Sylvanie and Temple.

"What's going on? Is something wrong? It's mega hot in here. And somebody's been smoking something totally rank."

The dogs were going wild. They had heard her voice.

"I believe, Miss Hart," Temple said, "that our work here is done."

24 (There)
Remembrance

It had been the longest of the journeys, not least because it looped them almost back to their starting point. A good day's walk would bring them to the town with the Hall of the Handless Clock at its centre and the Barrow Ship safely hidden. They invariably knew little about where they were going until they got there and Eleftheria professed to know no more than the Hexemore Hares had told her. Nothing was written down; it was all in her head, along with some of the purpose and some of the meaning.

Finch, Danny and Maisie had all lost a little weight. They looked fit, healthy and scruffy. Not once had Danny or Finch shaved. Danny's beard was big and bushy, whereas Finch's was wispier and more pointed. Finch had taken to stroking it, apparently unselfconsciously, prior to answering even the most mundane of questions.

Maisie loved Danny's long hair and had taken to tying it back, like her own, with a piece of pink ribbon she had begged Eleftheria to buy. Danny always complained, but secretly enjoyed the fact that they had matching ribbons in their hair. He was happy about his mended boots and pink ribbon, but he would have been unable to find words to describe the joy that his crystal axe brought to his heart. Everywhere they went, people stared at them, but they pointed, wide-eyed, at Danny in particular. Their jaws dropped in wonder and disbelief and people often applauded. Danny had always had an aspect of swagger when he walked, but now his solid stride was emphasized by the shining axe laid nonchalantly upon his shoulder.

He jumped down from the train holding his axe in one hand and Maisie's hand in the other.

They had been on the roof of the train for more than sixteen hours. There were two toilets; both were roughly cut holes in rotting floorboards and both were hell to get to. At one point a man had climbed onto the roof with a lidded bucket full of broad bean and wild garlic soup. Eleftheria bought a heavy rye loaf to accompany this delicacy, cutting it into quarters with her knife. The soup was ladled into big enamel mugs. Maisie thought it was the most wonderful thing she had ever tasted. Danny hated it. He soaked his bread in his mug and gave what was left of the soup to Maisie. When she kissed him, people on the roof of their carriage applauded.

They got off the ancient steam train at a place called Remembrance. The stop had taken Eleftheria by surprise and their disembarkation had been a scramble. There was no platform, or station buildings, only a sign made from whitewashed wooden letters staked unevenly into the mossy siding.

"It looks a bit like a scaled-down version of the Hollywood sign," Maisie said. "From a model village or something."

"Hollywood?" Eleftheria looked puzzled.

"The place where they make the films."

"Films?"

Finch did the explaining.

Three other people got off. A middle-aged man and two older women. They carried no baggage except what appeared to be bundles of white-painted number eights and balls of thick jute twine.

Eleftheria asked for directions to the Chapel of Sleep.

"You can come along with us," one of the women said, "as far as the Wooden Hill. From there the path winds quite steeply to the chapel."

"Our work is in the woods," the man told them. "You can go on from there. We'll point you in the right direction."

"Are you on the Pilgrimage Trail?" one of the women asked.

Eleftheria smiled. "You could say that."

Since selling the horses, they had pared their luggage down to two canvas kit-bags, so they were able to lend a hand with carrying the string and the wooden numbers.

"Why is this place called Remembrance?" Finch asked as they walked through lush meadows beside a meticulously-laid hedgerow.

"It is a memorial," one of the women said. "The whole place is the memorial; the wildflower meadows of Blanket Fair, the stream and the hedgerows, not only the symbols in the trees around Wooden Hill." The woman's hair was cropped very short. Her eyes were limpid, blue. Finch thought that she looked like a person from whom only good could come. He wondered how many people like her he had met in his life.

"What are the symbols in the trees?" Maisie asked. "What are they for?"

"Children," the man said, holding up his bundle, but saying nothing more.

Twenty-or-so paces into the woods, they halted. It was a forest of fine silver birches, tall and slender, pale as lines chalked on a wall. As far as the eye could see, elegant trees stood like rays of moonlight in dappled sunshine.

"They're not eights," Finch said, surveying thousands of the wooden figures hanging from the trees. "They're infinity symbols. If they were eights, they'd be upright."

The symbols appeared to hover between chest- and head-height above the bluebells, sorrel, celandines and wood anemones.

"Each of these figures," the woman with the blue eyes said, "represents a child that was either killed by, or at the behest of, Nicholas Temple. But it is undoubtedly an inadequate representation of the true historic total."

"It's like trying to number the pebbles on a beach," the man said. "Or grains of sand in a wheelbarrow."

"We have been coming here to do what we do for a very long time," the other woman said. "We come at least once a month. If we didn't, we'd simply have far too many to carry. These figures, depicting the partnership of the Spheres and eternal remembrance, represent only the deaths that are brought to our attention."

"And none of the adults at all," the sky-blue-eyed woman told them. "We have sadly lost count of the years since we lost count of those."

Many of the suspended wooden memorials had long since rotted and broken, leaving little more than pale curves and cracked circles turning slowly and swaying gently, or empty strings hanging frayed and doleful in the spectral birches.

25 (There)
The Chapel of Sleep

They worked with the women and the man to hang the wooden symbols. Using long, tapered, fruit-picking ladders and heavy hemp ropes, they climbed into the trees and hung fourteen symbols representing recent deaths of children. Five others to replace symbols that had rotted away.

"We always bring extra," the man said. "People carve and paint them and bring them to us, even if they haven't lost someone themselves."

They walked together to the grassy path that meandered through Wooden Hill. It was not a heavily-trodden thoroughfare. Danny noticed roe deer slots in mud that had hardened in the dry weather.

"Follow it," the blue-eyed woman told them, making a fish shape from her hand and swimming it along her sighting of the winding pathway ahead, "out of the woods and around the hill." She raised her hand to wave. "We give you thanks for your kind help."

"Thank you for allowing us the privilege," Eleftheria replied.

"And thank you for sparing our trees, woodman," the other woman called to Danny, smiling.

"She's talking about your axe," Maisie explained, pushing him along the path.

"Two or three hours' walk," Eleftheria said as they moved off. "We'll eat the last of the cheese and green onions with some dry biscuits before we leave the shade of the forest."

Later that afternoon they found the tiny chapel nestling in a combe blushed with light from the sun setting in the east. There were no gravestones, but fruit trees and wild flowers in profusion. The combe was brimming with birdsong and the low hum of insects.

"I can smell the sea," Danny said. He had been to the sea four times in his life. All of those times had been with Sylvanie, Finch and Maisie.

"It'll be just over the hill," Eleftheria informed him. "Twice I caught glimpses of it from atop the train."

"Oh. I thought I did," Finch said. "But I wasn't sure."

"Where are we?" Danny asked no one in particular. He went and stood by the tiny chapel's big door. "What is this place?"

"It's somewhere we're supposed to be, to see something we're supposed to see," Maisie responded, turning to Eleftheria.

"Let's find out," Eleftheria said, stepping forward.

"Look," Finch said. "Read that." He pointed to the name carved into the ochre sandstone arch above the door.

"Chapel of Sleep," Maisie read out loud.

"I don't think it says that," Finch said.

"Chapel of Sleep," Danny read, stepping back and looking up. There were small birds flying in and out between wooden slats in the sides of the little tower on the steep slate roof. "That's what it says."

"It doesn't," Finch said. "Or at least that's not what it's meant to say."

Danny shrugged. He and Eleftheria were closest to the door. Maisie was looking at the plain leaded windows reflecting the sunset.

"Are we going in, then?" Danny asked. "Or are we going to stand out here all night waiting for the owls and bliddy weasels to tell us what to do next?"

He gripped the twisted wrought-iron ring that lifted the latch. The door was unlocked. It opened soundlessly. The interior of the simple building swam with fuchsia-pink light.

They saw the young red-haired woman, ghostlike, pale as a silver birch, standing by a table in the centre of the room. She appeared slight enough to blow away with the breath from the open door. Apparently blind, and thin as a hazel switch, she turned.

"One, two, three, four. Miracles standing in a row," she said, her voice as light as the scent of a primrose.

Maisie wondered how she knew that there were four of them.

"A very old friend once told me," the young woman said, "that all you have to do if you wish to witness a miracle is watch and wait until the miracle that is due to happen there takes place. Most miracles go unnoticed. People are impossibly impatient."

Her lips were dry and cracked, her tongue unused to the shaping of words. Her milk-white eyes were unseeing. The long robes she wore were ash-grey.

When she moved her head, Eleftheria saw, the dusty, drab uniformity of her hair divided above her shoulders to reveal red amber and burnished copper streaked with filaments of gold.

Finch noticed that there were hundreds of faded butterfly wings on and around the table.

The woman's feet were bare. She looked brittle enough to shatter if touched. "I counted you in. One of you is carrying something unthinkably heavy, yet it weighs as little as a bunch of cowslips to you."

"How did—" Danny began, before Eleftheria cut him off.

"We can't say, exactly, why we're here," Eleftheria told her, "This is our final destination on the itinerary told to me by the Hexemore Hares. Forgive our ignorance. We are feeling our way."

The young woman smiled. "Ignorance is the clay from which all knowledge is sculpted. You have to start somewhere. Ignorance is bliss. Enjoy it while you may."

"I think I know why we've come here," Finch said, stepping forward. "It's something to do with that." He pointed to a slim rectangular object on the table. It was the size of a pencil case, covered in a thick grey felt of dust. There were butterfly wings upon it also, fluttering in the light breeze from the open doorway.

"How long have you been in here?" Danny asked. Maisie tugged at his sleeve, but he continued, undeterred, "Who feeds you and brings you stuff you need?"

"I have not been here very long at all," the wraithlike woman said. "All of my short lifetime. I was here before you dreamed of me, before your dreams were born. I have been here in this timeless place. I ask for little. People bring morsels, like offerings to a god they are desperate to believe in. They don't come in. You are the first."

"So now what happens?" Danny asked.

"Miracles," she said. "Everywhere we go. The miracle of the wren and the miracle of the rose-bellied stickleback. The miracle of ivy-leaved toadflax and the miracle of our loves."

"I think we need to take a look at the box," Finch said, his gaze fixed. "We've got to open it." He took four or five steps forward. Beneath the dust and the insect wings, he could see that it was an insubstantial metal tin.

"It has been waiting for you," the blind woman said. "I ask you now to take ownership of the miracles it holds."

Maisie wondered if the young woman was becoming more real, more alive.

They all drew closer to the table. A robin flew in and flew out again. Night, dressed in capes and cloaks and overcoats of silky shadow, was closing in around the little stone chapel.

"Light the candles, if you wish," the pale woman said, "though the tender darkness means us no harm. It has served me well throughout my countless and seamless daylessnesses." She indicated four pillar-like candlesticks standing away from the corners of the table.

Maisie wondered how the woman knew that it had grown dark. Perhaps, she thought, the robin had told her.

Eleftheria took a match from a tinder pouch in her pocket, struck it with her thumbnail and lit all four wicks. The chapel door remained ajar and the cool night air sauntered in, coaxing the naked flames to bow and curtsey. Shadows waltzed around the walls like ravens on strings.

"If you touch it," the woman said, "you must open it. If you open it, you must take ownership of what lies within." She sounded a little breathless, as if her words had run a long way.

Finch felt sure she was addressing him.

Maisie had noticed a wooden chair, painted white. Other than the table, it was the only piece of furniture in the chapel.

"Would you like to sit down?" Maisie asked the woman.

The woman nodded.

"Take my arm." Maisie breathed in sharply when the young woman's icy hand touched her forearm. The woman's fingers were so cold that they felt like they were burning her skin.

"What do you feel?" the woman asked. "What is it?" She had begun to shiver.

"Nothing ... No, I ..." Maisie faltered. "It's just that your hands are cold."

"Am I alive?" the woman asked Maisie, gripping her arm tighter. "I am unsure. It is a question I have asked myself many times."

"Yes, you are."

"I feel cold. Perhaps I was dead. You feel so warm. And I have never felt this cold."

Eleftheria pulled her coarse blanket from her kit-bag. She doubled it and wrapped it around the woman's shoulders, embracing her.

"You'll soon warm up." Eleftheria's voice had a tenderness that the friends barely recognized.

"You have a gun," the pale, red-haired woman said.

"Big gun."

"Why?"

"There are wolves out there. Mister Wolf is everywhere."

"Not here."

"No." Eleftheria rubbed the woman's arms and shoulders and pulled her closer. "Not here with us."

"Who shall open it?" the woman asked, colour visibly returning to her lips.

"I will," Finch responded.

"You go ahead and fill your boots, matey," Danny told him. "If anybody has the muscle power to get that little tin open, it's you."

"Open it," the woman said. "Then I can return to my footprints in the sandy mud by the riverbank and the minnows can nibble my toes. That's where the light is, and the scent of wild peppermint. That's where all the light is, curling and unrolling on its way to the sea, on its way to the sky. I remember it." She was almost singing.

Finch picked up the tin, turned it on its side and let the many years of dust fall away. He blew dust from the lid as Danny and Maisie came to his side.

"Get on with it," Danny told him.

Finch wiped the lid with the back of his hand. There were letters scratched through the commercial printing. It had once held goose quills for dipping and writing.

The scratched letters read: 'SLEE P'.

"I knew it," Finch said.

"What?" Maisie asked.

"What did you know, matey?"

"That's what it says above the door," Finch explained. "It says 'Chapel of Slee P', not 'Chapel of Sleep'. This was hers." He tapped the tin with his forefinger. "It belonged to Mrs Slee."

Finch paused. The others gave him some time. "It's about us. I think it's either about us … or, anyway, meant for us." He looked at Danny and Maisie in turn, then over at Eleftheria and the phantom woman. "I'm going to open it." *It's full of the unknown*, he thought. *And I know what that smells like.*

"Get on," Danny said, as if ushering bullocks through a gateway.

Finch had to pull hard on the side of the lid. He turned the quill tin around several times in his hands before it started to move. When the lid came off, he put it straight down on the table for Maisie and Danny to see.

There were four beautiful bisque-headed dolls, approximately the size of a clothes-peg doll, but a little longer and slimmer, all lying still and with their eyes closed. Their faces had been painstakingly painted and they were dressed in perfect handmade clothes.

"They're us," Maisie exclaimed. "How did they get here?"

"How did any of us get here?" Finch asked, tilting the tin upright to allow the four effigies to open their eyes. He took out a figure. "This one's you," he told Danny, holding it out to him.

Danny was reluctant. "It's bliddy creepy," he said, inspecting the doll, but keeping his hands behind his back, holding the shaft of his axe.

Maisie held out her hand to take the miniature model of Danny. "Oh my God." She held it up. "It looks exactly like you. It's unreal. Your boots have been mended and you've got a pink ribbon in your hair."

"And you've got your axe," Finch said, carefully passing Danny a crystal replica that was almost the length of his doll.

Finch passed Maisie her doll. It had the same pink ribbon tied in a tiny bow at the back of her head.

"Mrs Slee stitched them," Finch said, "and all of their clothes, before we were even born."

Eleftheria stood beside the red-haired woman. She put her hand on the woman's shoulder. The woman smiled knowingly and turned her face to meet Eleftheria's gaze.

Finch took the dolls that were him and Sylvanie out of the tin. The little figure of him had long dark hair and a pointy beard. Sylvanie's doll wore jeans and a T-shirt and her pullover with really long sleeves.

"There's something around her neck," Maisie said, pointing at the doll's T-shirt collar.

Finch had seen it. Picking very carefully with his forefinger and thumb, he pulled the fine cord from beneath her pullover. Though Sylvanie had shown it to him only once, he recognized it instantly.

"What is it?" Maisie asked. "Is it a Hare? It's lovely."

"It's something Mrs Slee made for her," Finch said. "She gave it to Syl ages and ages ago."

Danny leaned in to have a closer look. "What is it?"

"A Hare," Finch said. "Syl said that Mrs Slee carved it. She's worn it ever since."

"It's a fantastic thing," Maisie said.

"A Phantastic Mystery," Finch said.

Maisie felt the sweater that Sylvanie's doll was wearing. "Mrs Slee must have knitted that with a pair of matchsticks."

"It's hard to get your head round any of it," Danny said.

"Slowly but surely we are, though," Maisie said, wrapping her doll up with Danny and his axe in a cotton rag. They felt like the most important things in the world.

"We need to *know* it," Finch said. "We don't need to *understand* it." He carefully placed the dolls of him and Sylvanie face-to-face in his jacket pocket.

"There's something else," he said, looking over at Eleftheria and the red-headed ghost-woman.

They were watching him. They were holding hands. Finch imagined for a moment that the blind woman's eyes might be holding him in focus.

He lifted the tin from the table and took out a scrap of yellowish lined paper that looked like it had been torn from a school exercise book. It had lain in the bottom of the quill tin, beneath the four dolls, for countless years.

The woman came to Finch's side. He had the folded slip of paper in his hand. Maisie and Danny leaned closer. Eleftheria followed.

Finch held up the piece of paper so that they could all read what it said.

One word.

Written in rook-black ink with a dipping quill.

The young woman's eyes had cleared.

Her pupils shone like emeralds in a mountain stream.

"Hope," she read. "It says 'Hope'."

26 (Here)
Sold

Nicholas Temple was just a man. A man who had found a way to slip like a note beneath a Door into another world. Another time. He had the ability to walk off the face of the earth and evade all justices.

It was raining. The floor-to-ceiling windows along one wall of the hotel dining area were misted with condensation. Indistinct shapes passed hurriedly by outside. Groups of people? Animals? Monsters?

There were bucolic scenes of rural life, agricultural labour and country fairs on the walls, misappropriated from other people's lives in other times and other worlds. Sylvanie studied a grainy monochrome photograph of an assortment of farming folk, young and old, seated in the shade of an enormous haystack, having their lunch break, tilting back cider flagons, doorstep sandwiches in hand. She looked hard at the picture in the vain hope of seeing someone she recognized, someone she knew, someone she loved. Did the grinning boy in the flat cap look a bit like Danny? Not enough.

Sylvanie turned away from the picture, from her food, from Temple. She looked up into the plastic brightness of the lights.

She looked over at the driver. He was seated alone near the window, his hair plaited, his shoes shiny, his suit pressed and his skin corpse-washed. He wasn't eating. Was he even alive? Should she despise him? She wondered what Temple had done to render him so completely lifeless and joyless. Would she have the strength to stop him doing the same to her?

Sylvanie ate her breakfast, forcing herself to connect with her hunger. She had to be strong. She poured herself more coffee, adding milk and sugar. She didn't take sugar. "More coffee?" she asked Temple.

He smiled. Slowly. His whole face lit up gradually and his piggy eyes twinkled. "I will, Miss Hart. How thoughtful. How perfectly civil."

Sylvanie sat back in her chair and looked at him. She could imagine herself strong enough to outwit him, to outmanoeuvre him when the appropriate moment presented itself, to catch him unawares, to catch his last breath and clench it tight in her fist while he looked helplessly on with no friend in any world to turn to.

Sylvanie watched Nicholas Temple eat his breakfast. He disgusted her. It was, she thought, bound to show on her face. But she wanted him to see that she could be more than one person at a time. Could she be more than one person, looking for the gossamer thread with which to snare him?

I am her, she thought. *And her.*

"I had felt inclined to remove all of your privileges." Temple placed a rough brown sugar lump on a spoon and lowered it to the surface of his coffee. "But I am willing to give you the time it takes for this to dissolve. If you tell me that you want your balcony, and you want to swap all potential and prospects for a miserable demise, then I will take you back there. But you must respond to my ultimatum before this toothsome cuboid collapses." He smiled. "I'm giving you this final chance because you very sweetly offered to pour me more java."

It was happening quickly.

"You need me," she told him, her mouth filled with darkness. "There is no going back. For me. Or for you."

Temple laughed. "Splendid. And quite remarkably ... *spirited.* I would not dream of taking one step backward. The past is mere shadow. The past is buildings filled with rooms full of shadows turned to stone." He was looking sideways into her eyes. There was something he wanted to tell her.

"Say it."

"You were so lucky to have such a loving mother. She was a—"

Sylvanie cut him off. "I'll give you until this sugar cube has dissolved," she said, taking a lump and lowering it into her coffee between her forefinger and thumb, "to stop talking about my mother."

"Forgive me, but I ... I never had the privilege of a mother's love. Please, don't misunderstand me, Miss Hart. I had a mother. And I had all the hatred she could possibly bestow upon a child. I think she loathed my sister and I because we simply got in the way of the life to which she believed she was rightfully entitled. I come across an awful lot of very indignant people who believe their tawdry lives to be some sort of inalienable entitlement. I consider it part of my professional remit to disabuse them of such fancies."

Temple called for more coffee by raising the pot in the air. Fresh coffee was quickly brought to the table and all used china whisked away. Temple didn't speak to any of the staff. Sylvanie could see that other guests were being turned away at the dining room doors. Temple lit a large, greenish cigar. The whole hotel was a no-smoking zone, but no one came to admonish him. He rolled the end of the cigar between his pursed lips, moistening and darkening it.

"My father, also, got in her way. He was a weak man, woefully lacking in any form of clarity, be it moral, political or emotional. She despised him. I am certain she despised herself. And perhaps she saw in my sister a potential mirror image of her own utterly contemptible existence."

Sylvanie wondered if Temple had ever said these things to anyone before.

He was frowning deeply, not looking at her. Looking inward.

He belched. "Pardon me for being rude. It was not me, it was my food." He smiled at the inanity.

Killers, Sylvanie thought, were the weakest of people. They constantly had to prove themselves, robbing people of the strength they've earned over the course of their lives.

"My father was too weak to choose to leave of his own volition, and my mother hated him for it. She decided to have a party, filling the house with loud, obnoxious people who told my father that it was a private function to which he had not been invited. They pushed him around and pushed him out of his house." Temple laughed. "It sounds comical, doesn't it? But my father was not laughing."

He leaned toward Sylvanie, as if to draw her further into his revelations and confessions.

"My father cried, and he kept asking where he was supposed to go. 'Go to Hell. Go to your grave, for all I care,' my mother told him. It's funny the things that stick in your mind. Perhaps it was evening. I remember that the world seemed to be fading away, disappearing beyond my reach, getting darker and darker. Neighbours were coming out into the street to see what all the commotion was about. My sister and I watched. She said that our mother wanted us to ask to go with our father, and that we should pretend that we didn't want to go. But I didn't want to go with him. Later that night my mother told me that I couldn't have gone with my father even if I had expressed the wish to do so, because she had sold me to a couple who couldn't have children of their own. I never saw my father again."

Sylvanie watched Temple's face the whole time he was talking. It felt like he was looking right through her to some nebulous land beyond.

"The couple who bought me tried their damnedest to love me. I tried to be someone they – with all their agonizingly methodical kindnesses – could learn to truly hate."

"Is this intended to make me feel sympathy or pity for you? Are you offering this up as some kind of feeble excuse for your stupid, greedy little life?"

"I need no excuses, no forgiveness or absolution. My only motive now is my chosen profession, my honed craft, my true vocation. My work shows people the real nature and consequences of their wishes and desires, Miss Hart. It is that simple. There have always been unscrupulous scoundrels in abundance. There has always been violence, extortion and murder, blackmail and torture – " he rolled his hand while looking for the right words. "– mundane and unoriginal criminality. Whereas, what I have sought to do, throughout my illustrious career, is elevate the rotten darkness to the form of pure art. I am currently working on what will surely go down in history as my greatest masterpiece. You should feel very honoured."

"You are pathetic," Sylvanie told him, trying to find words that could not be twisted.

"My mother, I was informed, poisoned my younger sister over a period of several months. She apparently died wordlessly and in terrible pain. She was never able to tell any physician what the matter was. My sister died alone, in a kind of sickbed limbo of lovelessness. But I don't care what happened to her. I never liked the little bitch either."

Temple relit his cigar. "Are you following all this?"

Sylvanie blinked. It felt like an unintended response.

Temple nodded. "I was packed off to school each day. At first I spoke to no one, but Valentine and Slee felt it their duty to befriend me. Being befriended is not quite the same as having friends. I hated them. I hated their charity. They were dreamers. Daydreamers. I stole their dreams, exchanging them for nightmares in the same way that sandwiches might be surreptitiously swapped in a lunchbox. I became their worst nightmare. And I don't think they have, as yet, woken up."

Temple folded his hands over his belly. His face and his eyes had reddened.

Sylvanie looked away.

There was another black-and-white photograph. In a blaze of slurred motion, a carousel of painted horses was spinning, rising, falling, their nostrils flaring and their eyes wild with adventure. Sylvanie scoured the image, sifting through every swirling grain of fractured universe for something to hold on to. There were crowds in the foreground; families, all in their Sunday best, with greased-down hair, waving.

Sylvanie focussed. The girl in the frilly meringue dress, leaning forward into her horse's mane. She had blonde hair and an Alice band. She had something on her back. What was it? A coat buttoned around her neck, flapping out behind? A bag, like an open satchel, or a package? A pair of wings? And who was the young man behind her? He looked a lot like Finch with his long hair rolling and flying. Older, though. And he had a beard. Like a goatee. Like a little professor's beard.

Sylvanie knew who they were. They were the people she had been searching for. They were the people she loved. They were the people she so desperately needed to see again.

It's at times like this, she thought, *that you must choose whether or not you're going to believe in something.* She made her choice.

"Do you want to know what became of my darling mother?" Temple asked.

"No," Sylvanie lied. "I'm not interested in any of it."

"I killed her. She was very beautiful. Her beauty had a blue, icy quality. She had no good side to her nature; no loving, sympathetic, empathetic, caring aspect to her character. I inherited everything from her." Temple chuckled. "Except her beauty, obviously. I have to pay people to tell me I'm beautiful. People charge very little for lies. Fortunately, I'm very rich and therefore very beautiful."

Temple brought his gun from its holster and placed it on the table beside his coffee and the saucer he had been using as an ashtray.

"I killed her with this. I bartered with an elderly gentleman in Austin, Texas, for this six-shooter. He was most reluctant to part with it. It was part of his family history. But we managed to agree on a price eventually. I gave him the life of his faithful old dog and he gave me the gun. He'd only kept it in a cabinet anyway. He was singularly unaware of the weapon's true potential. I fell in love with it. True love. Unconditional love."

Temple picked up the gun.

Sylvanie saw two male members of the hotel staff stand with their backs to the glass panels in the dining room door. The driver rose and went to guard the kitchen door.

"My mother tried to talk me out of her death, of course, Miss Hart." Temple pointed his gun at Sylvanie and poked his chubby finger in over the trigger. "You wouldn't believe the rewards potentially on offer. Despite all the fuss and painful histrionics, I took her life with a silver bullet."

Sylvanie stood.

Temple followed the action with his pistol.

Sylvanie could hear herself breathing.

"I wonder," Temple said, "if when my father was alive, he might have felt some perverse sense of pride upon hearing my name?"

Sylvanie picked up her coffee and threw it over Temple. He made no attempt to shield his face.

"It would be no fun at all if you were merely to comply," Temple told her, unfazed. "I want you very slowly to give up. I don't care if it takes years; I want to see your resistance drain slowly away like blood drawn from a freshly-killed hind, Miss Hart, until you no longer have the strength to remember why you hated me in the first place."

"I will remember."

"That's the spirit." Temple wiped his face with a starched white napkin.

27 (There)
Liss

They remained in the chapel all night. Eleftheria cradled the red-haired woman, wrapped in her blanket, in her strong arms. Maisie and Danny were sat side by side with their backs to the cold stonework. They were each wearing all the clothes they possessed; Finch's legs were stuffed knee-deep into one of the kit-bags. The blankets barely insulated them from the flagstone floor. The young woman insisted that the door be left open; she said that she wanted to be able to hear the foxes and the owls.

When dawn broke, Danny woke and went outside for a pee. Finch followed him. They peed together into the nettles and burdocks.

"Stinging nettles are a sure sign that human beings have urinated here loads before," Finch said.

"Your piss'll probably kill 'em off, then, matey," Danny told him.

"You're a twat," Finch said. He lifted up his face to the sky and laughed.

It was going to rain.

The young woman was next to exit the chapel, followed by Eleftheria, who enlisted Finch's help with packing up.

Danny fetched his axe from the doorway and went to stand beside the woman.

"What's your name?" he asked.

"I don't remember anything being so beautiful," the young woman said, looking out over the landscape. "Wooden Hill and Blanket Fair." She turned to Danny. "My name is Liss. And I can see."

"It seems like a proper miracle," Danny said.

"She's a miracle," Eleftheria said, clasping Liss tightly in her arms.

"And you are," Maisie said, doing the same to Danny.

"And I am," Finch said, hugging himself.

They all laughed. Liss applauded.

Finch watched them laughing, holding each other, their laughter falling head-over-heels down the bracken- and furze-covered slope. He felt for the quill tin in his jacket pocket, turned away from the others and put the dolls in the tin with the word on the piece of paper.

Then he was struck by the notion that the tin was like a coffin.

In a cold sweat he took the two dolls out again and tilted them upright so that their eyes opened.

The two dolls stared back at Finch.

Him.

And the two dolls.

The three of them.

Waiting for a miracle.

28 (There)
Betrayal

It was there, beneath the avenue of great trees, in a barrow-shaped enclosure that had been planted generations ago and had been awaiting its presence. The track didn't lead right to it, but passed on the lower side of the coombe, and it would be a scramble to get up the bank.

It's there, Finch thought. *I can't see it, but I know it's there, hidden in all those trees.*

"It's up there," Danny said, nodding ahead. "We must have put it there. It must be where we left it."

There were derelict buildings on the outskirts of the town, with dark ponds and fractured areas of concrete, bordering on steep, scrubby fields and unmanaged woodland. The Barrow Ship was well hidden.

"It is there," Finch said. "I can feel how close we are to it. It's got a kind of magnetic power. It's like when we found the first lumps of it up on the moor."

"I can feel it," Maisie said. "You're right. It makes me feel a bit light-headed."

"Or," Finch said, "just *light*."

They had been walking in the rain all day: an hour or so after they left the chapel the skies had comprehensively darkened. The rain chimed on Danny's axe, providing a delightful musical accompaniment to their journey.

Liss had rinsed her hair in a stream, laughing like a child the whole time. All the dusty shadows left her hair, leaving the ginger strands copper-bright, shining like darting fish in a stream, polished and charged.

Eleftheria couldn't take her eyes off their newfound companion. The two women walked hand in hand.

Maisie and Danny walked arm in arm.

Finch walked side by side with someone who wasn't there.

"A penny for your thoughts," Maisie said as Finch drew level.

"I'd bite her bliddy hand off, matey," Danny told him. "You won't get an offer of anything like that kind of money from anyone else. Pocket the cash and piss right off, sharpish, before she realizes she's been conned."

"I was thinking about the Barrow Ship," Finch said. "How Mrs Slee said Sylvanie was meant to stay behind to be like a beacon for us to find our way back."

Danny shifted his axe off his shoulders and balanced it at his side. Rain had been running down his arms and inside his sleeves.

"Not for *us*, Finch," Danny said. "A beacon for *you*. If you want to go back, you'll be going it alone."

Maisie couldn't remember Danny ever using Finch's actual name in all their years of friendship.

"Don't be stupid," Finch said, looking to Maisie for help. "I don't know why you'd want to say something like that."

Eleftheria and Liss were some distance ahead, walking together through the taller vegetation in the centre of the track. It was still raining. They were all soaked, but not cold. A herd of long-eared goats was ambling down the hillside to meet them.

"I'm not going back," Danny said. "Nor Maze."

They had all stopped walking.

"This is where Danny wants to be," Maisie said. "And I want to be here, too, with him."

Finch was trying to process their words.

"I don't have nothing to go back for," Danny said. "You know that. And loads of kinds of shit that I *don't* want to go back for."

"Yeah, but I do, though," Finch said, his voice rising and wavering. There was panic in his eyes.

Liss and Eleftheria had stopped and turned.

"I've got Syl to go back for," Finch said. "I don't know what she's been doing all this time. I don't have any idea what might have happened to her. I want to make sure she's OK. I … I just want to see her."

"We're not going back," Danny told him. "You'll have to go back – to Syl – on your own."

"We know that the Barrow Ship will take you back to her," Maisie said. "Otherwise there's no way we'd ask you to go back without us."

"What about your family?" Finch asked Maisie. "You've got all sorts of people who'll be completely desperate to see you."

"Finch," she said. "You'll have to tell them that I love them. And you'll have to … Will you explain why I have to stay here and be with Danny?"

"Tell them," Danny said, "that she's OK. She's here with me."

"It's just idiotic. You've both lost your fucking minds. You're not thinking about anyone but yourselves. You'll break their hearts."

"I'm never leaving Danny, Finch," Maisie told him.

"And I don't want her to," Danny said, reaching for Maisie's dripping hand. "I've told you: I'm never going back. We're going to find a few good fields here, and—"

"I'm not interested in any of that happily-ever-after farming bullshit. It's like you two have completely betrayed me."

With that, Finch turned on his heels and ran. Recklessly. Back in the direction they'd come from.

Eleftheria and Liss walked back to Danny and Maisie.

"I can guess what's happened," Eleftheria said. "I'll go after him."

"I'm going," Danny said. "You lot all stay here."

"You can leave your axe with us," Maisie said.

Danny laughed, swung his axe onto his shoulder and marched back down the track in the drizzle, scattering bleating goats as he went.

29 (There)
Homing

Maisie, Liss and Eleftheria waited for an hour before deciding to go after Finch and Danny. The rain had eased, but the sky remained grey and there looked to be little sign of any weather that might dry their clothes.

"We'll have to take serious shelter somewhere tonight," Eleftheria said as she shook excess rainwater from her hair and jacket. "We'll need to get dried off, fed, bathed and get a decent night's kip. Once, that is, we've bade our fond farewells to our man Finch."

They heard Finch and Danny in raucous conversation before the two of them came into view with their arms around each other's shoulders and broad smiles on their faces. Danny's axe swung easily in his right hand. They looked like drowned rats.

"We've talked about him going back," Danny said as they met up, "on his own and everything. And he's up for it."

"Are you, Finch?" Maisie asked. "Are you sure you're OK with it?"

"What Danny says is absolutely right," Finch replied. "He says that this is the life that you two were meant to find together. And I guess it all makes sense. Like you two being meant to find each other as well." He looked at Eleftheria and Liss, and smiled. "But I've absolutely got to go back. I mean, if I don't, Sylvanie will have been waiting for all this time for nothing. And I'll be alone, without her, forever."

"All you have to do," Liss said, "is wait until the miracle that is due to happen, happens."

"Well, sometimes," Finch said, "you know that you've got to give the miracle a little nudge."

"Or a kick right up the arse," Danny added.

"I know it's all been worked out to be exactly like this," Finch said. "If it wasn't, then Syl would be right here with me. I get it. I'll go on my own. I'll get into the Barrow Ship on my own and go back to her."

"You are a brave and lovely man," Liss told him.

"Yes, you are," Maisie said. "I know that if you don't go, nothing at all will ever fall into place or make sense for you, and none of us will ever see Syl again."

"And you'll always be the wrong person," Eleftheria added, "in the wrong place at the wrong time."

"And words won't fit in your mouth," Liss said. "And thoughts won't fit in your head."

"No bliddy change there, then," Danny said, as they moved along the track toward the arbour holding the Barrow Ship.

"Feel it now," Finch said, looking ahead into the trees.

"Stronger than any of us," Maisie said. "Stronger than anything."

It was true. Finch could sense the hidden vessel taking hold of him. Drawing him to it. He couldn't have fought it.

Now they could hear it humming. There was singing. As if the Barrow Ship had given the giant beeches, oaks and elms their lost voices.

"I could hear it," Liss told them, "when I closed my eyes and floated on the cold, dark water alone and looked down at the sky. I could hear it singing."

Maisie went forward with Liss and Eleftheria, linking arms as they entered the vast green cavern of trees.

"We are all children," Maisie told the other women. "The Barrow Ship makes you feel like a kid. Being with it is like catching a snowflake on your hand for the first time. But instead of watching *it* melt, you feel *yourself* turn to liquid."

Finch and Danny were close behind. Danny's axe was ringing and humming.

It was – once more, all over again – impossible to believe the magical beauty of the Barrow Ship. Impossible to deny it. It was rainclouds bound with sunlight, a mirror of everything in the woodland, everything in nature, everything in the sky. It was breathing and breathless, singing and silent. Almost invisible, it was a pebble in a pocket of trees.

Vegetation grew around, about and even under it. The branches of the trees above seemed to shield and cradle it.

"I know we've been here in this other world for a long time," Danny said, "but that thing looks like it's been here a hell of a lot longer."

"Maybe it has," Finch responded. "Maybe it's not about *one* time, or the *same* time. Maybe it's just about the times when times meet."

Danny lowered his axe to the ground, took ten or twelve paces forward and turned.

"I'll show you something that'll blow your tiny minds."

He brushed aside creepers and vines cascading from branches above, slapped both hands flat on the surface of the Barrow Ship and leaned slowly in.

He hit his nose and forehead hard, as if he'd head-butted a plate-glass window.

Maisie's gentle laugh floated like smoke into the canopy of the trees.

Ribbons of light emanated from the Barrow Ship, bypassed Danny and wound round and round Finch.

"You were right," Finch said, stepping forward to touch the living skin of the immense crystal. "I'm the one who's going back."

30 (Here)
A Long Chalk

Pony threw his door wide open and jumped down into the pull-in by the lych gate, landing surprisingly lightly in his old work boots. He whistled like a blackbird all the way up the serpentine cobbled path to the church. As well as a reddish-brown corduroy jacket with leather patches on the elbows, Pony sported a black homburg with a sturdy wide brim. He looked like happiness. A man content with his kit-bag-of-a-life stuffed full of nature.

Mrs Slee and Lilian were sat on the bench at the side of the church. They had heard Pony's old David Brown chugging along the lane.

"Hello, Pony, dear," Mrs Slee said as he appeared around the corner. "I do very much like your hat."

"Good day, Mr Chalice," Lilian said, sitting upright with her hands on her knees.

"Ladies," Pony said, taking hold of the brim of his hat and sweeping it almost to the ground as he bowed. "Lady Jeffers give it me. Some dignitary must have left it behind. 'If the cap fits, wear it,' she told me. And it does. And I be."

"Lilian has made custard tarts," Mrs Slee informed Pony. "We've eaten ours already. We couldn't wait. We were simply famished. But we saved one for you."

Mrs Slee held the delicacy out on the flat of her palm as if feeding a horse.

Pony paused to smell the nutmeg grated onto the surface of the egg custard before seeing it off in three swift bites.

"You're a domestic goddess, you are, maid," he told Lilian, blowing out crumbs of buttery shortcrust pastry as he spoke.

"Less of the *domestic*, if you please, Mr Chalice," she replied, smiling.

"Tell us what you have been up to this morning, Pony, dear," Mrs Slee said.

"I've been making wild bee hives by hollowing out a couple of big larch logs. I hung 'em up in the ash trees in the copse this morning. It's just for the bees. I won't be taking the honey."

"That's wonderful," Lilian said. "I hope you get some bees to take to them. What a splendid idea. And what a marvellously selfless service to provide. I would really like to come and see them sometime."

"You can come up there anytime you want, maid. You'd always be more than welcome. Both of you, of course," Pony added, to be polite.

Lilian thanked him for the open invitation to the copse, but then had to look away.

"So, what's all this about, then?"

"We have to make some magic in order to save the world," Mrs Slee told him. "Or at least in order to save everything that really matters in this world. And the next. We have no one else to turn to, Pony, dear. You are most assuredly the only man for the job."

"Quite a job it is, too," Lilian added.

"You'll need your fastest, most agile and intelligent horse," Mrs Slee informed him, "and you'll need to bring it here to walk it round a course that we hope – with your expert help – to plot out today."

"That'll be Jess," Pony said. "She's the swiftest I've ever had by a country mile. She'll fly like shit off a shovel. She'll dream about galloping when she's bedded down in her straw, she will. I've seen her laid in the meadow, kicking and snorting in the moonlight. I never met any other bugger daft enough to get up on her."

"She sounds to be quite the mount for the task," Mrs Slee said.

"Jess is short for Gesso. I gave her that name when I was given her. She looks like the gypsum treatment the old boys used to give the carved wooden horses they made for fair roundabout rides. She's as pale as the moon and a thousand times prettier."

"She'll be perfect," Mrs Slee told him.

"So, are you going to tell me what it's all in aid of, then? What is it you two have been brewing up?"

"Sit down, Pony, please," Mrs Slee said, patting the space on the bench between her and Lilian.

Lilian shuffled over to give Pony enough room to seat himself.

He leaned back until the brim of his homburg touched the lichen-encrusted stonework at their backs. His hat tilted up over his brow.

"I have something to show you," Mrs Slee told him. "I think it might help you to understand our reasons for asking you to attempt to do something almost unfeasibly audacious."

Mrs Slee lifted the blue plastic flap on her raincoat pocket, withdrew an old postcard and placed it in Pony's bark-brown and calloused hand.

It looked to Pony like something she'd had forever and a day.

He looked briefly at the picture: a black-and-white photograph of the village church outside which they were currently seated. Pony turned the postcard over. It was addressed to Mrs Slee at her cottage. There was a message written in blood-red ink, probably with a dipping pen or quill.

It read: 'I have her'.

As far as Pony could make out, the postmark was a date in 1959. The card was unsigned.

Pony looked from side to side to the two women for help.

"It was sent by Nicholas Temple," Mrs Slee said. "The man you struggled to identify on the cover of your old equestrian magazine. The *very* bad man we told you about."

"He's referring to Sylvanie Maud Hart, Mr Chalice," Lilian explained. "Informing us that he has her in his evil clutches."

Pony scratched his ear, then held his nose as if about to submerge.

"We have to rescue her, Pony, dear," Mrs Slee told him. "And we can only do it by working together."

"But," Pony began, rising to the surface of the situation and taking a big breath, "this was posted way back when."

"But it arrived this very morning," Mrs Slee gravely informed him.

"The plan is," Lilian said, allowing Pony no time for analysis, "for the three of us to work out a rideable route anticlockwise around the church, obviously avoiding all hazards and obstacles, like vergers and gravestones. Then, once you think we've sufficiently tested an achievable circuit, you get in as many practice runs with your Jess as is possible in the available time."

"Well, what about the vicar?" Pony asked. "There's those new houses at the top end that can look in over the wall. They won't—"

"Let us worry about them, dear," Mrs Slee said. "We'll take care of all of that sort of thing."

"You'll have to put Jess into a field nearby," Lilian said. "You'll need her on hand for practice runs, but she'll need to be fresh as a daisy for the actual night of the ... *event*."

Pony took off his hat and scratched the back of his head. "I'm not expected to understand any of it, am I?"

"All will be made abundantly clear by our actions," Mrs Slee said. "Now, let's go and see if we can map out a course for a race against the clock."

31 (Here)
Banker of Souls

There had been a queue of people to see Temple all morning. Sylvanie counted at least twelve sets of desperate or scheming folk who had come to beg him to do some sort of business with them. Temple had not told Sylvanie that these meetings were in any way private; on the contrary, he seemed happy for her to bear witness to his rolling programme of transactions. She knew that every meeting that concluded in gratitude and praise would one day end in abject despair.

The terrace outside the hotel was massive. They had it to themselves. Temple appeared to have hired one entire wing of the hotel and, judging from the way the staff behaved in his presence, it was clear that it was something he had done numerous times before.

Sylvanie perched on the stone balustrade and observed Temple's dealings from afar.

If the Devil existed, Sylvanie thought, people would go to him, in dire need and merciless greed, and sell their souls – just as they were doing out here on this vast terrace, overlooking the perfect blue lake, with majestic snow-capped mountains in the distance.

What would Finch do? If she walked away from the hotel right now, would some henchmen come after her? Maybe she could get a Batman costume and just run away? If she got away, she'd never see Finch again. That's why she was here, observing these repellent routines: to get to Finch. Would it end there? Would Temple be satisfied? Could Sylvanie fool herself into thinking that she was any different to those deluded fools walking out to meet the man in the shade of the pretty white parasol?

He had his coffee. His cigars. Iced water. The stage and scenery. An audience before whom he could enact his dramas.

Sylvanie turned and looked out across the water. The vista was a vast landscape garden where the appointment of every dark conifer and each luxury villa was painstakingly chosen.

The mountains were like gods, Sylvanie thought, despairing gods dressed up to dance for a mad emperor.

Would Finch try to kill Temple, if he was in her position? Would he think that she should actually try to kill the man if the opportunity arose? If she was actually able to kill Temple she would never see Finch again, because Temple couldn't then take her to him. Was it her moral duty to rid the world of this banker of souls?

She would kill him if she could.

How did she become someone who even entertained the idea of murdering another person? What would her mum say? Stupid, stupid, stupid question. But, really, what would her mum see her do? Sylvanie thought she was far beyond all that anyway. Temple had killed her mother. Why would she even think that Temple was telling the truth?

How did she know that Temple hadn't already killed Finch? And Maze and Danny?

Sylvanie looked down into the pines. Was she a fool? Had he simply duped her?

A young woman in a black skirt and white shirt made her way to Sylvanie. She looked a little like Maisie. Maze in another life. She looked too innocent to have any idea of the atrocities that Temple was capable of.

"Mr Temple requests the pleasure of your company for a little light luncheon. He told me to tell you that in his humble opinion you've had quite enough sun and that you look lonely, forlorn and hungry." She smiled sweetly at Sylvanie then turned on her heels and walked back across the expansive terrace.

What would it be like to have a uniform? To know your place in the order of the grand everyday scheme of things?

Sylvanie watched the waitress report to Temple. He said something and the waitress laughed. They looked in Sylvanie's direction.

Where was a crummy supermarket selling cheap Batman suits when you needed it?

By the time Sylvanie had walked over to where Temple was seated, lunch had been brought to the table.

Temple had not once asked Sylvanie if she wanted to change her clothes or have new ones. She had kept – and repeatedly washed and dried – her own clothes. This had led to her feeling scruffy and out of place. She was deeply grateful for that feeling.

"Did you get all your foul business done?" Sylvanie asked as she took her seat facing Temple, now with her own parasol and her back to the view. "Did it all go as well as you hoped? Will you be richer? Sicker?"

Temple ignored the questions. He was preoccupied with piling fried baby octopus onto his plate, buttering chunks of crusty baguette and quaffing chilled German white.

"What next?" Sylvanie asked. "How much bloody longer here? Then where? I don't mean to sound ungrateful, but I truly hate being here with you in this hollow place in this museum landscape."

"Rudeness comes very naturally to you, Miss Hart," Temple told Sylvanie with a wry smile. "I can't pay for someone to fake those heartfelt sentiments, because it seems that people are invariably timid, no matter how rich the reward. They always harbour the fear that I'll suddenly take umbrage. And yet you never fail to amuse and delight, Miss Hart. You really should eat. Keep your strength up for further vitriolic barrages and petulant foot-stamping."

Sylvanie looked at the platters that had been brought to their table. It was mostly seafood, but there were olives and tomatoes and salad. She put a few things on her plate and buttered some bread.

"If there is something that isn't on the table," Temple suggested, waving his knife loosely over the food, "something you would prefer, then you can click your fingers and a waitress will come running. Your merest whim is their command."

"There's enough here to feed ten people."

"Luckily, I have the appetite of ten people. It has been a long but productive morning. I won't bore or shock you with the details and scar you forever."

"Too late," Sylvanie said.

Temple ate six raw oysters, slurping and gulping them. He ate langoustines and caviar. There were fish-eggs on his plump lips. He glugged more wine. There were fish-eggs on the rim of his lead crystal goblet.

"We fly back to England tomorrow."

"Then what?"

"Through the Door," Temple told her. "You will be very close to home. All sorts of pieces – light as snowflakes – will fall softly into place for you, Miss Hart. Your friends have been gone a long while. It will make me so happy to have played a tiny part in such a triumphant reunion. Everyone else has stopped missing them now. Everyone else has lost hope. Except you. I am sure that your love for Mr Finch remains as strong as ever. I pray it is reciprocal. Wouldn't it be simply dread—"

"I don't care what you hope. You can't twist my feelings into something you think you can begin to understand, you arrogant bastard."

Temple smiled and looked at his wristwatch. "I am awaiting an important call," he said, scanning the main building and the attendant staff loitering in the vicinity of the open doorway. "It will round off this morning's work quite nicely, if all has gone according to plan. I will take the call inside, but I will be gone for no more than a minute or two. It's already overdue and people know how I dislike to be kept waiting."

"I'll sing hymns quietly to myself to try to fill the void while you're gone."

Temple laughed. "Bravo, Miss Hart. You're honing your skills, stropping your blade."

A house sparrow and several chaffinches were hopping about in the margins of the shade of the parasols. Sylvanie threw a generous crumb. A chaffinch got to it first and took to the air with its prize. Sylvanie threw more breadcrumbs and flakes of crust and word quickly spread. She rose from the table and sat on the warm flagstones.

This is the life, she thought. *Going all over, eating lovely grub, feeding little birdies and killing people. He would get an amazing Batman suit made for me if I told him I wanted one.*

Shut your deluded and delirious mind, she told herself. *I am her.*

A waitress marched hurriedly from the hotel, her heels clicking on the shimmering flagstones. It was getting very warm. Temple stood and the birds flew away. He threw his white napkin on the table and turned to meet the waitress.

"Ten minutes at most," he called over his shoulder. "Forgive me."

Sylvanie sat back in her chair. She noticed Temple's gun, partially visible beneath his discarded table linen.

Temple had disappeared inside. She could see one waiter. He wasn't looking. It would be easier to go around the table than to try to reach across. Sylvanie made the move and slid the pistol from beneath his napkin.

It was heavier than she had expected. The barrel seemed very long.

Sylvanie sat back down with Temple's gun in her lap. She broke more baguette and threw it on the ground in the hope that her birds would come back. She squeezed her thighs together and brought her knees up to stop the weapon from sliding to the ground.

The situation had changed completely. She had changed it. She had taken control over the surreal nightmare.

She held the gun. Due to the length of the barrel, it would be difficult, she realized, to bring it quickly up past the rim of the table. She would have to pull the weapon right back into her abdomen to ensure clearance.

Sylvanie held the gun with both hands and put her finger on the trigger.

Nicholas Temple was going to get the shock of his life.

She must breathe. She must force herself. In through her nose and out through her mouth.

The crumbs remained untouched on the flagstones.

When Temple re-emerged he was walking quite slowly, apparently deep in thought.

Sylvanie decided to keep her hands where Temple could see them, until he was seated.

Then she would shoot him.

Or she could run to the parapet and hurl the pistol out as far as she could, down into the trees and shrubs below. But she'd seen an old man down there, raking up twigs and leaves. She might hit him. Anyway, where would any of that get her? The gun would be retrieved and she would feel stupid.

She felt stupid now. Rigid with stupid fear.

She had to take him by surprise. She must not give him a moment to gather his thoughts and defend himself.

"So sorry, Miss Hart," Temple said, pulling back his chair. "That took longer than I had hoped, but it's all turned out significantly in my favour."

He sat. He did not pick up his napkin.

Sylvanie knew that he knew his gun was not there. She knew that he knew she had it.

She pulled out his gun, levelled the lengthy barrel across the table at Temple and pulled the trigger.

Buh-lamm!

The sound of the explosion fused in the centre of her brain. The barrel jumped. There were sparks crying in the sun. The whole weapon was smoking.

There was a knowing look on Temple's face. He saw the bullet begin its journey across the table. He moved the wine bottle so that it might eventually pass unhindered.

He lit a cigar.

Sylvanie watched the bright silver bullet revolving slowly, making barely any progress toward Temple.

Smoke billowed out across the table in the bullet's wake.

"It takes," Temple said, waving the flame from his match and puffing on his cigar, "a measure of courage to do what you just did. I applaud you for it, genuinely. I was unsure, when I left you my precious Remington, what course of action you would elect to take. But your laudable bravado is misplaced, misused and therefore wasted – like so many plucky strays before you."

He glanced at the bullet. Perhaps it had made some progress?

Sylvanie couldn't breathe.

Temple looked at his watch. "Lesson time. You be pupil and I'll be teacher."

He leaned his head onto his left shoulder and removed the cigar from his glossy lips.

All the volume of the shot returned like an Atlantic breaker crashing against Sylvanie. The smoke was moving again, unfurling and falling over the table.

She watched the bullet gain momentum, passing fractionally to the left of Temple's right ear.

She watched it travel through the still air hanging above the terrace.

She saw alarmed employees looking their way.

Temple did not turn to follow the bullet's trajectory.

He was content to watch Sylvanie watch it.

He wanted to see the look on her face when she realized that it was her finger that pulled the trigger of the gun that killed the waitress who had reminded her of Maisie.

32 (Here)
The One with the Return Ticket

Finch pulled his knees right up under his chin and hugged his legs. He had a belter of a headache.

The huge, dark bulk of the third barrow was at his back. It seemed only right. Covered in whortleberries, gorse and bracken, it might have been there for centuries. The Barrow Ship was once again inside the ancient earthwork.

Finch looked at the fat moon. He wanted to rise and follow it. But, all in good time. He first had to learn to move. He looked at his hands. They were full of light. He tried to stand, but the moonlight weighed so heavily upon him.

He saw the lights of a vehicle coming along the contour road around Dunkery Beacon and heard the hollow thrubbing noise as it sped over the cattle-grid at Dunkery Gate. He watched its lights flooding the deep lane and bursting the banks of the hedgerows on its way to the Exford road. Then it was gone.

The Barrow Ship would allow him to move when the time was right. A strong wind barged past him, nudging him, trying to shape him, but the moonlight weighed him down.

Where was Sylvanie? He was stuck up on the moor in the middle of the night. He was almost paralysed, too cold to unfold his legs. How long till warm sunlight? He straightened one leg at a time and tried to unlock his glowing fingers. He rolled onto his front and pushed up from the brittle heather and cotton grass. His head throbbed.

He heard the truck before he saw it, its diesel engine loud and raw. It followed the same route as the previous vehicle, but slowed almost to a stop before turning right onto the track to Worthy Airfield. It halted for a while at the gates, the engine idling. There was shouting and laughter before it was driven through. The truck's headlights were turned off, doors were slammed and lights went on in a low building to the left of the gates, past Des's old office.

Finch thought he could make it that far. He tried to steady himself, stop himself from rocking. The moon was swaying like a pendulum. There must be people at the gate. Soldiers? They would give him a glass of water and something for his pounding headache.

He was going to look strange, he thought, staggering through the rough heather in the dead of night with glowing hands. He wondered about his head, his face? He felt as though every particle of his being must be a tiny individual light, every taut sinew a glowing wire.

Where was Sylvanie? What would his mum and dad make of it? Would Sylvanie be in the village? Would she have had to go back to college? It didn't matter. She'd have finished college by now, surely? When had he stopped counting the days and the months? There was no point in trying to think about any of that right now. She would be waiting for him.

He was going to kiss her full on the mouth before she could say one word.

He was very thirsty.

The two soldiers on gate duty saw Finch's face shining and swaying like a lantern held high. He was singing, and asking himself questions. They decided somebody was probably just winding them up.

He was cold. He couldn't fasten his jacket because his fingers wouldn't cooperate. He shoved his bright hands deep into his pockets. His headache was beginning to subside.

I am full of light, he thought, *but I feel heavy, like I'm full of water.*

Both the soldiers had their mouths wide open. They were backing off. An elderly Alsatian with dodgy back legs strolled out of the little wooden gatehouse, barking and whimpering at the same time. The soldiers had backed off as far as the gate. Finch stooped and stroked the dog. One of the soldiers had an automatic rifle slung across his abdomen.

"Stay back," the soldiers told him.

Finch rubbed the dog's ears. The Alsatian sat upright and swept the dusty tarmac with his tail.

"I'm freezing. I think it might be a good idea for me to have a hot drink. Then maybe I won't die. Can I have hot chocolate with whipped cream and marshmallows? And sprinkles?"

"You look like a fucking ghost," the soldier with the gun informed him. "What the hell's the matter with you?"

Finch laughed, which made his head hurt. He rubbed his temples with his cold, bright hands.

Slowly but surely the soldier with the rifle came around to the idea of pointing it at Finch.

"No need to shoot. If you can wait five minutes I'll have died of hypothermia and you won't have to waste valuable ammo." He stooped again to pat the dog. "I need a hot drink and I have to make a phone call."

"Don't fucking move," the unarmed soldier shouted at Finch. "Where've you come from?"

"Ring the office," the soldier with the gun told his comrade.

"I came out of the Barrow Ship. It's up there, buried under a big pile of Exmoor. It's been up there forever." He laughed and shivered at the same time. "I'm one of the ones who went off in it. Now I'm back."

"What the fuck are you talking about?" the unarmed soldier demanded.

"I'm saying that I've been and gone and come back again. I guess I'm the reason you guys are here. Please ring the office, like you suggested, before I get frostbite and bits of me start dropping off like fairy lights off a Christmas tree."

The soldier with the rifle gave it to his mate. He then took off his heavy greatcoat and handed it to Finch.

"Here. You'd better put this on."

Finch dived into the big coat, warm from the soldier. He managed to fasten all the buttons and hoist the collar. He felt more human.

"Thanks. Can I go in there and sit down and warm up a bit?"

There was one plastic chair in the gatehouse hut. Finch sat down and hugged himself.

"He's one of them kids who went off in the Barrow Ship thing years and years ago," the coatless soldier said. "Tell

Sarge right now. Go on. Tell both of them." He opened the gate and pushed the other soldier through. "Go on. Wake 'em up. Run."

The unarmed soldier with the coat did as instructed.

"I was a kid," the coatless soldier told Finch, "when you lot buggered off. I was nine, maybe ten. If you really were who you say you are, you'd look a fair bit older than you do."

That made Finch think. He looked at his hands. They were fading. The Alsatian came and laid down on his feet.

"I've come back. I've been away ... seems like some considerable time. I've got to see my girlfriend and my mum and dad. I don't know what they'll make of any of it. They won't know I'm here. They didn't even know I was going anywhere. Come to think of it ... I didn't either."

"If you was one of the kids who went, then you ain't gonna find your parents around here anymore. I thought you lot was meant to be teenagers when you went. The families got mobbed by the press for ages. I mean, they couldn't carry on with their normal lives when everything went batshit crazy. Honestly, mate, if they was your families, then—" He stopped himself. "What about the other kids what was with you? What happened to them?"

"They stayed. They liked it there."

"Where?"

"The place we went to. The other ... world. You can't see it from here, just like you can't see here from there. It's not like Jupiter or Mars or somewhere, but it's there."

Lights were going on in the newer airfield buildings. Doors were being opened and slammed.

"I watched this show about it on TV, ages ago. Loads of people who said they was there was being interviewed. In some countries they still can't talk about it. I mean, it's against the law."

"They'll have to talk about it now."

"I thought you was a pissing ghost when you was coming down the track."

"I felt like one. I've felt like one for ages, to be honest. I just look pale now, like I've dipped my hands in a bucket of whitewash." Finch had kept his head down, but now looked the soldier straight in the eye.

"Christ," the soldier said. "You're enough to freak anybody out."

"I need to make an urgent phone call. And I'm going to need a lift to the village."

"You can ask these two about all that," the soldier said. His comrade appeared at the gate followed by two sergeants who looked to have thrown their uniforms on in a hurry.

The female sergeant stepped into the gatehouse. "What's going on with you, chap? Did you get lost on your way home from a party? Or did your mates drop you off on the moor for a giggle?"

Finch looked at her.

"Holy shit," she said, flinching from the crystal light in his eyes.

"I've come back in the Barrow Ship. I'm very thirsty. My two friends stayed behind. I need to find my girlfriend and my family."

"What's your girlfriend's name?" the male sergeant asked Finch. He looked like he was trying to hide his fear.

He looked like he was racking his brains to remember something.

"Begins with S," Finch said.

"Sylvanie," the female sergeant said. "Sylvanie Hart."

"She couldn't come with us. She had to stay behind so that we … So that *I* could find my way home. Do you people know where I can find her?"

"Nobody knows where to find *her*," the male sergeant said, then wished he'd kept his mouth shut.

"He's been bloody cold, Sarge," the coatless soldier said. "And he's been saying how thirsty he is. Maybe it'd be a good—"

"Let's get him in the office," the female sergeant said. "The heating's on. And we can sort out drinks and a sandwich." She looked in turn at the two soldiers. "You'll have to finish your watch. Both of you."

"Security's been stepped up since I was last here," Finch said. "The fence is massive now. I thought it was just the gates, but …"

"Back in the day," the male sergeant said, "when all of the so-called Barrow Ship crap kicked off, loads of cult followers used to keep cutting through the fence to try to get to what was left of the third hang—"

He heard the telephone ringing in Danny's uncle's old office.

"We'd better get that," Finch said, walking toward the steep flight of concrete steps.

"You don't need to worry about that," the female sergeant curtly informed him. "Nobody's been in there since forever."

"I'll have to answer it. It will be for me."

The phone inside Des's old office kept ringing.

Finch went up the steps. The handrail had rotted away.

"I don't know why the bloody hell you think you'd be getting a phone call," the female sergeant said. "How would anybody even know you're here?"

Finch ignored her and turned the wobbly, white doorknob. The door was locked. He could see the key on the inside through the glass panels in the upper half of the door.

"Come down, fella," the male sergeant ordered. "Let's get you somewhere a tad warmer, eh?"

Finch broke the glass panel nearest to the handle with his greatcoat-padded elbow.

"What the hell do you—" the male sergeant shouted.

"Don't worry," Finch said, holding his hands up. "All damages will be paid for." He then extracted enough shards of broken glass to get his hand through.

The sergeants seemed reluctant to climb the steps and get too close to Finch.

The phone sounded louder and more insistent with the glass gone. Finch reached through and withdrew the long brass key from the lock.

"Let him do it," the female sergeant told her colleague, barring his way as he stepped forward.

"How can it be locked from the friggin' inside?" he asked her.

Finch unlocked the door and went in. The air inside was stale, but the fresh night air rapidly muscled in. The sergeants came up the steps and switched on the light. Finch was standing by the vacant desk with a faded, green telephone on the corner, still ringing.

Not only was the cord to the old landline unplugged, but the obsolete bundle of wire was hanging with an elastic band around it beside the leg of the desk.

Finch picked up the receiver.

"Hello."

"Hello, Finch," Mrs Slee replied. "How good it is to hear your voice. How are you, dear? I know you must be feeling somewhat confused and exhausted. How was your journey? *All* your journeys?"

"The journey was incredible. I don't know where it began or where it's supposed to end, but it's certainly been nothing short of amazing so far."

Mrs Slee laughed. "I always knew that you were the right people for the job."

"It's not over yet, though, is it?"

"No. Now comes the difficult part. Lilian is waiting just outside."

"Say hi," Finch said.

"Finch says hi."

"Where exactly are you?"

"We're at the telephone box in the village," Mrs Slee replied.

"Is it still working? I mean … or, has it been mended?"

"There are times when it works and there are times when it refuses to work," Mrs Slee told him.

Finch looked down at the disconnected wire to the phone he was using.

"The Barrow Ship has buried itself up here on the moor. Pretty much where we found all the pieces. I'm in Danny's uncle's old office up at the airfield. But you knew that, otherwise you wouldn't have known where to ring. I've got soldiers with me right now. I think they're finding the whole night pretty strange. Anyway, what's the difficult bit that happens next?"

"We have to rescue Sylvanie," Mrs Slee told him.

"What? What do you mean? Rescue her from what? Is she in danger? Where is she?"

"With Nicholas Temple. We have to act fast. Lilian has already left. She's on her way to you. She'll be turning around at the cattle-grid in her red Volvo in a few minutes."

"Nicholas Temple ... I ... He has ... *my* Sylvanie? How did that happen? Why?"

"I am so very sorry, Finch. We will have to allow forthcoming events to explain themselves. I must go. I have to bring Pony up to speed on certain matters. You and Lilian can pick me up at home."

Mrs Slee rang off.

"Can I trouble you for a cup of tea, please," Finch asked the sergeants.

They backed down the steps.

Finch banked off right and legged it through the unlocked, high-security entrance gate.

33 (Here)
A Very Poor Loser

His champagne had a plump red strawberry in it. Sylvanie watched silver bubbles clinging to the fruit.

"I win," Temple said. "I invariably do. Though it does feel particularly rewarding in your case."

Sylvanie closed her eyes. She had never felt so lost.

"You have been defeated," Temple pointed his finger at her. "I have seen the look on countless previous occasions, upon innumerable faces. I would feel infinitely more inclined toward sympathy if your sort were not perpetually predisposed to taking the moral high ground in such an inherently rude and arrogant fashion." He was wagging his fat, pink finger. "You … are a very poor loser."

Sylvanie opened her eyes. The interior of the small private jet was made up of textured plastic panels and cream-coloured leather.

Her chest ached where the Hare amulet lay against her skin. It felt like it had given up, as if whatever life force it had once contained had ebbed from it. Now it felt like loss. The exact, measured weight of grief. If there had been somewhere she could have thrown it – out of a high window or into a raging river – Sylvanie would have ripped the jewel from her neck.

Temple knew she had it. He had told her that he wanted it. He had seen the thong around her neck, but he had never seen the Hare itself. How had he known it was there? Why would he want it? She could imagine Temple taking the Hare from her by force, and smashing it to pink dust with a hammer. Worse – much, much worse – she could imagine Temple slipping the thong over his head and wearing it.

It was the last piece of *her*. It was the last possession from her previous life. No mum. No boyfriend with a motorbike. No journals or pens or pencils. No Satyajit or Georgia. No friends.

The pebble in her pocket. Of course, she had that. These things were like bones. All she had left were two stones like bones. Relics from another life. Someone else's perfectly stupid little life.

"You chose to play the game. You looked down at the hand of cards I dealt you and decided to pick them up. It was a fatal mistake. You imagined that you could beat me at my own game."

Sylvanie thought that he laughed. She thought that it sounded like bubbles of bile deep in his throat.

A steward came from the front section of the plane and stood at a polite distance.

Temple picked up his champagne flute and glanced at the man.

"Twenty minutes to Bristol, sir."

34 (Here)
Barefoot and Bareback

Sylvanie had made the decision to cry. He wouldn't be able to see her, and her tears were silent. It was dark in the car and mostly dark on the motorway. She had completely lost track of time.

Sylvanie made the decision to grieve. For Hannah. Georgia and Satyajit. For all those unfortunate souls whose paths crossed with Temple's. And for the waitress.

Her tears tasted like the Atlantic. They ran down her cheeks and into the corners of her mouth. Her tears and her stone and her Hare were all she had. Were all she was.

The Hare amulet upon her chest. The pebble upon her unfeeling palm. The tears that burned her face.

"Nearly there," Temple said.

She turned to the window and wiped her tears with the back of her hand. She made an involuntary move to sit more upright.

Sylvanie knew that they had been off the motorway for some time. There was light in the sky now. A veil was being pulled slowly from a reluctant material world. There were shadowy masses, shapes shifting into being something that Sylvanie could perhaps recognize. It had been so long since she had been here. There were beech trees shouldering the crawling sky, identifiable curves in the lane, and hedgerows and embankments in familiar sequence.

She was home.

She looked out of the window at the place she had carried with her everywhere she and her mother had been forced to go.

There was Mrs Slee's cottage. There were wan lights within. Candles? The door was wide open. Sylvanie quickly turned to look out of the rear window. There was Lilian's Volvo.

Temple's limousine turned up toward the church. He shuffled in his seat and twisted to face Sylvanie.

"I am a man of my word. I am a keeper of promises." He laughed. "I preserve them in jars of formaldehyde."

Sylvanie did not look at him.

The car pulled in just after the lych gate and the driver turned off the engine and lights.

"Here we are then, Miss Hart." Temple waited for the driver to fetch his hat and coat and open his door.

"Now, let's be absolutely clear about this. We have to do this together. You have to get out of the car and take my hand. You must then keep hold of my hand as we proceed along the path, past the church, to the Door in the wall. We must go together. You will be holding my hand as we pass through the Door. Do you understand?"

Sylvanie said nothing.

"I am taking you to your poor Mr Finch. I gave you my word and my word is my bond. I cannot allow you to besmirch my immaculate record. We have come a long way, you and I."

The driver opened Temple's door and helped him into his long, black coat. Temple took his hat and placed it with great care on his head. He walked under the lych gate and waited, looking up at the church tower and the tide of racing clouds. The driver opened Sylvanie's door and stood back.

Sylvanie sat perfectly still.

"You'll get out," the driver snarled, "if you know what's good for you."

"Clearly," Sylvanie informed the man, "neither you nor I know what's good for us. If we did, we wouldn't be here."

Sylvanie climbed out and the driver closed the door.

She straightened her back and watched the noisy jackdaws circling the tower. *Just as this world is being born,* she thought, *I am leaving.*

The Hare amulet felt warm. It was getting warmer. Sylvanie grabbed it through her sweater.

She went to Temple and took his hand.

I can't live without Finch, she thought. *I can't be without him.*

"That's right," Temple said, as if he had been reading her thoughts. "That's the spirit. And from the very moment you two reunite, you can begin plotting your revenge."

He squeezed her fingers until he hurt her. He pulled her through the gate and along the cobbled path, past gravestones and crosses on both sides, between the dark masses of the ancient yews.

They turned the corner of the church and saw Pony Chalice, bareback and barefoot, upon his pale horse.

Sylvanie gasped. "Pony!"

Temple stopped dead in his tracks.

Pony nudged Jess forward to bar their way.

Another vehicle screeched to a halt at the lych gate.

Sylvanie felt the world fly by.

She saw time howling in every sinew of Pony's being. He had thrown himself from his horse to get to her. But he was now suspended in mid-air like an acrobat pegged out on a wire.

Sylvanie turned to look back as Temple dragged her and swung her violently around Jess's raised head, past her wild eyes.

Sylvanie saw Mrs Slee and Lilian arriving too late.

But ... Finch? His hair long. A beard. Finch was with them. And he was too late.

"Finch!" she screamed. But the world was already unravelling.

Temple gripped Sylvanie's hand so tight it felt like he was going to break her fingers.

"Finch!" she screamed.

Too late was too late.

There was the black Door in the wall.

I am the Door.

Temple was panicking.

Sylvanie jerked her hand in his. She twisted and fell, forcing him to take her full weight. She bent her body and kicked his legs. She pulled her hand frantically, until it felt like her wrist would break, but there was no release from his vice-like grip.

"Finch!" she screamed. And time held her voice like a tadpole in a jar.

The locks fell away. Temple slid the rusty bolts and opened the heavy black Door.

Pony fell to the path like a sack of limbs thrown from a railway bridge. Jess reared and whinnied savagely.

Temple was running out of time.

Finch was racing across the churchyard.

Too late.

Temple shoved Sylvanie through. Her fingers were numb in the man's desperate grip. He was right behind her now, pushing her and pulling the Door.

She heard Finch screaming her name before the Door slammed shut.

35 (Here)
Widdershins

He had fallen very badly. Having leapt from Jess's back, intending to grab Sylvanie or tackle Temple, real time had been wrenched away. Pony had then lost control of his descent, hitting the unforgiving cobbles face-first, breaking his nose and cheekbone, several ribs and his left wrist. He was in agony; blood was pumping from his nose, streaming down his chin and neck.

Lilian got to him first. She seized his right arm and hoisted him slowly to his feet. She took him in her arms as he rose. He yelled out in pain.

"It's a wonder you didn't break your neck. I'm glad you didn't."

"You and me both, maid," Pony replied, as Mrs Slee arrived, more than a little out of breath.

Finch was beating wildly, with both fists, on the Door in the wall, screaming Sylvanie's name over and over.

"Can you get back on your horse?" Mrs Slee asked Pony.

"Don't be ridiculous, old girl," Lilian exclaimed, reaching out for Pony's shoulder. "He's terribly badly injured, and—"

"I can," Pony said, shifting his weight from one bare foot to the other to ease the pain that racked his body. "I can do it, but this strapping maid'll have to give me a leg up."

"Then do it now," Mrs Slee ordered, "and we'll have a chance of saving Sylvanie and restoring some semblance of balance to our forsaken Spheres."

"He's slammed the door tight shut," Finch screamed. "I tried to—"

"You can't do it, my love," Lilian begged Pony. "You'll fall again, doing yourself much more serious—"

"You'd do the same, maid, in my shoes."

They both looked down at his bloody and filthy feet.

"What's he got to do?" Finch asked, howling. "We've got to get—"

"Please, Pony," Mrs Slee implored. "There is less than no time at all to waste."

Pony shook himself as if to wake from a nightmare. He stepped toward Jess, who turned her head to him, her eyes insane, savage. Lilian and Finch stood to either side of Pony.

"Lock your fingers like that," Pony said, painfully attempting to show Lilian the stirrup-cradle she would have to make for him to step into. "I'll pull on Jess's mane, but you have to boost me proper."

Lilian did as she was told, planted her feet firmly apart and leaned forward. Pony placed his right foot in her hands. He roared with agony, but in the blink of an eye was sat once again astride his white horse.

"Ride like the wind, Pony, dear," Mrs Slee implored. "We will go to the Door. Do not stop, or even slow down, until we are gone from sight. Do you understand? Everything has come down to this."

Lilian burst into tears, making no effort to wipe them away. "Please don't get more hurt," she begged.

"Stay here, maid, if you will. I may be in need of some nursing when this all be done."

"Is there a way to open the door?" Finch asked in desperation, "and let us get through? I can run like hell and get a bar or a post or something to lever—"

"You and I will go together, Finch, dear," Mrs Slee told him, "but only if Pony can stay on the carousel of time."

Pony and Jess turned toward the church. He leaned forward onto broken ribs, and whispered into her ear, "Fly, girl," and they were off. They headed for the nearest corner of the sandstone building and veered left, galloping the practised course anticlockwise.

In a breath, they were back around, racing by at breakneck speed. Pony was not looking at them. Lilian cheered him on.

Mrs Slee and Finch took up their positions at the Door in the wall.

"When you look at it now," Finch said, his eyes wild with desperate fury, "it looks like it's never been open. But I saw it. And I saw him take Sylvanie through it. How can we get it open?"

"We wait," Mrs Slee told him. "If Pony keeps going as fast as his young horse can carry him, we can push the tide of time back just far enough."

"Then we can get to her. We've got to get her away from him. I … I can't even think …"

"Concentrate all your thoughts and energies, now, on getting the Door open. Do not be distracted by Pony. I don't know how long this is going to take."

Mrs Slee linked her arm tightly through Finch's and they stared at the black-painted Door together.

"Stand with me outside all time for a time," she said.

Pony went careering twenty-six times around the church. The churchyard, the yews and the headstones darkened almost imperceptibly. Pony rode like his beautiful world depended on it. Horse and rider were a pale, ragged blur.

Twenty-seven.

Finch could hear Pony screaming. He could hear Lilian yelling and crying. He fought to concentrate solely on the Door.

There were sounds on the other side. There were voices.

Twenty-eight.

Finch could hear Sylvanie's screams diminishing in the distance beyond.

Twenty-nine.

There was a breath when the Door yielded. It sounded like disapproval.

Then, before time had a chance to change its mind, Mrs Slee jammed a wooden foot in the opening.

36 (There)
Going to the Door

Danny knew. As soon as he woke, he knew.

Maisie and Liss thought the place was spooky. Danny had laughed. He didn't care. Eleftheria was on hand to protect Liss from all forms of fear or fright.

The building was an abandoned monastery. There was a chapel, a blue- and white-painted grotto with a statue of a woman in blue and white, and rows of plain cells where the monks had slept. The only things the monks had left behind were their shadows. There was a darkness lurking behind every door of every tiny room.

Eleftheria and the others slept on the cool blue floor of the painted grotto.

Danny knew. He knew because his axe had been telling him things all night. He'd slept like a log. Like a log that kept a monumental felling axe for company.

There was a latrine block, but it stank. Fortunately there was an old water pump with a long handle. Eleftheria managed to prime it with water from a stagnant pond and Danny and Maisie pumped until the pure water from deep inside the hill ran cool and clear.

Eleftheria had insisted that they hold back from entering the town until morning. She said that there was some kind of traditional festival that it might be fun to join in with.

She knew. Eleftheria knew because the Hexemore Hares had told her.

Danny could see the Hall of the Handless Clock, down in the middle of the town. He could see the window, facing west to catch the morning sun.

The first townsfolk to arrive were whistling, and clapping softly and rhythmically with their fingers on their palms. They whistled all the way up the winding path from the town. It sounded pretty, like a troupe of flageolet players applauding themselves.

The townspeople were dressed all in grey, with plaits and wooden clogs. They brought fresh, crusty bread; boiled eggs; walnuts; green onions; salty cheese; a whole roasted chicken and dried sausages made from wild boar meat.

Eleftheria, Maisie and Liss joined in happily with the whistling. Danny was more reticent.

"It's called 'Going to the Door'," Eleftheria told them. "It's a festival, a procession. This year we can take part."

More and more people arrived during their outdoor breakfast. By the time Danny had finished eating they had an audience of more than two hundred adults and children.

The sea of people parted for the Hares. Garlanded with daisy-chains and dandelions, they looked stately and beautiful. People threw petals and fragrant leaves onto the stony path before them.

Danny saw children carrying axes made from sticks and papier mâché. They had flags with Doors painted or stitched on and long, pink ribbons embroidered with the words: 'I Am the Door'.

The swelling crowd hushed as the Hares approached the blue-and-white grotto.

"We are Going to the Door," the Hares sang sonorously.

"We are Going to the Door," the crowd chorused.

"Will you follow?" the Hares sang.

"We will follow," the people replied.

All faces turned to Maisie, Liss, Eleftheria and Danny.

"Will you follow?" the Hexemore Hares and the townsfolk called.

"We will follow," sang Maisie, Liss and Eleftheria Mutt.

Danny was pulling on his boots and munching a dried sausage.

Maisie elbowed him in the kidneys.

"What?" he said. "Alright ... Gimme a bliddy minute."

37 (Here, There, and Neither Here Nor There)
Reflect Upon Your Sins

Finch plunged his fingers into the jaw-like gap between the open edge of the Door and the jamb, and pulled with all his strength. It did not give. Mrs Slee's foot was trapped. She twisted and leaned back, and Finch managed to force his left arm into the gap, but he couldn't squeeze his shoulder in.

"Syl!" Finch called desperately into the thin strip of blackness.

"Lilian! Pony!" Mrs Slee called. "Shout for them, Finch."

Finch turned to see Lilian and Pony weaving hurriedly through angels, crosses and headstones. Pony was bent almost double as he ran, clutching his chest and crying out in pain.

Lilian got her fingers into the gap above Finch, Pony above Mrs Slee's foot.

When they pulled together, the Door began to yield.

It was a mouth, opening wordlessly, gasping. Air rushed past, taking hold of their hair, their clothes and wrenching chimes from the moon-faced clock and alarmed voices from the jackdaws wheeling about the tower.

Using every ounce of their combined strength, they forced the black Door wide.

* * * * *

The procession came to an abrupt halt at the top of a short, but very steep, side street. Little more than an alley, it differed from all other roads and thoroughfares in the town because of its colours. Every wall, arch, lintel, mullion and kerbstone was brightly painted. The little street was a festival of vibrant colour.

All except for one rather unassuming black Door.

Into the massive granite lintel above it, four words were carved: *I Am the Door.*

The Hares went to it first. One after another they stood on their hind legs and boxed, fought and scratched at the unyielding black. It was a purely symbolic effort, resulting in cheers from the crowd.

The children were next. They were ushered into the alley to confront the Door in groups of four or five, to throw their little wooden and papier mâché axes at it. Their toys clattered to the ground. All the while, the cheering and clapping of the pressing crowd grew increasingly uproarious.

Danny stopped eating his little red apple.

* * * * *

Sylvanie felt Temple's grip loosen on her hand and she wrenched free.

She stopped moving. There were lights in the tiled ceiling of the tunnel. Most were broken, but some were flickering sickeningly, and sparking.

Sylvanie knew that Temple had panicked in the churchyard. He had seen the pale horse. He had seen Mrs Slee, Lilian and Finch coming for him, coming to rescue her from him. She had seen the fear in his eyes and felt the tightening of his grip.

After a few paces Temple stopped and turned. He looked shaken.

"Look around you," he said, intense anger saturating his words. "You are nowhere."

Sylvanie looked down at the black mud beneath her feet, at the filthy walls and dangerous lights. She sensed malignant shadows thickening about her and heard the wailing of the lost dead.

"In this forsaken place there is no life. Young Mr Finch cannot get to you, but all the deceased who are in limbo in this interminable wilderness can. They need you. They will suck all life from you. They will consume you, you ungrateful little bitch, and you will abide here with them in this no man's land of ceaseless remorse for all stinking eternity."

I am going back to the door, Sylvanie told herself. *Finch is there. I know he is. They are waiting for me.*

"You lied," she screamed at Temple. "You said you'd take me to Finch. You're not a man of your word. You're a liar. You're a murdering liar."

"Actually, a trick has been played here. Not by me. I did not lie. I cannot take you back through that Door. It is closed. If you go back, Miss Hart, you will only journey along an endless, Doorless tunnel to perpetual purgatory."

Needful shadows were forming. And there was the awful, sweet scent of death, filling Sylvanie's nostrils, catching in her throat and stealing her breath.

"I'm not going anywhere with you," Sylvanie said, feeling the appalling chill of undeath about her, waiting to embrace her. "I won't make that deadly mistake ever again."

"Stay, then. Behind us, I do solemnly swear, lies nothing. Not your world, nor those interfering witches. Not your beloved Mr Finch. My way is the way to the next life."

Sylvanie breathed in the cold shadows.

"If you fall here, they will walk over you for the rest of eternity. If you stand here forever, they will stand with you, protecting you from any form of life or love. I cannot take you to Mr Finch, but I can take you to your mother."

"You disgusting liar," Sylvanie yelled, moving toward Temple with cloaks of shadow peeling from her clothes and from her skin. "You killed my mother."

She ran past Temple, barging him as she went. How could she have allowed it to come to this?

"You need me," Temple cried.

Sylvanie turned. He was already a long way back. Shadows were lifting from the walls. The tunnel was not still; it writhed like a snake. There was a bend back there, beyond Temple. He was walking toward her with the hem of his coat dragging in the mud. The bend in the tunnel – like a wave cast down a long rope – was following him. She saw his fear and distress. He was terrified of being alone, terrified of facing his own death.

Sylvanie clutched at the Hare amulet. It was hot against her skin. She pushed her hand into her pocket and grasped the grey pebble that Finch had brought back for her through the sea cave at Hurlstone Point.

Hurlstone. Point.

She held the little stone tight in her fist. Temple had crushed her hand. He hadn't broken her fingers, but he had bruised every bone and tendon.

The Hurlstone felt good in her hand. It felt just right.

She looked behind her as Temple caught up. The curve in the tunnel had followed him. It was like being in the belly of some venomous serpent.

Temple wrenched her arm. He walked around her, forcefully turning her.

That was all that was needed. A new fear threw itself upon her, poured like molten lead into her heart.

"You don't know," Temple said.

He was right.

She didn't know. She didn't know which way they had come in.

"You need me," Temple said, walking arm in arm with Sylvanie.

All the lost souls of dust and dirt, ash and shadow needed her.

They needed to pour her reflection into a looking-glass and drink it.

They needed to press the air from her lungs and gulp it.

They needed to wrest the pebble from her hand and squeeze the blood from it.

* * * * *

"It's your turn," Eleftheria told Danny.

Danny knew.

384

He lifted his axe from his shoulders, lowered the head to the ground and leaned the shaft toward Maisie's waiting hands.

She felt the impossible weight of it.

The crowd fell silent.

Danny walked to the Door. There were colourful mock axes strewn before it, piled against it. He started to shift them, throwing and kicking them aside. Folk stepped forward to help with the task.

When his way was clear, Danny stepped up.

I am the Door.

The Hexemore Hares were watching.

Danny looked at the Door. It hadn't been opened for an eternity. It had massive wrought-iron hinges. It had weighty bolts and locks.

Danny turned to the Hares.

He knew that Sylvanie was behind the Door.

He knew that Finch was behind the Door.

They were in there in that other world. And they needed his help.

"You are the Keyholder," the Hares told him.

Danny nodded. He knew that Temple would also be waiting.

"Amen," the Hares said as one.

Danny went to Maisie to retrieve his shining axe. He balanced it in his right hand and strode back to the Door.

The crowd remained silent. Breathless.

Danny heaved his axe high, then brought it down on a fat brass padlock. The metal sheared and twisted and the lock somersaulted to the steps.

The crowd erupted in rapturous applause.

Danny broke the second lock. He pulled at remnants of the bolt housings, but the Door was solid. With the next two blows he sheared the hinges on the right-hand side of the Door. Again he pulled at the contorted metalwork, but the Door remained immovable.

He aimed a mighty blow at the centre of the Door. This time a crack appeared and splinters fell to the ground at his feet. At the next blow Danny's axe stuck in the Door. Using the slender shaft as a lever, he worked it free.

Through the fissure in the woodwork, the voice of a plaintive wind was calling.

Danny kept going, pulling large splinters and split planks free as his axe bit hard into the Door. Maisie, Liss and Eleftheria came to his side.

A cowering, frightened darkness was being pushed toward the light by the growing wind. The shadowy dead were being pushed to the mercy of the sunlight.

The Door surrendered, suddenly loose in the frame. Danny hooked the head of his great axe through and pulled the Door down.

Royston Quantock trotted out into the light. He was emaciated, filthy, crow-black with dust and slime.

Maisie scooped him up into her arms and he yelped with delight.

* * * * *

The ghosts kept coming. Finch saw that the churchyard was full. They were cowering in the shadows, clinging to the yews and monumental masonry.

"We must go in," Mrs Slee told him. "We have to get to Sylvanie before Temple can drag her through, or they'll both be gone."

Finch dashed headlong into the sordid darkness.

Lilian picked up Mrs Slee and followed with the old woman in her arms. Pony staggered after them, clutching his chest and howling like a beaten dog.

"Syl! Syl!" Finch roared into the rank dimness.

Sylvanie heard him.

Temple heard him. It was impossible to imagine how the infuriating brat had come to be on their side of the Door. It would have something to do with that cursed witch who had carved herself a pair of pretty new feet.

Sylvanie once more wrenched herself free from Temple's clutches. Before her, the tunnel was thick with the breath of death. Wraiths peeled from the walls and dark forms rose from the mud.

Sylvanie ran with the fleeing dead. They passed by her and through her, leaving her tainted with their fathomless grief.

"Finch!" she screamed.

He heard her. Running against the flow of filthy shadows, he could see almost nothing.

"Syl!" he roared, shielding his face with his arms as he ploughed on.

$$* \; * \; * \; * \; *$$

Temple turned his back on their noise. He was certain that both ends of the tunnel were now open. It was something he could neither have foreseen nor imagined. What was this? Who could have predicted this insanity?

New Doors would have to be constructed.

New hasps and clasps. New bolts and locks.

New rules would have to be made. New orders issued.

Fresh graves would have to be dug.

He took out his revolver.

*****

Some of the townsfolk stood their ground, bearing witness to the unfolding events. Others ran in fear for their lives, sweeping their children up in their arms, as the denizens of that reeking labyrinth surged out into the street.

Danny held his axe across his body.

Maisie cradled Royston Quantock. He was shaking.

Eleftheria held her gun. Liss held Eleftheria.

"Enter," the Hexemore Hares commanded. "Amen."

"You stay out here with Roy," Danny told Maisie, striding over the smashed Door.

Still the torrent of dead poured unabated.

"I'm coming with you," Maisie told Danny, handing her precious bundle to Liss.

Eleftheria followed Danny, gun in hand, Maisie close behind.

From deep within the dense gloom, Danny heard voices. The voices were names. The names were 'Syl' and 'Finch'.

"Hey," Danny bellowed as if into a bottomless well, "we're coming."

He raised his axe to chest-height. It was humming and blazing.

"Charge!" he roared, slicing through the rotten air.

*****

Temple clearly heard voices from *both* directions. He stopped and pointed his antique firearm one way and then the other.

Which way had he come in?

He saw the wild light from Danny's axe before he saw Danny. He heard Danny roaring. He loosed two shots, the first skittering harmlessly along the tiled wall of the tunnel, slipping past Danny, Eleftheria and Maisie like a wasp. Danny saw the second silver bullet heading straight for him. He raised his axe as a shield and the missile hit the shaft. Fat sparks fell like yellow raindrops to the black mud and expired.

Danny turned to Eleftheria and Maisie. They were still at his heels.

"Don't shoot," he yelled. "Finch and Syl are along there somewhere."

Temple fled from the flaming light. Which way should he go? Fear replaced the blood in his veins. He threw off his hat. He was confused. His long coat was slowing him down. His gun felt strangely heavy in his hand, too big for his chubby little fingers.

He saw Sylvanie. Far past that most difficult child, someone else: an equally youthful figure, filled with strange light. And beyond: unidentifiable others, no doubt intent on causing chaos in his orderly existence.

Temple had planned none of this. He had sprung a trap. He would punish someone for this. Someone would pay very dearly.

Danny, Maisie and Eleftheria were fast gaining on him.

Temple fired at Sylvanie. She threw herself down into the slime. The bullet hit two lights in the roof of the tunnel above Finch's head. Temple turned and shot at the screaming staff of burning gold. Danny stopped the bullet dead with the side of his axe.

Sylvanie picked herself up. She had no idea what the incandescent light might be. She turned and ran toward Finch.

She didn't have far to go.

They flew into each other's arms, colliding and falling.

Lilian and Pony had closed the gap, supporting Mrs Slee between them.

Temple loosed his last two shots over the heads of Sylvanie and Finch, directly at Mrs Slee.

In front of Pandora Slee, the two bullets – one at shoulder height, the other at eye-level – halted. Everyone watched. She picked them from the air. She shook them like rune stones in the cup of her arthritic hand then cast them aside.

Temple wondered if he had ever known fear – fear that he could call his own. Had he ever been frightened as a child? For sure, he had known other people's fear. Vicarious fear had always felt sublime. Divine.

Finch and Sylvanie were standing together, holding hands.

Lilian and Pony were holding hands with Pandora Slee.

How many people had been playing this game? His game? He'd had a hundred opportunities to take their lives. Who did they think they were?

Temple started walking. He emptied his gun and put his hand in his pocket for more ammunition. He looked at the trinity with the flaming axe. They slowed and froze. They would be sorry their paths had crossed.

Sylvanie took the Hurlstone from her pocket and threw it with all her strength. Using all the power of her mind she sent the little grey pebble flying like lightening through the fetid air.

Temple turned. He looked surprised. The Hurlstone struck him right between the eyes. Sylvanie watched him collapse heavily into the mire.

Mrs Slee went to him. He was unconscious, but moaning, resurfacing. She brought the folded moonskin from the frayed pocket of her blue plastic raincoat, calling to the others as she spread the gossamer mirror, casting it like a shroud over Temple.

"Roll him over. Roll him up."

Temple began to struggle, but the moonskin completely enveloped the man. Danny, Finch, Maisie, Eleftheria and Sylvanie pinned him down in the mud.

"Reflect upon your sins, Nicholas," Mrs Slee said.

And, in that precise instant, he was gone.

38 (Here)
One Word

"Mrs Slee, I have something for—" Finch began.

"I understand how people are reassured by a label, but I never have been . I wish you would always call me Pandora."

She looked wistfully out of her kitchen window at dancing light and leaves.

"Soon," she said, "to become Pandora *Valentine*. Do you think we're silly, Finch? Douglas and I, at our time of life?"

"Yes. Very, very silly indeed. You're perfect romantic role models for Syl and me."

"Romance has had to be patient, Finch. You'll try to be back in time for the wedding?"

"Yes. Of course. Syl and I will bring the others back in plenty of time. We wouldn't miss it for the world, any of us." He smiled at Pandora. "For the *worlds*."

"Danny, with his wonderful axe?"

"And his wonderful Maisie. And Eleftheria and her wonderful Liss."

"So many heroes, Finch. And so many miracles."

"Yeah."

"Did you want to ask me something? I mean, before I so rudely interrupted you?"

"Well, I have something for you. A souvenir from the other Sphere."

"I want you all to have the dolls, Finch. I thought that was understood."

"Thank you. But it's not the dolls. It's this." He drew from his jacket pocket the old quill tin they had found in the Chapel of SLEE, P. He placed it in Pandora's hands.

"I think it might be important," he said.

"Oh," Pandora exclaimed, clutching the tin to her chest. "Everything is important, Finch, dear."

"I know that, but there's something inside, Pandora. You must have put it in there a long time ago."

"Did I? I don't remember." She struggled, with arthritic hands, to prise open the tin.

"Can I ...?" Finch opened it and handed it back with the lid resting lightly in place.

Inside was the twice-folded scrap of lined notebook.

Pandora unfolded the piece of paper with the word written on it. Her eyes welled with tears.

"I remember writing the word. I remember the quill I used – even the ink's dark aroma. I had forgotten the *meaning*, though," she told Finch. "I had buried it. I had burned it a thousand times. I thought it was lost to me."

39 (Here)
The Awakening

Out of the blue, Finch laughed.

"What is it, kid?" Sylvanie breathed the question into his ear.

"I was thinking about Pandora and Douglas getting married. I can picture her walking down the aisle in her blue plastic raincoat."

"And do you know what? When she does, everyone in the worlds will want to get married in blue plastic raincoats for evermore."

Finch laughed again.

Sylvanie lay her head on his chest and closed her eyes. They had opened all the windows and doors in the cottage. They had picked more flowers than they had vases for. A male blackbird was singing its heart out on the telegraph pole at the bottom of the garden.

"Just sit up a minute, my love," Finch said.

They sat cross-legged, facing each other.

"I brought us something back. One each."

"What have you—"

"Close your eyes and hold out your hands."

Sylvanie did as requested.

Finch slid his hand under his pillow and pulled out both their dolls from the quill tin.

"Don't open your eyes until I tell you."

He lay the Finch doll gently down on her palms.

He lay the Sylvanie doll in his hands, so that the effigies were toe-to-toe.

"Open your eyes."

Sylvanie opened her eyes. She saw themselves asleep in each other's hands.

"Now stand me up, so that we're face-to-face."

Sylvanie followed his instructions.

As the dolls were lifted, so too were their eyelids.

And they looked into each other's eyes.

And they looked into each other's eyes.

About the Author

John Wilkinson was born in Yorkshire in 1959, but grew up in Somerset. Having studied sculpture at Saint Martin's School of Art, he went on to take creative writing, as part of his degree at the University of Lancaster, and printmaking at Bradford Art College.

John frequently paints and draws on Exmoor in all weathers. He has travelled in North America, Europe and Africa. From his book stall at South Molton's award-winning market he also sells original artwork, antiquarian maps and historical printed ephemera. He has written poetry and short stories all his life, but *The Barrow Ship* is his first published novel.

John lives in North Devon with his partner, Deb, who is a teacher. They have one son, Tom, who is an architecture student.

Finally

If you have enjoyed this book, please tell people. Tell your friends or tell Blue Poppy Publishing. As a very small business, we need every review and every recommendation we can get. Even constructive criticism can be valuable. Something that you didn't like about the book might be exactly what another potential reader is looking for. Reviews on Goodreads and blog posts are especially valued. Thank you.